To Carol,

May you find mu[...]
and inspiration from this
volume of Regeneration!

Sharon McElhaney

Regeneration!

A Journal of Creative Writing

Regeneration Writers

Penfield College at Mercer University

When we tell our stories authentically, it is not only important to us: our stories become an inseparable part of those who hear them and how they view the world. We change the world by telling our stories.

Regeneration Writers Press, LLC

2016

Macon, Georgia

Published in 2016 by Regeneration Writers Press, LLC
1177 Adams Street, Macon, GA 31201

www.regenerationpress.com
editor@regenerationpress.com

Margaret H. Eskew, Publishing Editor
Jerome Gratigny, Technical Editor
Sharon McElhaney, Student Editor
Terri DeFoor, Alumni Editor
Duane Evans Davis, Review Editor
Yvonne Gabriel, Art Editor
Jan Crocker, Photographer

Student Editorial Team
Karl S. Adams
Robert (Bob) Mathis
Sharon McElhaney
Anna M. McEwen
Ray Sapp
David D. Toliver
William M. (Bo) Walker
Maximo G. Wharton

Order *Regeneration! 2016*
from regenerationpress.com
or amazon.com
or Regeneration Writers Press, LLC
1177 Adams Street
Macon, GA 31201-1507

ACKNOWLEDGMENTS

Seven years have passed since that first generation of Regeneration Writers demanded writing classes, organized themselves, recruited other writers, created course syllabi, labored through multiple versions of their stories, poems, and essays, read their works aloud before diverse audiences, and brought forth the first edition of *Regeneration! A Journal of Creative Writing.* Without their sustained vision, consistent leadership, spirited recruitment, abiding forgiveness, and unfaltering energy, this current volume would be languishing somewhere in student folders or forgotten on some outdated computer. Their writings have inspired each new class of writers and journal contributors, whose combined accomplishments are myriad and legendary, proof positive that their journey through writing lifted them off dead center: doctoral programs, master of fine arts, law school, master of business arts, master of leadership studies, contributions to journals and newsletters, published books, art commissions and exhibits, community leadership, etc.

It all began with five students, led by military wife Diane Lang and egged on by cohorts Jan Crocker, Gloria Jordan, Terri DeFoor, and Barbara Sellers Bryan, raising their voices at 10 p.m. after an evening class on the literature of the South. Chair of Liberal Studies J. Colin Harris heard those voices, empowering those five and the many who came after them to find their voices and use them. Finding our voices became the rallying cry of the classes along with the obligation to listen attentively to the voices of others. Then came the discovery that listening to the diversity of the voices in the classroom brought about a greater awareness of the world and of ourselves in the world. The power of story was made manifest in those classrooms as authentic education emerged.

In this issue we pay tribute to two of the forces at Mercer who so generously supported the fledgling efforts of the small tribe of working adult writers whose dreams might have seemed at that point to outpace their abilities: Drs. John Colin Harris, who charitably agreed to allow the piloting of new writing courses, and Duane Evans Davis, who contributed hour after hour to leading in the effort to make the volume as error-free as possible. Both have since retired, but continue their unwavering commitment to the writers and the journal. Their leadership goes way beyond writing to the edification of the human spirit.

The Dean of Penfield College at Mercer, Dr. Priscilla Danheiser, has found innumerable ways to recognize the Regeneration Writers, championing their determination to continue to put writing in the forefront of a liberating education. Dr. Fred Bongiovanni, current chair of Penfield's Department of Liberal Studies, has led in the effort to formalize the writing courses so creatively initiated by the formidable five. Dr. Melanie Pavich, Penfield's coordinator of writing, has labored hard to sustain and elevate student writing. Dr. R. Kirby Godsey, chancellor of Mercer and for twenty-seven years president, and his wife, the inimitable Joan Stockstill Godsey, continue to inspire and encourage Penfield writers and faculty. Chancellor Godsey's words in a 2002 chapel service at Mercer resonate strongly with students and faculty: "You are God's gift to the world. It is your task to live out that gift." The Godseys are indeed gifts to all of us through his exemplary writing, her gift of music, and their penchant for creating, sharing, and encouraging beyond all walls.

Truly a community effort, this volume has been several years in the making. In addition to students in writing classes, the authors include the larger Mercer family–local pastors, Mercer faculty and staff, family members, and colleagues from other universities. It is impossible to point to the efforts of one single individual as foundational. It is truly a grand chorus of voices, reminiscent of a great choral work with many movements.

Our alumni editor, Terri DeFoor, served as the student editor for the first edition of *Regeneration!* She is in demand as a writing tutor in Mercer's Academic Resource Center. Her gift for writing short stories is equaled by her gift for perceptive and careful editing. Student editor Sharon McElhaney is self-selected. Proficient in the use of spreadsheets and endowed with incredible attention to detail and managerial skills, Sharon volunteered to undertake the organization of the different contributions. Her labor of love spilled over into many days and nights. In the process, she learned to create indexes and tables of contents electronically, in addition to contributing stories and formatting the volume for electronic and print publication. The diligent and insightful Regeneration Writers editing team added tremendous value to this collection of voices.

Jerome Gratigny has collaborated in the publication of ten books by Regeneration Writers Press. His can-do spirit, his sometimes dogged determination, and his artistic vision have been an invaluable resource. Amazingly, all of the founding Regeneration Writers–Cliff Brown, Janet Crocker, Terri DeFoor, Elnora Fluellen, Yvonne Gabriel, Gloria Jordan, Diane Lang, Andrew Legare, Kevin Reid, Barbara Sellers Bryan, and Zach Wells–have made enduring contributions to this volume. In addition to writing, Janet Crocker has served as photographer. Yvonne Gabriel painted the magnificent tree of life that graces the cover. Terri DeFoor edited portions of the content and proofread the final version of the entire book.

Although the poster was destroyed by flooding in the wake of Hurricane Katrina, the words inscribed beneath the portrait of an African woman cradling a child have become the enduring mantra of Regeneration Writers: "I may not be able to do great things, but I can do small things in a great way." A miracle of inclusiveness and diversity rooted in a common reality, these works increase and enrich the great body of enduring Southern literature.
--Margaret H. Eskew, Publishing Editor

TABLE OF CONTENTS

DEDICATION

to

Duane Evans Davis

&

John Colin Harris

Duane Evans Davis: One Who Holds the Lamp

For nearly forty years, I have enjoyed and benefitted from a personal and professional association with Duane Davis. I am honored to offer from that experience some thoughts on the significance of his life and work as teacher, colleague, and friend.

One of Duane's favorite stories, which he cites often with appreciation as a gift early in his teaching career from our late teacher and friend Jean Hendricks, is poet Robert Louis Stevenson's memory of watching as a child the village lamplighter going at dusk from lamppost to lamppost illuminating the darkening street. "Look," he called to his father, "that man is punching holes in the darkness!"

Those of us who have worked and studied with Duane Davis readily see the effect of this image in his philosophy of education. Quietly, perceptively, gently, and effectively, he has lit many a lamp in many a dark spot in the streets of religion, history, and philosophy, as well as in the darker places in the personal journeys of many a student and colleague.

Modifying that image slightly, but keeping the theme of light and darkness, I'd like to suggest that for all of us–students, colleagues, and friends–Duane has been throughout his life and career as a teacher "one who holds the lamp" for others to see by.

There is the kind of light that calls attention to itself – the lights of a holiday decoration, for example, or the lights of an advertisement, designed to impress us in such a way that we will respond by buying its product. And, there is the kind of light that focuses on an object to the exclusion of its surroundings – the spotlight on a stage celebrity. Then there is the kind of light whose purpose is to illumine the area of something previously in the dark so that it can be seen for what it is rather than for what the shadows sometimes make it appear to be. When this kind of light does its job well, it often goes unnoticed once the illumined subject is seen more clearly.

We who have been fortunate to be traveling companions with Duane Davis in our personal and academic journeys know well the benefit of his holding the lamp for us as we have navigated the complex paths of our lives and careers.

One who holds the lamp does not presume to tell us what we

will see, but helps us have the clarity of vision to discover it for ourselves.

One who holds the lamp does not require particular answers to life's challenges, but helps us to see and understand the questions more clearly.

One who holds the lamp does not require honor or even appreciation, but unselfishly offers a service for the benefit of others' growth and development.

One who holds the lamp seems to say, "Look at this and tell me what you see," and, in the conversation both discover new levels of understanding of what is illumined.

In an academic world too easily vulnerable to "look at me" scholarship, it is both refreshing and inspiring to know that there continue to be followers of the "masters" of teaching – those whose focus is on the "leading out" (*e –ducere*) of the capabilities inherent in every student. The "bright lights" on one generation are easily superseded by the brighter ones of the next, but the carefully held lamps of one generation enable the developing understanding of what is true and good to continue to evolve from one generation to the next.

Those who have read Duane's *Light in Dark Places* know how generous he is in his appreciation for those who have held the lamp for him along his journey. Perhaps it is that kind of awareness and gratitude that creates an effective "lamp holder" for others. If that is the case, there is a legacy of thousands now who are serving in that role in their everyday places, having as a model of "how to do it" our friend and teacher Duane Davis.

--J. Colin Harris

JOHN COLIN HARRIS: LIBERATOR

Colin Harris joined the faculty of Mercer University, his alma mater, in the fall of 1977. He retired from his faculty position in the spring of 2013. During his thirty-six years at Mercer, Colin served as full-time Professor in both religious studies and philosophy, chair of several faculty committees, and for a number of years Department Chair in liberal studies. Throughout his career at Mercer, Colin received repeated recognition from his students as

Faculty Member of the Year on the Atlanta campus, and most recently, in 2010, he was honored as the first university-wide recipient of the Joe and Jean Hendricks Excellence in Teaching Award.

In his role as classroom teacher, Colin endeared himself to his students, who continue to remember him as a thoughtful, challenging, and liberating professor. They speak of him with gratitude for introducing them to new ways of thinking and for helping them see, perhaps for the first time, that a life of serious thought and reflection is not incompatible with a life of genuine faith. Teaching is not only about instruction, and Colin continually helped them understand and take seriously the fact that they have been gifted with how to engage both heart and head.

Colin had a way of helping his students see in themselves talent and potential they didn't know they had. Several years ago during a serious classroom discussion about education, one of Colin's colleagues listened carefully as one of the students acknowledged and expressed deep appreciation for a teacher she had had who helped her, after years of self-doubt, begin to believe in herself. That was for her, she confided, like an escape from a debilitating prison. Following the discussion, during a class break a couple of hours later, her teacher asked her if she had been talking about Colin Harris. "Yes!" she said. "How did you know?"

Colin's work as a teacher is not confined to the classroom. For several years Colin has been busy writing and submitting, a couple of times a month, carefully stated arguments about thoughtful and courageous Christian participation in critical ethical issues of our time. In the *EthicsDaily* website, readers will find wise counsel about responsible citizenship in today's troubled world.

Colin is a courageous participant in the ongoing debate not only about how the University can achieve its objectives, but also about what those objectives should be. He has served as a quiet but persuasive leader in the effort to frame the questions and consider the options regarding where the University should go in the years ahead. For both his classroom teaching and his thoughtful faculty leadership, Colin Harris continues to serve his alma mater as a grateful former student who has returned to his roots to continue the tradition from which he himself found both educational guidance and a deep and abiding commitment to paying it forward.

--Duane Evans Davis

INTRODUCTION

Regeneration! A Journal of Creative Writing demonstrates once again the powerful impact of a unique learning space that both intentionally and accidentally accentuates the life experiences and encounters of its students. Partnering with teachers dedicated to mentoring their students and learning from them, students in Mercer University's Penfield College build a love of learning sure to last a lifetime.

Central to our work in Mercer University's Penfield College is underscoring the beauty, power, and impact of writing. Critical to our work is connecting with our students and connecting them with one another so they come to understand that writing strengthens their ability to lead and serve others with an integrity that emerges from valuing and telling their own stories.

--Priscilla Ruth Danheiser, Dean of Penfield College

HONEST WRITING AND READING

A writer writes. An honest writer displays his or her heart for inspection, and there isn't much that is braver than that. Within the pages of this journal are many displays of such bravery. Through reading the essays, stories, and poetry within this collection, you the reader have the opportunity to contemplate viewpoints from varying positions in the landscape of the human experience, and to listen to authentic voices. You may laugh at the antics of hens and goats, or chipmunks in a mattress. You may be sad watching a family break apart or a little boy miss his mama. You may get angry at the injustice of those who try so hard and still haven't quite gotten there. You may discover something about yourself and the way you may have treated others in the past, as I did. The offerings here are not just about reading for entertainment, although you certainly will be entertained. They are about giving voice to a variety of writers and giving contemplation opportunities to readers.

Honest writing is about throwing off fear and allowing

growth. But as I think about it, honest reading is about the very same thing: setting aside one's own closely guarded binoculars and picking up someone else's. Giving these opportunities to writers and readers is what *Regeneration!* is all about.

Joining the editing process as the alumni editor of this journal is a privilege and a joy. I am proud to be a small part in this latest edition of *Regeneration!*

--Terri DeFoor, Alumni Editor

A MERCER MIRACLE

As a little girl, I walked across the campus of Mercer University. As an adult, I drove through the campus to my job at the Post Office on College Street until the street was closed off. An African American, I felt the negative vibes emanating from the campus, seemingly whispering in my ear that I did not belong there–that I was not capable of doing the academic tasks successfully executed by Mercer's white student body. Never did I imagine that my mindset would be completely turned around.

When the little girl walked across the campus, she wasn't greeted with smiles, but shooed away. Even though she was among the smartest and brightest students in Macon, Mercer admissions did not attempt to woo her. She eventually concluded that the consensus at Mercer was that she was just not good enough. It was the consensus in the black community that at Mercer white was far superior to black. The little girl began to hate Mercer–and white people.

The little girl grew up, eschewing college for the workforce. Passing the exam for the Post Office with an almost perfect score, she spent the first half of her career ensuring the timely and accurate delivery of the daily mail to Macon residents. In the second half, she served as district analyst in Operations for the South Georgia District, covering from the Middle Georgia area to the rest of the southern half of Georgia and parts of South Carolina, including, for example, Savannah, Valdosta, Albany, Columbus, and Hilton Head, South Carolina. As district analyst, she had an enormous amount of responsibility that included managing operations in all the post offices in the South Georgia district–the motivation for her development of cutting-edge computer, analytical, and managerial skills. About one-third of the way into her tenure at the Post Office, the now grown-up little girl encountered a life-changing force. A religious experience motivated an intense study of the message of Jesus and a fierce dedication to learning the ways of God, resulting in a fifteen-year home ministry to Macon's children.

Retirement brought with it the challenge of how best to invest her time and talents in her post-retirement years toward addressing the issues and challenges her spiritual rebirth had awakened within her. Realizing her need of knowledge and skills, she attended the Crossroads Institute of Biblical Studies for almost two decades. In November of 2013, recurrent thoughts of attending Mercer University began to invade her satisfaction with her life's journey. She immediately dismissed the thought of attending Mercer. However, it was as if the voice of God was whispering in her ear: "Mercer University." She prayed, asking God, "Are you trying to tell me something?" Sensing a big "Yes," she went to Mercer the next day to see what would happen. To her great surprise, Mercer welcomed her with open arms and the financial assistance she needed.

She became a Liberal Studies major with a concentration in Religious Studies and eventually added a second concentration in writing, reuniting her with an earlier love for writing. The selection of readings, introspective assignments, and the student-centered and open teaching style of the professor brought about a genuine reflection on her past life and education. Honest, reflective writing helped her put her life experiences and attitudes in perspective and pointed her to a more redemptive path. The quality education she received in the area of language and racial history brought a new awareness and understanding. She experienced a new freedom. The burden of hatred and recrimination was lifted. Her energy level increased as her creativity was engaged. She experienced regeneration.

Her regeneration spilled over into the social arena. A deferred dream of establishing a fulltime shelter for the homeless in Macon, Georgia was rekindled, leading to her involvement at Daybreak, a resource center that provides Macon's homeless population with critical services all in one place. She volunteered to help those on the outer fringes of life write their personal stories. At Daybreak, she began facilitating a writers' group that meets weekly. Daybreak participants share personal stories as she shares the writing skills she is learning at Mercer. At the urging of her Mercer professors, this effort turned into a research project, "Narratives of Homelessness," that she presented at the 2015 Mercer University Atlanta Research Conference. She subsequently led a student-initiated community of writers, Estuary Writers International Guild (EWIG), whose purpose is to change the world through writing. They meet regularly to share their works and receive feedback and support from each other.

On that first visit to Mercer, the admissions counselor, Angel Horton, happened to show the little girl (now a retiree) a beautiful book that had been written and published by working adult students. The pictures of the writers on the back cover testified to the full inclusion of all races and ages. It sealed her decision to cast her lot with Mercer. Wistfully, she thought about how wonderful it must be to work with a group of writers to write, design, and publish such a book. Miraculously, she voluntarily took the two beginning writing classes required for all Penfield graduates, then enrolled in additional writing courses, and volunteered to be the student editor of the 2016 volume.

Regeneration! A Journal of Creative Writing 2016 includes some of the stories, essays, and poems that writers birthed and polished in EWIG and in Penfield classes. This collection of works by students, faculty, staff, and friends of Mercer is a testimony to the regeneration that opens minds to change and catalyzes new energy and engagement. This volume epitomizes the repeated miracle of regeneration that students experience in Penfield College at Mercer. It is our sincere hope that our words and sentences will open up your world such that you can experience with that little girl the miracle of regeneration.

--Sharon McElhaney, Student Editor

A REGENERATIVE COMMUNITY OF WRITERS

Regeneration! A Journal of Creative Writing (2016) represents a journey of discovery. Writing our stories, poems, essays, sermons, and plays evinces both a communal effort and personal discipline. We write to learn–to discover patterns that are invisible until one phrase, sentence, feeling, or fact juxtaposed against a second and a third reveals a relationship or connection. The writers form a community across generation, gender, religion, race, and class. We wade into the shallow waters together and sometimes jump into the deep end. We wait silently, speak softly and exuberantly, laugh long and loudly, and weep. We listen to the authentic voices of other authors and celebrate their compelling honesty. Together we expand the worldview of each other and develop a greater awareness of ourselves, our world, and ourselves in the world.

Regeneration! writers embody the strengths of diversity. As many as sixty years separate the youngest author from the oldest. Collectively, the writers speak at least six languages natively. Although Georgia is a common denominator, they come from all across the United States and several foreign countries and represent a broad range of disciplines and professions. In addition to working adult students from Mercer's Penfield College, writers include Mercer staff, professors, alumni, and friends, including a professor of speech and theater from Albany State University in South Georgia. Topics emerge from the writers and from courses taught in Penfield or from Mercer programs, such as Mercer on Mission.

The dedications honor two beloved faculty members who are now retired: Duane Evans Davis and John Colin Harris. Duane graciously and magnanimously volunteered to help proof the first book. Colin was the chair of Penfield's Department of Liberal Studies who genially consented to provide creative writing courses upon multiple student requests. Both men have supported the writing efforts of students by their gifts of presence at student readings and their participation in classes as guest writers. Both Duane and Colin contributed essays to this volume, unaware that they are being honored.

When it came time to write dedicatory remarks, there was no question but Duane would craft the text for Colin and vice versa, each under the impression that the other was being honored. We are indebted to them for the examples they set for us. Duane wrote and published *Light in Dark Places* to articulate the role that key books have played in his spiritual journey. A regular contributor to the online journal, *EthicsToday*, Colin Harris has recently completed a book with his son and granddaughter, *Thirteen Heroes*, about the integration of a school in Georgia and the principal who individually welcomed each of the thirteen students to *their* school.

Our sincere desire is that the voices radiating from this volume will add momentum to your discovery of value and sustainable community.

--Margaret H. Eskew, Publishing Editor

I, Too, Have a Dream . . .

. . . that everyone who needs a place to live will have somewhere safe that he or she can go.
--Sharon McElhaney

. . . that we never stop dreaming. We should set our dreams and goals sky high, never accepting less than what we deserve.
--Anna M. McEwen

. . . that acceptance and tolerance will rule the land, toppling inequality and bigotry.
--Maximo G. Wharton

. . . that we will stand up against injustice anywhere.
--Margaret H. Eskew

. . . of a world where respect, integrity, truth, and love reign.
--Ray Sapp

. . . of tolerance, of equality, of the meticulous dismantling of systematic partitioning.
--John Steele

. . . a dream where history is remembered without being used to divide people, where our past is used to improve our future, where people's religious beliefs and resources are used to unite and care for all people, where religious texts are no longer used as weapons to hurt and ostracize those who may look or believe differently. I dream of a world that works for our children, where both the physical earth and the cultures that we cultivate are acknowledged as crucial and inseparable components for a better tomorrow--not just for humanity, but for every living thing that shares this world with us—of a world of awareness, where we think beyond ourselves—most importantly perhaps, of a world filled with fellow dreamers.
--William M. (Bo) Walker

. . . that we will live as equals and not judge or be judged.
--Robert (Bob) Mathis

. . . that our differences will no longer overpower our similarities.
--David D. Toliver

. . . that one day technology will repair the damaged body and allow the blind to see, the deaf to hear, the crippled to walk and run, and the hearts and minds of all to reach their fullest potential.
--Karl S. Adams

. . . that my children and grandchildren will achieve every life purpose for which they were created. I want to experience the fullness of life, teaching by example through faithfulness instead of empty words, echoing Shakespeare's immortal line: "To thine own self be true."
--Annie Stephens

. . . to one day have my own classroom of children, to one day fall in love and have children, and to take my family overseas and teach in a foreign country.
--Michael Northrup

. . . of owning my own home one day, of using this education to help people with substance abuse issues or victims of domestic violence, of loving my job and making a good living.
--Linda Southward

. . . that one day each person will receive the help he or she needs to overcome the obstacles that prevent him or her from becoming his or her best self—perhaps something as simple as day care so a young mother can work without worrying about her children or a trip to the dentist for someone with a toothache; . . . that someday people will realize that we are here to help each other.
--Jan Crocker

. . . to conquer my fear of public speaking so that I can help battered families or individuals who have been in domestic-violence relationships.
--Ashley Campbell

ALL IN THE FAMILY

What can you do to promote peace? Go home and love your family.
--Mother Teresa

All happy families are alike; each unhappy family is unhappy in its own way.
--Leo Tolstoy

The family is the nucleus of civilization.
--Will Durant

The strength of a nation derives from the integrity of the home.
--Confucius

Family life is too intimate to be preserved by the spirit of justice. It can be sustained by a spirit of love that goes beyond justice.
--Reinhold Niebuhr

I have found the best way to give advice to your children is to find out what they want and then advise them to do it.
--Harry S. Truman

A family is a place where minds come in contact with one another.
--Buddha

You can kiss your family and friends good-bye and put miles between you, but at the same time you carry them with you in your heart, your mind, your stomach, because you do not just live in a world but a world lives in you.
--Frederick Buechner

I sustain myself with the love of family.
--Maya Angelou

Nobody has ever before asked the nuclear family to live all by itself in a box the way we do. With no relatives, no support, we've put it in an impossible situation.
--Margaret Mead

REGENERATION

Winds blowing from the northwest against a colorful back-drop of the American landscape signal the arrival of the fall season. The farmers have gathered all of the bountiful harvest of food for the upcoming winter. New seeds of growth will soon be planted in great anticipation of next year's harvest. The sun and rain will combine to nourish the seeds as they mature and regenerate the fields with next year's crops.

Ring, ring, ring–that can only be the sound of my faithful rotary-dial telephone. Ever faithful, the bulky device serves as a reminder of times past. *Click, click, click*–I always like numbers with a nine in them–the more clicks to listen to as I spin the numbers on the telephone. The communication device that sits on my bedside table today is a creation of modern art. The clickety rotary dial with its loud-bell ring has been regenerated into a series of push-button tones on a sleek device absent of any bell sound.

The elementary school teacher commanded, "Come to the chalkboard and complete this math problem." Why is it every time I visit the chalkboard, the only chalk available is small and worn down? It's like writing on the board with my knuckles. Why can't someone invent something other than this nasty chalkboard to write on? Technology has since regenerated a new crop of utilities that some might say has successfully retired the dusty chalkboard. Smart boards connected to projectors with wireless interfaces make chalk smudges a matter of history.

A few years ago my best friend's wife gave birth to a little boy. He has his whole life to look forward to. A baby's birth symbolizes the start of life. The years will expire as this child grows in physical size and mental ability. As I continue to mature mentally and enter the middle years of adulthood, I look enviously at the wisdom the years have granted my father and grandfather. In time, my grandfather and father will dim their lights for the last time. Our children will continue the cycle of life, carrying a part of us into future generations. Life is a continuing practice of regeneration.

--Cliff Brown

PINKY

Pinky's head popped up, "Where, where?" She had missed seeing the wild rabbit spotted by her brother, Phil, as it darted across the road. Rita saw it, though, sneering at Pinky's slow reaction. Pinky couldn't respond fast enough to catch the type of excitement that only occurred once a year when the family traveled the country roads of Powersville, Georgia.

Taking their children to live in the country for three months' summer vacation was the Jones's way of giving themselves and their children a break from each other. The children didn't mind sacrificing the conveniences of electricity and running water for the unequaled freedom of living in the country. The father sat at the wheel of their black Pontiac, the mother at his side, and the children in the back, as they rode twenty miles south of Macon to their relatives' home.

On this trip, Rita, age seven, hugged the driver's-side back window, and Phil, age six, almost leaned out the opposite side, as the children quietly soaked in the changing scenery when the car turned off the paved road onto the dirt. Shortly thereafter, one of the tires went flat. This didn't dampen their spirits. Their father effortlessly changed the tire, and the trip continued along the long, narrow country road until they reached the stop sign. Slightly to the right sat the general store that also served as the courthouse, city hall, post office, bus stop, and train depot. It was Powersville's all-in-one stop.

They turned left up a steep hill, adorned with plantation-styled homes and barns about a mile apart on both sides, until they reached the top. At the hilltop, a right turn led to Mr. Thomas's two-story house, which seemed smaller than its actual size because of the distance it sat back from the road. Around the curve, a fence ran along both sides of the road. The uncultivated thin brush on the left contrasted with the thick woods with tall trees on the right. The white, powdery dirt road was long, narrow, and straight, its straightness seeming to add to its length. Finally, it ended at a "T" where the mailboxes stood. Down about two miles and to the right resided the Sugar family, an elderly couple who were their relatives' only neighbors.

Their relatives, the Nelsons, lived to the left down another long, narrow road, where the ground was harder with rocks and debris strewn about, and the woods were thicker. Branches and limbs almost reached into the car. The Nelsons' house of wooden boards stood at the end of the dead-end street. Its four rooms had two front doors, two back doors, a porch, and windows on the sides. Aunt Dora came out on the porch, wiping her hands on her apron. Her wide smile, bright and complete, complemented the colorful scarf that tied up her hair. The absence of their car meant that Uncle Judge was not at home. Welcoming chatter filled the air as Doll Baby, their only daughter, and their three sons, Richard, Troy, and Willie C., all teenagers, came from around the house at the sound of the car. Immediately, what seemed like two-inch thick clouds of gnats surrounded Rita, Phil, and Pinky, getting into their mouths, eyes, and noses. The children quickly learned to fight them off and after a few days no longer noticed them.

When Rita, Phil, and Pinky roamed about the farm, they observed the chickens, some running free and others in their coops. Their cousins demonstrated the daily egg-retrieval method. Even rows of crops grew in the back on the right side of the house behind a huge black boiling pot. In the middle of the backyard and behind the hog pen stood the dreaded outhouse with its Sears and Roebuck catalogue minus about half of its pages. Pinky knew why they kept the catalogue in the outhouse. Farther to the left were the woodpile and the path that led to the gate of the cow pasture. The gate had a clothes-hanger wire lock that looped over a four-by-four post. The path to the well led through the cows and then down a steep hill. It was imperative to keep the gate locked so the cows could not get out.

As soon as the children began searching the woods for something edible, Aunt Dora called them for supper. Food cooked in a wood-burning stove was beyond compare: fried chicken, fresh from the backyard; peas and greens, picked out of the field; and homemade biscuits and preserves. After supper, everyone gathered for homemade ice cream in the living room, which doubled as Aunt Dora and Uncle Judge's bedroom. Each child had a turn at spinning the crank of the ice cream maker. As the day came to an end, the father and mother kissed their children goodbye, trusting them into the capable hands of Aunt Dora.

A strict disciplinarian, Aunt Dora kept her "enforcer," a two-inch leather strap, hanging handily on a nail in the middle of the doorway between the living room and the kitchen. The children bedded on the other side of the house. Rita and Pinky rested serenely in the warmth of hand-sewn quilts in a full-sized bed with Doll Baby. Phil and his cousins, Troy and Willie C., slept on bunk beds in the same room, while the oldest cousin, Richard, slept in the back pantry.

The Nelson kids had their cousins to help with the chores. Rita helped Doll Baby feed the chickens, clean the coop, and gather eggs. Phil helped with slopping the hogs and toting wood from the pile. Since Pinky was only four years old, she played around the house with Aunt Dora, who wouldn't allow her to go near the hogs.

Pinky was, however, included in the daily trips to the well, although she did not carry any water. The walk through the cow pasture terrified her. Towering over Pinky with big round eyes, the cows lowed at the most unexpected times. Rita and Phil teased Pinky because of her fear, with their cousins, Troy and Willie C., playfully joining in.

The descent to the well required a balancing act down the wide, rocky pathway. At the bottom of the hill next to the well was a trough filled with water. Cousin Troy opened his palm, skimmed the surface of the water so that the water spread on both sides of his hand, and announced, "Here go my motorboat." Willie C. stood beside the trough with his arm outstretched, gliding his palm across the water. He likewise declared, "Here go my motorboat." Rita and Phil mimicked them. Then they looked at Pinky, standing on a brick at the end of the trough. Feeling compelled, she announced, "Here go my motorboat," trying to do what the others had done. Her arms were not long enough. She fell face first into the water. All the while they were at the well, the siblings and cousins laughed and teased Pinky. The thought of her splash entertained them as they carried buckets of water up the hill. As they passed by the cows, they didn't neglect the opportunity to tease Pinky once again.

Not long afterwards, Pinky took a chance at climbing the hog pen. Aunt Dora caught her red-handed. Pinky knew she had done wrong. As punishment, Aunt Dora told her she had to get a bucket, go to the well, and fill it with water–all by herself. Pinky began to cry as she obediently picked up a bucket. Crying louder and louder, she approached the gate that led into the cow pasture. Pinky unlocked the gate and was about to open it when Aunt Dora yelled, "Ah, Gal. Com' on back. You don't have to go git no water." Pinky was so glad. She happily skipped back to the house with bucket in hand.

That night all the cows got out of the fence. Aunt Dora woke up all the children with the belt: "Somebody left the gate unlocked, and all the cows got out. Git up and go git them cows," she ordered in a high-pitched voice, while slicing licks on their behinds.

Cousin Troy wore glasses. Whenever he went to sleep in his glasses, he got a whipping. He frantically patted his eyes, protesting, "I ain't got my glasses on." Aunt Dora continued to beat him, and he jumped out of the window.

Aunt Dora wailed, "Git up! Somebody left the gate unlocked, and all the cows got out. Go git 'em, and count every one."

Everybody got the strap that morning, including Rita and Phil–everybody except Pinky. No one knew who had left the gate unlocked. All the children had to find the cows–everybody except Pinky. She was the baby.

The house was quiet that day with everyone gone to round up the cows. They did not return until late that evening after all the animals were accounted for. Following supper, Willie C. called Pinky to come to him.

"Panky, 'member when Muh told you t' go git a buckit of water?"

Pinky answered, "Yeah."

"An' 'member when you walked up ta de gate and unlocked it?"

She replied, "Yeah."

Willie C. continued his examination: "An' 'member when Muh tol' you you didn't hafta git dat water?"

"Yeah," she smiled.

Then he concluded, "Panky, you didn't lock dat gate back."

Pinky's eyes widened. She gasped, realizing she was the guilty party.

Before long, everyone knew that Pinky had been the one who had left the gate unlocked. The unfolding events caused the teasing to backfire. It wasn't as pleasurable to the others to pick on Pinky the remainder of the summer.

14

On the trip back home, the long, country roads seemed somehow shorter. Pinky alone caught a glimpse of a wild rabbit. "I saw a rabbit," she proclaimed exultantly, standing on the back seat and peering out of the window of their black Pontiac.

--Sharon McElhaney

Nobody to Tell

The South presented a time of frequent violent protests against racial segregation by blacks and the ensuing protests against integration by whites. Blacks wanted schools integrated. Whites fought and protested against the integration of schools, neighborhoods, buses, restaurants–against everything, it seemed. Outside, a war was raging among people of different races, while inside the old three-bedroom frame house lived a family–all of the same race—with a raging war of its own–and nobody to tell.

Except for a simple letter to the editor–Ceci's lone memory of affirmation from her parents—she did not actively participate in the "Black Struggle"–the demonstrations, protests, and the violent verbal and physical racial exchanges between whites and blacks. Yet, she clearly knew what injustice felt like and sensed that the state of affairs in black households was somehow connected to the injustices inflicted upon the black race.

She was just a child—an observant and obedient child who had learned as a safety mechanism to bend her wishes to those around her. She would say whatever they wanted her to say and act according to their dictates. Perpetual violence loomed all around her–indoors and outdoors. Her perception of the outdoors was skewed–the violence there waned in comparison to what went on daily indoors. Both were out of her control. What should have been a time of childhood innocence for her was filled with the constant threat of violence and the resulting insecurity concerning her immediate future. Her parents' house was a house divided–just like the community and the nation.

Ceci needed a way to deal with what was happening. When her grandmother introduced her to the Bible, she held on to it for dear life. Sensing the authority of the scriptures, she became quite familiar with many of God's promises. She began to read the Bible daily, eventually lighting on Psalm 70, which became her fervent prayer for deliverance from the situation in which she found herself trapped:

Make haste, O God, to deliver me!
Make haste to help me, O Lord!
Let them be ashamed and confounded that seek after my life.
Let them be turned backward and put to confusion that desire
*   my hurt.*
Let them be turned back because of their shame who say:
*   "Aha, aha!"*
Let all those that seek You rejoice and be glad in You;
And let those who love Your salvation say continually, "Let
*   God be magnified!"*
But I am poor and needy; make haste to me, O God!
You are my help and my deliverance;
O Lord, do not delay.

As a five-year-old, Ceci and her mother claimed the great promise of Matthew 5:8: "Blessed are the pure in heart, for they shall see God." At this tender age, she fervently desired a pure heart more than anything else. She expectantly and dutifully walked the mile to the church on the hill, where her grandparents and mother worshipped. Going alone, she talked aloud to God and listened attentively for a response. Even though she acknowledged that God was everywhere, she rarely experienced Him at home or in their neighborhood. Once, during a violent storm when her father was away for the night, her mother gathered all the children in one room, praying ardently for their protection. She felt strength come out of their gathering together. However, this occurrence was not enough to meet the need she had for relationship.

Ceci's neighborhood did not offer her a sense of belonging or safety. On cool summer nights on the old wooden porch swing where the mother and her children sat until way past dark, they had no peace of mind knowing that boys gathered to sell and use drugs just a block away. Whenever she rounded the corner to go to Perry's Grocer, fear caused shivers to go up her spine.

Ceci's only solace was the gatherings at church on Sundays, when the church doors were always open. In welcoming visitors who came to worship, her mother would proudly tell them that her daughter walked to church all by herself. The praise of her mother did not compensate for the fact that her parents owned several cars, but she had to walk everywhere she went. In fact, she could not remember ever riding with her father.

Her parents must have enjoyed some togetherness early in their marriage, when they had been quite young. She saw no remainder of the love she thought must have motivated their marriage. There were no conversations of substance, no hugs, no birthday celebrations, not even an "I love you."

In the summers, she and her siblings either watched television sitcoms or played outside. Since their parents did not buy them toys, they learned to create their own playthings. Together they constructed "stick children," using candy wrappings for clothing and recycling the twine from bunches of collard greens for hair. They designed houses and cars for their stick children and became the voices for them, almost endlessly redirecting their own thoughts into the combinations of sticks and twine. They reluctantly left their "children" to eat their daily allotment of collard greens and cornbread, washed down with Kool-Aid. During berry season, Ceci and her siblings were permitted to go a whole block away to pick blackberries for their mother to make pies.

Although her father was physically present in their home, he was emotionally absent. When his car pulled up in the driveway, all the children immediately scampered off. He did not like for them to sit in the front of the house. His dictum reminded Ceci of the social practice relegating black people to the back of the bus.

At mealtime, her father received special treatment with the fan trained on him and a loyal wife at his beck and call. On weekdays, he left each night and returned early the next morning to catch a ride to work at the military base, where he had a leadership position. He never came inside to greet his wife or his children. He ran the house like a boot camp. His wife and children did not know real freedom. They had to endure in their home what most blacks endured in Southern society.

Their house had belonged to their maternal grandparents. Their father paid the bills on time and bought their ration of groceries, although there was seldom more than the basics. Outwardly a fine man, her father fit the image of the good family man: he went to work every day, he did not drink, and he did not do drugs.

He prided himself on not having to depend on welfare to care for his family. But there was no consistency.

His weapon of choice was cutting language. He assaulted his family verbally, cursing them for what they did and what they didn't do. His disrespect toward his family carried over to whites. He would look white people straight in the eye and curse them out. When he cursed out the white woman from the Department of Family and Children Services who came to investigate, she never returned. Because of his threatening personality, no one dared interfere. Not content to keep people at bay with his bad humor, her father also kept several mean dogs, which he carefully tended, reserving for them one half of the yard to roam freely.

"Get me my #*&! belt," he would yell at the slightest infraction of his wife or one of his children. It was not the one he wore, but a thick black leather strap that would wrap itself around the body. In accordance with his belief that children require regular discipline, the children lined up for their daily beatings. The boys had to drop their pants, and the girls had to take off their blouses, exposing even their bras. Intelligently, Ceci escaped daily beatings through obedience. She learned early how to stay out of trouble.

Their mother received the worst of the beatings—those that were unannounced. She was threatened with knives and guns. She was shoved, hit, beaten, and called a bitch, the source of Ceci's recurring nightmares. Once her father just walked in, picked up the water bucket, and poured the water onto her mother's newly styled hair.

"He said he's going to get the gun," their mother cried to her children on another occasion. The children advised her to leave, but she refused. Once, when the police were finally called, her father showed his "nice" side to them. Afterwards he gave all of his family a stern warning that no one was ever to call the police again. They had to shift to plan B—run down the street to a cousin's house and, without telling her what was going on, ask her if she could come—that mother needed her. Afterwards, their father would then leave their mother alone for a while and go away.

On one occasion, they had left their father for all of one day and had gone to live with another cousin about two miles away. When the father found out where they were, he called and asked them to come home. None of the children wanted to return, but the mother told them that she couldn't take care of all of them by herself. Sadly, she held on to an extremely abusive relationship because of the security she thought it provided.

Although no one took notice, Ceci did exceptionally well during the elementary grades but became discouraged in junior high. Art gradually became the vehicle for her voice. Her high school art teacher persuaded her to enter her work into a competition. When she asked her father for art supplies, the answer was a resounding "no." Later, the newspaper sponsored an art competition with the winner to receive a scholarship to an art school. Ceci practiced and practiced with pencil and paper and finally got up the courage to put her drawing in the mail. To her surprise, she received a phone call that she had won.

"Get off that #^*n phone," her father bellowed.

"But, but–" she tried to explain. The person on the other end continued to explain more about the scholarship and Ceci's winning entry.

Her father threateningly sidled up to her. "Now!" he yelled and slammed down the phone abruptly ending the conversation. "Next time, I won't ask you to get off the phone," he uttered menacingly.

Friends weren't allowed to visit but for very short periods of time. "Run along home," her father would admonish. Fearing his reception by her father, she met her boyfriend for a ride on the way to school. No matter how cold the weather was, her father insisted that she and her siblings walk to school.

One cool morning, her boyfriend surprised her with the suggestion, "Let's go to the woods and make love." It was more of a command than an amorous request. He was at the wheel, and she was at his mercy. At age fifteen, she was still a virgin with no desire to be intimate with him. All she had wanted was a good friend.

"I want to go to school," she whined.

"We are going to the woods to make love," he stated unequivocally.

"No! I want to go to school. I'm not going to the woods," she shot back.

He continued to drive on, accelerating to over 55 mph. Observing the road's shoulder, she decided to take her chances. Without warning, she jumped from the vehicle, nearly losing an eye in the process.

"Are you out of your #*!^ing mind? Get back in this #^*n car!" he ordered.

"No," she stubbornly shook her head as she trudged, shaken, back up the road with her injured eye. She never spoke to that boy again.

At home, she wanted to confide in her mother, but she knew that her mother would feel compelled to tell her father–all of them always had to answer to him.

"You've been in a #^*n fight," he accused.

He did not allow fighting outside the home. She made up a story that he didn't buy. He was a smart man who often bragged, "I got dollars and sense with it!" She reasoned that if she told her parents, they would likely press charges. The boy would then deny everything and go free. He would go free, and she would get all the backlash–literally.

Nobody knew what had happened except the boy and her. There was nobody she could tell.

--C. C. Engram

TREASURES

She saw them–tiny stars throwing light as they tumbled from the lap of the lady in the steel gray dress with white narrow-corded trim as she scooted off the buttery leather passenger seat and stood up. And she saw the pretty lady in gray keep walking, the driver of the shiny black car right beside her with his hand on her waist.

Mavis waited until they had disappeared through the glass entrance doors of the mall, then eased up carefully, first looking around. No one else had seen it–of that she was certain. She shuffled over in the old Nikes that her daughter Emma had brought her from a yard sale a year or so ago. Her snagged and uneven black skirt caught the warm spring breeze. Mavis felt antsy–like a daredevil kid waiting in line for a roller coaster ride and trying to look teenage-bored. She drew her eyes into a scan of the asphalt around the passenger side of the shiny black car. She quickly spotted them both. And she knew at once that there were only two. They were matching stud earrings, big diamonds mounted in silver.

Forgetting the need to look inconspicuous, she stooped stiffly and reached for both at the same time, each hand grasping for treasure. She almost lost her awkward footing. Hungry eyes knew immediately what she now had in her possession. For the most fleeting of moments, while she slowly drew her small and life-worn frame upright, the thought to hurry toward that glass door crossed her mind. She saw herself finding the pretty lady in the gray dress with white trim. She saw herself being hugged by the lady who enveloped Mavis with breathy gratitude, and then backed up to look at her with blue and gray eyes, smile lines around them deepening in admiration. Then Mavis saw her pull a couple of hundred dollar bills out of a turquoise and gray purse to show just how much she appreciated honest Mavis. Blue and gray eyes looked into Mavis' soul.

Mavis looked around again as she stood still next to the car, a diamond earring in each hand. Doing her best to look as if nothing spectacular had just happened to her, she transferred the diamond in her left hand to her right, now holding both together, protected by a fist so tight that the posts were threatening to poke through her lined and leathery palm. She adjusted the wide strap of her tattered brown shoulder bag so that it hung straight over the pink cardigan with the stretched-out front. It gave her something nor-mal-looking to do as she scanned the parking lot once more.

Then she broke into a smile—a smile so big that all of her front teeth were exposed, and not just the two in front that had always slightly protruded. She just couldn't help herself. This was better than winning the lottery, Mavis thought. And because sometimes her really great thoughts needed to be spoken, she uttered aloud: "This is better than winning the lottery!" She examined the park-ing lot again, reminding herself to keep quiet and squinting her eyes as the sun appeared from behind one bumpy gray cloud and headed toward another. No one was even close to her. There were a few in the distance, and that was all. Trembling inside, she slow-ly opened her hand to view the two stars in the emerging sunlight. She gasped: "So sparkling!" They threw off so many fragments of light that she feared that their brilliance had drawn someone else toward the treasure in her hand. She narrowed her eyes and clamped her hand around the diamonds once again, and turned to walk toward the highway crosswalk and toward home, forgetting why she had come to the mall in the first place.

Mavis lived a half-mile or so from the mall, in the same trailer park where she had lived for thirty-one years–ever since George had divorced her to marry his second wife. Last she had heard, he was now between wives. She had also heard that his hardware stores were doing well now–the same string of stores that had kept them on the doorstep of the poorhouse while George pretended to be well-off, spending money on watches and shirts with his initials in block letters on the pockets and expensive dinners for what he claimed were potential investors, while stuffing the regular bills in the deep bottom drawer of his desk. The reports about George's good business fortune and bad marriage decisions had come from her only son who now lived in Atlanta with his skinny, stylish wife and three sons. She could never tell if Danny was proud of his father or disgusted with him.

The white trailer was really a pretty little home when she had first settled in and begun substitute teaching for the county school system; the fork-shaped neighborhood was clean with little manicured front lawns and metal A-framed swing sets in the back yards. Her neighbors were mostly young couples, many with children, working and saving money for a down payment on a real house. A few retired couples had also lived there. There had even been a community vegetable garden at the back of the neighborhood, tended mostly by Mr. Molter and Mr. Jacobs, both of whom had kept a large garden for years before downsizing and moving to the trailer park. They didn't have tractors anymore, but had gone in together to buy a used Troy-Built rototiller. The summer tomatoes that they had grown had made the best sandwiches! Mavis had been closest to Brenda, who lived by herself, one street over. Mavis and Brenda used to trade rotten ex-husband stories and daylily bulbs. They had gone together once a week for a shampoo and set at another neighbor's house, whose name Mavis could not now remember, although she never forgot how the woman had scolded her toddlers while doing their hair.

Over the years, things had deteriorated. Mr. Molter and Mr. Jacobs had died the same year, several months apart. Their widows hadn't stayed around long. She hadn't seen Brenda since Brenda married a man she met at Calvary Baptist Church and moved into what Mavis imagined was a brick house with a long tree-lined driveway and an in-ground pool. Nowadays, young married couples rented newer apartments with swimming pools, dishwashers, and landscaping crews.

Into the aging trailers gradually came groups of people who wanted a cheap place to crash, sometimes living together to divide the rent. No one had planted flowers in so long that even the perennials had given up and stopped blossoming. The most anyone did to a yard was run a push mower haphazardly across the grass and weed patches, meandering around parked cars and stirring up dust across the ever-widening bare spots. Fading white trailers covered in mildew and dirt stood out starkly in the midst of ugly little yards. The few old trees that had survived the years were not enough to hide the dreariness of the park. For a while Mavis had continued to keep up her yard, but more and more she had retreated inside her dreary trailer, away from the riffraff, and away from their children who didn't seem to have anything better to do than gather around and tell her she looked funny and that she was old—which she already knew. She certainly didn't need any unmannered children around to tell her.

Mavis had stopped working as a substitute teacher five years ago when she turned sixty-eight and had to have back surgery to alleviate nerve pain. The recovery had been long and hard. She had spent two weeks at Emma's house after leaving the hospital, knowing the entire time that her son-in-law hated her presence. Emma pretended not to know this, but she didn't protest much when Mavis announced she was well enough to go back to her trailer. The eventual result of the surgery was a stiffer walk and less mobility, but less pain and a better night's sleep. Now she scraped by on a little less than $600 a month in social security and her daughter's constant handouts of pantry items, used clothes, and garage sale household goods.

Mavis clutched the tiny treasures in her right hand. She had stopped twice on the sidewalk to make sure they were both still there. At the entrance to the trailer park she turned down Magnolia Lane, her street. She had to walk past five trailers. There was nothing but quiet at the first one. It was the early afternoon when most residents were just beginning to come to life for the day, or really, for the night. At the second yard she spotted a scraggly-haired man–a boy, actually–with an open plaid shirt and a concave abdomen. His dark shorts were past his knees, the crotch sagging with several inches of light blue boxers showing. The skinny boy peered over the open hood of a dilapidated car. Mavis squeezed her right hand into a tighter fist. Was he new to the neighborhood–or just crashing at a friend's place for a few nights? Who in the world could keep up?

No one else was around, so Mavis hurried past, although her hurry was not what it used to be. She had one more trailer to pass to get to her own driveway when she heard the noise of neighbor kids on bikes approaching from behind. Almost instantly there were three squeaky bikes circling Mavis.

"Where you been, Crazy Mavey?" The big one had short chubby arms and long flat feet, a combination that Mavis thought was quite comical. His stiff dark hair that stuck up on each side of his head looked to Mavis like devil horns as he swung his bike so close in front of her that she had to stop.

"Someone should teach you some manners, Young Man!" Her substitute-teacher voice cracked, and her heartbeat rose, as she waved a pointed finger at the impertinent scoundrel. "Who is your mother? Where do you live?" They were the same questions she always asked, knowing she would get nowhere, and not wanting the answer bad enough to really find out where he belonged. She knew from past experience that nothing would change anyway.

A string of vulgarities and laughter were let loose in the breeze. Devil Boy could cuss a blue streak, and his two little yes-men imps thought it was hilarious. Mavis passed her mailbox, which used to say Mavis McVee, but had been graffittied into Mavey McCrazy sometime last week. There was not much question about who was responsible, but the police she had called had yet to put anyone on the case. "Mrs. McVee, why don't you move out of here?" That was the officer's solution.

"I could call the police on you boys, you know," Mavis called back the empty threat as she reached her front stoop. "Now get!" She held up her fist, then turned and slowly climbed the two concrete steps.

"You don't scare us, Old Bitch! Crazy Mavey!"

Little did these rascals know what treasure she had in that upheld fist. Once inside, Mavis ambled over and sank down on the worn sofa that had just a whisper of hunter green left in the threadbare fabric. The tiny living room held the old trailer-sized sofa and a matching loveseat, and one broken chair covered in a plaid fabric that used to coordinate with the green in the other pieces. These and all the other furniture—the faux tile coffee table and end tables and the two gold lamps with pleated and cracking ivory shades, and even the stiff floral drapes that now hung crooked—had come with the new furnished trailer thirty-one years ago. Furnished "mobile home," they had called it. And the neighborhood was named "Sunshine Mobile Home Park," with a pretty little stone entrance.

That's what she had gotten in the divorce settlement. She was supposed to get the house, but George had borrowed so much against it that the judge had insisted it wasn't enough—the judge had pointed this out to her own lawyer. So George had bought her the trailer, and he made the payments for fifteen years until it was paid for, because the court had said he had to. Mavis had always paid the rent on the lot.

"Why didn't they make him pay the mortgage and just give you the house, Mama?" her daughter Emma had asked once, many years after. Mavis didn't have an answer, had never even wondered, until Emma had asked. Mavis had walked mechanically through that time in her life, stunned by the reality of it all. Her family fell apart. Her husband moved into his girlfriend's apartment; her son and daughter, only a year apart in age, had moved into apartments close to the state university they were both attending a couple of hours away. And she had moved into her trailer.

"That's the kind of nonsense that happens when trusting wives are blindsided, Dear." That's all she knew to say after she thought about it. "Don't you be so trusting," she had warned her daughter.

Everything around her, including herself, had worn out with passing time. But in her left hand were two diamonds that had been transformed by time into something ageless—from carbon lumps to magical stars. Mavis peeled open her right hand slowly, leaning her face in to behold her treasure without worrying who might be watching. There they were, smoothly faceted and flawless—and quite large. Mavis didn't know much about carats, but she knew these were big. She knew they were very special. She turned them over and over, studying them from every angle. She laid them down on the peeling tiles of the coffee table to move the lamp over. When the short cord wouldn't allow the move, she scooped up the diamonds and put them on the same table with the lamp. She leaned the lamp on one side and then decided to remove the shade to get more light. There was a sudden sharp knock on the door. Mavis jumped and dropped the lamp. When the bulb popped and shattered, the knocking became frantic.

"Mom? Mama? Open the door!" Emma's frantic voice boomed over the knocking. "Mama! Are you okay?" She continued to knock. "Mama! Can you open the door?"

Mavis tried to gather herself as the knocking stopped. "Mama, hold on! I'll get my key."

She knew Emma would be bursting frantic through the door any moment. "I'm fine, Emma," she called weakly, as she bent stiffly over and scanned the carpet around and under the end table. The metal base of the bulb was still in the lamp socket, now looking a bit like a crown with sharp glass in the place of spires. One diamond sat in the middle of the tiny shards of thin glass on the end table, but Mavis didn't see the other one. Finding her new treasure was more important, more immediately necessary. She wasn't sure she was ready to share her secret treasure with Emma.

Emma opened the door with her key and rushed in with Jingle right behind her. Mavis had not heard her grandson for the noise Emma was making, but Jingle was always with Emma–always would be.

"Granma! Granma!" The tall and bumbling form of Emma's only child rushed toward Mavis with his arms out for a hug, the spread of his good-natured facial features a clear indication of the extra chromosome carried by his kind.

Mavis struggled to stand and turn. Jingle's hug threw her off balance, throwing both of them down on the sofa.

"Jing, Honey! Be careful with your grandmother," Emma admonished as she pushed him onto the sofa and off of Mavis. "Mother!" She turned to face Mavis, taking in the broken mess at the same time. "What happened?"

What could she do at this point, but confess the treasure? "Oh, I was just trying to see the earrings in better light. The knocking startled me and I dropped the lamp."

"Did you forget I was coming today? It's Tuesday, Mama. We always come on Tuesday, remember?"

Mavis had thought it was Monday, but she didn't tell Emma. Emma worried enough about Mavis already. Jingle pulled two matching plastic giraffes out of his pockets and held them dancing inches from his grandmother's face: "Look at my 'rafs, Granma!

See, they can run!" The giraffes galloped in front of Mavis' eyes.

"Oh, they are lovely, Jing! Where did you get them?" Sweet James had been nicknamed Jingle when Emma and Mavis discovered that jingling things calmed him as a baby. They had known from the beginning that he was different. He was the result of a surprise pregnancy years after Emma had given up the idea of ever becoming a mother. The next surprise was that he would be born with Down's syndrome.

"I got them at the mall toys! The mall toys!"

"You were at the mall today?" Mavis turned to Emma.

"Just a little while ago. I had to go to Belk's to buy a wedding gift." Emma was picking up the overturned lamp. "Did you cut yourself, Mama? What earrings?"

Mavis opened her hand to reveal the diamond that had been on the table. It was now tinged red.

"Mom, you did cut yourself!" Emma plucked the earring from her hand and tossed it onto the coffee table. It bounced a couple of times, but landed on the table. Emma headed for the kitchen sink. She snatched the paper towel roll, then had to tear one off with the other hand and wind the extra back hurriedly on the roll. She wet the towel, wrung it out, and brought it back to Mavis, all the time fussing about the need for her mother to be more careful, and then switching to talking about the kitchen sink.

"We need to try to fix that drippy faucet, Mama. Maybe I'll bring a new one next week. I can google how to install it."

She grabbed her mother's hand and studied it to see if any glass had stuck in her flesh, and then wiped gently with the wet paper. Blood oozed from a tiny break in her skin, but Emma could find no glass. "It's probably that blood thinner the doctor has you on that is making this tiny cut bleed so. Billy has the same problem." She pushed the wet paper towel into the cut and closed her mother's hand around it. "Hold it there. I'll go get a band aid."

She headed down the hall across rippled carpet to the miniscule bathroom and opened the creaking mirrored door of the medicine cabinet, which almost came loose from the sagging hinges. She grabbed a bandage from the box, then saw herself shaking her head in the mirror as she closed it. This place was falling apart, and she hated that her mother was still living here. Billy ignored her with a grunt every time she brought up moving Mavis in with them.

"Mama!" Mavis was off the couch and leaning over the table, trying to spot the missing earring. "You are going to cut yourself again. Jingle, stay on the couch until I sweep this up."

"I need to find the other earring, Dear." Emma offered to look for it, to get Mavis to sit back down.

"Let me put the band aid on your hand, and then I'll find it. Okay?" There was an exasperated twinge in her voice. Mavis sat down.

"I need a band aid, too, Mama. I need one, too!" Emma and Mavis exchanged a smile.

"You want to be like Grandmama?" Emma asked. "I'll get you a Band-Aid, too."

Once Mavis' bandage was in place, Emma headed back to the bathroom to retrieve another one to put on Jingle's palm. She then turned her attention to the mess. She got the kitchen trashcan, the broom, and a dustpan, and began to remove the glass. "Y'all just stay on the couch." Mavis played with Jingle and his new giraffe twins, but her mind was on her own treasure.

"Be careful, Emma. Look for the other earring." She kept one eye on the blood-covered one still on the edge of the coffee table.

"Found it, Mama." Emma held up the lost diamond to show Mavis, then drew it in for a closer look. "Were these in that box of jewelry I got for you from Julia's yard sale?" She picked up the other one and looked at both together. "It's amazing how real they can make cubic zirconium look."

Mavis didn't answer, but continued to keep Jingle entertained. "And they can be in the circus with the elephants, Granma! Under the tent!" The giraffes rose as Jingle formed the outline of a circus tent with his outspread arms, and a little drool formed on his chin. He had big plans for his two long-necked friends.

"Yes they can, Jingle–and with the monkeys, too!" Mavis watched as Emma carried the earrings to the kitchen sink, leaning her head around Jingle to see what Emma was doing with the diamonds. Emma felt the anxious gaze of her mother.

"I'm just washing the blood off, Mama. I'll put the stopper in the sink." She returned to the living room with the earrings, and dropped them into her mother's bandaged hand. Mavis inspected them as carefully as she could in the low light.

After running the vacuum over the area to make sure she had not left any glass in the carpet, Emma plopped down on the lumpy love seat, glad to be done with the chore. She turned her head to look at her mother and her son. There was precious Jingle, now sixteen years old, his almond eyes on his talking giraffes, one in each hand. Right beside him was Mavis, in her seventh decade, just as happy with her yard sale treasure, holding the earrings up in an effort to catch light, one in each hand, pinched between forefinger and thumb. "To be so easily content," Emma sighed to herself, then smiled.

"Take your old earrings out, Mama. I'll help you put in the new ones." Later, as Emma backed out of the driveway, she spotted the mailbox and made a mental note to bring black paint back with her next Tuesday, and to mention once again to Billy the possibility of bringing her mother home to live with them.

--Terri DeFoor

DELIVERANCE IN GEORGIA

Where was I? I awakened in a room I had never seen before. The luxurious softness surrounding my body conveyed to me that I wasn't in my lumpy bed at Grandma Simmons' house. The smooth sheets gently caressed my skin, unlike the rugged feel of the much-patched quilt that had been allotted to me. The sun was shining brightly through the frilly pink polka-dotted curtains. There were little pink roses on the wallpaper and a little white chest of drawers with rosebud drawer pulls. I had never seen such a beautiful bedroom. And I was wearing a pretty pink nightgown with hearts all over it. Was I dreaming? If so, I wasn't ready to wake up. I closed my eyes tightly to preserve the beauty of the moment, afraid that I would soon hear my cousins forcing their way into the room–and the nightmare of my daily life would resume.

If it was a dream, it was the best dream I had ever had–and it seemed so real. The smell of waffles and ham wafted into the room, teasing my taste buds. I heard the door opening softly and felt a hand tenderly stroke my face. It had been years since I had felt that kind of touch—a touch I often craved during my forced exile in the country. "Good morning," crooned a soft but resonant voice through the sheets covering my head. Where had I heard

29

that voice before? The events of last night gradually began to come into focus.

Realizing her limitations, my mother had put seven-year-old me on a train by myself to go from Philadelphia to Georgia to live with my step-grandmother, Grandma Simmons. All I had known my whole life was the big city of Philadelphia. I pleaded with Mama, "Please come with me. I am afraid to go alone." She assured me that I would be fine. "Grandma Simmons will be waiting when the train stops, and this nice man, the porter, will be sure that Grandma Simmons gets you." As I sat by the window, a steady stream of tears ran down my cheeks until I fell asleep from the emotional exhaustion.

The porter woke me up as the train began to grind to a halt. I realized that I didn't have any idea what Grandma Simmons looked like. The grandmas I had seen on television always spoiled the grandchildren, taking them special places and buying them treats their parents wouldn't. Just maybe I would be lucky enough to have a grandma like that. Through the train window, I spied a weary-looking woman with clothes that were clean but had seen better days. The lady's mouth was set firmly, giving the impression that she had an iron will. I looked in vain for someone else in the waiting area. My heart skipped a beat when the porter handed me over to her.

I thought for a second that the dejected-looking lady was just picking me up for my grandmother. However, she jumped in right away and began to lay down the law at her house. She cautioned that she didn't brook any nonsense—that I would have to follow her rules strictly if I wanted to live in her house. There were consequences for infractions. There was no "Welcome to my house. I'm so glad to see you." Then came the long ride to her house.

We passed up all the houses, with a dirt road every now and then leading into the bushes. Finally, we turned down one of those dirt roads and then down a second one. It was scary. It wasn't at all like Philadelphia with its bright lights and houses so close that you could yell from one house into the next. I couldn't believe she was taking me so far out into the country and so deep into the woods. At long last, the truck pulled up in front of a ramshackle house that looked like somebody had forgotten to finish it.

Two boys about twelve and thirteen sidled out of the house, insolently looking me over with what appeared to be permanent sneers ingrained upon their faces. A shiver went unbidden down my spine. I couldn't tell if Grandma Simmons had seen how they had looked at me. I followed as close to her as I could.

As she showed me to my room, I asked her where the bathroom was. She pointed through the window at a small building outside. For bathing, she told me we would have to haul water from a well that belonged to a neighbor. She showed me how to light the kerosene lamp, warning me that kerosene was dear: we would have to blow the lights out early. To cook, we would have to build a fire in the cast iron cook stove. I was amazed. In the short time it had taken to get from Philadelphia to Georgia, my life had taken a drastic turn. I felt completely alone in a hostile and unknown world.

Rural Georgia was a real cultural shock for a city child. I didn't know that chicken came from real live chickens. It was hard to eat the first chicken I watched my grandmother kill. She wrung its neck right off its body—and its body kept jumping wildly around the yard without its head. Then she made me watch as she gutted the chicken and stripped the feathers off. I woke up in the middle of the night traumatized by images of that chicken. Grandma Simmons also had a smokehouse. Until my first hog-killing day, I thought bacon came from the store. I wasn't spared from any of the work. Taking care of these tasks meant the difference in eating or starving for the family. It wasn't only the workload that was difficult.

My relatives took a huge toll on my childhood. To say it was difficult to live with Grandma Simmons and my two older male cousins is a gross understatement. She was a very strict disciplinarian, whose whipping switch was always at the ready. Rarely affectionate, she did not fit my rosy picture of the perfect grandmother. I shut down emotionally. I was afraid to tell her when my two older male cousins were abusive to me in ways that destroyed my sense of being. I have suppressed the events of that year so deeply in my subconscious that I have no memory of attending school. I dreaded not having any relief from the oppression that seemed to dog me–and the summer would be even worse. I lived daily in hope of deliverance from my personal hell in the backwoods of Georgia.

Even though it was extremely hot that summer, I stayed outside as much as possible trying to avoid my demon cousins.

The heat was unbearable—causing us all to move in slow motion. Late one morning as I sluggishly came from behind Grandma Simmons' house, I saw a brown truck pulling into the driveway. For a moment, I thought I must have been having a heat stroke. We almost never had company. I closed my eyes tightly. When I opened them again, the truck was still there. I wondered who could be coming this deep into the woods in the dog days of summer. As I watched surreptitiously from behind a corner of the old wooden house in bad need of painting, there emerged an unfamiliar–yet friendly and kind-looking–man and an even kinder-looking older lady. A painfully shy and unassuming child, I was determined not to be noticed. Yet I was curious to hear what had brought these kind strangers to my home.

Wiping her hands on the front of her apron, Grandma Simmons trudged out to meet the strangers. From my corner of the house—afraid to move closer—I could not hear, but I could tell from the expressions on their faces that Grandma Simmons and the older lady did not see eye to eye. Suddenly Grandma Simmons turned and called out, "C'mere, Gal." At that moment, time stood still. I wanted the ground to open up and swallow my entire body. It was Grandma Simmons' tone that had stopped me dead in my tracks–the tone that meant "You're in trouble." Yet I inched closer, anxiously reflecting on the day and my behavior. "I cannot possibly be in trouble," I reasoned. "I've been good all day." I had practiced "being good." Being good was necessary for my survival. Once again the voice rang out, "M'ere, Gal." Only this time, the voice seemed a little softer.

As I moved closer, I breathed in the airy fragrance of magnolia blossoms. The scent seemed to come from the kind older lady. She invitingly reached out and took my hand between the softest hands I had ever felt: "Hello! I'm your grandmother, Nannie Lee. You may call me 'Granny.' I've come to take you home." Right at that moment, Grandma Simmons looked away, her face displaying a sadness I had never before seen there. In a monotone, she told me to go pack my things.

Before I had time to move, the kind older lady softly whispered, "That won't be necessary. I'll buy her all the things she needs." She turned to me with gentle eyes and an even gentler voice filled with love: "Just go get in the truck."
--Jacqueline Smith

UNCLE GEORGE

Rumor had it that Jacqueline was a "Funderburg," although neither her mother nor her Uncle George's brother, Charles, had ever confirmed the relationship. Finally, when she was an adult, she met Uncle George and Aunt Lois Funderburg for the first time at his 126-acre farm in Middle Georgia, although they lived in a retirement community in Gladwyne, Pennsylvania. That summer, Uncle George, a retired real-estate millionaire with his black cowboy hat, southern cowboy clothes, and striking figure, decided that it was time to get to know his niece. The farm was beautiful, boasting a vineyard, three large pecan orchards, a variety of animals, and two lakes–one of which had the biggest and best catfish in the world. Each of the lakes was fully equipped with fishing gear, docks, and boats. Uncle George loved the country. He loved to laugh. He loved animals. He loved fishing–and he loved Jackie.

She had been an adorable little girl, he remembered, when her mother brought her to Monticello. He would see her when he was home on leave from the service and always thought to himself, "She is such a darling child and so full of energy. Why can't we acknowledge her?" As time passed, he lost track of her and her mother, but learned that the child had been adopted by her young mother's new husband, taken to Pennsylvania and, through life's circumstances, had been abused both physically and mentally. He felt bad. She was an adult now and still so full of energy. He was determined to develop a relationship with her.

Uncle George and Jackie would get in his truck and start on their daily adventures. The trips were always exciting. Once they traveled to Fort Valley, Georgia, where it is said the best Georgia peaches grow. As they traveled, their talks were endless. He would tell her about growing up in Monticello with four siblings. The softness in his voice as he spoke of her grandparents revealed the affection and love that he had for them. At times, he would stop in the middle of a story, and she would look over at him, his wide eyes misty and his thin lips curved slightly upward. How she cherished that smile. During those pauses, her mind would drift, and she would imagine that her Uncle George was actually her father speaking–the father who had never claimed her, who was telling his daughter of all his wonderful childhood memories, calling her his "princess." She had always wanted a loving daddy who would pick her up and spin her around in the air, just like her friend Elaine's dad did. During those precious times with Uncle George, she could actually hear her father's voice. Sadness would fill her soul because she could never have those fun and loving times. Somehow, Uncle George sensed that and would change the conversation, telling her how proud he was of her and her accomplishments. He encouraged her, advising her to "Live well, laugh a lot, and never waste precious time with regret."

Upon arriving at their destination, they walked the length and width of the peach orchard with their basket dangling between the two of them. The stories continued as they slowly surveyed and chose the best and brightest of "Georgia's finest" to take home. The sweet smell of the orchard permeated the car as they made the trip home in the late evening with baskets of peaches for various neighbors, family, and friends.

During other days of that lazy summer in 1995, they stayed at the farm all day long. They would get up early to the sounds of roosters crowing, horses bellowing, and the most delightful sound of all–the braying of Papa George, their donkey. Papa George was lean, tall, and brown, with the longest and furriest tail she had ever seen on a donkey. He was the protector of the farm; no coyote, fox, or other intruder would dare touch any of the animals in Papa George's charge. The air smelled crisp, fresh, and invigorating as the birds awakened and began their daily song, humming melodies that rivaled the greatest music ever composed.

For excitement, with their snack pack in hand, she and Uncle George would walk down the path to the fishing lake past the old barn where they would stop to speak to Papa George. She laughed with glee as Uncle George taught her how to bait a hook, even though she kept a watchful eye out for crawling things. She was never afraid when she was with Uncle George. Her first catch was exciting and memorable. As she pulled the line in, Uncle George guided her with his gentle baritone voice, "Go slowly, Honey. Step back. Hold on tight. Reel him in. Slowly, slowly, back, back. Ohooooooo–there he is." It was a bream about as big as a hand palm, but it belonged only to her. Of course they couldn't eat him. They just threw him back. That is the stuff smiles are made of.

The best times of that unforgettable summer were the evenings. The farm sat at the highest point in Jasper County, enabling them to see all the way into Butts County while sitting on their back patio. On one summer evening, Uncle George, Aunt Lois, and Jackie curled up in their favorite chairs with a glass of wine and watched in wonder as the sun turned from brilliant yellow to bright orange, before fading into the eastern sky. The blue and white of the sky slowly turned to an unbelievable midnight blue as the biggest moon they had ever witnessed rose in the east.

Years would pass. One night, as she was riding home from work, Luther Vandross' voice crooned from the radio, "Dance with my father again." She became teary-eyed at the thought of her father–the father she had never actually had. Then a still small voice whispered to her, "You are always my princess. You are my little girl and you are a queen." Silently, she voiced a prayer of thanksgiving to God for sending her Uncle George.

--Jacqueline Smith

A DECEMBER ROSE

It's a sunny yet chilly day, typical for the week before Christmas in Middle Georgia. As I pull into the driveway where my parents and my "Grandmommy" live, my mother is waiting, and my children hurry to unbuckle and run into Grandmommy's arms. I take my time getting out of the car, and when I finally gather my belongings and shut the car door, I see it—a single, beautiful pink rose on a rosebush. My mother had already told me it was there, but the full impact of it does not occur until I finally see it in person. Memories come flooding back to my mind.

Grandmommy was a character. If you asked her how she was feeling, she always had some ailment to tell you about. She even seemed proud to be depressed at times. Her television was always turned to a home shopping channel, and at Christmas, you'd better believe, that was where your gifts came from. In addition, the price was always still on your gift. If she bought the present on sale, she removed the sales price and left the full price sticker for everyone to see. No matter how old my cousins and I got, we always received porcelain dolls. We had to open them one at a time, so Grandmommy could tell a story about why she chose each doll. I was her first and favorite grandchild. I know this because she would tell everyone–even my aunt who had given her two other granddaughters. Although it was horrible for her to say out loud, knowing this gave me a small sense of importance.

One day when I was about seven years old, I was surprised to see Grandmommy and Papa waiting to pick me up from school. I rode home in style that day in their like-new Cadillac. When we arrived, my grandparents and I hopped out of the car. I was so excited. I didn't see my grandparents that often, and I never saw them in the middle of the week. I soon found out they had come to give me a present. Grandmommy opened the trunk and pulled out what looked like a bouquet of twigs. "This, Amanda, is your very own rose bush. Papa and I have come to help you plant it anywhere you want." I was disappointed, expecting a toy or some-thing grand. Instead, I was getting a bush. Trying not to show my disappointment, I agreed to plant it under the window to my room.

Papa dug the hole, and Grandmommy and I placed the bush in the ground and covered the roots. Afterwards I was allowed to use the garden hose all by myself to give the bush its first taste of water in its new home. When my grandparents were ready to leave that night, Grandmommy bent down to my level and said: "Now whenever a rose blooms on your rose bush, you will know how much I love you." At the time I didn't think much about that rose bush or what Grandmommy had said.

The last true event Grandmommy attended was my high school graduation. I cherish every picture of her that was taken on that day. She was there feeling fine while I got dressed. She was there to watch me walk across the stage and receive my highest achievement at that time. Sadly, as we were exiting the Macon City Auditorium, Grandmommy fell and hit her head on the cement steps. She was rushed to the hospital, and I was told she would be okay. I went on with my night celebrating, while in the intensive care unit Grandmommy was having a stroke.

The rose bush no longer sits under my old window; instead it greets me in the driveway. As I walk closer to admire the beautiful rose, I remember my grandmother's words: "Now whenever a rose blooms on your rose bush, you will know how much I love you."

--Amanda McCranie

The Road to Homeless

The road to homeless began with my giving up the apartment I had been renting for fifteen years. My daughter wanted us to share expenses in an apartment where we could live together. Although I agreed, things didn't go as planned. I ended up living with my sister who was dealing with end-stage renal failure, while my daughter rented a place for herself and her children. When I moved in with my sister, I had to help her with her bills and medications. She had to go to dialysis three times a week. I was also trying to help my daughter and her children.

Unfortunately, one day my daughter left her children alone and the Department of Family and Children Services (DFACS) was called. The police also got involved. I ended up having to volunteer for the custody of my grandchildren, resulting in my having to run back and forth between my sister's house and my daughter's apartment. In family court, I was made legal guardian of my grandchildren. We moved twice the first year, incurring significant expenses each time. When daycare was dropped, I had to begin paying for childcare. Later, my sister died without any burial insurance, and I dealt with that.

In the meantime, my daughter was supposed to be paying for the utilities. First, the water was cut off for nonpayment, and a few months later the electricity went, too. After I managed to get everything back on, my daughter and her husband moved out without any notice or warning whatsoever. Not able to continue to pay the utilities, I became depressed living alone in a house without water or lights.

I had begun to pray about how to get out of my lease of $750 per month. When I returned one Saturday morning, the ceiling in my kitchen had fallen in. The landlord promised to get it fixed. After I confronted the landlord with the lack of insulation in the house, she released me from the obligation. I just couldn't continue to live in a house with no water, no lights, and a fallen ceiling.

I still had unpaid bills from Georgia Power. I saw on television that the Salvation Army would help people with energy bills. I filled out the paperwork and began living there a few months later. I still owe Georgia Power. The transition to homeless happened pretty quickly. Just barely scraping by means there is no money to save for an emergency.

--Unsigned

THE BROKEN BOY

The three-year-old boy sits quietly while his mother talks to the nice lady. He likes the nice lady; she always has a smile for him and never looks at him with the bad face. He does not know why his mommy and daddy look at him with the bad face sometimes. Sometimes Daddy makes the bad face and follows it with a heavy hand. The little boy does not understand. It makes him sad and withdrawn without knowing why. The nice lady comes to him with a toy for him to play with: it is his first hearing aid.

In the year 1972, a hearing aid was a box that hung from a strap around the neck. Wires trailed from the box to the ears and transferred amplified sound through the wires to the custom-molded ear buds. This allowed someone with severe hearing loss to understand the spoken word. Without it, the person had to rely on lip reading. Lip reading was a necessary skill to survive—although it was a drawback if the individual was good at it. People often refused to believe anything was wrong with the boy because they could have a conversation with him until he lost sight of their lips. Then the people with normal hearing just thought the boy was being rude or not paying attention.

The nice lady attaches the strap around his neck. The box is funny-looking. While still smiling, she gently looks him in the eyes and attaches the custom-molded ear buds. She flips a switch on the box, and his world is never the same again. "Karl, can you hear me?" He gasps with astonishment and delight. Sound has been introduced to Karl's world for the first time. He immediately notices that sound moves in concert with the lips. He intuitively understands that it is her voice he is hearing. He does not recognize the language of the sounds because he speaks the language of the lips. Karl smiles at the nice lady. Forever will hers be the first voice he ever hears.

His mother is delighted with the results and promises the nice lady she will work with him daily on understanding sounds. His mother takes him home. Later the father comes home; the boy wants so much to show his daddy his new toy. All the father sees is a broken boy. The bad face stays.

Karl is in the middle of puberty. He has mastered his speech deficiency and learned to speak well. He still struggles on occasion to master listening to one voice in a crowd, but he is constantly improving. Karl begins to have trouble with his back. The doctors say it is just growing pains and that it will go away after puberty. When Karl is fourteen, his mother takes him to a specialist. They put Karl in a large tube called an MRI, brand-new technology recently available to the general public.

MRI stands for Magnetic Resonance Imaging. Technicians use this machine to take a magnetic, real-time photograph of the inside of the body. Depending upon the frequency with which it resonates, it can show everything from muscle tissue to bone density and even chart the layout of the brain. This has greatly reduced the need of exploratory surgery to find out what is producing the symptoms of many types of ailments.

The doctor comes in to speak to the mother and son: "I am afraid I have some bad news." He then explains that the boy has a congenital defect in the base of his spine. According to the scans, the lower lumbar region is not correctly lined up with the sacrum. To make it simple to the boy, the doctor explains that his butt and his back are two pieces of a puzzle that do not quite fit. This is why the boy has constant pain in his lower back. He recommends surgery to correct the problem, which would require Karl to spend six months in a body cast after the surgery. The body cast fits from below the hip to the upper chest. They thank the doctor and go home to discuss it. The father comes home from work and listens to the mother relate all they have learned. The father turns and looks at the son. All he sees is a broken boy. The next day the boy tells his parents that he will not have the surgery. The bad face hurts more than the back ever will.

Karl is in his late thirties now with a family of his own. He has worked in factory jobs for nearly twenty years. Standing on concrete all day and picking up heavy items repeatedly have taken a toll on him. He can no longer hide the pain from his wife. He has missed too many days of work. The back that should have lasted seventy years has barely made it to forty. He sees the bad face everywhere: his boss, his coworkers, his wife. All they see is a broken boy. It is time for the surgery.

A spinal fusion is a process by which an orthopedic surgeon and a neurosurgeon slice the back open over the problem area. Working in concert, the two drill holes in the spine and simply attach screws and a plate made of titanium to reinforce the spine so that the person can go about a reasonably pain-free life.

He slowly comes out from under the anesthesia. Twenty-five years of back pain is waiting for him when he wakes up. The pain is horrible. His mother, wife, and sister are there. After Karl cries and begs almost an hour, the nurse administers painkillers. The broken boy has been patched back together.

I stand at my father's gravesite. I miss him terribly. It has been nine years since he left my mother for glory. The frustration of this broken body will always be the chains I have to carry with me in this life. I hope one day, in a better place, to look up into his eyes and see the bad face gone, replaced with the sheer love a father has for his perfect son. But for now, when I look in a mirror, all I see is a broken boy.

--Karl S. Adams

CAREGIVING

"Jane, where are you?"

"Mama, I'm sitting right here beside your bed."

"I can't see you, Jane."

"Here is my arm, Mama. Can you feel it?"

"Yes."

Mama and I never got along, not for as long as I can remember. Now we are the only members of the family still living.

How did we get to this point?

Mama was Dr. Loreen P. Overstreet, Professor Emeritus, Georgia Board of Regents. The best Registered Nurse I ever saw was counting on me to make decisions for her life and death. It was my turn to see that no one interfered with Mama's dying. Now that I was her court-appointed guardian, I was standing vigil to protect her wishes. She had died several times before and been resuscitated. She did not want any more life support machines. She had taught me since I was a child that there was nothing unusual about dying. The best thing I could ever do for Mama was going to be in these last few weeks. I would allow her to leave without interference.

This was the first time in months Mama had known my name. Dementia is such a thief.

"Jane, I love you."

"I love you too, Mama."

"I really mean it."

"Yes, Mama, I know you mean it. I mean it, too."

I put my right arm into the bed, and Mama hugged the arm that she could no longer see. She went to sleep. I stood guard so that no one interfered. Mama died just as she had wanted–in her sleep.

--S. J. Overstreet

THE BIG LITTLE MAN

My father was known in our family as "the little man who does big things." He was five feet five and a half. I'll never forget the "big" things he did that earned him his title–like the day we were being delayed by the train station and his attempts to persuade them to get moving–by what means I can only imagine. Or the summer that he organized a Little League farm team because I was so disappointed at not being drafted.

Papa's drive and determination sometimes came at the expense of style and grace. He always claimed that if there were two ways to do something, he'd find the wrong way first. And he seemed to be plagued with vehicles that were held together with paper clips and chewing gum. His track record with boats is probably the most infamous chapter in his history of misadventures. The basic problem was that Papa never accepted defeat at the hands of an uncooperative watercraft. If it leaked, he patched it up in a hasty sort of way and forged on ahead. If the motor wouldn't stay in gear, he tied it or had someone hold it in place. I don't think he could ever have felt comfortable with a smooth-running, well-maintained boat.

On one occasion, Papa's dauntless determination to make it go somehow or other was nearly his undoing. He later felt fortunate to be able to look back on it and laugh. He and my brother-in-law Phil took the four grandchildren to ski at the lake near Rockmart. When the rope had been thrown out to my daughter Jenny, Papa had to climb back to the motor to crank it manually, since the electric starter wasn't working. He yanked on the rope, and, sure enough, the old Evinrude 35 horsepower began to roar, but it also jumped immediately into forward gear, hurling Papa head over heels out into the water as it lurched ahead. Katie, my six-year old niece, was left in the boat with my nine-year-old son Michael, neither having no idea how to stop the runaway ski boat, affectionately christened *Ladybird* in honor of my sister's nickname. Michael gallantly comforted his cousin: "Don't panic, Katie. It'll be okay," and then immediately yelled, "HELP," at the top of his lungs.

The situation with Papa was going from bad to worse. He first tried to climb into the boat, but it was now plowing around swiftly in circles, the outer edge guarded by the menacing blades of the propeller. So he proceeded to grab the ski rope as a way back on board. That move of course was highly ill advised. The rope wrapped itself around him and pulled him under water for a dangerously long moment. Managing to free himself, he decided to climb up the prow. By exerting all the strength he could muster, he climbed halfway up the prow. His legs, however, still trailed in the water, which threatened to pull him into the path of the deadly propeller. He thought he was about to breathe his last breath.

The story does have a happy ending–even a comical one, if you can get enough distance from the dire danger that it held for those involved. Thankfully, a young man in another boat was able to get into the Ladybird and choke the motor in time to save the day. When Papa emerged from the water, he had to scramble fast to save the modesty of the stunned group of spectators who had gathered. It seems the pull of the water–while he was clinging for dear life to the bow of the boat–had stripped him of his swimming trunks. He ended up serving as a rather vulgar hood ornament for the wayward Ladybird. He had to resort to a little pink stretch terry-cloth sun suit that my six-year-old daughter Jenny had worn over her bathing suit. One of the wonders of modern technology–a size six girl's sun suit forced to fit the hips of a grown man!

Papa's return to Rockmart was less than grand that evening. The only time I've seen him more beat looking was in the hospital after his heart attack. He had lost his glasses and false teeth in the lake, was wearing a two-day beard, and had the expression of death all over his face. After telling the whole story several times over a good meal and a glass of wine, he began to enjoy embellishing it and appreciating its ridiculous hilarity.

One particularly memorable remark overheard from the spectators to these strange goings-on went something like this: "What's that man doing?" asked some fellow when he saw a nude body hanging to the prow of an unpiloted ski-boat. "Can't you see he's trying to save those kids?" replied the next witness. Whereupon the first witness couldn't help wondering aloud, "But why is he naked?"

--John Dunaway

ANOTHER TORNADO DREAM

The sounds of the storm had diminished. When she realized she was in a dilapidated old barn and was still alive, she closed her eyes and prayed a silent "thank you" to God. As she opened her eyes, she felt movement beneath her. The child she had been protecting with her body was still alive! She quickly lifted him into her arms and began speaking softly to him. When he smiled up at her and said not to worry, that he was okay, she burst into laughter. She had weathered the fierce tornado, and they had made it together. It would certainly take more than a storm to get her down, and she would always be there to protect her child.

She opened her eyes. She was in her nightgown, wrapped in the sheets on her bed. The tornado dream had returned but wasn't nearly as disturbing as it had been on other nights. She began to think of her life. Nothing serious or disturbing was taking place right now, so why was she having the dream again?

As the days passed, she began to feel stronger and more invincible. Her son grew into a handsome, strong teenager. He was a good kid–one who never gave her much trouble. She leaned on him for strength when her husband was sent to fight in Afghanistan. Although he supported his mother by helping with chores, running errands, and encouraging her to be strong while his father was overseas, he couldn't fill the void his father left behind. His mother needed someone to reassure her constantly that her husband would be returning home safely. She was insecure, frightened, and lonely. She could not sleep at night. Her days were spent in a daze; she was like a robot as she performed the tasks necessary to get her through the day.

She slipped into a deep depression. Her doctor prescribed medication for the condition, but it did little to help. Her friend told her to buy a bottle of alcohol and mix a strong drink before bed. This should help her get some rest. She thanked her friend and headed straight for the liquor store, where she purchased a small bottle of tequila and mix to make margaritas. She wasn't a drinker, never had been, but the desire to get some much needed sleep was greater than any reservations she had regarding drinking. She began to mix a drink each night before bed. When she saw how much it helped her sleep, she began making them stronger. Soon, she could not fall asleep without a drink. She would never admit that she had a problem, but the demon of alcoholism reared its ugly head.

One night, while in a deep, alcohol-induced sleep, the tornado dream returned. It was as before–she was outside with a young child, laughing and playing. She didn't notice the storm until it was almost upon them. She picked up the child and began to run–only there was nowhere to run to. Buildings had disappeared. There was nothing but flat farmland as far as she could see. With rain hitting her face, she blindly began to run, desperately seeking refuge for herself and the child. She suddenly stumbled and fell into a shallow hole. Sobbing, she lay there as the storm violently spun around her. Then she sat straight up.

When she opened her eyes, a storm was raging outside her window. She was sitting in the center of her bed, shaking uncontrollably. Since she hadn't dreamed of a tornado in quite a while, she wondered what it meant. Instantly, she thought of her husband. Was he okay? Did the dream have something to do with him?

Without a thought, she climbed out of bed, went into the kitchen, and poured a stiff drink. A few hours passed as she continued to drink. After a while, she began to feel the relaxing sensations the alcohol caused. She lay down on the couch and closed her eyes for a few minutes. She did not awaken until her son called her as he shook her shoulder gently. She struggled to open her eyes, and in a drunken stupor asked him what was wrong. He gently shook his head and said, "Mom, I need you to drive me to school. I overslept when you didn't wake me up this morning, and I missed the bus. Get up. Let's go before I'm late for class."

She arose from the couch and found she was unsteady on her feet. The room was spinning, but she was able to clear her head enough to make it to the bathroom, wash her face, and slip into some clothes. Feeling a little better, she emerged looking haggard but awake. She grabbed her keys and purse and followed her son out the door. Pulling out of the driveway, she told him she was sorry she did not wake him on time. She explained how she had struggled to sleep and after being awakened by the storm, she had gotten out of bed for a while. He smiled at her and told her it was okay. She glanced over at him proudly, and smiled. At that split second, a car coming in the opposite direction around a curve was in the middle of the road. Her reflexes were encumbered by the alcohol; she was slow to react. Sideswiped by the car, she lost control. Her car left the road and plunged down into a deep ravine off the right shoulder. The car finally stopped when the passenger side slammed into a huge tree.

The next thing she heard was the insistent blowing of a car horn. She lifted her head, opened her eyes and realized her head had been resting on the center of the steering wheel. As she moved her head, the horn stopped blowing. She gently shook her head, trying to clear her muddled thoughts. What on earth was going on? Why was she sleeping in her car? When she began looking around, she saw her son. He was crumpled on the seat beside her with blood oozing from his head. She began to scream hysterically.

She suddenly heard voices. She continued to scream, calling for someone to help. She was pinned behind the steering wheel, and her son was not moving. Blood continued to pour from a gash in his head. It ran down his handsome face, making rivers of red. She suddenly noticed his head was leaning in an incredible angle. She called to him, begging him to wake up and talk to her.

It seemed like an eternity before the ambulance arrived. The rescuers had to use the Jaws of Life to cut the mother and son from the car. They gently lifted her son, put him on a stretcher, and left for the hospital. It took longer to get her out, since she was pinned behind the wheel. When they finally pulled her from the mangled wreckage of the car, she was thankful to look down and see that she was still in one piece.

She immediately began asking about her child. Was he okay? Why wouldn't he wake up and talk to her? What had happened? How long would it be before she could see him? They had no answers for her. The rescue workers loaded her into another ambulance and sped to the hospital. After several hours of tests and x-rays, they told her she would recover from her injuries. Relieved, she began asking about her son again.

The doctor sadly shook his head and told her that he didn't survive the accident. The impact of the car hitting the tree had snapped his neck. In addition, the multiple internal injuries he suffered would have killed him. He would have suffered from brain damage if he had lived. He offered his condolences, and added that he wanted her to remain in the hospital for a few days. They were already in the process of contacting her husband in Afghanistan, and he would be returning home as soon as arrangements could be made.

Numbed by what the doctor had just told her, she could only shake her head. Her brain could not process the information he had just given her. Her son was sleeping in another room–that was it. He was resting. He was going to be fine. She always protected him from danger and evil, and nothing would ever take him from her. She would make sure of that. Nothing bad would ever happen to him as long as she was alive.

--Barbara Sellers Bryan

Letting Go

One of the most vivid memories I have of my mother takes place in a grocery store when I am about six years old. She is legally blind by then, having been struck with early-onset macular degeneration when she was twenty, an injustice made more poignant by her tremendous physical energy. She was a first-class athlete, a good enough tennis player to have gone professional, a woman who needed to move and exert herself physically. Losing her sight meant losing a huge portion of what brought her joy, fed her spirit, and relieved her stress. Nevertheless, she proved to be indomitable, walking with great strides from one end of Richmond, Virginia to the other, cutting the grass, gardening with a vengeance, and making herself head of every organization she could join–from the Episcopal Church Women to the Garden Club to the school recess monitors to the Volunteer Guild of the Virginia Society for the Blind.

Yet all of this mental and physical exertion was not nearly enough to sate her overwhelming energy. She was prone to expel what was left of it in occasional eruptions of anger that leapt out of her without warning like a striking rattler, accurate and fast as lightning. Just as quickly, these outbursts utterly dissipated, leaving behind not a trace of any atmospheric disturbance. My calm and dignified mother would reappear as quickly as she had disappeared behind the rattler.

Meanwhile, I stood inexplicably bleeding, stunned by the poison, yet wondering if it was a dream. Had I made it up? The evidence was nowhere to be seen in my mother's placid demeanor. It was completely gone, out of sight, out of mind–deftly driven underground, deep inside my sacrificial veins.

Thus, our weekly trips to the grocery store have a dual life in my memory. Right next to the real version is the imagined scene, rehearsed over and over again in my mind throughout my childhood whenever my anxiety needed soothing. In this scene the good little girl is dancing through the store, her hand lightly balancing on the cart her mother pushes, as if it is the *barre* in her impromptu ballet class. Together, the pair swings around the corner onto the soup aisle, and suddenly, there it is–the never-ending shelf stacked with red and white Campbell's soup cans all exactly alike, except for the dim gold letters that identify each flavor.

Knowing that her mother is too blind to read the labels, the girl asks cheerfully, "Mother, may I help you find something?"

"Why, yes, my darling," the proud and grateful mother replies. "Can you please put four cans of Cream of Mushroom soup in the cart?"

"Of course, Mother. It's done!" says the remarkable, dancing, dutiful, soup-fetching daughter.

"Why, thank you, My Dear. I do so appreciate your help!" the mother chirps lovingly.

The two continue in this way throughout the store, enjoying their happy day of shopping and bonding. The girl enjoys being trusted, being relied upon by the one on whom she depends so much, being appreciated, and feeling powerful and competent enough to have something of herself to offer.

That's the beautiful dual. Right next to it in my brain's storage bin is the actual event that transpires somewhat differently.

In the real version, the mother leans into the cart, powering up and down the aisles. The little girl races breathlessly along, trying to keep up. The mother has faked her way through the shopping trip pretty well so far. She is amazingly adept at disguising her blindness, at "passing" for a person with normal sight. She knows most of the products she wants to purchase by size, shape, color, and location in the store. Occasionally, she will hold up an item and ask, somewhat rhetorically, "This *is* the Bisquick, isn't it?" just so that she can hear her little girl affirm that she has once again defeated her so-called "handicap." The mother takes great pride in knowing what is said about her all around town: *"That Virginia Trice is so amazing. Why, if you didn't know she was blind, you would never be able to tell. She is just so independent!"*

As usual, everything is moving along smoothly until that one turn that takes Supermom and her admiring sidekick daughter onto the interminable soup aisle, that endless wall of almost identical red and white soup cans. In this version of the story, the aisle is dark, and the shelves seem to tower over the little girl. There must be a thousand cans stacked there–a million!

The little girl feels a tightening in the pit of her stomach as she stands by, watching as her mother picks up the first can at the far right end of the aisle. Her mother lifts to her eyes the half-inch-thick, pink-framed glasses she always has hanging from the jeweled chain around her neck. She practically scrapes the red and white can against the fat glass as she holds it right up to her nose, sliding it back and forth across her face, pulling it slightly up and down, twisting it this way and that. The girl watches the ritual helplessly, knowing that her mother cannot possibly read the faint print. But the daughter waits. Her job, as she understands it, is to give her mother only the thumbs up remark when she has guessed correctly. Stepping in without being asked might insinuate that her mother is–well, *blind*–a topic no one except Supermom herself has permission to broach.

After a few minutes of hopeless glaring, the mother stops and asks a little huffily:

"What does this say? Is this the Cream of Mushroom?"

The girl hesitates, though she can easily read the label: "No,

Mom. I–I think it's the Tomato."

"*Oh, damn*," says the mother, under her breath as she shoves it back onto the shelf and picks up the one beside it. The rattle begins to whisper.

The little girl watches, frozen, as her mother eyeballs the can, struggling to read the letters that are so clear to the girl: another Tomato. The girl's eyes span the length of the shelf and she sees a familiar pattern. The cans are arranged alphabetically from the left. The mother is struggling with another "T" can at the far right. The chances of making it to the "C" cans at this rate seem doubtful. The rattle becomes a little more intense.

The girl's tummy tightens. She remains frozen. She sees the Cream of Mushroom. It is right there in her sights. She could just walk down and get it so very easily, but her stomach tells her that any move now could be a wrong move when that rattle is buzzing so dangerously. Her anxiety at this point is making her nauseous. Should she–

"*DAMN!*"

The strike happens before the girl can finish her thought. The mother slams the soup can on the shelf and spits, *"JUST GET ME THE DAMN SOUP!"*

"How many?" the girl whispers tentatively as she slinks, invisible, down the aisle.

"*FOUR! FOUR DAMN CANS OF CREAM OF MUSH-ROOM. JUST FIND THEM AND PUT THEM IN THE DAMN CART!"* the mother snarls as she hurtles past the girl and disappears around the corner.

Four soups–four *"Damns,"* five, counting the first quiet one. *Damn* is the only curse word I ever heard come out of my mother's mouth, but that one usually came in clusters.

The little girl grabs the four cans, clutching them precariously as she scuttles clumsily out of the dark soup tunnel after her mother. She looks around, stomach churning, heart racing. Where did her mother go? Relief begins to creep into her as she sees her mother placidly strolling amongst the giant square tables of the fruit and vegetable section. Here, everything is brightly lit, and the items all have distinct shapes, colors, and smells.

The mother is perfectly at ease as she wanders through this safe and sensory world, the menacing wall of red and white homogeneity seemingly forgotten–along with the *damns* and slamming soup cans. The girl slips her cargo silently into the cart, as if the absence of words and clinking tin will wipe out the strike of the dreaded soup snake once and for all. She quietly absorbs the poison as usual, maintaining the family pretense that nothing is awry in their world. She files the bitter memory right next to its antidotal dual, which she pulls out and recites yet again, applying it like a poultice to the brand new wound.

It is December 25, 2001. The girl is a woman now–fifty years old. Her mother is dying, in the last stages of pancreatic cancer. She has vowed to make it through one more Christmas and *damn* if she didn't bulldoze her way right through to it. The family is gathered in the hospital room: husband, children, and grandchildren, all celebrating the day with her, bringing a final outpouring of packages for her to open.

My mother has instructed the hospital staff to dress her and put her in her chair before we arrive so that she can receive us with dignity, despite the haze of pain and morphine that envelops her. We are all participating in this one last pretense that she is not blind–that she will get well, that our world cannot be shattered by that thing called "Life"–that includes that inconvenient thing called "Death."

My mother opens gift after gift, as the giver tries to describe it without hinting at the fact that she is too blind and drugged to know what she is holding in her hands: *"I just knew you would love this throw when I saw it in the catalogue. The trees and the sunset are just like the ones you could see from the porch at the River House!"*

The festivities go on and on with lots of laughter, and soon we are all talking to one another, and my mother is just a ghostly presence at the rollicking Christmas Party–to everyone except me, that is. I am watching her, as usual. I notice that she has become tense. She is clutching the soft bundle of bright blue pajamas, the last gift she was given, with every ounce of strength and will that she has left in her frail body. Her face is strained with exhaustion and anxiety. I go over to my mother and kneel beside her so we are eye to eye. I put my arm on her shoulder and ask, "Mom, can I help you with that?"

Relief floods her face as she turns her eyes towards me.

"Oh, yes. Please. Please take it."

I gently lift the bundle from her cradling arms and place it on the bed beside the rest of her gifts. I go back and kneel beside her and take her hands.

"I didn't want to drop it," she murmurs quietly. "I was so afraid it would break."

"It is safe and sound," I assure her. "You took very good care of it."

She squeezes my hands. "Oh, thank you," she says, unseeing eyes speaking worlds. "Thank you so much."

"You're welcome, Mom." I answer, smiling. "I love you."

The pajama moment immediately eases its way into my memory, parking itself arrogantly beside the soup scene–the real one, boldly edging my beautiful invented one out of the picture. Although I am grateful to my invention for serving me well so long, I find I am not sorry to see it go. Like the palliative poultice it has turned out to be, its usefulness has expired. I no longer need it now that the real healing has begun.
--Mary Palmer Legare

My Mother's Eyes

Kubler-Ross is wrong. Grief is not a series of steps from stage one to stage two on through to the final stage at which point you are done with it. Grief is a strange and cyclic thing. It burns and aches, but it has much to teach us about living, about love, and about gratitude.

It has been nine years since my mother died. I never expected to "get over" it, but I had assumed that time would somehow lessen the sense of loss. Instead, what I am experiencing now is an intense flood of memories that brings with it not the howling grief that brings you to your knees, but rather a deep longing of the soul. This is, perhaps, what it feels like to simply *miss* her.

Why now? Why this September am I sharply reminded that 9/11 happened in my mother's last September on this earth? She was still in her own apartment at Westminster Canterbury then, hypnotically glued to the endless loop of footage and cascades of inadequate words blasting away at us through the TV–reeling in shock, just like the rest of us. She was watching it all unfold again and again and again from her own bed, in her own room, in her own apartment. She was still very much a part of the wide world then.

Within a month, she was moved to the healthcare unit, a move that she hoped would be temporary. But by November, by the time her last birthday rolled around, we all knew she would live out the rest of her days there, her world pretty much reduced to that little room. Still, the room was peopled with visitors. National and international events may have become more distant and less relevant to her, but she was still very present to her family and friends.

By the time December rolled around, it was sheer grit and determination that kept her on this planet. She had made up her mind that she wanted to have one last Christmas with us and, although she was in and out of clarity, riddled with pain, and addled with drugs, she made her goal.

Three days later, she was gone—but she did not simply waste away. The night of December 27, my mother was quite agitated. Although too weak to stand on her own, she kept trying to get out of bed, demanding imperiously:

"Get me my shoes and coat. It's time to go. Where's my hat? This nonsense has got to stop! I need my pocketbook. I've got to get home!"

She was so ready to get on with it, this dying—but she did not know how to do it without being completely in charge. She did not know how to let go and drift away. She had lived her life in great, vigorous strides, erect and purposeful. She simply knew no other way to move or be.

So she stormed out of this life. It took her all the way until the next morning, around 6:00 a.m., to finally hem and haw her way into eternity, and I was with her for a good part of that time, but not at the end.

Around midnight or so, I decided that I had to leave in order for her to get any rest at all. She had been extremely intent on giving me "the baby" over and over again, all evening long, and no amount of pantomime or placating on my part would convince her that I had ever actually received "the baby" from her. As she became increasingly frustrated, I began to have a sneaking suspicion that maybe, in some way, I was "the baby." Despite whatever dim vision or distant echo I sent her way telling her otherwise, it was clear to her that "the baby" was still standing alone before her, no cradling arms in sight.

I did not want to leave her. For some months, I had been nursing a vision of being with my mother at the time of her death, helping her to cross over peacefully. As I tried unsuccessfully to convince her that I had "the baby," and it was safe and sound, it became very clear that she would have none of it, and that the vision I was striving for was perhaps more about the death I wanted us to have together than about the death she was actually having. It was her dying, after all, and she was bound and determined to do it her way. She seemed to need to do this task on her own, to bulldoze her way into death the same way she had bulldozed her way through life, independent and self-sufficient to the end. So I left my mother to die alone.

Was that the right thing to do? It would make a much sweeter story if it had happened my way, but to my knowledge, "sweet" is not a word that was ever used in reference to Virginia Brown Trice. Generous, yes; gracious, loving, loyal to the end, dependable, certainly; courageous, competitive, down to earth, funny as hell–my mother was assertively and aggressively all that and more. But "sweet"? Not so much.

And in her own bawdy way, she was an intensely private person. (Around me, she never closed the door when she was on the pot, insisting on carrying on a conversation while she did her business.) There were doors in my mother's heart and soul that were simply never open for viewing. I asked her once towards the end if she believed in heaven and received a glare along with the stern admonition, "*That* is between me and my God."

So I have come to believe that, being the mother tigress she was, my mother simply could not take leave of this earth with any of her children present. The call to stay and take care of "the baby" was just too strong in her. No one else could be trusted to do it correctly, least of all any "baby" itself. Only if "the baby" went home and put herself to bed could my mother begin to quit fussing about her and get on with the business at hand.

I have also come to realize that death, along with heaven, was one of those things between my mother and her God. Like it or not, I was not invited to the final dance. I left my mother to die alone–stubbornly, fiercely, boldly, privately–in her own way, in her own time, on her own terms. I no longer regret that decision.

But here it is September again–the beginning of the final trek to her grave, and I think I am not so much mourning as I am cycling through that journey of loss with her–her autonomy breaking off shard by shard, her world diminishing, her ability to connect eroding. Pieces of my mother, crumbling away from that last September until the final night in December when I decided to walk away and leave her to duke it out with her God in private.

And I am left wondering: since Kubler-Ross is wrong about the linear thing, will I circle back around to this grief every September through December for the rest of my life? Maybe it's a nine-year cycle and won't spiral back around until 2019. Will it be different next time, if there is a next time? With Kubler-Ross as the sole misguided guide, I have no answers.

I only know that this cycle of sadness does not feel like a bad thing. Along with the ache of missing her comes the gift of getting to know Virginia Brown Trice a little better, to understand what she meant to me, and to appreciate everything she gave to me. And that gives me a better understanding of who I am and maybe even what I might have to offer.

A few weeks ago, I was watching the videos my husband made of the Three Divas here at church singing *Lift Thine Eyes* and *Down in the River to Pray*. The music was nice, but the visual–all I could see was the train wreck of this inappropriate alto woman, bobbing and weaving, making strange faces, music pages flapping this way and that, just a mess of disorganized motion. What was she doing in the same frame with these two perfect little sopranos, so still and so proper, standing just so, music held just so, beautiful voices floating clearly and effortlessly up and out of the perfect little o's of their perfect little mouths. But that bizarre alto–what in the world was she doing up there with them? It was not a pretty picture.

Then suddenly out of nowhere came this vivid memory of my mother describing my performance as one of the angel band of five-year-olds in the Christmas pageant. She was telling the story to a rapt audience of my teenage friends. I thought I would die of embarrassment right there on the spot.

"There's Mary Palmer," she said, shaking her head in mock despair, "halo off-kilter, tripping over her robe, chewing on the gold rope that was supposed to be around her waist. All the other little angels' wings go up; Mary Palmer's stay down. There she is looking all around everywhere all over that church–except where she needed to—at her wildly gesticulating Sunday School teacher motioning and mouthing, "*UP. UP.*" Finally she notices that the other wings are all up, so up go Mary Palmer's wings, just as everybody else's wings go down. There she is, wings up, halo crooked, soggy gold string stuck to her cheek, but just grinning like she's the greatest thing since sliced bread." Belly laughs all around, which at the time I thought were at my expense.

But looking back I see that even though my mother ended the story with that clicking sound of disapproval with her tongue, she was also stifling a smile—a kind of *proud* smile. Suddenly I saw that it was not I who thought that little angel was the greatest thing since sliced bread: it was Virginia Brown Trice.

So what does this have to do with this current cycle of grief? There's certainly the ache of longing for and missing Mom as I make this trek towards December, but intertwined with it is a kind of *newness* to these memories that are flooding over me now, a sense of *surprise*, followed by an *of course*, as if I had always known these things, but had simply forgotten them.

And it is quite possible that in the turbulence of adolescence and in the conflicts my adult choices seemed to always bring into our lives, a lot of the really good stuff just got lost somehow. Perhaps the first big cycle of grief, the tsunami that swept over us all for the first couple of years after Mom's passing, was about letting go of all that stuff I was holding, so I could just swim and survive. This time around, with that baggage for the most part swept away, the good stuff is all coming back to me, pouring over me in big, healing doses.

So back to that distracting, discombobulated alto that didn't seem to belong in the musical picture–well, she looks different to me now. Now, when I look at her, I see her through my mother's eyes and the picture is not nearly so disturbing. Through my mom's eyes, that alto looks more like an exuberant angel, halo definitely askew, slobbery string stuck to her face, completely out of sync with the rest of the angel band, but making beautiful music, and, oh, so happy with herself and the world at that moment– and that, My Friends, well, that just may be all that a person can ask for–and I guess that's the very definition of the greatest thing since sliced bread.

--Mary Palmer Legare

Heroes and Villains

With great power comes great responsibility. This is my gift, my curse. Who am I?

I am a father–hero to those who adore and depend on me, a soldier fighting for justice, hope, and the American way, an unwavering leader in the face of danger, never backing down.

But I have a secret–a dark secret, one that could shade the sky and make the earth tremble beneath those who worship me.

I am an egotistical skeptic of the way things are. I doubt myself on occasion and for many, many years, I laid to waste any fantasies of me being brave.

I am a hero despite myself–a villain in conflict, a father afraid for his children. How dare I sleep at night, after lying to them all day? What right do "I" have to be the guardians of beings so precious? Picture my hands, calloused and horned, holding the very thing that I least understand. But they need me.

I pray for them to a God that I have limited faith in, and I pray to God that the sins of the father do not spill onto the plates of the children. Unfortunately, I can already see pieces of myself in them. Anger! Resentment! They share my unyielding ability to bolster hatred, so much so that the hands of one attempted to smother the head of another. I fear for their lives, their futures, their souls, and as God is my witness, I will never forgive myself for the pain and misfortune I will surely bring to them. I don't deserve them, but I have them, and as a result I must do right by them. But how? How do I halt the inevitable?

One day they will come to face the real me–the liar, the sinner. The example I have forged for them will be shattered, and the villain will be exposed. The children, my children, will learn the truth about their beloved hero and see me as the majority does–as poor.

--Tobias Croom

56

LOVE

Love is friendship that has caught fire. It is quiet understanding, mutual confidence, sharing and forgiving. It is loyalty through good and bad times. It settles for less than perfection and makes allowances for human weaknesses.
--Ann Landers

You can't blame gravity for falling in love.
--Albert Einstein

I like nonsense, it wakes up the brain cells. Fantasy is a necessary ingredient in living, it's a way of looking at life through the wrong end of a telescope. Which is what I do, and that enables you to laugh at life's realities.
--Theodor Seuss Geisel

I have decided to stick with love. Hate is too great a burden to bear.
--Martin Luther King, Jr.

Love is life. And if you miss love, you miss life.
--Leo Buscaglia

Love is composed of a single soul inhabiting two bodies.
--Aristotle

Being deeply loved by someone gives you strength, while loving someone deeply gives you courage.
--Lao Tzu

I have found the paradox that if you love until it hurts, there can be no more hurt, only more love.
--Mother Teresa

A new command I give you: Love one another. As I have loved you, so you must love one another.
--Jesus of Nazareth

Love takes up where knowledge leaves off.
--Thomas Aquinas

Cold Showers of Paranoia

In the cold light of the morning, no palm birds sing. Perhaps someone got a gun before I did, Travis thinks. He sits bemused as silence creeps across the tile floor, and hours roll away. Ice droplets fall onto his skin before inevitably seeping through his pores. He wishes they would clean the layers of soot formed atop his brain. Instead, he shakes his head, trying to scrub it clean and get it working. The water spins around in whirlpools creating hallucinations he does not want to see. There in his mind, he is sitting cross-legged on a dusty porch. He shakes his head again, refusing to succumb to that memory.

Red is smeared across the tiles in failed attempts to write her name–to sketch her face and bring her back again. If only he could hear her sing again. Nobody sings like she did. He wants to cry, but can't, in fear of being watched like he always is. He only wishes it were with more love than suspicion. Besides, she never did like tears. The memory sneaks back. He sees her running toward the road with smiles in her eyes and white ribbons in her hair, spinning around in her purple dress–so lovely.

Once again he struggles to drive the memory back, but at last he can fight it no longer. She floods back into his senses and courses through his veins as the memory grows stronger. He's struggling to his feet, waving and calling, "Emily!" But she runs, not looking, not staying behind for him. That day he lost his little sister, locked within the doors of her childhood. Though she is gone, her laugh remains–one that will never cease to stalk his nights.

--Anna M. McEwen

Finding Love Where There Is None

The words coming out of my husband's mouth hit me like ice water. I couldn't catch my breath. The room started to spin in slow motion as panic worked up through my chest. His lips were still moving, but I had fallen deaf after he announced that he wanted a divorce. I stammered as I tried to put words together, but he didn't stick around. He walked out the front door without glancing back.

Sitting on the sofa, I wondered how I had missed this. I felt like a fool. I moved around the house aimlessly from room to room, like a pinball slowly making its way back down the alleys after being slammed into the playfield. I touched the empty drawers where his clothes had been. His things were missing out of the bathroom cabinet, too. He had been planning this for a while.

My daughter didn't understand why her daddy wasn't home. She cried for him every night. She didn't understand why I couldn't make him come home. It's not that I didn't try. I called and begged him to come home, but he was busy with his new girlfriend.

My insides felt like they had been through a blender. It was hard to breathe. I slept on the sofa every night and cried until I fell asleep. I wondered sometimes if I'd wake up the next day. I was sure that my heart would just stop beating.

I had to pull myself together and get a job. Most of the bills were in my name. I knew that I had enough money in the bank to carry me through at least six months, but I needed to establish an income. Coming home after my first day on the job, I stopped at the mailbox as I made my way to the house. There was a stack of notices from the bank. I sat down on the steps and opened the envelopes–all twelve were bounced-check notices. I could not fathom how that could be possible. It was after work hours so I couldn't call the bank. I sat up all night worrying. The next morning I got up and went back to work without any sleep.

On my lunch hour I went to the bank. The woman behind the desk was very kind as she explained to me that there was no money in my account. It had actually been overdrawn by $1,000. She explained that my husband had made a substantial withdrawal and showed me the documentation. It was dated the day before he had told me that he wanted a divorce. The next day, I met with an attorney to see what I could do. His answer was another blow. There was nothing I could do. Even though it was my money, my husband's name was on the account. He had not broken the law by taking it. I reached an anger level that was so intense that I was afraid of what I was capable of doing.

The intensity of my hatred and bitterness toward the man I once loved grew every day. When I found out that his girlfriend was pregnant, I hated him even more. And I hated her and her bastard baby. Thoughts of hatred and revenge ravaged my mind and body. Months later I received a phone call from him out of the blue. Obviously upset, he asked for my help. His young girlfriend was drinking while she was pregnant. He wanted me to explain to her the devastating effects that drinking could have on her baby. I took great pleasure in laughing in his face and slamming the phone down. I thought to myself, *"Good. I hope her baby is born severely deformed–or even better–dead. I hope the baby dies, and she is so devastated that she kills herself. It would serve them all right for what they have done."*

I reveled in my sense of justice, picturing how terrible it would be for them to have a deformed child when he had abandoned our beautiful, healthy child. I tried to put the thoughts out of my head, but they sprang back with more intensity. Surely, God would understand. I was right. They were wrong. They deserved bad things to happen to them. I wanted them to suffer.

Something surreal happened to me that day. It was as if I rose out of my body and watched myself from above. I could see myself smoldering in hatred. I didn't recognize myself. I couldn't believe that this was me. Being consumed by this kind of hatred was not setting well with my soul. But what could I do? The answer was clear to me. I couldn't do anything by myself. I knew I needed help.

I got down on my knees. I put my head in my hands and sobbed and prayed: *"God, please help me. I know what I'm feeling is wrong, and I'm not able to get a handle on it. Take this hatred and bitterness out of me. Give me your love for this baby because I don't have any of my own."* After saying that simple prayer, I stayed on my knees for over an hour. I was exhausted. As I knelt there, I felt a heavy weight lift off of my heart. The hate was fading, but forgiveness was still out of my reach. That would be a much longer process.

The baby boy was born the day before my birthday in June. When he was six months old, they brought him over for my daughter to meet her new brother. They walked through the gate with the little guy in a stroller, and my daughter bounced out the front door to greet her dad and the baby. I decided to meet the situation head on. I took a deep breath and followed her out.

I examined the baby, thanking God that he was all right. I ran my hand over his smooth, perfectly shaped, round head. I counted his fingers and toes. I looked into his tiny face and I very clearly saw God's love shining through his eyes. It was as if he knew me. I held him in the swing on my front porch and I felt God's love for him and God's love for me move through us both and envelop us like a soft breeze.

This little baby has grown into a handsome young man. He calls me his aunt. It seemed to him to be the most appropriate term for the mother of his sister. He is a blessing in our lives.

God helped me find love where there was none. He channeled his love and strength through me and helped me deal with circumstances that were too much for me to bear on my own.

--Jan Crocker

THE WAY IT WAS: THE BABYSITTER

Lawd! Lawd! What dese white wimmens be thinkin'? Ain' no way us black wimmens gonna put up wid what dese wimmens tol'rate wid dere mens. White wimmens, dey haf problems wid dere mens? Dey go jump in de lake. Black wimmens? Dey gonna trow dere mens in de lake.

Me and de neighbors set out in de alley every morning together. De kids can run 'roun' and git dey energy out. Dey wait for de trash truck to pass each week. De garbagemens always saves out some of de ol' candy dat de candy store trows away and gives it to de kids.

I likes to talk to de other mamas to find out what be goin' on in de neighborhood. One of 'em tol' me 'bout dis white man dat moved in de junk apartment down de street. Say he try to kill hisself when his wife up and leave him. He kinda unfriendly and keep to hisself. Mus' be way down on his luck to move into de black quarters. He ain' de only one down on his luck.

Dat poor, young blond woman move into de neighborhood a month ago wid her two chirrens. De boy de older one. He play hard–he ain' no problem. But dat girl, she be hard to watch. She always be breaking de rules. She wanna run after her brotha. Spankin' her jus' help for a lil' while. Then she run off after her brotha again.

Dere mama so poor she don' know how she gonna makes ends meet. She 'splain to me dat she be tryin' to make a new start.

I wants to help dis young gal. She ain' got nobody else to help her wid dese chirrens. Poor thang–she jus' tryin' to make ends meet. She gotta go to work ever'day. De pay ain' hardly 'nuff fo' her to afford a babysitter. She aks me to hep her out.

I got dis new baby dat still be on de breas', but I tol' her I hep her out wid de chirrens while she be workin' at de box facto-ry. Dis mornin' I be sorry dat I make dat offer. De lil' sister wait till I turns my back to chase after her brotha and de udder boys. I calls her back, but she 'tend she don' hear me. I tol' her I cain' be runnin' after her ever' minute.

I breaks me a switch from dat peach tree and I switches her skinny white legs. She go to squallin' like a stuck pig. Her brotha come a runnin' to see what de matter be. Befo' I kin calm dem down, I looks up and sees dat crazy white man from de junk apart-ment come a barrelin' to'rd me.

"Nigger," he 'rupts like a cannon, "don' you never hit another white chile." He pick up de lil' girl, order de boy to follow him, and tramp off. He turn back jus' long 'nuff to tell me to tell dey mama where to git her chirrens.

De mama she come home an' go gits her chirrens. I waits and waits fo' her to come back. In 'bout two hours, she come home wid a li'l spring to her step. 'Fo' long, de crazy man be movin' in wid her and de chirrens.

All I can say dey be some bad storms a brewin' down de road.
--Ray Sapp

MAMA MEETS STEPDADDY

The day started like many others for the little boy. His moth-er went off to work in a box factory and left his sister and him in the care of a nice black lady in the community. The siblings pretty much spent the days outside, mostly in an alley with other children playing games such as hide-and-seek. While they watched the children play, mothers breast-fed their babies and visited with one another.

The arrival of the trash truck on its regular route was a high-light of the week. The garbage men gave all the children candy from a local candy maker. The children devoured it without a trace. Each day seemed to be much the same as the next one.

Without any warning, a blood-curdling scream exploded, signaling an abrupt end to that comforting sameness. Recognizing his sister's screams, the little boy ran as fast as he could to see what had happened to her. Running back to the alley, he found her on the ground crying. Their sitter had disciplined her for breaking one of the rules.

No one could ever have anticipated what followed. Out of the blue, a strange white man materialized and picked up his howling sister. His voice rose as he began to threaten the black sitter. The man claimed that he had been looking out his apartment window and witnessed the lady spanking the little boy's sister. He warned the sitter strongly about the consequences if he ever saw her hit another white child. Shockingly, he picked up the sister and began to carry her toward his apartment, indicating to her brother that he was to follow. Almost as an afterthought, he turned back toward the sitter and instructed her to tell their mother to come to his apartment to pick the children up.

After work, the little boy's mother went to the apartment and demanded to know where her children were. The man calmly told her that he had already fed the children, and they were now engrossed in watching television. Her fears somewhat assuaged by the seeming kindness of the stranger, she allowed herself to be drawn in by his attention to her children. The children were all but forgotten as the man and woman began to get acquainted.

The man became a daily visitor to their apartment, always bringing candy and playing with the children. He seemed like the answer to their prayers. When their mother asked them if they liked the man, they giggled and replied, "Yes, Mama."

It wasn't long before the stranger began to stay overnight in their mama's room. He soon asked her to be his wife. After a quick courthouse wedding, the stranger became their father, at the outset bringing stability and filling a big void in their lives.
--Ray Sapp

'Twas the Day after Christmas

'Twas the day after Christmas, and on the living room floor the three younger siblings played intently with their new toys–a pleasure rarely available to them. Christmas Day had been a nice day with no outbursts of anger. The children had let down their guard as they enjoyed their gifts. Holidays helped them relax a little more than usual. Eager to get back to their gifts, the children had dressed hurriedly on the morning after Christmas. Gathered on the living room floor, the three youngest children were completely absorbed in their new toys. To have new toys with time to play made the day special. Ignoring breakfast to get in more playing time, the boys had not yet ventured out into the yard. The weather was in the low thirties with strong gusts of wind, making the living room the ideal place for the children to hang out and play. Only a brief trip for something to drink or a quick run to the bathroom paused their play.

Adults spent the morning around the dining room table drinking coffee and chatting. The oldest girl cleaned the dishes and hung out at the table with the grown-ups. One of the gifts that the two young boys had received together was a toy named Creepy Crawlers that needed to be plugged into an electrical outlet. It baked a liquid mixture that could be poured into different molds. It solidified after heating. Once baked, the finished product was a jelly-textured creature that was scary-looking. Molds that varied in shape and size gave the children multiple options that kept them experimenting with different mixtures of colors. The liquid concoction gave off a burning plastic smell that their mother did not like.

Playing with her favorite gift from Christmas, the youngest girl dressed her doll in different outfits and mumbled her lines and the doll's lines in their conversation. She had watched her brothers briefly make a bug with their toy before she wandered over to the chair with her doll. Her older sister, interested in cooking and jewelry, left the seven-year-old little girl alone to play dolls by herself. Engrossed in their play, the little girl and her brothers were oblivious to the passage of time as morning turned into afternoon and then into evening.

The children noticed as their father turned on the television and settled onto the sofa to relax. They began to sense his agitation as he constantly monitored their actions. Their father had been smiling on Christmas morning as he and the children's mother exchanged gifts. Now, he was acting as if the holidays were over. They began to wonder if one of them had done something to displease him. However, the call of their new toys was so strong that they delayed acknowledging the tension that had filled the room with the entrance of their father. Lulled by the joy of the day before and the joy of the holidays, the children played on, oblivious that their father was watching the movement of the clock.

Each child knew the rules about doing chores and the strict 5 p.m. deadline their father had established for feeding the chickens and the dogs. The warmth of the room, the companionship, and the new toys so mesmerized the children that they failed to register the passage of time. They had observed the clock at 1:00 p.m., thinking they had the whole afternoon with plenty of time to do their chores before the rigid deadline.

The children continued to play on the living room floor, relishing every moment of the special holiday when time seemed to be suspended for them. Startled back to the reality of their existence, they heard their father's threatening question: "What time is it?" Looking up from their infrequent time of play, they saw him standing in the doorway and heard the ominous tapping of his fingers as he repeated the question: "What time is it?"

Immediately rising from the floor, they began to look for the wall clock to check the time. They panicked when the hands of the clock indicated it was almost 5:30 p.m. All three scrambled through the door where their father stood. They raced down the hall toward their rooms to get their shoes and coats.

Before they reached their rooms, they heard the menacing command of their father: "Stop! Leave your coats and shoes alone and come with me." They obediently followed him as he strode toward the chicken coop. They wondered what was about to happen. Opening the gate to the chicken coop, the big man turned and grabbed the little sister by the shoulder and forced her into the coop with the chickens and closed the gate with the harsh words: "I want you to see how it feels to go without food and water." The little sister began to sob and fell hopelessly to the ground.

The two brothers instantly realized that their fate would be similar to their sister's. They marched behind their father toward the dogs at the back of the yard. Reaching the motor where the first dog was chained, the man pushed the older brother to the ground and chained him to the motor and allowed the dog to run free. He repeated the same words he had said to the little sister: "I want you to see how it feels to go without food and water!"

The younger brother recognized immediately what was to befall him. It was his turn to walk toward the second dog. He kept pace with the man in an effort to avoid being pushed to the ground. Instinctively, he collapsed on the ground as the man turned to grab him. The chain was ice cold as it made contact with his flesh. His stepfather then repeated the same words again: "I want you to see how it feels to go without food and water!" The man walked away from the boys without a backward look, leaving them shivering from the bitter cold, crying, and scared.

The children had no idea how long the man would leave them in the cold without shoes and coats. The back door opened and their older sister came out with their coats and shoes. Before she could reach any of her siblings, the man stopped her and forbade her to approach the freezing children. He threatened her with the same punishment if she attempted to help them. "Dogs don't have coats," he roared at the older sister as she headed back toward the door. As she entered the warm house, she turned and looked toward the children sympathetically before she closed the door.

As their hope died with the closing of the door, the brothers huddled close to the ground to try to minimize the wind's brutal shear. As the sky began to darken, they saw a car pull into the drive up close to the house. A lady got out and opened the back door of the car. She noticed the older boy and called out his name. She needed help to carry the Christmas gifts she had brought. The older boy replied that he could not come and help her because his dad had chained him to a motor.

Incredulous, the woman with the gifts asked loudly: "What?"

The older brother repeated his explanation: "Dad chained me to this motor."

The older brother's biological mother, the lady with the gifts, became furious. Within minutes of her threats to call Family and Children's Services, the boys were unchained and allowed to enter the house again. Still sobbing and with chicken feathers in her hair, their little sister was also permitted to come back into the warm house. It was the day after Christmas.
--Ray Sapp

THE JUNKYARD BOY

No matter what he had to endure, the five-year-old boy's naturally sweet spirit and his finely honed sense of humor enabled him to cope. His beautiful brown eyes glowed like smoky quartz gemstone when he was able to bring a smile to the faces of his family. Somewhat skinny and tall for his age, he wanted most of all to please his mother and stepfather. Yet the little boy had many dreams of his own about what he wanted to become when he grew up. His dreams multiplied as his experiences broadened.

The little boy's stepfather worked as a foreman over a construction crew and frequently brought blueprints home with him. The detailed blueprints captivated the imagination of the little boy. He asked his stepfather multiple questions about what the lines and figures on the drawings meant. He soon progressed to copying the drawings as exactly as he could. His drawing skills increased as he reproduced the blueprints of the buildings his stepfather's company built. He began to imagine designing futuristic-looking buildings like he had seen on The Jetsons cartoons. He started to dream about becoming an architect.

When he wasn't sketching designs for buildings, the boy and his brothers loved to reenact the football games they saw on television, although his stepfather thought work was the only constructive activity during daylight hours. Blessed with the ability to run faster than any other family member, the young boy often thought of becoming a pro-football player. Playing pass-and-catch football with his older brothers only expanded his imagination of what it might be like to become a famous football player. The boy and his brothers had to steal time for football whenever his stepfather was gone. Even with the disapproval of his stepfather, the boy's ambition to become a football star continued to grow.

As the boy's experiences increased, his ambitions multiplied. The family gathered nightly in the living room with the television tuned to the local news, followed by the world news with anchorman Walter Cronkite. It was this nightly ritual that instilled a great patriotism in the little boy. He watched the young American soldiers flying into rice fields on helicopters and imagined himself there. His dreams of becoming a soldier were as vivid as the images he witnessed on television. He practiced battle strategies with the little green plastic army men his mother had bought him, staging a veritable living-room war. The Vietnam War had touched the young boy's life and influenced his aspirations for the future.

The little boy's mother also had a dream for him. She admired the two young doctors from their small town and wanted her son to be like them. One had even delivered the little boy. Hearing his mother tell family and friends of her dream for him to one day become a doctor, the young boy began to embrace his mother's dream. To please his mother, the boy would do anything, including owning her dream. He began to aspire to become a doctor.

The young boy's life was in a state of constant change. His plate was full just dealing with the realities in front of him. The family junkyard and the rigid rules of his stepfather limited the time available to him for personal pursuits. The five-year-old would-be architect-football player-soldier-doctor poured cheap, dry dog food onto the pans of table scraps to take out to the two junkyard dogs that guarded the area. His stepfather's warning that some people would try to take automobile parts without paying replayed itself in his head. He knew that some men would even come back at night to retrieve the parts they had found on their earlier tour of the junkyard. Being a junkyard boy was no easy task.

The boy stopped for a moment as he surveyed the junkyard. Old junk cars covered the large field next to their house. Business could take place anywhere–in their house, in the driveway, in any corner of the huge lot. Due to the high costs of auto parts at the dealerships, the junkyard always had plenty of customers trying to save a buck.

Saturday had a history of being the busiest day of the week. On one of those chaotic Saturdays, the junkyard boy saw a customer drop something as he got out of his car and headed toward the house. The boy ran to the driveway to see what the man had dropped. He found a big wad of money, which he immediately carried to his mother. Before returning it to the customer, she counted it–more than $400. The customer turned to the little boy, thanked him, and handed him a dime. The little boy looked at the dime, and the hope in his dark brown eyes dimmed.

To ensure the constant traffic of customers, the family had to maintain the junkyard stock of cars. The entire family had to remain on constant alert for old automobiles that were not working or had been abandoned. The stepfather assumed the task of contacting the vehicle owners to work out a deal with them for the purchase of the vehicles. Wreckers or rollback trucks picked up the newly purchased vehicles and brought them to the junkyard.

The junkyard boys had the job of hooking the cable from the truck to the newly acquired cars—a task that required intricate knowledge of the anatomy of vehicles. They could attach cables only to the parts of the vehicles strong enough to tolerate the pressures of the tow truck. The junkyard boys often had to navigate kudzu, insects, and snakes to secure the cables to the cars. The boy had no idea that he was amassing a body of practical knowledge that would be invaluable to him as he sought at a tender age to make a living for himself and eventually for his family.

The job of junkyard boy required much more than an understanding of the structure of vehicles and of the danger of the woods. Junkyard boys had to develop a mental catalog of cars and their locations to help customers locate parts for a certain car model. They maintained a list of parts they had to remove before salvaging vehicles. The boys also had to become proficient at stripping parts off the vehicles and prepping them for burning. The burning removed anything that was not metal. Burning an automobile required flipping it over and puncturing the fuel tank with an ax to prevent it from exploding. Early on, the boys had set a car on fire and watched in amazement as the drive shaft took off like a rocket and circled the field around them before coming to rest— one more important lesson in the anatomy of the car.

Once the car was burned and cooled, the junkyard boys stripped the cars of their copper wiring and deposited it in barrels kept close to the main house. They removed the heater coils from the burned vehicles and loaded the vehicles onto the trucks going to the salvage yard. The severed parts were stored close to the house and guarded by the junkyard dogs.

The junkyard boy lived in a constantly changing landscape. As one vehicle was removed, another was unloaded in its place. Junkyard tasks kept the would-be architect-ball player-soldier-doctor so busy that he had little time to dream of his future. Making a living for the family consumed his energies and time. His hopes went underground as he struggled to survive in an environment that became increasingly more brutal and demanding. It seemed that his family disintegrated more with each vehicle going up in smoke. It would be years before he would begin to realize the value of the many skills he had mastered in his youth in the junkyard. But somehow the embers of his dreams still cast a glow in the deep brown of the eyes of the junkyard boy.

--Ray Sapp

THE SCENE

"That movie was really good."

"I know. Right? Angie M got dat body!"

"Seriously, Bobby, do you think of anything other than girls?"

"Nope. You see her? Look at all dat wiggle and giggle in dat skirt! Uhmm mm mmm. I'll be right back."

Tasha shook her head and rolled her eyes as she watched her older cousin dart across the theater lobby to catch *another* one. She began to unzip the oversized jacket that he had let her borrow during the previews. *He might as well just let me have his jacket. I'm always taking it from him anyway.* While she prepared herself for the sweltering heat outside, she shivered as she noticed somebody watching her. It was Him–Q, the hottest, smartest, cutest boy in school–and he was staring right at her. She tried not to make her glance so obvious by looking away and smoothing back her long black ponytail.

She quickly headed towards the door, head down, trying not to let anyone see her blush or giggle. She knew that she would just die if he or any of his friends talked bad about her on Monday.

She rushed to reach for the door, but a larger more muscular hand beat her to it. She looked up, and her heart dropped. There he was–smiling that same bright smile that she'd admired in school. *He's more perfect up close.*

"Excuse me, please."

"No. Excuse me, Tasha."

Oh, crap! He knows my name. He ushered her out of the door, and she swore that she could feel his eyes studying her every movement. *God, please. If you're listening, PLEASE don't let Momma pull up ANY time soon. Thank you in advance.*

"Thanks."

"Anytime. I was wonderin' what you be doin' on tha weekends. I figured that a girl like you would prob'ly be at home doin' next month's homework while watchin' the History Channel or somethin' like that," he chuckled.

She smiled at his acknowledgement of her good grades. *He watches me.* She couldn't believe the fact that the infamous Q was actually talking to *HER*.

"No. I do other things than homework."

"Reeaally now? Like what?"

She took a brief pause and then replied, "Like singing, dancing, obviously the movies. You know, just hanging out and stuff."

"And stuff, huh?"

"Yeah. And stuff." She couldn't contain her laughter. She knew that he knew that she was lying.

"Well, you never hang out with me."

"You've never asked me to."

"If I had yo number, I would ask."

"Well, if you'd ask for my number, you could have it."

"O.K. Lemme get yo number."

Tasha loved that he was quick in conversation. She rushed to pull a torn piece of paper from her pocket. He held her jacket as she began reaching for a pen, but through all of her nervousness, she'd forgotten that she didn't have one. She'd left her purse in her mother's car. Q could see the frustration in her face and moved beside her to lay his arm across her shoulders. *Dang. I never knew that he smelled so good.*

"I'll just get it from you on Monday. Hall 3?"

"Sure. Meet me by my locker before first period. My bus drops us off a little early."

"I know," he grinned.

They stood there, propped up against the brick wall of the theater–him watching the people, her holding on to the moment. She leaned against him, her eyes closed, her head resting on his sweaty shoulder–the perfect moment with the perfect man. Nothing else mattered.

Her moment of pleasure was abruptly ripped away by the loud sounds from a group of boys coming towards them.

"I see you, Nigga! I told you we was gon' find yo ass!"

Tasha's eyes shot open trying to determine who they were and who they were talking to. Q quickly let her go and took off running at full speed, trying to use his All American status to his advantage. Unfortunately for him, human speed couldn't outrun the speed or force of either bullet propelled from their guns. The entire crowd scattered. Everyone ran–except Tasha. She stood there with her eyes opened as wide as her mouth.

Bang! She watched his running stop. Boom! Bang! Pap! He dropped to his knees. Boom! On the ground. She wanted to run, but could not move. Everything on her body was frozen but her eyes. They turned towards the group of guys who had just killed who may have been her first boyfriend. She locked eyes with one just as her mind began to process what she'd seen. PAP! PAP! Bang! were the last sounds that she heard as her body slammed to the ground on top of her tears.

"T! Get up! Please, Tasha! GET UP! We have to go. Get up!"

She could feel her body being pushed, hit, and shaken. Tasha opened her eyes to the sight of her cousin pleading with her to stand.

"Aunty Jay gon' be here any minute, so GET up!"

He helped her stand as she stared at the puddle of blood on the concrete down the sidewalk. She slowly scanned over her body. Her clothes were clean. *I must be dead already.* Bobby grabbed her hand and started to drag her towards the parking lot, but she yanked away to go and pick up Bobby's dripping jacket.

"Jus' leave the damned jacket there. It's covered in his blood anyway!"

Tasha dropped the jacket a few feet from Q's still warm body. As they ran, Q's eyes seemed to follow her until she was too far away to see them. When they reached the top of the parking lot, Bobby let her have it.

"What's wrong wit' you! You jus' standin' there while dat man gittin' shot! You ain't s'pose to stand there. You s'pose to run! Girl, you coulda been shot! Are you listenin' to me?"

Tasha stood there staring at the distant body that had been holding her only moments ago. *He's never fallen before. Not on the court. Not on the field. Not even on the track. Why here? On the concrete? Why now?*

Bobby continued pacing back and forth in front of her, giving her a full-force tirade. Tasha tearfully looked up into his eyes, causing him to stop. He grabbed her arms and face, hastily examining her from top to bottom and began to dust off her back and side.

"Look. If she asks, tell Aunty that you scraped yo face and arm 'cuz you tripped from runnin'. And we didn't know the guy and we didn't see what happened. Okay?"

"Okay, Bobby."

"Aunty'd kill me if she knew you was this close to bein' shot," he took a deep breath. "And T, I'm sorry dat I slammed you so hard, man. I was scared and jus' didn't know what to do."

"Uh-huh."

After a brief pause, Bobby's face went again from worried to mad.

"Tasha?"

"Huh?"

"What the hell was you doin' talkin' to dat damn boy anyway? I saw y'all ovuh there all hugged up. You ain't got time for no boys. You have to go to school–college. Be somethin' otha than somebody's baby mama. Dat way you and yo kids don't evuh have to be 'round a scene like this. You wasn't made for this."

§ § § § § §

Tasha stood straight up in the mirror, fixing her hair and adjusting her blazer. She wiped the tears from her eyes, careful not to smudge what was left of her eyeliner. *High school. Check. College and med school. Check. Awesome career and even more awesome condo by the water. Double check. Husband and kid by 35. Maybe. There might have been a slight error, but there's still time.* The buzz of her doorbell startled her. She closed her eyes and gave a long sigh. *I guess it's time to go.*

She slowly headed down the stairs where Joe was waiting patiently at her front door. Young, black, gorgeous, and scared, she took her first step in nearly fifteen years into the ice-cold dating pool. "Love Jones generation," she mumbled sarcastically to herself. "I swear to God I'm gonna kill Emily if this guy is horrible."

Taking in one last deep breath, she reluctantly opened the door to a man whose eyes stared directly into her soul past the memories of a chance at love once lost. Taking her time, she stepped out as calmly and confidently as she could, not able to deny the shifting of the blues in her left thigh into the funk in her right.

--Katrina Croom

MOM'S BEST FRIEND

I am standing in the doorway to Steffi's bedroom, watching as she makes preparations. The small blue pill is placed in a teaspoon and crushed. Great care is taken not to lose any of the precious powder. She adds water from a syringe, mixing and letting it dissolve. A small piece of cotton from a Q-tip is placed in the spoon; the liquid is drawn through this cotton to serve as a filter. Now she ties her arm off with a hair band and searches for a vein. This proves difficult. Her arms are scarred with tracks from previous uses. She finally succeeds and injects the solution into her arm. She cleans her rig out and then licks the blood off her arm. The blood tasting, along with her pale, wan flesh and deep circles under her eyes does more than suggest vampires–it screams it. These opiate addicts are the actuality of which vampires are the types and shadows. At last an expression of relief appears on her face. She looks up at me and smiles. It's a pretty smile on the face of a pretty young girl. It is also one of the saddest sights that I have ever seen.

Steffi is twenty-four years old. We are talking about her past. She shows me trophies she won playing softball in high school. On her wall are a few pictures of kids in her family–she says she loves kids. There is a sacred heart of Jesus prayer card, though she is not Catholic. She just likes the picture of Jesus. There's a poster of MLK's "Dream" speech, an unusual item in a redneck trailer park in southeast Georgia. Her past seems fairly normal. She is really interested to know that I am a writer.

Digging under a pile of clothes, Steffi locates a notebook and invites me to read some of her writing. The thing that leaps out at me is a poem scrawled out in the hand of a child: "Mom's Best Friend."

> Mom's Best Friend is a secret she keeps
> When it comes around all she does is sleeps
> Small and secret in the palm of her hand
> Now you know her friend isn't a man
> Not another woman, a boy, or girl
> Mom's new best friend takes her to another world
> Dropping her cigarettes, while sitting in her chair
> Although you know you can't see it you know that it's there
> Look at her eyes half shut with a stare
> Her friend could cause her life to end
> Does that sound like much of a friend?
> Wish it would scare her so she could see
> The best friend she could ever have is me
> If you don't understand the way that I feel
> Then your Mom's best friend probably isn't a pill.

"Did your little girl write this?" I ask.

With a shake of her head, she points to the name at the bottom: "Stephanie Rhymes."

"You wrote this?"

"Yeah, when I was ten."

Her green eyes shine wet through the tears she struggles to hold back. The poignant moment is broken by a clattering sound from the living-room area of the trailer. I see a small gnomish body sprawled on the floor. There is also a cell phone lying there, its battery jarred out by the impact of falling.

"Mom's nodded out again. Will you help me get her up?"

We help the little old lady up and prop her in her chair. She tries to say "thanks," but it comes out slurred and mixed with drool. Steffi isn't nearly this high.

"How many did she do?" I ask.

"Oh, she mixes hers with Xanax when she can."

This sort of mixing has been the cause of many deaths. The mom, Roxanne, stirs enough to ask for a smoke. Steffi lights the cigarette and places it in her mother's mouth.

I retrieve my drink from the counter and start to sip when I notice a roach has fallen in and drowned. Steffi notices and apologizes profusely. I can tell she is embarrassed. I tell her it's okay.

"Mom!"

Steffi rushes to her mother's chair and beats out the embers that are starting to burn from where Roxanne has put her cigarette down.

"Mom, if you gonna nod, you can't smoke. You're gonna burn the house down one day."

Roxanne lifts her hand to her mouth and takes a drag on the cigarette. She drops her hand–cigarette and all–into the green glass ashtray on the table beside her chair.

"There," she slurs, having solved the problem. She leaves her hand in the ash tray, her head nods forward, and she crumples into herself–not falling this time, but headed to the edge of her seat.

You can see how the falling works in stages. This is only the beginning; the process will end with her on the floor again.

In the night a horn sounds.

"That's for me," Steffi explains.

She opens the door and hollers, "Just a minute!"

"Can you stay and watch her for me?" she asks me. "I'll only be gone a few minutes. I promise."

I try to refuse, but can't resist her pleading. I imagine lots of men must fall for her charms. She dashes out the door, hops into a late model Ford Lariat, and rides off into the night. I look at Roxanne, crumpled in the chair and close to falling again. She is very small and thin. Her unkempt hair is pulled back in a band. She doesn't stink, but you can tell that she doesn't bathe much, and her personal hygiene is lacking. What do I know about her? She has been arrested numerous times–the worst for murder and armed robbery. She got out of that somehow. She has been to prison on drug charges. Now she mostly sits in the chair and nods on pills.

A truck pulls up. Steffi hops out, says "Thanks," and blows into the trailer. "See, that didn't take long."

It has been less than an hour.

Roxanne stirs in her chair. "You bring me something?"

"Mom, you don't need anything. You're nodding out now."

"Don't you tell me what I need, Bitch. I know you been out whoring. Now give me my medicine."

Steffi goes to her room and closes the door.

"You get your slut ass out of my house," Roxanne is pounding on the door and yelling.

This is the most animated I have seen her.

"You think you can stay here and turn your tricks and not give me a damn thing? Get your ass out now."

She turns and spots me.

"Who are you? One of her tricks?"

"No, I'm a writer. We met earlier. Remember?"

She clearly has no recollection of my arrival.

"You got pills? You want to party wiff me?"

She tries to grope me, and I step back.

"Screw you then, you bastard."

The bedroom door opens. Steffi motions me in, quickly pulling the door shut behind me.

"Get out! Both of you! Leave now!" Roxanne yells as she pounds on the door.

"Ignore her," Steffi commands. "She'll run down in a minute."

The raging continues like a full-force hurricane.

"I'm sorry," Steffi mumbles and begins to sob. "I hate when she's like this. I hate what I have to do. It feels like I am selling my soul."

I hold Steffi in my arms while she cries. A long time later, the storm finally begins to wind down. Steffi pulls two pills out, sets one aside, and prepares to shoot the other one.

"How much are those?" I ask.

"Twenty dollars each. Sometimes twenty-five, but if I can buy enough at one time, sometimes I can get them for fifteen."

"How many do you take a day?"

"I can get by on two. You know—not to get sick or anything. But to get high, I need six or so."

"That's over one hundred dollars per day. You don't work, so how do you manage it?"

"Like that," she says, nodding towards outside.

I catch the reference to her earlier trip.

"Every day?"

"Pretty much. Mom's got a script for ninety pills that she can fill every twenty-eight days. That's what she gets by on, and I help her. Of course, she gives me some, too."

I wonder exactly how much help her mom gives—very little is

76

my guess. Ninety seems like a lot.

"Well, she doesn't get them all. She's got a guy who takes her to the pain management clinic. He pays for the doctor visit and for the script to be filled. For that he gets half of the pills. When she runs out, he *loans* her a pill for two back. By the end of the month, she's lucky if she has twenty left. Usually it's closer to ten."

"So this guy's got all the money?"

"Yeah. He has several others that he does the same deal with."

"So he just uses them, and they are too addicted to get out of it."

By now it's quiet outside, and we go out. Sitting in her chair, Roxanne cries out, "Nobody cares about me. I am all alone." Steffi soothes her, "You know I love you, Mom. Here, I brought your medicine." She hands Roxanne the other blue pill. Roxanne grabs it, swiftly crushes it, and snorts it up through a straw.

"Steffi's my best girl," she announces proudly. "She's all I got left. The others left long ago. Don't know what I'd do without her."

The Jekyll-Hyde transformation is too much for me. As I leave, Steffi is killing roaches on the wall with a slipper, and Roxanne is nodding–cigarette in hand, putting the whole place in danger of burning.

Holding my eyes open so the wind can blow them dry, I walk to my car. I keep telling myself that it is just smoke irritating my eyes, just cigarette smoke–that's all.

--Joe Chafin

Animal Stories

Man is by nature a political animal.
--Aristotle

I care not for a man's religion whose dog and cat are not the better for it.
--Abraham Lincoln

Until one has loved an animal, a part of one's soul remains unawakened.
--Anatole France

The greatness of a nation and its moral progress can be judged by the way its animals are treated.
--Mahatma Gandhi

It is just like man's vanity and impertinence to call an animal dumb because it is dumb to his own perceptions.
--Mark Twain

The average dog is a nicer person than the average person.
--Andrew A. Rooney

Any glimpse into the life of an animal quickens our own and makes it so much the larger and better in every way.
--John Muir

Experience demands that man is the only animal which devours his own kind, for I can apply no milder term to the general prey of the rich on the poor.
--Thomas Jefferson

If a dog will not come to you after having looked you in the face, you should go home and examine your conscience.
--Woodrow Wilson

If you pick up a stray dog and make him prosperous he will not bite you. This is the principal difference between a dog and a man.
--Mark Twain

THE BEAR

On the way out of town, we stopped at a gas station with a small grocery store attached–a last chance for needed items, or for a fifteen-year-old boy to procure any items that might provide additional entertainment around the campfire late at night. Several years ago, my friend Timothy and I had hidden a rubber snake beside my dad's tent. When I pointed it out to my dad and began reaching for it, he freaked out. He made quite the spectacle of himself trying to get to me before I could get my hands on the serpent. We all thought it was hilarious–even my dad. Unfortunately, there weren't any rubber snakes for sale–or any good prank-type items for that matter.

I decided to buy a copy of the *National Inquirer* that promised a great cover story, advertised in large caps and bold text: "**MAN FINDS JESUS!**" The story wasn't about a man finding any spiritual enlightenment, but rather about Jesus supposedly working at a laundromat in Des Moines or somewhere. How do they think this stuff up? Sophomoric entertainment maybe, but I was hoping for a gem hidden in there somewhere.

The hike started off like most every other hike or camping trip I had ever been on. My buddy Timothy and I hung back with our dads until eventually we broke ahead so we could talk uncensored. Timothy had recently hooked up with an older girl and was itching to tell me about it. Earlier in the week, he had gone to a friend's pool party. With little to no supervision, things escalated quickly. Handholding under water, shy kissing, heavy kissing, and then the curious hands. I hung on every word. Being drastically less experienced in such encounters, I found a sense of vicarious masculinity through his tales of promiscuity.

We were barely into his next tale of astonishing bravado when the side of my left calf lit up like someone had skewered it with a red-hot poker. A lengthy and impressively diverse trail of expletives poured from my throat–the kind of vulgarity born from that dark place only visited during times of sudden anguish and thought only accessible to men from the grimiest of backgrounds. By the time I looked down to see the gargantuan hornet ass still hanging from my leg, my right hand took a hit–a second stinger between my index finger and thumb. It looked like a tiny little goblet holding the creamy bowels of one of nature's most selfless warriors. I screamed bloody murder, and we took off running, waving our arms and shrieking like a pair of wild animals. I still have no clue how Timothy got out without a sting. It was totally unfair.

Eventually we stopped and I examined the damage. I'm not allergic or anything, but never in my life had any bite or sting had such a powerful impact on me. My hand swelled to the point that I could barely close it. My leg sported a distinct red circle the size of my fist that started to rise and seemed to be widening. It was also around this time that I started to notice some distinct and worsening blisters forming on both feet. A rule I had never really heeded was to break in new hiking boots before wearing them on an actual hike. Not only was I dealing with some nasty hornet stings, but I was also nursing bum feet–not exactly the way to start out on a camping trip.

I made it to our campsite, but not without multiple stops to apply bandages and re-lace my boots. At the first opportunity, I abandoned what are now orthopedic torture devices and opted for my comfy flip-flops. In addition to the blisters on my big toe, I had blisters on each heel that had worn through my skin to the red meat. Both of my pinky toes were raw. My feet were pretty much shot, and my hand resembled a bright red baseball glove.

I quickly became the butt of all jokes. "Hey, I sure hope a bear doesn't come up on us! But if one does, all we have to worry about is outrunning you!" "Good thing you brought something to read–it might be days before you can hike out with those bloody stumps!"

After dinner, we began cutting up around the campfire. It was just before reading some random passages from the *National Inquirer*, when we hear a branch snap. I'm not talking about a little twig on the ground either. This was a live and healthy branch, a still-attached-to-a-tree kind of snap. At first we held our breath, and no one uttered a word. You could have heard a pin drop, if it hadn't been for the terrifying noises coming from the darkness.

We tried to joke briefly, but the aura of fear was already palpable and distracting. It–and we were pretty sure we knew what *it* was–was headed right towards us. The cracks and snaps got louder and closer. I swear I could hear heavy exhales and grunts as the brush up against our campfire began to rustle. I was beyond screwed. Our fun-loving group had jinxed me. I had feet that were no damn good and hornet stings rendering one of my hands nearly useless. As the small trees and bushes split like the Sea of Reeds, we caught our first glimpse of this proverbial Moses.

The bear was massive. We panicked. What were we to do? We weren't more than fifteen feet away from the magnificent beast, and despite everyone having joked that they were planning on leaving me for bear food, no one moved. The bear stood up on his hind legs, as if he were preparing to roar or attack or make some violent movement. Barely even thinking about what I was doing, I threw the *National Inquirer* onto the campfire. As it left my engorged digits, I glimpsed the article about Jesus being alive and living in America. As the paper touched the fire, I hollered out, "Sweet Lord Jesus, save us from the bear!"

The campfire flashed quickly, and the flames jumped high into the air. The newspaper material the tabloid was printed on couldn't have been much more flammable. As fast as this horrific scenario had descended upon us, it was resolved. With the burst of heat and bright light, the bear vanished–not a roar, no swiping paws, no charging the campfire–just gone.

We all tried to sleep with one eye open, half awake and waiting for the return of the bear. He did just that. He didn't make the same grand entrance as before, but crept into our campsite stealthily under the cover of darkness and in the ambient buzz of the forest at night. The bear sniffed around Timothy's tent as my dad and I watched through the mesh windows of our own tiny pup tent. It felt like we were the filling in a great big human burrito.

The bear was suddenly nowhere in sight. We heard him. He was close, but we had lost visual contact. I could barely hear Timothy trying to whisper something to us when I realized that the bear was outside our tent. He was right beside me. I could almost feel the warmth of his body through the cheap tent fabric. We were done for. Even without being trapped in our makeshift domicile, we were hopeless with my laughable injuries and all. My poor dad was going down with me. We held each other tight and braced for the vicious impact. Under my breath, I whispered, "Back in Des Moines already, Jesus?"

The whole car ride home we laughed about the bizarre ordeal–everything from my feet to the mysterious vanishing bear. I can't for the life of me remember hearing him leave the campsite.

Maybe I heard a footstep or two, but nothing that gave us much assurance that he was gone. It felt like he had just sat outside our tent until we fell asleep and then had casually taken his leave.

We stopped at some random gas station to fill up and take one last bathroom break to get us the rest of the way home. To my surprise, I saw a stack of *National Inquirer*s by the register. It was the same issue that had saved our lives the night before. I asked the guy working there if he had read the article. "That garbage! Ha! I don't know why we still carry those stupid, fake newspapers." I laughed and bought a copy.

He looked me up and down. I was still a sweaty mess. The hike back down the trail with my damaged feet and hornet stings had been a brutal trial of endurance. Yet I was grinning like a kid at Christmas. It was an insane juxtaposition, I'm sure. The worker cocked a sideways glance at me like I was crazy.

As I limped out the door, I turned back toward him and said, "Mister, you have no idea."

--William M. (Bo) Walker

Delivery Six

A few months ago, I was sitting at the main computer and entering in my inventory adjustments for that week. When we used spare frames, center supports, adaptor plates, and such directly off the delivery truck, we had to go back and make sure they had been added to the right tickets. Beyond the computer were the big glass front doors of "Better Bedding." I heard some kind of land-yacht pull right up to the front–a cream-colored Buick, I think. It had a deep maroon interior and top and looked in tremendously better condition than it sounded.

An elderly couple struggled to get the doors open all the way and climb out of their vintage ride. As they made their way into the store, Venom approached them with his usual "How you folks doin' today?" Even though he was the manager, he still worked the sales floor just as much as any of the other employees.

"Y'all got any'a them chipmunk covers?" she hollered at him.

She was a tiny lady and wore a raincoat like a blanket over her shoulders. Enormous outdated framed glasses covered half her face, and ironically she looked very chipmunkish. She had a giant salt and peppered cotton ball of a hairdo that added at least three or four inches to her height.

"Do you mean–Alvin, Simon, and Theodore chipmunk?" I could hear his voice asking more than one question with just his tone–the other question being, "Are you going to be some kind of problem?"

"Naw, Sonny. I got critters. I can feel 'em runnin' aroun' under my bed. They're livin' inma box sprang." She shook her head and acted exasperated at his misunderstanding.

I got comfortable shielded by the computer screen and tried to stay as still as possible. This was about to get good.

"Ma'am, are you sure–"

Before he could finish, the husband jumped right in:

"I done told you it ain't no damn chipmunks! This man ain't got nothin' fer chipmunks."

He was potbellied and wore a pair of action slacks that looked like blue jeans, but were closer to some kind of fancy pair of sweat pants. We saw the action pants all the time when these older, more country types, would come to the store. He didn't have belt loops on his action slacks. They were held up by a pair of suspenders that were so wide that they looked like a part of some kind of back brace or harness. The stains on his undershirt made me think it had either been worn a hundred million times–or one really disgusting time. Or maybe he just loved mustard.

Venom was in the pressure cooker. He had a set of customers who were going to make any kind of sale difficult. What's more, he was going to really have to play his cards right just to get out of this without saying the wrong thing and further angering these two already volatile forces.

"Well, I think we could sell you a new box spring and just keep tha plastic on it. Or we could order you a zippered heavy duty mattress cover that you could use on your existing box spring." He used hand gestures that made him look like he was trying to calm a two-year-old.

The old lady looked at Venom and tilted her head. She leaned in close like she was about to tell him a secret, and then made a loud chipmunk-type noise right in his ear.

"SSST SSST SSST! SSST SSST SSST! I can hear 'em!" She ended her sentences like a judge slamming a gavel. She turned to her husband with a sharp intention, speaking faster the more she talked, "I told you how many times? You know I heard 'em! I ain't crazy and I ain't sharing my bed with no critters no more. Ya hear!"

"Well, Ma'am, like I said–"

The husband interrupted him again, "Come on, Beatrice. I ain't wasting this poor boy's time no more! An' I damn sure ain't buying your chipmunks no expensive heavy duty cover protector–er, whatever it was."

I don't know how prevalent it is in other types of retail, but in bedding they claim there's no such thing as a "be back." In other words, if the customer leaves the store without buying, you have basically lost the sale. We had strong success with returning shoppers, yet I admired Venom's tenacity. He always tried to save the sale: "No, it's no trouble at all. An' it ain't that expensive–"

Before he could finish, the woman became so fed-up with the fight she was having with her husband that she turned around and stormed off, heading for the door. I could tell Venom was at a loss for words at this point. He just kind of stood there.

"Thanks anyways for ya time." And the old man turned to follow his feisty little wife to the car.

Venom turned to me as the door closed behind the man.

"Tell me you heard all that!" He must not have realized I had been right there the whole time. Although they had been standing less than ten feet away, I had remained mostly obscured by the computer.

"What the hell! Chipmunks? Really? On a scale of one to Ted Kazinski, how crazy was that lady?" We were both laughing so loud the owner came out of his office, already starting to laugh himself.

"What'd I miss?" he inquired.

These type experiences were both the crown jewels and the thorns in the side of retail work.

We relayed the story, with minimal embellishments, and we all laughed so hard we were folding over. The speed and brevity of the whole thing made it all the more comical–like life had dropped a commercial for the bizarre right in the middle of our day. But like almost all commercials, if you see it once, you're probably gonna have to see it again. And so they came back eventually and bought a new box spring. I had just finished reliving the whole initial scenario for Lurch's entertainment when we pulled into their driveway.

The house was actually quite picturesque. There were fancy birdhouses set up all around the side and back of the home. They were brightly colored, and many of them were impressively constructed. There was even what appeared to be a birdhouse version of the White House out in the back, complete with a little miniature American flag. There were a male and female cardinal bouncing around the birdhouses and trees at the edge of the yard. The lawn was very well manicured, and there were beautiful azaleas along the front porch with various flowers elegantly punctuating the space. The small covered garage was tidy, and everything clearly had its own place. I was actually excited to find out these people's deal and learn what was going on with this lady's supposed chipmunk situation–especially now that they didn't seem to live in depraved conditions.

We knocked on the door and only had to wait a few seconds. The husband must have heard us pulling in.

"Hello, Boys. C'mon in." He was wearing the same exact clothes that he had been wearing the first time I saw him. And I discovered he must really wear this shirt all the time. I wondered how expensive he thought plain white undershirts must be–or if perhaps the practice was based on some strange set of principles, or maybe even some superstition.

"Yessir, Mr. Sanderson," Lurch politely replied as we followed him in. Thomas and Beatrice Sanderson were their names, and their home felt just like my grandparents' house. They probably hadn't changed much of anything since the late seventies–lots of modest furniture with plaid fabrics and Georgia Bulldogs knick-knacks here and there. It was just like a solid fifty percent of the homes we visited–one level with a long hallway off the den. That was always our direction.

Mrs. Sanderson was waiting in the room for us. She was wearing a nightgown, the kind I wouldn't even guess are sold anymore. She had her hair in curlers and her bedroom slippers matched her gown. It was immediately apparent we were to be the ones to help her get to the bottom of all this critter business.

"Just lean the mattress up o'er there. I want you boys to see if you can figure out what's going on here."

As we moved the bed, Lurch jumped right in, "What seems to

be the problem? Your salesman mentioned something to us about critters?"

"Yeeeah. I got sumpin' gettin' in here an' I can feel it at night an' hear chitterin'."

"Hmm …" We both gave our default "I'm-thinking-about-it" hum.

As we pulled the box spring off the bed frame, an impressive series of cameras and mirrors came into view, peppered with a few strategically placed mousetraps.

"This is quite a little labyrinth you've got here!" I chirped before I thought. It looked like the work of a beautiful mind–like the Russell-Crowe-crazy-math-guy kind of beautiful mind.

"We done tried everythang. These here are my son's motion de-tect-or cameras he uses when he hunts. I had Tommy set-up them there mirrors 'cause them critters keep dodgin' the cameras," she explained.

"Were the cameras being set off in the night?" Lurch inquired.

"Huh?" She did that head tilt thing again, and I remembered her making that noise right up in Venom's ear. I hoped Lurch wouldn't fall for it.

"The cameras? Have the motion detectors been going off at all? Have they taken any pictures in the night?" Now that he had asked the question, I was curious too.

"Tommy! Where you at?" she yelled toward the door. "You got them pictures from these here cameras?"

We could hear him yell something back, but couldn't make out what it was. Then we heard him coming down the hall. He was a heavy guy, and the house had plenty of creaky floorboards.

Before he got to the room, Mrs. Sanderson explained, "It took a few, but they all came out blurry. Couldn't see nothin'. I think them critters jus' too fast."

"I thought you had 'em!" Mr. Sanderson finally answered as he squeezed through the doorway.

"Huh?" Mrs. Sanderson wasn't keeping up very well. I was starting to question this poor man's mental state just from dealing with this day in and out.

"The pictures, Beatrice–the pictures. I told you I wadn't keepin' up with 'em. Now you put 'em somewhere, and I don't got no clue. But don't matter anyway. We couldn't see anything in 'em."

He seemed tired of all this. He turned his attention to the intricate gauntlet under the bed and said, "I built a little speaker that was supposed to play this high-pitched frequency and run 'em off. But she says it ain't doin' nuthin' but makin' whatever it is mad."

"Drove 'em inta a frenzy's what it did! They was runnin' aroun' like you had the rock'n roll music playin' just fer them, Tommy!" She placed her hands on her hips and shifted her weight from one foot to the other.

"Y'all see if ya can find where they're gettin' in on that box sprang," Mrs. Sanderson commanded, shaking a finger accusingly at her old box spring.

We looked all over it–flipped it, rotated it, held it up, laid it down, and generally made a great production of the whole thing. But it was immediately clear to both Lurch and me that there was absolutely zero evidence of anything, *anything*, getting into her box spring.

"I don't see anything," I reluctantly admitted.

"If something's been getting in, they've sure been covering their tracks," Lurch pontificated with an air of artificial frustration. "Did you want to keep this box spring or let us haul it off?" he inquired authoritatively.

"Good Lord, git that thing outta here! I wancha ta take it far away, an' you'd be smart to get it off your truck soon as ya can!"

"Yes, Ma'am, we'll wrap it up with some throw-away plastic and we'll be sure to keep an eye on it until we can dispose of it," Lurch diplomatically humored her.

When we came back in, the two of them were inspecting the booby-trapped, mirror-camera maze–not dismantling it, but rather, checking it for efficiency and making sure the traps were placed properly. I was surprised that Mr. Sanderson was so involved in catering to this part of her paranoia, but as we brought in the new box and observed their behavior, I could tell he was a tinkerer. He likely enjoyed building things, and this was some kind of common ground he could share with his often-cantankerous wife. It was albeit crazy common ground, but a shared experience, nonetheless. It was almost touching, and it definitely made me think about wanting to have a crazy lady to build chipmunk traps with when I got old.

"You got things how you want them?" I asked as they began to step back from the bed.

"I think so. We'll check it out tomorrow and see how it holds up," Mr. Sanderson replied with a subtle hint of pride in his voice.

We laid the box spring down on the frame still in its plastic. As we got her dust ruffle situated, Mrs. Sanderson turned her attention from the bed to us.

"Now if'n this don't work, what y'all gonna do?"

Lurch and I looked at each other, almost laughing at Mrs. Sanderson, even though we knew her question was far from a joke.

"I think if you continue to have any issues with these chipmunks or critters–or whatever they are, I'd maybe look into having a pest control company come by and take a look at things." I was really at a loss for what to tell her and was honestly looking for a way out of the situation completely for us as much as I was looking for a solution to her problem.

"We already did that, Sonny. Them jokers wanted damn near seven 'unnerd dollars to secure the house from any ol' thing that could sneak in here. You believe that? Seven 'unnerd dollars! I tol' 'em, "No way, no how." That's when I made Tommy figger us out a way to git right to tha bottom," Mrs. Sanderson piously replied. She might not care if we thought she was nuts, but she sure wasn't going to let us think she didn't have sense enough to check with some type of pest control.

"Yeah, that is pretty crazy," Lurch concurred–although we both knew that wasn't any crazier than the ordeal itself.

"You damn right," Mr. Sanderson fired back. I wasn't sure which part specifically he was agreeing with. It all seemed pretty crazy to me.

I could see Mrs. Sanderson was about to come back at us with a request to provide additional services if her little problem wasn't cured by the new box spring, so I tried to beat her to it.

"Ma'am, I tell you what–with this plastic on here, I reckon anything tryin' to get in will make considerably more noise than before. If it keeps up, try and pull the box off the bed and see if you can find where they're tryin' to get in. And if you have any questions, don't hesitate to call." *Please don't actually call*, I thought to myself.

She huffed a little and gave a slight eye-roll, but thanked us anyways.

We repositioned the mattress, and Lurch grabbed the clipboard and began getting the pen ready to hand over.

As Mr. Sanderson reached to grab the clipboard from us, he handed Lurch a fiver.

"You Boys, git ya a coke or sumpn'," he magnanimously mumbled.

We thanked him, and Lurch took back the clipboard with the signed receipt. As Mr. Sanderson walked us back through the den out of the house, I noticed certain shelves were decorated with what appeared to be little inventions–wind-up toys and what looked like train cars to a larger train set. I imagined he had a basement full of gizmos and gadgets, surrounded by a long train set that circled his workshop. It occurred to me that maybe this whole scenario was part of an elaborate plan to either drive his wife crazy or bring them together in a never-ending attempt to solve a made-up problem. There really had been a sweetness to them kneeling down by the bed working so fervently on their little chipmunk trap set-up. Who knows how long they'd been married, and maybe this is the kind of thing you end up doing when you've been together for a long time.

As we walked out the door, I could hear Mrs. Sanderson yelling at her husband from deep in the house.

"Yea, I'm coming!" he yelled back. "Thanks, Fellas, have a good day," he said to us as he shut the door.

"Make sure we shut the back, would ya?" Lurch cautioned me.

"Ten four, Good Buddy!" I yelled as I shot around the truck.

We had left it about halfway closed, so I yanked the strap and flipped the locking mechanism. As I jumped in the truck, Lurch was laughing to himself while programming the next address in our GPS.

"I'm not even telling you where we're headed next," he grinned impishly.

"Haha! That's fine by me. I don't mind surprises. But don't you think there was something kind of sweet to them working on their little camera and trap system?"

Lurch looked at me dead-faced for a second, then replied seriously. "Sweet? I was thinking more ..."loony." But I guess it's par for the course with what we've been having to deal with lately."

We pulled out of the driveway and headed back the way we had come. About a mile down the road, we heard something in the back of the truck. It sounded like something was scratching at the wall that separated the cab from the back where all the beds were.

"Did you hear that?" I blurted out. I could tell Lurch by his expression that Lurch had heard it, too.

"NO WAY!" he shouted. "So help me, God, if we've got a chipmunk in the truck, I'm gonna freak sure enough!"

"That crazy lady was right!" I shouted back, hysterically laughing.

About that time we were coming up on a small rural church on the right side of the road. Lurch jerked the wheel and practically squealed the tires pulling into their parking lot. We jumped simultaneously1, but stopped when we got to the door at the back of the truck.

"You hear anything?"

"Dude, there's something in there. We both heard it. Maybe it's just still now that we're parked." I didn't want to be the one to have to open the back. I couldn't believe there had actually been something in that box spring.

Lurch grabbed the handle and rattled the door with a quick shake. *BAM!* Something banged back against the door.

"Holy mother!" Lurch nearly toppled over.

"That's definitely bigger than a chipmunk! Mrs. Sanderson, I'm so sorry I laughed at you!" I exhaled as I stepped back. "Lurch, just open it quick–better to get this over with than deal with it at the next customer's house."

He looked at me, and his eyes got wide as he held back his nervous laughter and grabbed the handle. He took a quick breath and slung the door upwards. Before the door had even made it all the way up, a bright red cardinal came swooping out of the delivery truck. It practically brushed against Lurch's face.

"Gaaaaaaah!" the cardinal cried out.

I spun around to watch it fly away and let out a shriek that would have been embarrassingly feminine, had there been anyone else around. Before I could turn back around to look at Lurch, he grabbed my shoulder and jerked me around. He was laughing so hard tears were streaming from the corners of his eyes. I burst into laughter with him. He hugged his belly and bent over, catching himself on his knees.

When we had finally caught our breath, I asked, "Has that ever happened to you before on the truck?"

"I've had cats climb up on the truck a bunch of times, but

no birds–that was unreal," he testified, still wiping his eyes and climbing up into the truck.

"What kind of critter mojo are they working with at the Casa de Sanderson?" I joked.

"Well, they practically had a "birdtropolis" out back. Maybe she's like Dr. Doolittle and Mr. Hyde," Lurch muttered as he kicked against the mattresses to ensure we didn't have any other stowaways.

"How many more deliveries we got?" I asked.

"Just four. Let's get movin'. I want to get off on time today."

"Then quit wasting our time stealing the customers' animal friends," I joked, hopping into the passenger seat in the cab.

"If that cardinal finds a new home before getting back to the Sandersons, it'll be the best thing that ever happened to it. Any animal that winds up inside that house has just been handed a guaranteed death sentence–tortured first with a complex series of mazes and disorienting mirrors, with all of it captured on film! The horror!"

Laughing insanely, we pulled out of the church parking lot, cranked up the music, and rolled the dice of fate.

--William M. (Bo) Walker

DOWN ON A LITTLE FARM IN THE SOUTH

I live in the country where I care for a husband and a bunch of critters with interesting names. The chicken I eat comes from somewhere else–not from my chicken yard. But I do enjoy fresh eggs for breakfast. You just never know what might happen on my little farm.

§§§

The end of summer brought some new experiences for Boudreaux, the head rooster of the hen house. I was out one morning feeding Katiegoat, Paddygoat, and Rileygoat whose pen is next to Bou and the chickens. They were standing at the gate chewing last night's supper, shaking their heads, looking catatonic, and mumbling softly.

Katiegoat said to me, "Did you know our neighbors are nekkid? Nekkid, I say! Will that happen to me? I don't look very attractive without my goatee."

I reassured them all that their neighbors were merely molting, something to expect this time of year.

Suddenly, ol' Bou bolted from the coop, covering his eyes and screaming, "Don't look! I can't take it." He glanced my way. "I dun tol' you and tol' you about this. Just look at 'em; they do this ever' year. Nekkid, nekkid! So embarrassin'. No shame!"

"Bou," I explained, "The girls are molting. They can't help it." I tried to reassure him that this nudity was not permanent. "Don't get your feathers in a wad."

§§§

A new fall brought colder weather and a new robe of feathers for the gang. One morning I heard strains of music wafting from the hen house. "When a ma-ann lubs a wo-mann, keeps his mind on nuttin' else . . ."

"Boudreaux!" I hollered out toward the chicken yard. "I know Clothilde and Babbette have a nice set of new feathers, and they are no longer running around with their skin shining, but the goats are going to get tired of your caterwallin'. Try to control yourself."

When the singing stopped, I overheard Clothilde ask Boudreaux if her new feathers made her butt look big. Oh my, I thought. Hope he gives her the right answer.

Soon the new-feathered frocks brought romance back to the barnyard. Gathering eggs one morning, I saw the top of Clothilde's head sticking way up in the air above her nesting box. She had been collecting eggs for the past five days and was now sitting on a pile so high that her feet didn't even touch the hay. She looked like she needed a seat belt.

"The air is a little thin up here," she told me from her perch, "but at least Bou and the other boys can't bother me."

The girls began spending their days dusting the henhouse, fluffing the hay and then sitting down with their knitting, humming.

Feeding them one morning, I spoke with ol' Bou. "Hey, Bou, I see you are wearing your apron again this morning."

"Hmph! Clothilde is so grouchy since she started sittin' on our eggs. I have to do everything. If I get too close, she wonks me on the head. She's got me going out in the middle of the night to get worms. She claims her feet and wattle are too swollen to get around now."

Clothilde and the girls in the maternity ward were eagerly anticipating the pitter-patter of little feet and the cheep-cheep of little beaks–and Bou was top rooster.

"I've got bu-ugs on a cloudy day. When it's cold outside, I've got eggs to lay. I guess you say, what can make me feel this way? Bou-dreaux . . ."

The girls hummed and sang day and night. Boudreaux began to smoke cigars, and wondered if he could find enough bugs to support his coming family. Three weeks later came the announcement in the barnyard.

"Hear ye, hear ye. Announcement! Callin' all neighbors. The children are a comin'! Action in the henhouse. Clothilde's, Praline's, and Etoufee's babies are a hatchin'. Right now, the girls are concentratin' on their breathin' exercises–no action from Babbette yet!"

Bou was passing out fresh worms to the neighbors. Soon the cheep-cheeps filled the yard.

Evangeline Hen was still turning eggs and waiting, exhausted. One morning she spoke to Clothilde about it. "These roosters think if they bring home a bug or a worm, they don't have to help around the coop. Just look at Boudreaux and his buddies. When they get home from worm hunting, they just turn into roost potatoes. They don't realize we girls work, too, and how hard it is to stay home with all these eggs. We don't get any sleep because the eggs have to be turned all the time, kept warm, and clucked to. Do you think they would get up at night and turn just one egg? Noooo! And then they think when they get home, we should have all the worms on the table."

After having her say, Evangeline went back to tending her eggs.

§§§

Not long after most of the girls had hatched their broods, Paddygoat, Rileygoat, and Katiegoat decided they were not pleased

93

with their neighbors. They were lazily chewing their supper from the night before, ruminating and talking among themselves when I walked up.

"We've got new neighbors," Riley was complaining. "Yup, yup, the girls next door have a bunch of kids, a dozen or so, and that dad is no good. He just hatches them off and moves on. There goes the neighborhood."

Now Riley was tapping his foot at the gate.

"Babbette Hen has moved into a corner of our barn and she's taken over, fluffin' the straw, sharpenin' her knittin' needles, and tellin' us we shouldn't chew our regurgitated food. Before we go to sleep, we all run and butt our heads against the wall. You know, it helps us relax and sleep better," he reminded me. "But now, we can't do that neither." He shook his head. "She also said we had to be extra quiet, and when she thinks we aren't, she flies up and yanks our goatees. And it's *our* barn." He turned and ambled off.

"Where you going, Riley?" I asked.

"I just can't take it. I might go eat some tree bark."

§§§

One morning not too long ago, I saw Bou fretting and jumpy.

"Mornin' Bou. Why do you look so scared?" I greeted.

Bou explained in a low voice, "Well, the kids were asleep under Clothilde and we were watchin' *Animal Planet* and snackin' on a fresh bowl of bugs. But then, a commercial came on with these black and white cows, mooin' and tellin' folks to–to–to eat more chicken." He paced and fretted. "Oh, I'm so stressed. I don't know what to do. Why can't those cows mind their own business?"

§§§

In the early spring, after all the fall hatching in the chicken yard, I heard an awful sound coming from that direction–sounded kind of like one of my young roosters strangling on a worm. Going out to investigate, I met Katiegoat at the gate with her hooves over her ears.

"The neighbors are upsettin' our ruminations!" she yelled. "We can't even enjoy yesterday's lunch."

When I got to the chicken yard, Boudreaux had a class of

six-month-old roosters lined up and staring at him intently.

"Look, this is the tone and timbre you use to impress the chicks–not that screechy adolescent warbling. Watch me–feet flat, chest out, wings back, neck stretched, combs and wattles straight: EERRR, EEERRR, EEEERRRR! Got it? The girls will swoon when you get this down."

The little ones started getting into position to try again when Bou stopped them. "Uh–y'all go behind the coop to practice after class. Tomorrow our lesson is on the proper way to take a dust bath. Class dismissed."

The very next morning, Professor Boudreaux was in class again. I looked out the kitchen window to see what looked like the 1930s dust bowl. I thought maybe it was some sort of strange weather phenomenon coming from the chicken and goat yard. When I went to investigate, I saw Boudreaux on his side, scratching, kicking, and smiling. "Boys, this is basic Dust Bath 101. Find a spot with no grass, lay on your side, and kick like you're fixin' to be scooped up and taken to KFC." Bou's student roosters began to roll around at their professor's instructions.

"Don't shake too much dirt off, boys," he told them. "The girls like the smell."

§§§

A few weeks later those same young roosters were having a small meeting one morning in the barnyard, just after the change-over to Daylight Saving Time. Combs standing straight up, eyes wide, teeth chattering, they were nervously conversing.

"Look, the ol' blonde woman is threatening to make us into owl McNuggets," I heard one of them say. "We must be on our best behavior–no more crowing at 3 a.m. We will wait until at least 5 a.m., since she and everybody else should be awake by then."

"Hear, hear!" The cheer rose from the meeting.

§§§

When I ran out of goat chow one morning in early June, I discovered just how spoiled the goats are. They were just standing in the barn door with a faraway look in their eyes, staring and staring.

I heard Katiegoat ask Rileygoat, "What is it?" They were

staring at a strange pile in their troughs.

"Perhaps we should ask Clothilde Hen. Maybe she would know," Riley answered.

Paddygoat chimed in. "It's called *hay*. H-A-Y! Farm animals eat this."

"But where is our goat chow?" Katie asked.

"It's all gone. That ol' blonde woman must think we are common goats. Perhaps we could mail this weird hay stuff to the starvin' goats in Biafra."

Wow, I thought. What have I created?

§§§

One hot summer day, I decided the time to trim Katiegoat's front hooves had come. I got her dog collar on and tied her to the fence, and it was on. She screamed and snorted and butted. And then I screamed and snorted and butted. All this for a pedicure, for heaven's sake. Later that afternoon, I noticed she had recuperated enough to enjoy scratching her udders on a sawed-off stump. I decided I had to speak to her. If company came over, she must not smile so big.

I decided I would fix Katiegoat's skin problem to keep her from scratching those udders. I had been waiting on some used motor oil to rub on her–an old farmer's remedy. Meanwhile, I had the genius idea to coat her with the cooking spray. I tucked a can of Pam in my pocket and took their feed bucket out to the barn. While Katie was sweetly eating her goat chow from her little bowl, I whipped out my can and began to give her a good dousing. Her eyes began to roll around in her head; she snorted, bucked, threw her head in the air, and let loose other bodily functions. And then I did the same. I told her it was for her own good.

"Riiiight," she said, drawing out the word with sarcasm and rolling her eyes. "When folks use Pam, they are preparin' to eat somethin'!"

I tried to reassure her by telling her she was too old and chewy.

"This stuff will keep the flies away, and you will just smell buttery all day." I hesitated a moment. "But I wouldn't stand too long in the sun if I were you."

I then looked over at the henhouse and saw Clothilde hanging out the window, smacking her gum, pencil behind her ear.

"Wadda ya have? Make it quick," she was telling the other chicks.

I walked out and asked what was she doing. Clothilde told me they were making the best of the heat.

"You can order eggs fried, poached, or boiled at our drive-through window, and no wait time on Wednesdays."

§§§

A farmer always has to be on the lookout for intruders. One morning not too long ago I heard what sounded something like soldiers marching in a line: "Left, left, left, right, left!" It was the girls. When I checked with Babbette, Clothilde, and the others, they told me they had formed a fox patrol after hearing some frightening noises during the night.

"Great idea. I told them. "Where are Bou and the boys?"

"In the henhouse," Clothilde informed me. "They said we could be the first to watch and wait, look and patrol." She puffed out her breast. "We feel so honored they put us out here first."

It was then I decided it was time for a little heart-to-heart with the girls.

"Don't be so gullible, Ladies."

After my talk, I went back to the house. A little while later, I looked out my kitchen window and noticed that the fox patrol now consisted of every rooster in the yard.

"That's my girls," I thought, and then went back to washing all the eggs the girls had put in my basket.

--Becky Whitener

FREDDIE

It seems like a lot has been going on lately, and I've been distracted from my writing. I can feel the minutia piling up in my head, unorganized thoughts clanking together like pots and pans thrown together in a cabinet. I've been dealing with the illness of my spouse, an aging mother, a busted hot water heater, and a dying pet.

At fifteen, Freddie is an old man in cat-terms. His health has started to fail and I suspect he is nearing the end of his journey. I lay on the floor with him today, talking to him, telling him he was a good cat, soaking him up while he is still here.

My daughter, Meg, found him when he was only four weeks old–starving and freezing–hanging on to life in a storm drain. The vet said that he wouldn't have made it if she hadn't scooped him up and brought him home. I couldn't even object to her bringing another animal home. He was so tiny and frail. He could barely hold his head up. No one could have resisted his little silent mews and his big pleading eyes. We named him Freddie (Mercury), in keeping with our rock star-themed pet names.

Meg held him constantly. As he got older, she would drape Freddie around her neck and he would lie on her shoulders like a mink stole, front feet stretched out on her chest. They were odd birds.

Freddie is not an ordinary cat. He comes when he is called. He stands up on his hind legs and reaches up with his front paws like a child waiting to be picked up. That's how I knew something was wrong. He didn't come when I called. When I found him after hours of searching, he was hiding under a bush, huddled up and dirty. I brought him inside and cleaned him up. I thought he'd eaten a lizard or gotten into a fight. The vet said his kidneys might be failing. There's not much we can do.

Meg is grown and gone. She left Freddie with me. He's been a member of the family for fifteen years–a blessing disguised as a little black and white tuxedo cat.

--Jan Crocker

Taking Life

I think life is sacred, whether it's abortion or the death penalty.
--Tim Kaine

Had it not been for slavery, the death penalty would have likely been abolished in America. Slavery became a haven for the death penalty.
--Angela Davis

The death penalty is ineffective as a deterrent, and the appeals process is expensive and cruel to the surviving family members.
--Martin O'Malley

... there is ... one piece of moral ground of which I am absolutely certain: if I were to be murdered I would not want my murderer executed ... Especially by government–which can't be trusted to control its own bureaucrats or collect taxes equitably or fill a pothole, much less decide which of its citizens to kill.
--Sr. Helen Préjean

For centuries the death penalty, often accompanied by barbarous refinements, has been trying to hold crime in check; yet crime persists.
--Albert Camus

I don't think you should support the death penalty to seek revenge. I don't think that's right. I think the reason to support the death penalty is because it saves other people's lives.
--George W. Bush

You know, the Bible is so clear. Go to Genesis chapter nine and you will find the death penalty clearly stated in Genesis chapter nine... God ordains the death penalty!
--Rafael Cruz

Thou shalt not kill.
--Exodus 20:13 (King James Version)

It's harder to heal than it is to kill.
--Tamora Pierce

Becoming Real: Part I

I was christened into the Episcopal Church as an infant in Richmond, Virginia. At that time, it was a church that asked very little of its parishioners. It seemed to me that you mostly had to show up, stand up and sit down at the appropriate times, and read the assigned lines from the prayer book accurately and in sync with the rest of the congregation. Fortunately, this allowance for fermentation worked out well for me in the long run, but during my extended adolescence, it left me with a strong sense of wellbeing, but only the vaguest sense of "God."

In Richmond, I learned much about manners and mores, but intimacy remained a foreign concept–except when it was used as a euphemism for the sex act, as in, "Were they *intimate?*" whispered with raised eyebrows and a hint of disgust. For a curious and expressive young girl, it was confusing–this staid and separate way of being in the world. My salvation was books.

I embraced books hungrily, as they embraced me, with all of my being: heart, soul, mind, and body. When I finished a book I loved, I pulled it to my chest and squeezed it tightly, swaying slightly side-to-side, reluctant to let it go. Children's books spoke to me about God, about love, and about life in ways that the people around me simply did not. So it is not unusual that when I think about the story of Andrew and me–a long story, a love story, a redemption story, and ultimately a story of faith–that it all seems to come down to a simple truth given to me by a storybook from my childhood.

The story may be familiar. It is a tale of the secret lives of toys, *The Velveteen Rabbit*, written by Margery Williams. A brand new Velveteen Rabbit asks a very old and worn rocking horse what it means to be "real."

> "Real isn't how you are made," said the Skin Horse. "It's a thing that happens to you. When a child loves you for a long, long time, not just to play with, but REALLY loves you, then you become Real."
> "Does it hurt?" asked the Rabbit.
> "Sometimes," said the Skin Horse, for he was always truthful.
> "When you are Real, you don't mind being hurt."

"Does it happen all at once, like being wound up," he asked, "or bit by bit?"

"It doesn't happen all at once," said the Skin Horse. "You become. It takes a long time. That's why it doesn't happen often to people who break easily, or have sharp edges, or who have to be carefully kept. Generally, by the time you are Real, most of your hair has been loved off, and your eyes drop out and you get loose in the joints and very shabby. But these things don't matter at all, because once you are Real you can't be ugly, except to people who don't understand."

The Rabbit, of course, wishes "that he could become it without these uncomfortable things happening to him." Don't we all? That was the story of the *Velveteen Rabbit*. This is the story of two people finding each other through unlikely circumstances, in unlikely places, and perhaps helping each other along the road to becoming real.

I first started going to Clifton Presbyterian Church in 1977. Once you have a child in your life, you realize that your claims of believing in God, but just not in Church *per se*, won't fly anymore. If you want your child to learn about God, you need some help. I found myself turning to the idea of Sunday school for that help. Although Clifton Presbyterian Church was right down the street, it wasn't my first choice. At the time, in 1977, I had both a step-daughter and a young girl named Judy from the Georgia Retardation Center who came home with me on the weekends. Judy was deaf and hyperactive as well as retarded. I started calling Episcopal churches to see if any had interpreters.

"No," I was told repeatedly. "We don't have anything like that. Why don't you try the Baptists?"

"The Baptists?" this cradle Episcopalian thought. *"Aren't they kind of scary and fundamentalist? Don't they do that Holy-Roller stuff? I don't know if I can handle the Baptists."*

I thought I might try the Presbyterians. After all, they were kind of like Episcopalians, weren't they? So I started calling, but for the most part I struck out there, too–until I called Clifton Presbyterian Church.

"Why, no," said the woman who answered the phone. "We don't have anything like that here, but what a wonderful idea! I wish we did. I really do. Well, how about you? Couldn't you do it?"

She was so welcoming that I couldn't resist, even though I didn't really know enough sign language to interpret very well. It was only for Judy, though, so I could simplify the pastor's sermons a little to something like "Jesus dead–woke up! Alive! Death finished. You and me–winners!" It looked like a whole lot of meaningful hand activity. Nobody would know the difference.

God does work in mysterious ways. Actually, to quote Sister Helen Préjean, *"God is just plain sneaky, because if He wasn't, there is a whole lot of stuff we would never have gotten ourselves into–if we really could have seen around the next corner."* He leads us into the water one little toe at a time, backs us into things when we're not really paying attention.

The pastors of that little church were Murphy Davis and Ed Loring. They seemed like really nice people to me. I had no idea they were crazy Jesus-loving radicals out to tip the establishment on its ear. I was just trying to take my little girls to Sunday school.

My first Christmas at Clifton Presbyterian rolled around, and Murphy made an announcement. She had Christmas cards and a list of people on death row in Georgia. Would anyone like to send a card?

"Death Row?" I asked, truly bewildered and appalled. "What do you mean 'Death Row'? You mean that's a real place–not just in the movies? You mean they really put people in an electric chair and kill them? You must be lying. That can't be. Not in the USA!"

My naiveté must have amused them, but, nevertheless, I took a few names. I remember the personal way Murphy picked out one of them. "Oh, Andrew Legare! He is so precious with his blue, blue eyes. You have to send a card to Andrew!"

I went home, sat down, picked up my pen, and prepared to jot down a little note in each card and get those things in the mail. Good deed done–that simple. Then it hit me. *What am I supposed to write to these guys? Merry Christmas? Best Wishes for a Happy New Year?* It gave me pause. I realized that I could not begin to imagine the lives of these people–that I had no idea who they were, how they got to this point in their lives, what they must feel at this moment–much less when pondering Christmas or the New Year. I put down my pen and said to myself, *"Hmm. I'm going to have to think about this–maybe even pray about this."* Though, being an Episcopalian, I was unaccustomed to praying without reading from the prayer book.

My first little toe in the water–my first little movement towards becoming real: I was forced to ponder the meaning of the incarnation and the promise I believed it held for even someone facing death and alone. I wrote to each one prayerfully, and from my heart. Andrew and the two other guys wrote back. Both the other guys wrote praising Jesus and telling me how to send a money order. Andrew wrote an unassuming letter, thanking me for the card, and telling me a little about himself. This Jesus freak-phobic Episcopalian was far more comfortable with this normal, polite thank-you note than with all that "Praise Jesus, hallelujah" stuff. Although I wrote all three back, Andrew was the only one that developed into a friendly little correspondence.

Soon afterwards, I began making some big movements in my becoming-real process. My marriage, which had never been too solid, had fallen apart. My work was no longer satisfying. I was accruing the bumps and bruises of life at an intense and alarming rate. Despite a lot of partying and boyfriends and lots of social activity, I was very much alone. I seemed to be going through the "eyes-falling-out, getting-all-torn-up" part of the becoming-real thing without the being-loved part. So instead of becoming real, I was probably just becoming depressed.

Meanwhile, Andrew started writing to me about Jesus. He was reading scripture and learning theology for the first time. He was so bright and so young and so thirsty for intellectual and spiritual stimulation. At that point in my life, however, this did not impress me at all. I had been to an Episcopal girls' school where Old Testament and New Testament studies were required courses. I was completely over it. I didn't want to dialogue about all this religious stuff. We kind of fell off writing.

Then one day I got a call from a young lawyer named John Fleming. He told me that Andrew, who as a seventeen-year-old runaway had originally lied about committing the crime for which he had been convicted, had a hearing coming up, and that he had made up his mind to confess in open court. John thought Andrew needed someone–"a caring presence," he called it–in the courtroom. I told him Andrew didn't really know me and wouldn't recognize me, and that we hadn't even corresponded in a while. John said that wouldn't matter. It was just important that somebody be there. So I agreed to go.

I put on my Sunday dress and followed the lawyer's

directions to Butts County Courthouse. When I got there, I couldn't tell which was the front door. I went in the nearest door and up some steps and came into a little room where I saw a guy in a white uniform sitting and waiting. For some reason, he registered in my brain as a sandwich delivery boy. I guess I would have expected a prisoner to be in black and white stripes like they were in Elvis Presley's "Jailhouse Rock" video. At any rate, our eyes fell on each other. We searched each other out for a moment before an armed officer came rushing over to tell me I wasn't allowed back there and hustled me back down the stairs.

It wasn't until Andrew was brought into the courtroom in chains that I realized that he was the sandwich boy I had seen upstairs. It is still a little mystifying to me that I hadn't noticed that he was behind bars in a holding cell during that first brief encounter. I really didn't see the bars at all–just the boy–thoughtful and waiting. Andrew took the stand, forthrightly, courageously, and stoically recounting for the first time in court all the details of the very worst moments of his young life–the hours before and after the horror that he was too young to witness, much less to have his hands in. I could see the boy holding back tears, while the emerging man stepped up to take hold of his life by looking himself and his deeds squarely in the eye.

And there I was, witnessing this moment of passage, trying to be "a caring presence," silently cheering him on, trying to pray him through it, when I was really too young to receive this pain, this tearing apart of the safety and sanctity of life. But I caught it. I caught it. And I held it. I don't know why, but I loved it, like a broken child. I loved it, and then I forgave it. And it transformed me that day as I believe it had that young boy who had lived through the "unspeakable" and yet decided to move forward and make something of his life, instead of hating himself into hell.

I drove home, aware that I had been privy to a sacred moment. "Epiphany" is too small a word for it. It was a moment of redemption. For me, it was the beginning of forgiveness–of Andrew, of myself, of my family, of life, of all the hurts, real or imagined, that I had received or given, of God himself. It was the beginning of healing for me. The beginning of understanding what the Skin Horse had meant when he said, "When you are Real, you don't mind being hurt." I don't think I knew all this then, but I at least I knew what to do next.

I wrote Andrew to tell him he had done the right thing and to let him know what a privilege it had been for me to be present for this turning point in his life. He wrote back and invited me to visit. We began the process of getting to know each other, becoming best friends, and learning to love each other well. It took almost ten years for us to recognize our destiny. I had no idea on that day in that courtroom that we had started on this path towards becoming life partners. I just thought, *"Gee, the kid did the right thing, and that deserves a little follow-through."*

But, as Sr. Helen asserted, our God is a sneaky God. He lets us plow blindly on towards our destiny, knowing that if we could really see where this was leading, we'd never in a million years follow the path that turns out to be the road that leads us ultimately to Him.

BECOMING REAL: PART II

As I watched a television show, I thought about Toni Morrison's *Beloved.* In the show, a woman named Rosie, who had been repeatedly raped and beaten by her father throughout her childhood, went out the window of a second story apartment clutching her own little daughter in her arms–knowing she could not protect her beloved from the sexual advances of a corrupt and predatory social worker. She woke from a coma years later to find that, despite her intentions, she had survived, while her daughter had not.

In the face of these tragic scenarios, I found myself wondering: "How does one do it? How does one recover from such a vile incident?" The death of one's child is bad enough, but to survive after murdering your own child–that is unimaginable to me, a hell worse than hell. A song I know speaks of what it is "when the sacred is torn from life, and you survive." It feels as if we are not meant to survive–to have to put the pieces of our lives back together after something so horrific.

Yet I live within the miracle of that kind of survival. Both Andrew and I were too young to be scrutinizing this tearing apart of the sanctity of life that he described in that first meeting in the courtroom, as he confessed to the violent crime that drew us both to that place on that day at that time. It seemed to me a supreme act of courage for that young man to obey God's call–in the words of Maya Angelou–to "forgive life for having happened to [him]," to forgive himself when the world was saying he was not worth that forgiveness, to accept that he was a child of God despite his transgressions, to recognize that self-hatred is not some kind of penance, but rather an ugly form of blasphemy. It interferes greatly with one's ability to express the gratitude that is the only appropriate response to God's gift of this mortal life.

Did I know all that back then? Not a bit of it. There were no big epiphanies in my life at this point—just small steps of obedience to a God I was only just beginning to know. There was no big voice from the heavens telling me what to do. Somehow, I just knew the next right step. It was clear to me that the transformational moment in the courtroom was not one to squander. Some sort of follow-through was required, especially if we realize—which I didn't, of course, but by the grace of God did the right thing anyway—that God intends for all such moments to be transformational for all involved. There is no audience for God's plan. We are all on the court, at every moment, either playing, or waiting for the ball to bonk us on the head. "Be ye doers of the word, and not hearers only," says St. James, the patron saint of my childhood church. Play—or get trampled or whacked by the ball, frequently. It's our choice.

So I followed my nose to Jackson, Georgia—to Georgia Diagnostic Prison, to Georgia's death row. I did so without a lot of soul-searching. God said, "Go." So I just went. I had no idea what I was walking into—or out of, for that matter. I had no idea that I was walking away from my previous life and into a new one. I wasn't looking for a spiritual rebirth or anything like it. I was just doing the next thing I felt called to do. After all, this young man had just stepped up and faced himself, his God, and Georgia's broken-down justice system, confessing the excruciating truth about himself and his actions. He did it with courage and forthrightness. The least I could do was to go see him and let him know it was a job well done. I could go there and embody—incarnate, if you will—the idea that he had done the right thing, and that God continued to love him mightily through whatever repercussions that might have in his life and on his case. It seemed to me to be a no-brainer. Is that how the voice of God arrives—as a no-brainer?

And so I found myself standing at the foot of a square tower, shouting my name up to a guard, shouting Andrew's name, being glad that it was a balmy spring day without precipitation or bitter cold as I stood and waited outside for the clearance to go in. As per the guard's instructions, I returned my purse to the car and brought only my driver's license, car keys, and one unopened pack of cigarettes with me into the prison. I've always found it kind of ironic that no fruit, no green tea, not even a Bible, unless you are a certified cleric, can enter the prison—nothing life giving. But by all means, bring in more death to the already doomed.

Entering the prison in Jackson is a unique experience. Huge iron gates grind open by unseen hands, and you step into a cage. The gates grind and slam shut behind you, and now you are locked in, all alone. More grinding, and you step into a long, dark tunnel that leads you to the bottom of some stairs. The tunnel is all concrete, devoid of any pictures, furniture, or other signs of life. It's like some science fiction show, where Kirk and Spock are wandering through some apparently abandoned edifice on some unknown planet, wondering, *Are there beings inside, maybe around the next corner? Are they watching us? What will happen when we come upon them?* Of course, I don't have a phaser or any other space-age weapon ready for the encounter—only ID, car keys, and cigarettes.

"This is scary," I think, but it is more an observation than a feeling. The darkness that should be settling into the pit of my stomach is somehow lifted, suspended, dispersed into thin air by some combination of curiosity, innocence, and surreal disequilibrium.

My footsteps resonate on the hard surface reminding me of some old radio show where the sound-effects guy bangs shoes on a table to make the walking sound. There is literally light at the end of the tunnel, and as I arrive at the bottom of the steps, I have no choice but to go into it. So up the stairs I trudge, and suddenly I am in a different world—a world peopled with officers, one of fluorescent lights, uniforms, protocol, and procedures. There is an officer at a podium-like desk next to a freestanding doorframe that turns out to be a metal detector. These were the days before metal detectors in airports and public buildings. I had never seen one before.

The officer asks my name, whom I am visiting, and my relationship to him. I sign a little book, giving my name, Andrew's name, my relationship to him (friend), and my license plate number. Then I make several treks through the metal detector, removing this and that until I finally clear it. I have not yet learned the fine art of dressing for prison without buttons, zippers, certain types of shoes, underwear, and jewelry. I gradually learn to avoid any hidden metal components lurking in whatever I wear in order to clear the metal detector in one pass, without the repeated humiliation of removing items and going back through, a hand-wand check, or, most unnerving, a pat-down or strip search. Eventually, I become an expert at this game. That's not today. Today I am a little bewildered by the whole process, but dogged in my determination to remain upbeat and bring God's love and joy into that dark place.

The next stop is another officer in a glass cage who slides out a drawer into which I drop my keys and ID, in exchange for a metal chit that I will return for my things when I leave. Then another door grates open. I step in. It slams shut with a resounding clash. I am in a cage again. I stand. I wait for another grinding started by another unseen hand. I step out. More grinding and scraping, metal on metal, until I find myself in a large room full of couches and end tables—a visiting room: no carpeting, lots of Formica, no wood—just hard, cold surfaces. The couches are more like benches with dull-gold plastic cushions stuck on top. There is nothing to offer any feeling of warmth or softness. But the room is open and spacious—and empty. I wonder why there are no other visitors. I wait—and wait, and wait some more. Time drags endlessly because I don't know why I am waiting. It seems like an hour before Andrew arrives.

I see him on the other side of another cage, shackled hands and feet, accompanied by an "escort"—what they call the guards who transport UDSs—those under death sentence—one-on-one. I stand to greet him, only to watch him disappear past the cage I expected him to come through to me. The escort comes back alone, enters the cage, and after more grinding, scraping and slamming, juts his head out of the partially opened cage door and calls out loudly: "Inmate Legare for a visit!"

I look around. There is literally no one else in the visiting room but me. I am taken aback at the big announcement. I get up and walk to the cage. Step in. Grind. Slam! Grind. Step out. Grind. Slam. I am on the other side in a hallway facing three iron gates leading down three other endless hallways. One grinds open. I step through. Grind. Slam! I am standing in front of a heavy door that the guard unlocks. I step inside. He shuts and locks the door behind me.

108

And there we are. Andrew comes to greet me, politely. Even then, he assumes the role of caretaker. We are in a long corridor with a row of stools bolted to the floor. Along one side, there is a Formica ledge that extends the entire length of the corridor. Over that is a wire-mesh wall separating our corridor from an exact replica on the other side. Andrew leads me to a stool about half-way down the corridor. He stands until I am seated. He explains to me that during the week these visiting rooms are used for visits with "diagnostics"–those who have been sentenced and come to Jackson for testing to determine which prison they will be shipped off to for the duration of their time. They sit on a stool on one side of the mesh, while their visitors sit on a stool on the other side, and they talk through the mesh, a situation similar to the visitation in jails–no contact. They are allowed visits on weekdays, but not on weekends. The big visiting room, Andrew explained, is for the "permanents," inmates who are actually serving out their sentences at Jackson. They visit on weekends. Since this is a "special visit" on a weekday, there are no visitors in the big room.

Our little corridor, he tells me, is reserved for contact visits with death row inmates. On weekends, the four cellblocks that house Death Row inmates each get one corridor. This allows for inmates who have been separated by cellblock for various reasons to remain separated during visitation. On a weekday like today, the diagnostics get one set of corridors, and pastoral, legal, and special visits for death row inmates get the other set. In addition, there is a little room off to the side of the main visiting room for any inmate who needs to be segregated completely from the others. Although I do not know it then, this little room figures profoundly in my future. It is the room in which I will share visits with men in scrubs and paper slippers who will be executed the next day. It is also the room in which I will be married.

I do not remember what Andrew and I talked about that day. I do remember that the cold impersonality of the place evaporated as we sat down together and began to talk. Probably, we talked about Bruce Springsteen, because we were both fans of his poetry and music. We may have talked about Thomas Merton, because I was just beginning a period of obsessive reading of his works. I am sure we touched upon the confession, but I am also sure we laughed, and chatted, and learned a bit about each other. We talked about the process of getting onto Andrew's visiting list. I had to be put on as his "girlfriend" because there was no "friends" category then–only family and girlfriend. At that time, we were fudging: I am a female and I am your friend, so there you go. I do not believe either of us had an inkling that our lives were becoming inexorably entwined to the point that I would one day be not only "girlfriend," but wife. Back then, I was just a friend who dropped in for a few hours about once a month. We exchanged letters in between. Through correspondence and legal and pastoral visits, Andrew was beginning to develop a cadre of friends, including me. He and I had many, many miles to go before we even became best friends. For now, we were content to be slowly and shyly getting to know each other as friends, each hotly pursuing other love interests in our lives, with not a blip on either radar of what was to come many years down the road.

It was one of those other love interests who brought me to one of the biggest turning points in my life. I fell head over heels in love with a native of Columbus, Georgia. I dropped everything in my life to follow my heart to his hometown. Columbus also happens to be home to Fort Benning, with its prestigious Rangers and the School of the Americas. At that time, Columbus also boasted the highest number of death-row inmates of all judicial circuits in Georgia, so I knew I had my anti-death-penalty work cut out for me. I wasn't worried, though. This little Episcopal girl danced cheerfully into that Gothic environment, thinking, *"Gee, I can't wait to tell these people the facts about the death penalty; they'll be so shocked!"* They'll just come to their senses and change their mind about it–just like that, especially my numerous Christian brothers and sisters in the area. I bet they can't wait to have a little light shined upon the truth of the situation so they can see the error of their ways. I was happy, in love, invincible, and fired up for justice in Georgia–and in for a rude awakening.

Becoming Real: Part III

The best and clearest decision I ever made to drop everything and follow Jesus Christ was the moment I decided to follow my heart to Andrew. A few weeks ago, I was sitting in a church service listening to the story about the disciples' decisions to put down their nets and follow Jesus. I was imagining with some envy the crystalline clarity they must have experienced the moment they chose to simply throw everything else to the wind and follow

God's call. Suddenly it struck me: there was one moment in my life when I had experienced that same exquisite, unmistakable lucidity. It was the moment I knew that I was going to marry Andrew Legare.

I have to confess, though, that I did not then fall into the semi-hypnotic state the disciples seemed to be in when Jesus walked by and said, "Follow me." I did not just fall into easy steps with the rest of the band and march off blissfully behind the Master. I suspect that the twelve did not either, but the Gospels are not so much histories as dramatic portrayals of Jesus' life and teachings. We get the point about what it takes to follow Him. But most of us are much more like the earnest, rich young man who desires so much to enter the Kingdom and struggles to understand what the Lord requires, but in the end cannot "just do it." He wanders away sadly to think about it some more, we presume. Whether he ever comes around to doing what Jesus commands, we can only imagine. If he is like the rest of us, he begins with small steps, sharing more of his wealth, perhaps, and more actively using it and his life for better purposes. But to drop it all and just walk away from the person he thought he was in terms of status and money– that he could not do.

I had followed my heart for love several years earlier. Then it felt less like God's call than a young girl's romantic impulse. I dropped everything and moved from Atlanta to Columbus, Georgia to be with the one I thought was my true love. It did not work out, and four years later I found myself dumped and alone in hostile territory, and I soon high-tailed it back to Atlanta. But the years I spent there were like a refining fire. They were rich with joy and raw with pain, realization, and spiritual growth.

Columbus, Georgia is a strange and Gothic southern town. Even though I grew up in Richmond, Virginia, the capital of the rebel states, I don't believe I ever encountered the true South until I moved to Columbus. Virginia culture is much more rooted in Williamsburg. We view ourselves as British to the core. For us, the Revolution was not meant to throw off all things British, but rather was an honorable war to make us equals–a brother-sister nation of free and happy Anglophiles. We have always been Virginians first, then citizens of the Confederacy, and finally, the United States. In Richmond, however, the Civil War lives on as a quaint tradition of southern ladies and gentlemen, and dashing heroes who fought only for Our Fair State's rights.

It was in Columbus that I first encountered the bitterness of a lifestyle crushed and overthrown–of economic and social destruction resented openly to this day. While Virginia's racism is genteel and unspoken, you could cut the racial hatred with a knife in Columbus, Georgia. It was there that it first occurred to me that perhaps Flannery O'Conner and Carson McCullers wove tales not so much from rich imagination as from keen observation and sharp-witted analysis of the truth they had lived and breathed.

The weight of the repressed anger in Columbus is made heavier by the presence of the huge military base at Fort Benning. The town is overrun with young soldiers, teenagers really, tough and eager to prove their manhood with weapons and bullying. There, William Calley quietly lives and works behind the counter of a little jewelry store, accepted as one of Columbus's own. He took the fall for the massacre at My Lai, for doing what soldiers are all trained to do, what military outsiders can never understand.

At the time I lived in Columbus, the infamous Stocking Strangler was still at large, infusing a quiet fear into the already taut pall of racial tension and mistrust. He was thought to be a black man who had committed a series of brutal rapes and murders of elderly respected white women in Columbus–our sweet grandmothers. He had stopped the crime spree without being caught as suddenly as he had begun it, but, though inactive for several years, still held the community hostage, waiting in terror for him to strike again.

When I resided there, the District Attorney from Columbus held the distinction of having put more men on death row than any other DA in Georgia. The town had made martyrs out of the celebrated murder victims of all these men, hanging on tightly as a community to a collective anger and lust for vengeance. Since the death penalty had only recently been reinstated, no one had run out of appeals yet, so the men from Columbus sat on the row, invisible receptacles of the city's perfect hatred.

It was into this simmering swamp that I came barreling, alive with the joy, hope, and naiveté of new love. The world was a magic place in which good will always prevail, and it was my oyster. I was fairly new to the movement to abolish the death penalty and confident we would accomplish our goal in short order. I presumed, like Martin Luther King, Jr., that appealing to the best in people would bring about change. He was right, of course; but I conveniently overlooked a few of the facts. I forgot that the battle he fought had been going on for centuries before he picked up the gauntlet; I forgot that, although he certainly changed the face of the struggle, he didn't actually win outright; and I forgot that he and many others died in the struggle to make baby steps forward in the great movement towards justice that goes on to this day. I believed our cause was so just, so logical, and so morally incontrovertible that the battle would be short and the victory sweet.

Perhaps that is why God plopped me down in Columbus, Georgia. It was in Columbus that I first encountered the face of evil, up close and personal, again and again and again. I was dragged into a kind of spiritual warfare for which my little soul was ill prepared. It was in Columbus, Georgia, that I first encountered the kind of failure that results in death. It was breathtakingly devastating and most certainly life changing.

I began simply enough by asking the folks I had worked with in Atlanta who the contact person was in Columbus. I had been a faithful follower of the death penalty opponents, and was looking for a local leader to keep me in the loop. Their response was equally simple: *There's no one there. Would you do it?*

What? Me, become an organizer of some sort? I had never thought of myself that way, but what the heck—how hard could it be? Sure, I said. What do you want me to do? *Organize*, they said. Great. Where do I start? *We'll give you a list of the Columbus men on death row, and you can take it from there.*

Take it from there? Take it where? I had this list in my hand with no idea what to do with it, so I turned to the only expert I knew—the friend I visited on the row, Andrew Legare. I told him of my predicament, and he suggested that he talk to some of the guys on my list and find out what they might need from me. That could give me some direction.

Slowly, a ministry began to form. There was Bill, who had lost touch with his mother when she remarried. He gave me her new name—could I look her up and let her know he wanted to see or talk with her? Then there was Jerome, who had a family who used to visit regularly until the only one who could drive became too disabled to make the long trip and sit on the hard wooden stools for hours during the visit. His sister Shirley was eager to visit, but needed a ride. And Johnny had a sister somewhere in

Columbus. He had a phone number, but had been unable to reach her with the one phone call he was allowed per month. Would I try? William had no family, no visitors for years, and just needed a little human contact. Gradually, the ministry found its shape: putting together inmates with their families and other visitors; providing transportation and support for those families who needed it; and writing regularly to "my guys" from Columbus to stay in touch with whatever might come up for them. When one fellow asked me to contact his lawyer in Columbus, from whom he had not heard in a long, long time, I did so.

I learned then how overstressed and understaffed the legal resources were for those under a sentence of death, so I expanded my horizons and began making visits to his death row clients as a paralegal. I contacted the Southern Center for Human Rights, a law firm in Atlanta that specializes in capital cases, and began visiting their clients from Columbus as well. Through word of mouth, I developed a small mailing list to send out information (later alerts and pleas to write letters to the State Board of Pardons and Paroles) and to keep local people informed about the death penalty in Georgia.

As the ministry grew, something else was growing alongside it. A partnership was developing between Andrew–my friend inside–and me. It wasn't really my ministry–it was our ministry. We worked on it together–one on the inside, one on the outside. Andrew was not just a sounding board, but an active participant in building and improving this humble little mission.

As the DA from Columbus continued to send folks to death row, Andrew made contact with them, told them about me, gave them my contact information, which they shared with their families, and the little band of folks we served grew. As my relationship with Andrew deepened, I became one of them, not just the server, but one just as much in need. Andrew was no longer just a friend–he was my *best* friend. I was alone in Columbus in this world of death row, except for Andrew. He understood it and helped me navigate within it. And together, we were doing a bang-up job. We were winning! We were walking God's path together towards victory, sweet and sure.

Now, it's not as if there weren't plenty of warning shots. I remember the shock that shot through me when, as I sat and enjoyed a pleasant dinner at a local restaurant, someone saw my car in the parking lot and actually took the time to peel the "Oppose the Death Penalty" bumper sticker off it. I felt sick and violated when I came out and found it gone. What kind of insecurity produces venom so deep that any expression of an opposing viewpoint cannot be tolerated? I expected the bumper sticker to provoke a little controversy–but complete censorship? The message was clear: *Don't even THINK it–not in this town.*

Then there was the letter to the editor that I wrote. Of course, no one responded in support of my views, but that was expected. What I did not expect was the tone of the dissenting letters: no dialogue about the issue, simply murderous diatribes and personal attacks based on off-the-wall assumptions.

Even my so-called friends made fun of me, the resident bleeding-heart liberal. They were a mean-spirited bunch, whom I routinely forgave for the sick sarcasm that in their minds passed for intellectual repartee. Then one day the ante was suddenly ratcheted up. The always hovering storm-cloud of violence descended even more deeply on the town of Columbus, Georgia. The deep fissures between black and white and rich and poor split wide open. The black man assumed to be the Stocking Strangler was finally caught. Columbus's trial of the century was about to begin.

I immediately jumped over to the poor black side when I went to work for the lawyers of the accused man, Carleton Gary. My position on the situation embarrassed my lover and alienated my friends. Fairly soon, the judge pared Gary's defense down to a single lawyer with no funding–not one penny–for investigation or for interviewing witnesses, making the learning curve for me regarding how a death penalty trial is conducted in Georgia steep and fast. Still, I was unprepared for the monumental toxicity that came at me, day after day after day in the courtroom, through the media, and through conversations with people I knew. Carleton Gary, guilty or not, was the scapegoat for all of the community's fear, anger, bitterness, and racial hatred built up over the century since the decimation of the South in 1865.

As I looked at the faces in that courtroom and listened to the words of the people of Columbus, my friends included, I think I began to understand the meaning of demonic possession. The faces of my neighbors were transformed and twisted into those of an angry mob bent on destruction. Their minds were possessed with one passion: *Get this guy. Facts be damned. This man will pay for*

115

all the havoc wreaked in our community.

And then came the first death. While it's true several men had been executed before Jerome Bowden was put to death, those were men I only knew through others. Jerome was mine. He was my friend. His sister Shirley was my buddy who rode to Jackson with me every time I went to visit Andrew. The last letter Jerome wrote before he was killed was to me–to "My Sweet Mary." It was through Jerome's case that I met Randy Loney, who was working diligently on his clemency request to the State Board of Pardons and Paroles. I worked with Randy to track down school records, former teachers, and community members to help make the case for mercy on the grounds that Jerome suffered from mental retardation. As I became intimately familiar with Jerome's story, it also became clear to me that he was most likely innocent, that he was tricked into participation by a brilliant but sick younger boy who made the plan, did the killing and stealing, and then implicated Jerome. The prime mover, however, was only sixteen and could not be prosecuted as an adult. Jerome, though mentally and emotionally a child, was both old enough to be killed and helpless to defend himself, a perfect target for the relentless system of Georgia justice.

Jerome exuded love and cheer and gratitude, and his story was so compelling that I was confident he would get relief. Shirley and I even had breakfast with Sting, Bono, Lou Reed, Peter Gabriel, and various other stars who wanted to hear her tell Jerome's story before they signed a petition asking the State Board for relief. Now that we had God and the rock community on our side, how could we lose? And besides, I loved Jerome and Shirley mightily. Surely that love would cast a protective wall around them. Surely we would win this one. We had to.

I drove Shirley to the Board of Pardons review where she testified for her brother. I sat with her as the decision came down against him. I took her to the last visit with her brother before his execution. And I sat with her in her house, both of us filled with hope and dread, awaiting the phone call to tell us there had been a stay, or that the deed had been done. I held her helplessly in her grief when the phone call came. I attended the funeral. I drove her to the prison to collect his few belongings after prison authorities called and told her they would throw them out if she couldn't come and get them immediately. It was like a nightmare. I couldn't grasp it. Love had failed. Logic had failed. Good will had failed.

We could not save these men. We could not stop this bloodshed. The train was hurtling along at breakneck speed, and we could not stop it before it took out many, many more. Bill was killed. Chris was killed. Richard was killed. Joseph was killed. Friend after friend was going to the death chamber as I stood helplessly by, unable to abate the grief of the families I had worked with, hoped with, and grown to love.

During this wretched time, there was only one person I could turn to, one person who understood the pain completely, one person who could truly be there with me, one who was sharing the experience at an even deeper level than I could imagine. He sat on death row and watched his brothers fall one after the other. The grief, the fear, and the despair did not require words or explanations. He offered no platitudes or even words of comfort. We simply held each other through it all, often through long, deep silences that communicated volumes. We survived this onslaught, this terrible rending of the fabric of life, this thrust into the reality and surety of death together. In a sense, we came of age together. And together, we nurtured each other out of this dark place and back to life.

We became an indivisible pair then, though neither of us recognized it. We were still best friends, deeper and closer, but still pursuing other opportunities for romance. The notion of imagining a future together just wasn't on the radar, given the situation. It just didn't occur to us.

But slowly and gradually, the deep love began to win out over the absurdity of romance between us. We began to confess romantic feelings for each other, albeit in a completely analytical way. We hypothetically discussed whether every friendship between a man and a woman might have romantic overtones, but friends just chose not to act on those feelings. Or did they? Would it be wrong for friends to add a little romance to friendship, especially if neither was romantically linked to anyone else? Were the lines blurrier than we had thought? And all sorts of other nonsense, until one Easter Day, we just grabbed each other up in a joyful embrace and waltzed around the visiting room declaring our love for each other. He actually picked me up and swung me around, and I remember him saying, "You see what Andrew Legare can do for you!"

Indeed. He is my joy, my happiness, my center, my growing

edge–but we still were not on our way to the altar. The next week, when I visited again, we analyzed the situation. It was Easter. We both agreed that we were just so caught up in the joy and passion of the season that we had better step back and appraise the situation before jumping headlong into something we might both regret.

Thus began the long slow crawl to the altar, and I'm not talking about the marriage altar yet. Nope. Before that could happen, I had to make the long, slow crawl to that moment at the altar of total repentance, of total emptying out of my willful, controlling, disobedient self, of that primal reluctant cry of *Not my will, but thine, O God.*

But that is another part of the journey, another stretch in this long and winding path through the story of two ordinary lives made extraordinary only in their intertwining.

--Mary Palmer Legare

My Reflection of Grace

In the dark of the woods I sat and waited. I had been following him for the last couple of days—trying to determine his normal course of activities. As determined as I was, however, I remained angry as I sat there in the dark by myself, thinking too much about my reason for wanting to kill him in the first place.

I remembered my little brother complaining to me about school and how it wasn't safe for him—something about a fight over a girl. That's all I remembered, but as time progressed, his fear grew stronger and I started to wonder if this threat was real.

Unfortunately, it was, and the proof was given to me in the form of a young man's dead body on my mother's back porch. The young man was a friend of my little brother and, as I found out later, a witness to the threats my little brother was receiving. Watching my mother cry and listening to my little brother stutter filled me with a sense of invasion and anger that made my teeth chatter. I asked my brother who had done this. He said his name was Phat.

So here I am, sitting in the woods outside Phat's apartment waiting on him to come outside for his normal smoke so I can kill him. I had no doubt in my mind that he would die that night until I heard the hammer of a gun that wasn't mine. Slowly he motioned in my direction. He was behind me so I couldn't see his face. Nevertheless, I hated him. I hated him for interrupting my "dance with the devil." How dare he approach me in the cloak of darkness with ill intentions. I thought about turning around to see the face of my assailant, but before I could, his breath was on my neck. "I know your mother. I knew your father, and he would not approve of this," he said.

"Who are you?" I asked.

He wouldn't tell me his name. We both fell silent watching Phat smoke a cigarette outside alone. My arm tensed as I considered drawing my gun and trading my life for Phat's. No sooner had I thought that than I could hear the figure behind me whisper: "Violence begets violence and, despite the fact that you may not believe this, vengeance is not yours."

I tried to speak but was shushed instead. As I watched Phat finish his cigarette and go back inside, I listened to someone tell me that I was a great kid and that he admired the relationship I had with my little brother. He praised me for my courage and even promised that he wouldn't kill me if I went straight home and stayed there with my mother.

I did just that. I never heard that voice again. The following night on the news, however, I learned that Phat's body had been found dead in the kitchen of his apartment. I guess vengeance wasn't mine.

--Tobias Croom

I WONDER IF I TRIED HARD ENOUGH

"Stop!" someone screamed. I think that's what I heard in the dark. The air here looks more like the water at the bottom of the Chattahoochee River, a greenish black swirl surrounding me, making me afraid to open my eyes for fear of something getting in them and infecting me. I was drowning, gagging on the greenish black mist around me, afraid to speak when I heard that scream again. "Stop!" I was so afraid. I had to calm down. I didn't want to die, but someone needed my help.

"No! Please!" someone screamed.

"Wait! I'm coming!" I yelled.

Suddenly, my eyes are open, my feet are moving, and my heart is pounding harder than it had been at the thought of my dying. I had been here before. I know what is happening. I don't like it, but I don't know how to stop them.

Or is it that I'm too afraid to try?

It's always more than one of them–hideous creatures, at least in their actions. Scratching and pulling so violently, frantically attacking as the fluids of the lamb cascade across the bodies of the wolves, grunting and panting, grotesque gestures flailing in the dark–the very definition of abomination itself.

Yet, I run in their direction. I had to stop thinking about myself. Besides, they had never attacked me. I had witnessed numerous slayings and never been touched, but I am still afraid. Because I neglected to help my brothers, I am afraid I am just as guilty in the eyes of the Father. I need to help this person. But how? Do I get physically involved and risk being attacked? I can't reason with them. Not then, not there. This is insane! But this is the law in the dark–anarchy.

The screams stop, but I know I'm close. Unlike the aroma of sweet union, I can smell the stench of violation. And there he is, lying on the ground with his head behind the toilet, whimpering like a child. I consider reaching out to him, but eventually do not. What can I say to a man who has just been raped? Silently, I stand there, unable to speak. Watching him shiver reminds me of my son after a long bath, his knees colliding while his elbows are mashed together as if his hands are in his mouth.

"T? Hey!" a voice says behind me.

Uh, oh. It was one of them–talking to me in that tone, as if he doesn't know what he has just done. As if he doesn't know what he has done!

"What's up? You all right?" he asks.

Before I can turn around, I feel his hand on my shoulder. It smells like Coast soap and it is cold, but I am hot.

Like a balloon, I am swelling with anger. I should break his neck. I *can* break his neck, I think. My body turns slowly to try and position myself in a way to achieve my goal. In so doing, I can see figures against the wall. Faces point in my direction, smiling at me. Realizing that life beyond achieving my goal might not be realistic, I calm down.

I turn toward the beast that touched me and say, "Nothin'. Just chillin'."

He extends his hand for me to shake, and I take it.

I walk away, heading back to my bunk next to the green exit sign where the smokers gather. Later, I wonder if God was watching. I wonder if it is true what they say about God being able to see what's in your heart. I wonder if God thinks I tried hard enough.

--Tobias Croom

AND THE CHILDREN CRY

Most Americans go to bed at night thinking they are secure and are living in a free world. I wonder what the people on death row are thinking. We are living in a complicated world of laws, borders, and limits. The truth is that most Americans do not even know how to complete their own income taxes. How can citizens defend themselves with laws that take a three-piece suit to explain? Our lives are in the hands of attorneys who sometimes couldn't care less about the outcome of the trial. Most of the defendants in murder cases cannot afford proper representation. State-appointed attorneys are frequently inexperienced or too overworked to represent the defendant properly. Very few states pay enough to state-appointed attorneys for them to be competent or even effective.

Our system maintains that innocent people are not executed. How can they be sure when over ten percent of death row prisoners in the United States could be innocent, according to *Reprieve* (reprieve.org.uk)? If some inmates on death row are indeed innocent, the actual murderers are still at large in society. If we put one person to death who is innocent of a crime, then we are working with a seriously broken system. We are dealing with human beings who have equal rights to life and the pursuit of happiness.

We need to ask ourselves if the system is working. In states that have the death penalty, according to *Reprieve*, murder rates are forty-eight percent higher than states with no death penalty. For every state execution, three execution-style murders follow in its wake. Are we modeling for our children that killing is a positive way of dealing with a problem? Isn't there something inconsistent about killing to show that killing is wrong? Violence begets violence, whether it is violence perpetrated by the state or an individual.

The Romans believed in "an eye for an eye." Have we not progressed? There is no credible evidence that capital punishment deters crime. We are dealing with human beings and not just their crimes. Sister Helen Préjean preaches that we are all worth more than our worst act. It is likely that most of the people on death row have traveled a road of terrible abuse and have become broken products of society. Children are born every day into single-parent homes with little chance of making it in society. They are doomed in the womb.

The phrase "forgotten victims of imprisonment" describes the children who are affected by a system that turns a blind eye. The system rarely considers the effect it has on the children or the balance of the family. The system offers very little support in the damage caused to the family unit. This is where we should put our tax dollars to work. As a country and as a community, we need to stop this cycle. The prison system fails to even record information about the prisoners' children—or even whether there are any.

According to Christopher J. Mumola in "Incarcerated Parents and Their Children," a special report published in 2000 by the Department of Justice in Washington, DC, an estimated 1,498,800 children in America had a parent in prison in 1999. Since Sister Helen Préjean published *Dead Man Walking*, she has accompanied five men to their executions, counseled the families of murderers and victims, and spoken out against the death penalty in numerous settings around the world.

According to *Reprieve,* as of September 2011, the use of DNA testing has helped confirm the innocence of 273 people, including seventeen death row inmates. DNA is unique to an individual and unchanging throughout one's life and has become a reliable identifier. With this testing, we can ensure that some innocent persons will not be sentenced to death. But what about the death row inmates awaiting their execution with no DNA evidence?

At this moment, somewhere in America, a baby is born into poverty with a high chance of growing up abused and neglected.

Unable to escape poverty and low social status, these children experience unhealthy levels of stress hormones that impair neural development. If the children reach adulthood, it is very likely they will commit a crime—maybe a capital crime. And most likely, the victim will just happen to be in the wrong place at the wrong time. If the grown children draw the wrong lottery ticket, America, the home of the free, will put them to death.

Is this what the slogan "I am Troy Davis" means? It's no wonder that we have to go to the drugstore before getting a good night's sleep.

--Robert (Bob) Mathis

THE ROAD TO MERCER

Photography by Jan Crocker

THE PENFIELD JOURNEY: A PARTNERSHIP OF FAITH AND EDUCATION

If you are reading these pages that contain the reflections of some people who are using the gift of writing to share various aspects of their personal journeys, you probably have more than a casual interest in the process we call education. And, since education in the Mercer context is rooted in a rich religious tradition, you may also have more than a casual interest in the dynamics of the covenant faith underlying its particular history.

The journey from the Penfield of 1833 to the Penfield College of 2015 is a long one, but the continuity of vision and commitment between the two underscores an assumption that religious faith naturally leads to a process of education and that education is one of the ways that religious faith matures in a healthy direction.

The journey . . .

"Journey" has become a popular word or metaphor for referring to the life of faith. From its use in books and articles and its frequency in conversation, it seems to connect with what many experience the life of faith to be. It implies that faith is a *process* rather than a *fixed condition* or a *body of beliefs*. A journey has a starting point, a destination, a reason for travel, baggage, fellow travelers, significant landmarks and experiences along the way, various forms of guidance from those who have traveled before, and challenges that enrich, impede, and sometimes change the direction of travel. These parts of the analogy do seem to resonate with the experience of covenant faith that is shared by many.

"Journey" is also a fitting metaphor for the experience of education. Like faith, it is a *process* more than a *product*, even though its outcomes are specific steps that continue to be built upon. What can be said about the journey of faith can also be said of the journey of education, both formal and informal.

The assumption behind the following reflections is that there is value in having travelers along this journey study together the features of the pilgrimage. No travelers have exactly the same experience, yet all are part of the community of pilgrims; the perspectives and insights of others can enrich our journey.

Let's think about the features of the analogy of the journey.

1. Starting point: Every traveler begins his or her journey somewhere, with particular understandings of what the journey is about, where it will lead, and why one should undertake it. The earliest stages of the journey establish a travel pattern and either reinforce or modify expectations about what was in store. This foundational stage has a powerful impact on both the understanding and the meaning of the journey, and there is value in giving careful thought to it, for it is indeed a part of who we are. An important task in a faith community, and in an educational context, is to help one another both appreciate and analyze/critique our respective starting points.

   Reflection: Think about the "starting point" of your journey of faith. Was it your home? A church? A retreat or revival experience? What were the important things that surrounded you as you began the faith pilgrimage–ways of thinking and believing? Customs and traditions? The people who were with you?

   Consider the "starting point" in your process of education. Most likely it involved a school setting, but also included people who inspired you to do your best, value learning, and work toward fulfilling your potential.

2. Destination: Journeys that are more than just "riding around" or "cruising" have a purpose or endpoint. In a sense, a pilgrimage is defined by its destination, whether it be a holy place or an assembly from many places of a family of faith. A variety of images describe the destination of the journey of faith: a promised land, heaven, the kingdom of God, full fellowship with God, etc.

   The "educational pilgrimage" is often defined by a graduation, a degree, or a professional certification. A helpful question for each traveler to explore has to do with the destination of his or her journey: What is the "there" to which we travel?

   Reflection: As you have traveled thus far, how have you answered the question: "Where are you going?" Where do you see your journey leading?

3. Reason for Travel: Why make the journey rather than simply stay in the comfort and security of one's own place? Some choose not to–maybe a part of all of us chooses not to–because the appeal of comfort and security is often stronger than the invitation and the willingness to risk the uncertainties of the road. However, there seems to be a part of us–maybe part of the *image of God* in us?–that is drawn to the path of discovery, to the experience of new vistas, deeper understandings, and more profound mysteries than are available at "home." Is it part of being human to explore and investigate? The evolution of human history would suggest a positive answer to this question.

    There is another piece to the answer that is reflected in the biblical record of the experience of the covenant faith community. Recall those whose stories are the vehicles of the biblical testimony of faith: Abraham, Moses, the prophets, the early Christian disciples, the apostle Paul–all were called from their places of comfort and security to begin a journey, sometimes to other places, but always to other ways of thinking about God, themselves, each other, and life itself. Is their story a report of faith for us to admire, or is it an invitation to a journey for us to join? Our answer to this question has an important effect on the life of faith we live and on the process of education we choose to embrace.

    Reflection: How do you answer the "why" question to your choice to be a person of faith or to engage the process of education? Why would you leave the security of your previous way of thinking, believing, and relating to undertake a journey that will lead to unexpected discoveries that will most likely change some of your values and priorities? To make you richer? More popular? More prestigious? Happier? If not that, then what?

4. Baggage: The "baggage" of life consists of those experiences, influences, ways of thinking, habits, attitudes, likes, dislikes, phobias, obsessions, and animosities that have become a part of our lives and are "with us" wherever we go. Some of this baggage is essential and

helpful, and some of it just "weighs us down" and makes the journey more difficult. In the journey of faith, there are essential "tools" that enrich the development of our covenant relationship; and there are beliefs, ideas, and behaviors that interfere with effective travel. An important part of our responsible participation in a life of faith is our careful reflection on this "baggage" to discern the helpful and the unnecessary–the things we need and the things we'd be better off without. Some baggage is useful for a time, but then is no longer needed. Faithful judgment exercised in the process of education involves knowing what to keep and when to discard and replace.

Reflection: What baggage have you "left behind" in your journey thus far? What baggage do you suspect you might still need to discard?

5. Fellow Travelers: Unless one is on a solitary journey, travel involves companions. There is little to support the idea that the human pilgrimage is a solitary one. Personal? Yes. Private? No. Throughout the biblical record–and quite pointedly in the "greatest commandment"–to love God and to love one's neighbor (Matthew 22:34-40), our relationship with God is inherently connected to our relationship with others. This connection is both a blessing and a challenge, because we are at all times at different stages of the journey. There are those ahead of us, whose experience and guidance are helpful as we negotiate the path. And there are those not so far along, whose less experience reminds us where we once were and who need our help, carefully offered in terms of their readiness to receive it.

The journey of faith and education is a community effort, with no status or honor attached to any point along the way–only the delicate balance of the need for each other's help and the opportunity to be helpful. We're in this together, and faithful travelers are aware of their need for each other.

Reflection: Think of how your fellow travelers have

helped you in your faith journey. Who are they, and what contributions have they made? How have you contributed to the journey of others who have looked to you for guidance, inspiration, and encouragement?

6. Landmarks: Every journey has its combination of routine, uneventful stretches of the road that do not make significant impressions and those attention-getting sights and experiences that mark the stages of the trip and perhaps even interrupt its momentum and change its direction. The journey of faith and the process of education are seldom routine experiences–there are landmarks, figuratively speaking, in that journey that give us pause, change our progress or direction or both, offer vistas that reveal things we had not imagined, and become the "memory points" of the trip itself.

Reflection: What have some of these "landmark" experiences been for you?

7. Maps and Guidebooks: Though we journey into a wilderness in the sense that we have not traveled that way before, others have been there before us; and they have shared in various ways the wisdom of their experience. Maps and trail guides help us avoid making some mistakes and misjudgments, though they cannot guarantee a perfect trip. Again, figuratively, the journey of faith has available such maps and guidebooks in the testimony of those pilgrims who have gone before us. The Bible is a repository of such testimony, selected by our ancestors in the faith on the basis of its helpfulness with the questions of the journey: Where are we going? At whose invitation? For what purpose? How shall we travel and treat each other? After what or whom shall we model ourselves? What can we hope for at the destination? Faithful travelers do well to study the maps and guidebooks. Failure to do so exposes us to unnecessary risks. But it is good to remember that they are only that–maps and guidebooks–and no amount of knowledge of them can substitute for the journey itself.

The vast resources of the more general process of

education offer similar guidance. Rare is the question that has not been thought about before, with invitations to join the conversation that has gone on sometimes for centuries. Yesterday's answers may not fit today's questions precisely, but they do offer helpful lenses through which to study them.

Reflection: How do the Bible and testimony of other pilgrims affect your personal faith journey? How do they help you? How have the rich resources of your cultural tradition enriched your understanding of the customs and perspectives that you have embraced? Does your experience sometimes lead you to revise your previous understanding of the map or the guidebook?

8. Hurdles: Many trips are remembered in terms of the unexpected challenges that were encountered along the way. The snowstorm that brings a backpacking trip to a halt, the accident or breakdown that interrupts a weekend drive through the mountains, the illness that changes the schedule of a vacation–we could add to the list. The possibility, even probability, of challenges along the way of any journey, religious or educational, keeps us from being over confident that any trip will go as planned.

The journey of faith and the process of education offer a good illustration. We begin with the hopes and dreams that are part of the promise that accompanies the invitation. After a time, perhaps a very short or very long time, we meet the challenges that change the journey from smooth and easy to challenging and difficult; and those challenges change the journey–and us–as we respond to them. We can try to avoid the challenges, ignore them, deny them, or give in to them and quit the journey. Or we can respond to them with trust and the resources available to us, refining our journey and ourselves in terms of what we learn from the challenge.

Reflection: What are the challenges that have met you on your journey, both of faith and of education? How have they refined your understanding of yourself and your personal pilgrimage?

The past, present, and future pilgrims on the Penfield journey personify the legacy of Jesse Mercer's vision of educational opportunity for those Georgians whose location and economic circumstances would limit their access to it.

The wide availability of the Internet has replaced the rarity of available books, and technological wonders have replaced slate tablets and writing quills; but the experience of inquiry, examination, discovery, and transformation remain as the dynamic content of both faith and education.

And the journey continues . . .

--J. Colin Harris

FULL CIRCLE

Seven years ago, life as I knew it came to a screeching halt. A stay-at-home mom, I served with my husband of twenty-five years in full-time ministry. When he "fell from grace," I became a statistic–a middle-aged, divorced woman with two teenage children, no job, and no education. Devastated and scared, I had no idea what my life was going to be like in the future. It was through my education at Mercer University that I found hope to regain inner strength, determination, and the energy to turn personal striving into thriving that has brought me full circle.

Hope had not shown its face on my first day of class at Mercer University. Fear and intimidation were all I could muster as I sat in the classroom on the front row, pencil and paper in hand, ready to begin my educational experience. As I waited for other students and the professor to arrive, I reflected on how I had enjoyed reading and writing twenty-plus years earlier in high school. For this reason, I had chosen an English class to begin my college education. The only hope I had that night was that I would remember how to form a complete sentence and would find some enjoyment in this otherwise very serious time in my life.

Finally, the professor arrived. She appeared to be anything but serious as she entered the room. Without a word to anyone, she plugged in her boom box and started playing New Orleans jazz, swayed her way to the front of her desk, leaned herself on it, and closed her eyes. It was as if she were in New Orleans at that very moment. The playing of music and her silence lasted what seemed to be an eternity.

She finally opened her eyes and spoke. I thought for sure she was going to review the syllabus and explain her expectations, rules, assignments, and due dates. Instead, she spoke about her love of jazz music and how she first began that great love. I could not figure out for the life of me what that had to do with complete sentences and the seriousness of a college education. Then she gave time to the rest of the class to share something about themselves and a personal experience about writing. Time passed quickly as I listened to my classmates' stories. I shared two stories about how I had once illustrated a book for a friend while she was in college to become an elementary school teacher and how I taught my little sister to write cursive before she was in the first grade. After I shared my stories, the professor stood in front of my desk, shaking her finger slowly up and down, head slightly turned to the side, and said with a gleam in her eye, "There is something special about this one."

I felt anything but special when I learned that the following week's writing assignment was the description of another personal experience. What I was going to write about was heavy on my mind and heart. I was so proud of myself for speaking up the first day of class, but my joy turned to sadness as I had nothing to write about but the heartbreak from over twenty years of surviving the abuse from a spouse's addictions. I wanted to write about light-hearted events, but all that would come into focus was a journal of my most personal thoughts and feelings I had kept during my marriage. I would hide it in my closet under the carpet under my shoe rack. In my marriage, my voice had been silenced by abuse and the shame that overshadowed it.

I decided not to live under any more shadows of shame and to write about my personal journal entries. What I did not realize was how much I wrote, and wrote, and wrote. After I turned in my assignment, the professor asked to meet with me to discuss my writing. As I sat in the chair next to her desk, I was somewhat distracted by all the books in her office. I asked if all those books belonged to her. She replied with a perplexed "yes." She also told me that she had many, many more bookshelves full of books at home. I was in awe that one person could own so many books.

Books, magazines, and anything not related to the Bible had been considered evil in my home. Everything outside of the Word of God was deemed "worldly." I will never forget what my professor told me that day in her office. First, she assured me that I could borrow any book I wanted to read. She said I had a lot to say and the honesty in my writing was disarming. She compared my writing to popcorn popping everywhere out of an uncovered popper. She encouraged me to find my authentic voice and noted that my story would impact the lives of so many women who had been oppressed by their mates. She advised me to focus on one topic at a time. She had more faith in me that day than I had in myself–faith that I would be able to find my voice that had been silenced for such a long time.

After that visit I wanted to read every book and every word of each story we were given in class to read for our assignments. It was not until she assigned me to read "Sweat" by Zora Neale Hurston that I found the courage to find my voice and never be silenced again. In this reading I saw my life as a white woman through the eyes of a celebrated black folklorist and writer.

I shared many more stories through writing in her class. I stuck to writing about what I knew: abuse. Toward the end of the eight-week session, the professor asked if she could read one of my writing assignments in class. After she finished reading my story out loud, the silence in the room was so loud my ears were ringing. It was at that pivotal moment I began to see that I was no longer a victim of my experiences, but a survivor. This professor taught me how to find my voice. That's when I began to define my purpose and mission for the next stretch of my life journey to full circle.

My mission was even more defined when it came time to do my internship in human services. My advisor suggested I consider doing a study abroad program with Mercer on Mission in lieu of an internship. Cape Town, South Africa was on the list of study-abroad sites. Earlier in my life, I had tried several times to go to Cape Town as a missionary, but the trip had never materialized.

Spending the summer in Cape Town among the people of the shantytowns was a fulfillment of a lifelong dream. I delivered meals to the elderly and distributed food to women and children while they waited in line at a local clinic for their medical needs to be met. I held children in my lap who had lost their parents to

AIDS and colored with them in coloring books. I stood in Nelson Mandela's jail cell on Robin's Island. The stories of redemption and forgiveness that the people of South Africa shared with me resonated in the depths of my soul. The people of South Africa taught me how to truly forgive and move past any injustices that I had experienced.

Once I returned from Africa, I was even more driven to continue my education and prepare myself to give back in some way to help other survivors of abuse. I wanted to become the face of hope for those who had lost their voices. I applied for the Professional Counseling Program with Mercer on the Atlanta campus. The many years I had spent in ministry had not been extinguished. I only transitioned into a new direction–a new career: counseling. I was accepted into the master's program in counseling and finished it in December 2010. I sat for my licensure in October of the same year and became a Licensed Associate Professional Counselor.

Something was still missing for me on this journey to full circle. The desire to be in the classroom was persistent. In my graduate program I had been a teacher's assistant to Dr. Arthur Williams, Chair of the Professional Counseling Program. I loved it. I craved the connection I had with the students in helping them to become counselors. With Dr. Williams' encouragement, I applied for an adjunct position with Mercer. I started teaching in May 2011, serving as the Practicum/Internship Faculty Supervisor for the College of Continuing and Professional Studies, which has since been renamed Penfield College.

On the first day of class, I came early, prepared with pencil and paper, and this time, a class roster. The students came in one by one. My heart was not nervous, but full of excitement. I knew what wonderful experiences lay ahead for them because I had already traveled this road. This time I was the teacher. Instead of someone having hope for me, I now had hope for others. To my surprise, one student I knew entered the class. I felt my heart grow warm. She was one of my classmates who had started in the undergraduate program in Human Services and had taken that very same English class with me. She had also been one of the students who had embraced and comforted me after the story of my abuse was read in the class. I never forgot her. Her compassion for me soothed a tender, vulnerable, and insecure heart. I grew in faith within myself and felt I belonged to a new family–my Mercer family. Our ways parted until she walked into my classroom–still a student.

The adage "when the student is ready, the teacher will appear" entered my thoughts at the conclusion of my first class. I realized I had begun the process of repaying a debt to those who had helped me find my way by giving to those who now sat in the same seats I had occupied–in the same place where personal and professional growth had occurred for me. As I packed my bags of educational materials to leave the classroom, a sense of satisfaction, peace, and joy washed over me. The strains of jazz rhythms bounced soundlessly around the room. I swayed ever so slightly to their beat. I had come on a journey–a journey to full circle.

--Darlene Bowling

MY ROAD TO MERCER

I never dreamed I'd be back in college, especially in Georgia. Living in Indiana for thirty-nine years, I suspected that I'd always be a Midwesterner. I had never lived more than forty-five minutes from the city where I was born and grew up. I was married with three children, a good job, and immediate family all around me.

Over the course of several years as my marriage came to an end, I had to make a new life for my children and myself. As I ventured out into this new life, I met a man from Georgia. Deciding that we were not perfect, but perfect for each other, we married and I moved to Georgia with my children. My new husband Dave had five children of his own. Together we made a huge family with four boys and four girls.

I needed employment once we settled in Dave's home in Georgia. My daily routine consisted of applying for jobs online and going to the public library searching for jobs in the newspapers. I applied for several jobs, but didn't get many responses. I had heard from my husband's best friend that Mercer University was a good place to look. His wife, also named Brenda, had worked at Mercer for many years. The first interview I got was at Mercer University.

I was nervous, but determined to get the job at Mercer. I had previously worked at Ivy Tech and Purdue University in Indiana, so I hoped that experience might help me get the job. I prepared carefully, going over questions in my mind that I might be asked. Not being familiar with the area, I had driven to the campus the day before, making sure I could find my interview destination. Arriving early the next day, I was ready.

The interview went well. My experience at Purdue University, as well as my typing and Word skills, seemed to impress. I had done all I could do. The next step was waiting for a call or a rejection letter. Nearly two weeks went by with no word. I was sure I had not gotten the job. In the meantime, I was still applying for work. Then the call came from Mercer: I got the job!

Excited to have a job, I had never even thought that I would have the opportunity to further my education. I just needed a paycheck at that point. The plan was for me to work for two years, then I would be a stay-at-home mom–something I never thought I'd be able to do. Some of our children lived with the other parent, but as the years went by, more children would move into our home. It became apparent that with more children living with us, I would have to continue working. After I had worked one year at Mercer University, my husband asked about furthering his education. Mercer's tuition waiver was a great idea to help Dave finish his B.S. degree. Dave kept asking when I would take classes, but with teenagers in the house, I declined. I felt we had too many teens at home for both of us to be gone in the evening.

As the children grew older and began graduating from high school, we began to explore the options for them to use the tuition assistance offered by Mercer University. Dave finished his B.S. in May 2008, the same year my daughter Michelle graduated from high school. That fall, Michelle enrolled at Mercer in a double major in psychology and women and gender studies, and Dave began his M.S. degree. Now there were two family members benefitting from my job. As I settled into my job for at least another four years, Dave's son Joshua decided to transfer from Pensacola College to Mercer in the fall of 2009. He moved to campus and started his education in computer engineering.

At the same time in 2009, Dave's sister had become incarcerated, and we agreed to take guardianship of her children, bringing our total to ten. Because my sister-in-law and her children had been living under assumed names in Tennessee, we hadn't seen them for seven years. Bethanie and Christopher lived like fugitives, afraid to make a wrong move and be found out. They needed authentic birth certificates, immunization forms, and social security numbers just to get them into Houston County schools. It was quite a task getting it all worked out, especially legalizing the guardianship in court.

With more children at home to support, I began thinking I was destined to work at Mercer forever, so I might as well make it home. I hit the five-year mark at Mercer in 2010, and suddenly it felt like it was my time to take classes. I enrolled in the fall of 2010, happy to be on my way to finally getting my bachelor's degree. My husband and children were supportive of my educational efforts.

In January 2011, my second daughter, Anna, was accepted at Mercer. By the fall of that year, five members of our family were attending Mercer. Mercer is literally a part of my family now. There are great people working and going to school here.

Why am I here? This is where I want to be.

--Brenda J. Phillips

A SHOT OF ASHES

The man walks into the restaurant and has a seat at the bar. He is here to celebrate an important occasion. Looking to the bartender, he orders one shot of *Jägermeister*. After the shot is set in front of him, and his bill is settled, he looks at his watch. It is now 7 p.m. Graduation has started across the street. It is the culmination of his last two years. In the graduation hall, the presenter approaches the podium with his list. The audience quiets and waits for the prospective graduates to be announced. The first name is called: "Karl Adams?"

As the man sits at the bar, he remembers what had happened to him twelve years ago. The boy had walked into the Air Force recruiting office. He had asked to enlist in the military.

"Why do you wanna join the Air Force, Son?"

The boy had told him that he would graduate from high school in a month and wanted to follow in his father's footsteps. The recruiter had seen the boy's badge, the mark that rendered him unacceptable.

"Son, I'm afraid I can't use you. The rules say we cannot enlist people with hearing loss."

The boy had reached up and touched his hearing aid. He had not understood why such a ridiculous rule was in place. After further pointless discussion, he had left.

Over the next week, he had received the same answer from every branch of the military: *he wasn't good enough to serve.* His last hope had been a letter to Georgia Senator Sam Nunn. Two weeks later he had gotten his answer: "No."

The presenter looks to the end of the stage. He does not see the man standing there. He looks to the crowd. The teachers have their heads bowed. Once more he calls out: "Karl Adams?" The presenter cannot understand why the man is not there. The paper in front of him says that the man is graduating at the top of his class with honors. Why would he not be present for this important occasion?

In the bar, the man picks up the shot glass and stares at the amber liquid. He remembers when he first met his teachers at Central Georgia Technical College in Macon. He had met with advisors for the co-op program at Robins Air Force Base. The first question he had asked was if his hearing aid would be a problem.

"Nope, no problem at all." The staff had assured him that his hearing loss would in no way affect his chances of working on the base.

"The only thing they are looking for is skilled and responsible fabricators." He had grinned at the possibility of making a living wage. *Here was his chance to provide for his family.* He committed himself, heart and soul, to become the best student they had ever taught.

The presenter still sees no man coming forward. In the bar, the man sets the shot glass back down. Last month he had met with the panel at Robins that would interview candidates for co-op employment at the base. He had sat in a chair ten feet away from the panel. Flawlessly, he had answered every question they had posed to him. Some of the people on the panel had even cracked a grin or two.

"I think we've got a winner here. Report for your physical tomorrow and we will go from there."

He had been electrified. It had seemed that all was coming true. The reward for all of his hard work was at hand.

138

In the bar he picks up the shot glass once more. He remembers the physical.

A series of five tests had ensued. The first four had been no problem. He had had just one more to go and the job was his. *No more minimum wage jobs. He would be able to buy his wife their first house and get her and their little girl the things they deserved.* There had been one more test to go. The doctor had called him into his office. He was an audiologist. This doctor had to sign off on his hearing, and then the job would be his.

"I'm sorry, Sir, but I cannot pass you on this physical. You do not meet the minimum hearing requirement."

The man had told him that his instructors at school had assured him that his hearing loss would not be an issue.

"I am sorry, but you see your hearing aid presents a safety hazard. If something falls, and you don't hear the call to get out of the way, then the base is liable."

In shock and disgust, the man had left. He had once again failed his family–failed himself.

The presenter decides to call the name one last time and then move on: "Karl Adams?"

There is no one there. In the back of the graduation, the teachers sit in full regalia. One whispers to another, "We failed him, didn't we?" The others nod sadly.

When the man came back from his physical and recounted to them what had happened, they could not believe it.

"But you are our best student. No one knows the job better than you do."

The man agreed with them and shook his head. He finished his work quietly to receive his final grades. He had even thought about not coming back. In the end, he had to. He would not allow his performance to be affected by people who would not give him a chance.

The presenter gives up and moves on to the next name.

In the bar, the man gets up and leaves. Behind him, sitting on the bar is the shot glass, still full. He would not allow himself to drink a shot of ashes.

--Karl S. Adams

What's the Homework for Today?

"You should have done your homework last night, Mr. Baylis," my wife says to me as I scramble to complete an assignment at the last possible moment. Suddenly, it is as if my mother has come back from the grave just to say, "I told you so." I just smile at her lovingly and say, "Yes, Dear." I realize once again that my wife, much like my mother before her, is my greatest supporter. She, too, believes in my ability to reach heights beyond my own inflated confidence. You see, I am convinced that I can be president if I aspire to be. She believes the president should call me for advice today.

The confidence of others in my talents and abilities has always played a major role in my educational journey. In the early years of my elementary education, I participated in a program for gifted children. At the time, I assumed it meant that I had received good grades. It did not register in my mind that this meant I was above average in terms of intelligence. I did know that I was smart enough not to bring home grades that my father would not tolerate–in *this* subject, I am a genius. My mother encouraged education; my father demanded excellence.

My mother worked in the school system doing menial tasks. This allowed her to keep a close account of my schoolwork. She would speak with my teachers almost daily. She would inquire about my homework and stress to me the importance of practicing, even if I thought I knew the subject well. On the other hand, my father would hold his comments and concerns until report cards arrived. If I did not receive an "A," it meant one extra hour of study time each day for every five points away from an "A" average. I never dared drop below a "B" average. They both believed in my potential. At the time, I had neither the confidence that they had, nor the interest they thought I had. I usually made good grades, but there was usually an ulterior motivation.

I was the second-grade spelling bee champion for an entire year. This accomplishment was not influenced by my mother's nurture or fear of my father's fury. I didn't even care about the trophy or the three hundred dollar gift certificate. The credit for this feat rests solely on the desk of my classmate, Kai Spears. She was my reason for living. If she had asked me, I would have gone to school on the weekends. She thought I could spell every word in the dictionary. Allowing her to find out otherwise was not an option. Therefore, I studied as if my life depended on it.

Sadly, the divorce of my parents a few years later meant the divorce from the life I had come to know. This did not help my outlook on life. I found myself suddenly living in another state and in another state of mind. I may as well have been starting the fifth grade in a foreign country. I was a California kid who migrated to the deep woods of Albany, Georgia. Did I mention that Kai was not in Georgia? Sure, my mother still believed in me, but I figured that was just part of the job.

With this drastic change of venue came a severe change in the financial situation of my family. With no more fear of my father's fury and Kai clear across the world, where was my motivation? My mother was now raising four young men alone. Her work schedule allowed little time to check homework or attend parent-teacher conferences. By the time I reached the seventh grade, one of my mother's jobs was cleaning the laundry facilities of the low-rent housing project where we lived. Ironically, the facility belonged to Mr. Kelly, Principal of Southside Jr. High School where I was a student. As a result, from time to time she would get word of my mediocre B-minus and C-plus grades and remind me of the importance of my education.

I can recall thinking to myself, "You and Dad never even finished school. So get off my case!" Fortunately, I was gifted enough not to let the stupid people who live in my head speak out loud. My father's fury paled in comparison to my mother's wrath. I began to concentrate a little harder and pulled my grades up again. I began to understand that my mother wanted me to have better opportunities in life than she had had. But I still needed motivation. I found it in the dimples of Trina Williams. Trina was much more than a pretty face–she was very smart. Convinced she would not go out with a mediocre student, I turned it up a notch.

By the ninth grade, Trina and I had broken up, and my mother's health was failing. To maintain her income, my brothers and I would perform her duties of cleaning the laundry facilities and the empty apartments recently vacated. This meant less time for studying as we raced the sunset to complete our assigned tasks in vacated apartments with no electricity. By the time we finished, we would be far too exhausted to attempt to accomplish any effective studying. Sometimes I would try to get up early and finish my homework before school. "You should have done your homework last night, Mr. Baylis," my mother would say. I looked at her lovingly and said, "Yes, Ma'am."

It was this same year that I decided to join the Air Force. My oldest brother was in *Who's Who among American High School Students* and he had decided to go to the Air Force instead of college. I passed the Air Force entrance exam during the tenth grade and signed up for the delayed enlistment program. By my senior year of high school, I was on cruise control. All I needed was my diploma and I would be done with school. Little did I know that there are many other forums for education.

For the next two decades, the Air Force would prove to be an inestimable educational experience. From the beginning of my career, I learned about finance, leadership, world history, and social studies, etc. These lessons came by way of formal classroom training as well as day-to-day practical situations. With each promotion came a responsibility to impart these lessons to the subordinates who depended on my knowledge and guidance–a responsibility I took very seriously. I began to seek out educational opportunities and I encouraged my subordinates to do the same. I counseled many of them as if they were my own children.

As a parent, I try to instill in my children that education is critically important. I often tell them that someday they will appreciate the opportunities they have for a good education. Fortunately, my children seem to enjoy school much more than I did as a child. The exemplary performance of my eight-year-old and six-year-old daughters in all subjects gives me new motivation to continue my education.

A few years ago, my then six-year-old daughter challenged me to a game of "Upwards." Convinced that she had no idea how to play the game, I called her bluff and asked her to explain the rules. After explaining the rules to me, she continued, "I hope you know a few upper-level words, because I sure do." I suddenly remembered that there was something else I needed to do. It was an absolute affirmation that in order to stay above water with the younger generation, I had to keep striving for higher educational ground.

As a firm believer in the principle of leading by example, I enrolled at Mercer. I strive each day to exemplify the consummate student. I know how important it is to pay attention in class and how those lessons apply to everyday life experiences. Most importantly, I understand how essential it is to find educational experiences in virtually every opportunity that life offers. Now, I just stop and ask myself, "What's the homework for today, Mr. Baylis?" I hope that my children will do the same.

--Edwin B. Baylis

Go Back to School

After working in security for nearly eighteen years on a college campus, I did not have twenty-five dollars to my name once I paid my basic expenses each month. My two-bedroom apartment cost $625 per month. I knew that I needed to reassess where I was going with my life. As I studied the Bible and prayed about my situation for several months, I heard God's voice telling me to quit my job–that there was something else I was to do with my life. Because of my great financial need, I resisted what I had clearly heard. Yet I could not escape the conviction that the Lord was telling me to resign my job.

"Why? Why do I have to quit my job?" I asked God. The answer could not have been clearer: "You will never reach your full potential on this job." I turned in my resignation in September 2007, not knowing what I was going to do or how I would pay my bills. I took a giant leap of faith and walked into the unknown.

I doubted myself. I doubted whether what I had heard had truly been a message from God. For months I prayed. Had I been tricked? Had I fooled myself that the message I was so clearly receiving was from God? Had I mistaken the voice of God? So many questions went through my mind–questions that caused me to doubt myself and my relationship with the Lord. Each morning I awakened with questions: "What am I going to do? How am I going to survive?" I reluctantly asked my family for help.

My family called me lazy, crazy, weak, not ambitious enough, and a freeloader. They whispered behind my back. They mocked me and my faith in God. Throughout all the shame and humiliation of having to ask them for help, God faithfully provided for me. I kept on praying. I desperately asked God: "What if I missed you? What if I have been tricked by the devil to leave my job? Are you not still merciful?"

I came face to face with the possibility of finding out that I may have been living a lie. That humbled me. Prayer and scriptures became my strength. I reminded God of the promises in the Holy Scriptures. With fear and trembling, I waited each month for God to house, feed, and clothe me. In the midst of all my uncertainty, I heard God's voice once again: "I have called you into fulltime ministry. I want you to go back to school."

I could not believe it. I gasped: "School? I just resigned my job at a college, and you want me to go back to school?" God repeated the message: "Go back to school." For nearly eighteen years I had worked on a college campus and had not attempted to get a degree or continue my education. I had always been too busy raising kids, taking care of a family–too busy with life. I had never even imagined that education was my way of escape out of a preconditioned lifestyle of satisfaction with the mundane. Still incredulous at this turn of events, I filled out the application to attend Mercer University's program of continuing education.

In May 2008 I began my education journey at Mercer University's College of Continuing and Professional Studies in Macon, Georgia, renamed Penfield College. Math and English had never been my strong suits. From day one I remember telling myself that I was a fool if I thought I could attend Mercer University and get a degree. I was setting myself up for defeat.

One of the first classes I took at Mercer was a remedial communication and language class. I was so fearful of taking that class. I anticipated having problems with grammar. After three weeks in that class, I realized that I was sinking. The class consisted predominantly of African Americans. There was one young man from Saudi Arabia in the class. Each Tuesday the teacher would come to class exhausted from her day job. I heard students complaining about how the teacher was teaching and asking for help with the material we went over in class. They asked her to use the bulletin board to write out examples in hopes of understanding the material. The teacher arrogantly replied, "I teach my third graders this." Those words confirmed what people had been saying to me nearly all my life: "You don't belong here. You're not good enough. I'm better than you are." I went from struggling in that class to failing it. Those words from my professor almost shipwrecked me.

In my mind, I saw myself in the fourth grade in Miss B's class. She told the class I had to leave. That was the very first day that I had ever had a white teacher. I can still see her face so well. She was an elderly lady with gray hair pulled back and tied in a bun. Her name I don't remember. But I remember her trying to teach me English only because she had to–and hating every minute of it. She had been transferred from teaching in an all-white school to an all-black school that was just being integrated. As s black student, I was an inconvenience to her. I probably took the brunt of her anger at her being moved out of her comfort zone. In a small town in the South in 1965–where the Ku Klux Klan gathered and made their rides, burning crosses without worrying about who knew–she was probably just as afraid of us as we were of her. I was part of the generation that mixed confusion with misunderstanding. Little did I know at the time that her dreams were being shattered, too.

I attended an all-black African American school with a mean black teacher, labeled by my older siblings as the meanest teacher in the school. This black teacher made it her business to make sure that we learned something. She knew we had to be just as good as our white counterparts–or better. Ms. B and I had something in common–the color of our skin was black.

How ironic that experience in the fourth grade was. Because of it, I am able to understand the importance of tradition and the rich heritage that we learned about in our fine black colleges. Even having Barack Obama as the President of the United States does not make up for what we lost when blacks accepted the idea that white schools were better. The very idea sought to rob us of our rich heritage and what defines us as a people.

My mother had only a third-grade education. I had no father in the house. When my little sister and I started school, there were still marches on Capitol Hill. We became a part of the "nobody-left-behind" group," promoted even though we had not learned anything during the school year. Out of everything that happened that year, I only remember being in that classroom and the first day of integration at my school. Blacks and whites fought over integration. When the classroom was first integrated, no one considered the effects it would have on black students when white teachers overlooked them or caused them to feel dumb or incompetent, while they defiantly made sure that white students learned.

Most white teachers did not care about us.

I am thankful that God would not let me quit at Mercer. I had to take that writing class over again and passed it. In the fall of 2008, I had to take an academic writing class. Full of fear, I walked into that class on a Tuesday night, knowing that my pursuit for a degree at Mercer University may soon be over. I sat down in the front of the class. An elderly white woman, wearing glasses and a navy blue suit, stood in front of the class. She introduced herself and began to tell us something about herself. Caught completely off guard, I was immediately intrigued by her. All over the classroom students introduced themselves and told us their major and why they were taking the class–the universal reason: it was required. I could not take anything else at Mercer until I took this class.

We opened our books to an essay by Richard Rodriguez, "The Achievement of Desire." The professor read aloud to the class from the text: "I stand in the ghetto classroom–the guest speaker"–attempting to lecture on the mystery of the sounds of our words to rows of diffident students. 'Don't you hear it? Listen! The music of our words: 'Summer is a cumen'": clap, clap, clap. She stopped and looked at us. "Do you hear it?" she asked. Clap, clap, clap. "Listen to the beat. Listen to the sound."

From that moment on she had me captured. I began to see endless possibilities. From that moment I had a heartbeat and I knew through my leap of faith I had not made a mistake. I belonged here. Now, at this very moment and at such a time as this, I belonged at Mercer University in Macon, Georgia. I knew I had a purpose here.

I learned in her class that I had a voice and that what I had to say was important. I learned to listen when I read–to listen for the writer's voice. My voice is authentic, and only I can say what I have to say with my voice, experience, and passion. I found my rhythm. I have a sound and beat of my own.

I had never felt so inspired to learn and to pursue my education until I walked into her Tuesday night academic writing class. She plowed through all my resistance and defenses so that she could teach me what I should have learned in the fourth grade. Her compassion for me as a person and as a black woman gave her the courage and patience she needed to allow me to understand the lessons. God turned on the light inside of her for the entire class to be drawn into what our background said was impossible. The desire to reach my full potential was cultivated in her class. Learning was exciting, interesting, and fun. I would listen as she took us on a journey to Nazi Germany, Palestine, and New Orleans. Shhh . . . Listen! Do your hear it? Shhh . . . You will hear not the words I speak, but what my heart is saying–layers upon layers of suppressed images and thoughts that have never been spoken or written down inside of me. They are waiting to get out and wanting to be seen and heard. We never had a boring moment in her class. Every four hours and forty-five minutes was a learning experience.

I can't believe that I have now graduated. I'm so honored to be a graduate of Mercer University. I'm happy to say that Mercer's Penfield College has some of the greatest teachers in the world. I look back on my first year of college and thank God every day that I did not quit. I do belong here!

--Wylodene Adams

The Last Kid Standing

I have lived the majority of my life not being "picked"–well, at least not feeling accepted. Throughout my childhood, I never felt like I ever really fit in or that I belonged to any one group of people. In elementary school, I dreaded having to play kickball during P.E. The coach would pick two kids to be captains for the game. The chosen captains would then each alternate in choosing a member for his or her team. In the line-up with my friends–all of whom were thin and active–I was the chubbiest girl in the class. As I stood there, I repeated voicelessly to myself, "Please, please, please, don't let me get picked last."

Being picked last in elementary school was the end of the world for me. It was as if being picked for kickball determined my identity in school. The order in which students were picked signaled their social status. The students always seemed to be divided into four groups.

The "cool" kids were picked first, regardless of their athletic ability. I have to admit that if I had been chosen to be captain, I would have picked them first, too. Probably erroneously, I thought that if I picked a cool kid, some of his or her "coolness" would rub off on me. He or she might even feel compelled to hang out with me the rest of the day, almost decreeing that I would be popular for the rest of the day. A day in elementary school is like a week for the rest of the world.

I have no idea how a kid gets labeled "popular." It looks like popularity is based purely on the ability to adapt to different kinds of kids and the uncanny ability not to feel awkward–awkward in the sense that almost every child at the elementary-school age feels some sense of insecurity. The kids usually labeled "popular" seem to be secure within themselves. It's as if they simply declared themselves "popular." Many people lack the self-confidence it takes to declare themselves worthy of being popular. "If you speak it, you shall receive it." I don't know who said that, but I am a firm believer in this saying. I believe you have to speak it out loud to receive.

The second group, in order of declining social status, is the athletic kids. They automatically win cool points because they are good at sports. Who doesn't want to hang out with a natural athlete? I never strived to be in this group. I knew that no matter how hard I tried, I would never be a good athlete. Sometimes I find it a good virtue to accept one's shortcomings and move on. Why dwell on something you can't change? Move on to something you can change and give that a hundred percent. I learned that if I try to change something that I'm not any good at, I am just setting myself up for disappointment and depression. I am not saying that we should not force ourselves to do things we think we are not good at. Sometimes it is okay to accept that we are just not good at something. We should find something we are good at and focus on it.

The next group of kids waiting to be picked is what I like to call the "average Joes." These kids get picked because their friends just so happened to be picked–randomly, I might add, by the coach. This group of kids got the luck of the draw. They were no better than I was. It just so happened that their friends were in the same group, and one of them was chosen as captain. This third group of kids is average–not too popular and not too unpopular, just straight down the middle: regular kids with no standout qualities. At least being "picked" last is a memorable place to be. No one remembers the "inbetweeners."

148

The last group of kids standing in line waiting to be "picked" for one of the two teams is the "rejects." I was almost always in this group. It probably did not help that I wore a dress or skirt to school every day. I thought pants made me look too frumpy. I was always one of the bigger kids–even bigger than many of the boys in my class. And one of the hairiest kids, too. Since I was a girl, being hairy did not work in my favor. This most likely drove my desire to overdo my femininity. In line, waiting to be "picked," I stood there with two or three other kids. My stomach was in knots, and I was hoping and praying that my name would be called next and that I would not be the very last kid standing.

As a child I had frequent nosebleeds. I used to pray secretly to whoever was listening to please let my nose start bleeding to save me from the embarrassment of being the last one standing. This last-ditch prayer is an indicator of how anxiety can warp cognitive skills. Who in her right mind would prefer a nosebleed to having the distinction of being the last kid standing?

So there I was–the last kid to be "picked." Knowing that my new team did not really want me, I would slowly walk over to them and wait for my turn to kick the ball. I couldn't even claim to have been picked. The team captain didn't really choose me. It was the luck of the draw. I was the last kid standing.

--Sherry Johnson

On Mission

Gloria and Zulma, Mercer on Mission 2009

MY FRIEND JOSÉ

Settling into my seat on Flight 93 to Guatemala, I had no idea what to expect. This was my first trip out of the United States, and I was somewhat apprehensive. Although I had been informed that our destination was an orphanage in Huehuetenango, I did not fully understand what our mission would entail. Would we be successful in reaching out to the children? Would we be able to cross the language barrier? Would it be possible to bond with the children? I would find the answers to these questions and more during our three-week visit.

Our team, a liberal studies and sociology class from Mercer University, had embarked on a wonderful and rewarding journey. As our bus pulled through the gates of the orphanage, the children immediately gathered around. Happy anticipation glowed on their faces. As we clambered down the steps of the bus to meet them, the children swarmed around us like bees converging on a beehive. Eagerly approaching the children, we were met with hug after hug. The children were starved for attention, and the group happily responded to their needs.

This was the scene at the Fundación Salvación, an orphanage in Huehuetenango, Guatemala, on Wednesday, May 27, 2009. The faces of the children gathered around our bus were unforgettable. As I joyfully hugged the younger children, I suddenly noticed a group of older girls hanging back, watching us warily. Not wanting to leave them out, I immediately went over to them, greeting them with an "*Hola*" and giving them each a hug. They responded with smiles and returned the hugs, but did not follow me when I rejoined the group.

As I began spending time with the younger children, I noticed that the older ones kept their distance. Were they wary of trusting strangers? Were they shy? Could it be that they had grown close to visitors before, only to have them leave after a short time, never to see or hear from them again? In my mind, the last scenario was the most likely possibility.

I began to wonder what the story was behind the children being in the orphanage—not only the older ones but the little ones as well. Were their parents dead? Were they unwanted and put there because they were an inconvenience? If they had families, why weren't they with them? I could not comprehend a family not wanting their own child.

During dinner one evening at the home of the director of the orphanage, our group learned a few of the children's stories. Some truly were orphans. Some had run away from home and lived on the streets. The police had brought them there to live. The courts had placed some of them in the orphanage because of abuse at home. Others were simply unwanted and unloved.

It became obvious that although the children were well cared for, they needed much more attention. Several younger children bonded with members of the group and spent a great deal of time with them. One little boy, José, became my shadow after the fourth day of visits. On "Play-Doh Day," I spent quite a bit of time working with him and Jonathan making funny looking animals, buildings, and weird shapes. After that experience, I noticed him following me around. I looked down at him, smiled, and took his hand. He stayed with me the rest of the day.

When we returned the following day, he ran up to me as I exited the bus. I smiled and gave him a big hug. He then took my hand and led me to the area where we performed our silly dances. As I watched him, I noticed that he kept looking to make sure I was still close by. With each glance, my heart filled with love for him. Why was he watching me so closely? Had he experienced bonding with another person, or was this the first time he had felt loved by someone? I tried not to think about the fast approaching time that I would be leaving him.

Our team spent several hours per day with the children. Divided into groups, we taught the children crafts, sports and sportsmanship, and English as a second language. Due to the short amount of time we had to spend with them, we were limited in what we could do. I was assigned to the crafts group along with Gloria and Lisa. As we observed the children working diligently on the daily projects, we were amazed at how talented they were. Several showed artistic promise. Pictures they drew were creative and beautiful. When they constructed lanterns, some used decorations that made their work stand out. We praised them and made sure they knew that we thought they had done a superb job. The three of us were so proud the next day when we arrived and saw the children's work on display in the main arena.

We had a wonderful group of translators who assisted us in bridging the language gap. While we worked, they would relay our instructions to the children and make sure they understood what we wanted them to do. The younger children enjoyed drawing pictures, making crosses and lanterns, painting, and making shapes with modeling clay. The older girls enjoyed making pillows, while the older boys made tie-dyed tee shirts.

As I looked at the children's projects covering the walls of the orphanage, I began to wonder just who would see their work besides our group and the workers. I knew Wednesdays were visitation days for the children's family members, if they had any, but does the orphanage allow locals to come in and visit with the children? While we were there, I saw several people come and go, but it seemed as though they were visiting with the workers instead of the children.

Although I did see two mothers visit their children, I did not see anyone visit José. He seemed so alone. He would play with the other kids. Occasionally, I would hear him say a few words to another child, but I hardly ever saw him smile. Only when I prepared to take his picture would he sometimes smile. Most days he seemed so sad, and I wondered why. Perhaps he was one of the many who had no family that cared about them, or memories of abuse would occasionally flicker through his mind.

I began to reflect on my own childhood. My father passed away when I was only four years old. My mother had to work to support my sister and me. Luckily, our grandparents were there to take care of us. We grew up with love and stability. These children don't have much of either–maybe stability, since they have a roof over their heads, food to eat, and clothing to wear, and some could say love since the workers tend them, but they lack so much more. Stable relationships are necessary for a child to become healthy and happy. Without love, a part of them will wither away. With no family to provide for their needs, do these kids stand a chance at growing up happy, knowledgeable, energetic, responsible, and self-sufficient? Will José become a street child, involved in a gang, and just another statistic? For now, he is in a safe place. As he grows, I hope he realizes that he can become whatever he desires. All of the children at the orphanage are precious individuals who deserve much love and happiness in their lives.

As the bus left the orphanage the last day, several members of the team fought back tears. One of them, I opened the window as the bus began to pull out and looked desperately for José. I spied him near the gate and reached out to him through the window. He reached up, grabbed my hand, and held on tightly. As our fingers slipped apart, I mouthed the words "I love you." I hope he hears those words often in his life.

--Barbara Sellers Bryan

ZULMA, MY MUSIC GIRL

Byron, our driver, blew the horn, and the doors to the orphanage opened. Nothing could have prepared me for the sea of small bodies that stood against the wall on each side of the van. Chocolate-brown eyes, wide smiles, and waving hands greeted us as the van parked. Surveying the crowd of small bodies, I wondered if they were as excited as I was. A new adventure had begun!

Our instructor, Dr. Timothy Craker, introduced me to a little girl named Zulma. She was nine years old and had raven-colored hair, brown eyes, and a smile that melts the heart. Her younger brother also lived at the orphanage. When she learned that I would be doing music with the group, she became very excited. I soon discovered that she had a love of music. For me, that was our first bonding experience. We grew closer as the days moved on.

Each day Zulma would greet me with a hug and a kiss on the hand. Before I knew it, she had stolen my heart. I was concerned about communication, but found that love can be understood in all languages. Over the weeks at the orphanage I came to the conclusion that Zulma was a very complex little girl. As I looked deeper into those chocolate-brown eyes, I caught glimpses of pain, doubt, and fear. The pain I saw could have come from her past circumstances. Zulma lived with her mother, who is a prostitute. Her mother brought "Johns" home and "worked," at times, in front of the children. To keep the children quiet and out of the way, she gave them drugs to keep them in a sedated state. This drug would also keep them from feeling hungry. How many years has this beautiful little girl had to endure this situation?

Prostitution is a common occurrence in the lives of many children in Guatemala and other nations as well, including the United States. Hearing her story brought back many demons of my own. Her young life mirrors mine in so many ways. Our

154

mothers were similar: hers a prostitute, mine a party girl. Both left their children in horrible situations. Zulma's mother gave them drugs. My mother gave that same type of drug to my brother and tied me to the legs of the kitchen table. Can I relate? You bet!

Zulma did not yet realize how her mother's lifestyle had impacted her, already manifesting itself in her behavior. According to the director of the orphanage, she had been acting out and stealing. Some psychologists report that it is normal for many situations to trigger this behavior in children.

A trigger for Zulma was visitation day. These days were rough for her. I noticed a severe change in attitude. She became extremely sad. Her eyes lost that natural, happy glow I witnessed the first time I met her. She became very standoffish and distant and cried a lot.

Zulma had an episode during art time that caused tears to stain her brown cheeks. She lowered her head and hid her face. Several team members tried in vain to console her. Finally, someone came to tell me that she was calling for me. I went immediately, and she wrapped her arms around me. I walked with her, and we sat down on the slide. Dr. Craker joined us. I held her and kissed her gently on the top of her head. She kissed my head and placed her head in my lap. I was flooded with sad memories of my own children. I knew she was probably feeling abandoned and was missing her mother.

I wanted to let her know that I understood her pain, her loneliness, and her despair. I held her closer and looked into her eyes. I smiled and whispered, "I am here." I knew that I wouldn't need an interpreter because love is the universal language. She smiled as she always did and kissed my hand. Our souls were connected. She felt it, and I did, too.

When I learned about Zulma's background, I was not shocked. I now have an understanding of the hardships of Guatemalan life. Reading *The Americas* has opened my eyes to the horrible situations that many Guatemalans have faced over the past thirty years. Mass genocide has destroyed families, villages, and the economy. Many Guatemalans are competing for the few available jobs. Some women have turned to prostitution and drugs, Zulma's mother among them.

When Zulma is upset, she usually won't interact with the other children. She won't smile or play, but sulks and cries. She reportedly treats others in a mean fashion. I am at a loss as to what to do to help her. I know she has people in her corner who love her, but, at this time, she is not mature enough to understand. I am thankful to Mercer for allowing me to meet Zulma and the other children of the orphanage. With each smile and hug, a deeper understanding of the individual was my goal. I was aware that each child came with his or her own baggage, and each demanded respect and love. What works with Zulma may not work with the next child, but each child needs love.

Zulma's fate is not set in stone. She does not have to follow in her mother's footsteps. We must convince our children that they can achieve anything. Knowledge is the equalizer that will permit our children to reach for the stars and beyond.

Zulma's future as I envision it is filled with success. She will get a great education, find a challenging job, and display her talents. She will not forget her roots and will help others in need. I have confidence in Zulma and her caretakers to give her the best start possible in life. I would love to become fluent in Spanish and one day be able to share my story with her and help her understand that with hard work and persistence she can accomplish anything.

My mission will not be the last one in her life. I am hopeful that others will touch Zulma's life with the light that will aid her. Each hug will strengthen her in the areas where she is weak. Each positive word will lift her spirits and make her realize that she can dream–and dream big–because the future is hers as she reaches for the stars.

Meeting Zulma inspires me to be the best I can be. Inspiration is a two-way street. The give-and-take moments allow growth for each individual.

--Gloria Jordan

HAITI: A BEAUTIFUL AND BRUTAL PLACE

As our small plane crested the mountains, a strong updraft pressed us firmly to our seats, and then seconds later, a downdraft tested our seatbelts as we felt less than weightless. We all looked out the windows and saw the lush foliage below with hills and mountains not far from the frothy shoreline that extended as far as we could see in either direction. Then the plane banked hard and came in for a quick landing on a short runway. The grass was not mowed at the airport. Cows and goats grazed nearby, and a few people were roaming inside the airport grounds right next to the runway. As we pulled up to the terminal that had no electricity and was the size of two bedrooms, Dr. David Lane smiled and observed dryly, "We're not in Kansas anymore."

We had landed in the northern city of Cap-Haitian. From July 12-25, 2010, I was in Haiti with my colleague, Dr. Lane, and three students, Bloodine Bobb-Semple, Rose Donatien, and Oliver Clermont. We were on a mission to train 133 pastors on trauma responses in the wake of the earthquake on January 12, 2010 that had killed at least 300,000 people. Allen, our driver from the Christian University of North Haiti (UCNH), met us at the airport and helped us to his truck as pushy baggage handlers aggressively grabbed our bags, repeatedly ignoring our pleas of *"Non, merci."* Crippled children mingled throughout the crowd, begging in broken English and Creole.

Once we were tightly packed in the truck, we began the thirty-minute ride to Limbe, where UCNH was located. The trip to Limbe reminded me of an earlier journey to Bogota, Colombia, where the drivers had likewise exhibited a biggest-car-wins mentality. Unless you were able to discern the slight order in the chaos, the roads resembled an amusement park bumper-car ride. Allen cut to the right and then the left, dodging two- to three-foot indentations in the road, and honking at the pedestrians who walked or ran across the road with seemingly little concern for their lives. As the truck bounced along toward the university, I learned that the unemployment rate was above fifty percent, which explained the thousands of people milling around along the streets and in and out of the shoddy cement houses with tin-roofs lining the road. As we neared the university, I was grateful for the four-wheel drive of the truck that enabled us to negotiate trails that most Americans would not even consider roads. Once we arrived, I witnessed order, hospitality, hope, and purpose, which had seemed in short supply up to this point.

The Haiti Baptist Convention was meeting at UCNH for their annual convention. The following day we had our training with the pastors who were from all over Haiti. Each night, the limited five to six hours a day of electricity shut off around 11 p.m. We saw stars that we never knew existed. I concluded that we don't often see the bigger picture in life because we are either too distracted or self-centered to stop and notice God's handiwork.

The next morning we spoke to the pastors in a large group. Dr. Lane trained them on normal versus severe trauma responses, explaining a few effective strategies to help earthquake victims process trauma. It quickly became apparent that many of the pastors were wounded healers, as they shared the personal toll of the earthquake within their families, churches, and communities. One of the pastors in my small group asked how he could help a man at his church who continued to call his deceased mother's cell phone daily to hear the recording of her voice. They had retrieved her body and buried it, yet the man was still in complete denial six months later.

Clinically correct answers did not suffice as a response to many of the stories we heard, yet we achieved our goal of working with the pastors. Most of them shared their stories of loss, some for the first time. There were tears and sadness, but there were also numerous passionate and deeply hopeful exclamations of how Jesus Christ is now all they have. They talked about how God had comforted them in their grief in a way that would convert most agnostics. They had walked daily in the peace and purpose of Jesus, with death all around them. I did not envy their lot in life, but I did envy their faith. They lacked money, education, and facilities, but abounded in faith and zeal.

The next day we flew out of Cap-Haitian and into Port-au-Prince. Flying at ten thousand feet offered cooler air, which was welcome since air-conditioning is almost nonexistent in this hot and humid country. We spent a day in Port-au-Prince at the home of student Oliver Clermont. His family was unusual. They were all highly educated, entrepreneurial, and ambitious. Oliver related that most of the people in Haiti are just resigned to their conditions. Oliver and his very hospitable family maintained that poverty in Haiti is more than financial—it is a poverty of ambition, creativity, and desire, all of which reinforce the financial poverty. This perceived lack of ambition in Haitians created a lot of frustration for Oliver and his family over the state of their country, yet, at the same time, they are fiercely proud of their country and love it.

The next day we were in the air Haitian-style, in a twelve-seat turbo-prop plane headed to Jeremie on the southwestern coast of

Haiti. We stayed at the Auberge Inn, a bed and breakfast owned and run by Oliver's Aunt Juliette. For the next nine days we trained eighty-four teachers in disaster preparedness and trauma treatment for schoolchildren. Like the pastors, these teachers were wounded healers. As we taught them several treatment approaches to trauma, they told heart-wrenching stories.

One young man related how he was on his way to the university in Port-au-Prince when the earthquake hit. As he was about to walk into the building, it collapsed in front of him, instantly killing all his classmates and professors. Another man was injured in a building collapse and went with the surviving crowd to a large city park where no buildings could fall on them. When someone in the crowd shouted that the earthquake had caused a tidal wave that would kill them unless they got to higher ground, it triggered a panicked stampede, injuring even more people. As the teachers told their stories, some confessed that this was the first time in six months that they had allowed themselves to be under a roof.

Prior to our training on disaster preparedness for the schools, Haiti had no emergency plans in place in their public schools, not even fire drills. We proceeded to train them for a variety of disaster situations: earthquakes, fires, hurricanes and tornadoes, dangerous intruders, and more. We practiced drills with the teachers, which they found to be hilarious and novel–they had never done them before. Over half of the teachers had not graduated from high school, much less gone to college. However, some of the teachers were well prepared, and most were well intentioned. The lack of standards and organization was shocking.

Like the pastors, the teachers revealed a strong Christian faith. The teachers integrated their faith in the way they coped with trauma, although they continued to struggle with the question of why God would allow such an earthquake. To illustrate how God also grieves with us in our losses, I read aloud to them John 11:35, where we are told that Jesus wept over the death of Lazarus. The teachers responded very positively to the use of scripture. It helped them to make sense, theologically, of the disaster, although the "why" questions were rarely answered.

Haiti is both a beautiful and brutal place, where tragedy is so commonplace that the Haitian people have almost become inured to it. It is a study in contrasts with extreme poverty and a paradise of nature existing side by side. All kinds of fruit grow naturally and plentifully throughout the year, yet many Haitians congregate with very little food in the concrete jungle of Port-au-Prince. The aroma of jasmine and other tropical flowers wafts through the air, mingling with the smell of sulfur and burning trash along the putrid streets. Although almost everyone has cell phones, the teachers in our sessions suggested blowing a conch shell or sending someone on a donkey to announce crisis situations. There is so much need that each effort seems like a mere drop of water in the ocean. Yet the great natural beauty of the country and the unassuming warmth of its people invite us to return to this vineyard in great need of workers.

--Kenyon Knapp

A HIGHER POWER

There are only two ways to live your life: one is as though nothing is a miracle. The other as though everything is a miracle.
–Albert Einstein

Let every soul be subject unto the higher powers, for there is no power but of God. The powers that be are ordained of God.
–Romans 13:1

The two most important days in your life are the day you are born, and the day you find out WHY.
–Mark Twain

Faith sees a beautiful blossom in a bulb, a lovely garden in a seed, and a giant oak in an acorn.
--William Arthur Ward

When you have exhausted all possibilities, remember this: you haven't.
–Thomas Edison

Faith is taking the first step even when you don't see the whole staircase.
--Martin Luther King, Jr.

Be faithful in small things because it is in them that your strength lies.
--Mother Teresa

Faith is to believe what you do not yet see, the reward for this faith is to see what you believe.
--St. Augustine

What after all has maintained the human race ... despite all the calamities of nature and all the tragic failings of mankind, if not faith in new possibilities and courage to advocate them?
--Jane Addams

The art of writing is the art of discovering what you believe.
--Gustave Flaubert

To love another person is to see the face of God.
--Victor Hugo

TRUTH

Several years ago there was a movie called *Liar, Liar* that won the box office sweepstakes. More contortionist than actor, Jim Carrey plays a lawyer who makes his living telling lies. We can hope that Carrey's character is a caricature of lawyers. I have been in the business of educating lawyers, and perhaps more than many professions, I have found that most lawyers have a deep devotion to integrity. Even so, it is not an uncommon perception that truth is hardly the first order of business for a lawyer. The overwhelming view is that their point is to win. Truth be damned. Winning is everything.

In a culture where winning is the driving force, we get terribly confused about truth. It is no wonder we are confused. When the judge asks, "Do you swear to tell the truth, the whole truth, and nothing but the truth?" she is wanting you to assure the Court that what you say will correspond with what you actually know. Without that baseline assurance, the Court is left to wallow in a muddle of empty rhetoric. Witnesses must be trustworthy. On the other hand, if we ask whether someone is a true friend, we are using truth in a very different way. What we are really asking is whether his friendship is reliable and trustworthy. Will he be there in the morning?

In my former life as a full-time college faculty member, I regularly taught courses in logic. When I became an administrator, I learned that logic alone is rarely enough. Life–yours and mine– turns out to be a lot more than logic.

Logic's answer to "What is truth?" is very different, sometimes radically different, from life's answer to "What is truth?" In logic, "true" and "false" are characteristics of propositions. In order to determine whether a statement is true or false, we look to see if what we say corresponds to what is actually happening. Someone says, "It is raining today." If we want to know whether that statement is true, we look out the window or we go outside and see if we get wet. If we go outside without an umbrella, and it is raining, we will get wet. But logic quickly reminds us that getting wet alone will not be enough to establish the truth of whether or not it is raining. Someone could be working on the roof and spill water on our heads as we walk out. But soon, by sight and touch, we can determine whether it is raining. Observation establishes the truth.

Some statements pose a far greater problem to judge if they are true by observation. For example, consider the propositions: "Love endures." "God exists." "Murder is wrong."

There are no observations we can make to determine whether those statements are true or false. Observation alone is not likely to be enough.

Logic has one other avenue for establishing truth. Since some things cannot be easily observed, we try to determine if they fit with what else we know to be true. The truth and falsehood of mathematics depend upon this kind of coherence. Two plus two equals four is true because it fits with what else we know to be true. We cannot always know that simply by observation. Two apples plus two apples equals four apples. Observation is the key. But what about two raindrops plus two raindrops? They look like one small puddle of water. Their "fourness" is not nearly so clear. My point is that logic has its ways of determining truth, but logic's ways alone will not give us enough light to live by.

When logic leaves us feeling empty and cold, where do we turn? People often turn to religion, and even abuse religion, when we come to the end of logic's rope—when we cannot explain the unexplainable. As a matter of fact, some people have great difficulty dealing with religion and faith precisely because they cannot make faith fit into the canons of logic. They say, "Unless I can observe it or deduce it, I will not believe it." We should understand that faith is not a substitute for logic. We need all the logic we can get. Reason is better than nonsense. Reason pushes back the shades on some of our most challenging mysteries, helping us understand disease and tragedy, mapping the human genome, and exploring the universe—overcoming the eclipse of ignorance.

Reason enlightens us, but faith enables us to see even when the light of reason grows dim. We learn from faith that life is more than logic, and we learn that truth is more than a true statement. The most enduring lessons of life will not turn out to be lessons of logic. They are lessons about relating—relating to yourself, relating to other people, relating to what the world is all about. We do not diminish the power of reason, but we should remember that life cannot be lived by logic alone.

In our Western culture we are also quite enamored with the

power of facts. We even get consumed by the facts of our faith. Was the Virgin Birth of Jesus a fact? It is a trivial question. When Jesus said, "The truth shall make you free," he did not say, "The facts will make you free." The goal of religion should not be to get all our facts in order. Faith does not mean developing a neat set of propositions that we can believe to be true without a doubt. Faith is filled with doubt. Ask Peter about doubt. Faith can never be reduced to facts. The Christian faith is not about agreeing to anybody's set of facts. The facts of faith will never make us whole. The fact of Jesus, the fact of his death, the fact of his resurrection will not bring us life or set us free. Faith turns out not to be about facts. Moreover, believing in the Christian faith is not about accepting the facts of Christianity. Such a conclusion would be the ultimate trivialization of Christianity.

The Christian faith is about something far more compelling than facts or logic. It has to do with coming face to face with a whole new order of truth. The truth of the Christian faith is not a statement to accept or a fact to affirm. The truth of which Jesus speaks, the truth that will make us free, is a radically new way of engaging our being here. Isn't it interesting that Jesus did not say to his disciples, "Learn my teachings and you will be my disciples"? He said something far more direct and life-changing. Jesus said, "Come and follow me"–reorder your life. Change your priorities. Reimagine what your life means.

I do not discount the importance of facts. The facts of history are both interesting and very important. There are crops in the field, buildings along the skyline, asteroids in the heavens, and dinosaurs of long ago. The facts matter. Facts describe our being here. We must continually expand our almanac of information. A part of our education is getting our facts in order. Learn the facts. But when we get all our facts straight, we will not be educated. The facts alone will not set us free of ignorance.

Freedom: the facts do not liberate us. Hear again the rather strange words of Jesus: "The truth will make you free." To be honest, you and I probably long far more for freedom than the truth. We do not often long for truth. Indeed, we often hide from the truth. We obscure the truth. We lie about the truth–thinking that hiding or lying will make us free.

There is a yearning to be free that burns within us. We long for freedom because of an overpowering sense of being in bondage. It is not chains or shackles we fear. You and I live in bondage to silent chains. Uncertainty. What's next? Where do we go from here? Does she really care for me? Uncertainty. We are paralyzed by fear–the fear that we will be here, and no one will care.

We live in bondage to ignorance. All of our learning can be scary because it shines a bright light on our ignorance.

We live in bondage to prejudice–prejudice toward people who are different from us–different color, different ideas, different beliefs, different lifestyles. We are in bondage to our prejudice toward the poor, toward women, toward gays.

We live in bondage to our resentments. We hold on to our hurt and often will not let it go.

We live in bondage to bitterness–bitter because of some broken promise, bitter because of yesterday's disappointments. For all of us, life becomes bruised, our souls black and blue from bumping into another's harsh words and painful neglect.

That's where we find ourselves. We long more to be free than to be true, to be free of dread and uncertainty, to be free of fear and bitterness, to be free of resentment and anger that cripple us from within.

Longing to be free, we can reach for freedom in ways that can enrich us or we can grasp for freedom in ways that diminish us and make us lesser people–in the abuse of one another and ourselves through physical violence, so common as to be expected to fill each evening's news. The violence of drug and alcohol abuse numbs our sensitivities. Sexual abuse is growing, not declining. Abuse of those with different sexual orientation is not a sign of holiness–it is a sign of ugliness. We can grasp for freedom by using our power to put other people down. We can grasp for freedom by trying to control other human beings, making them serve our ideas and our priorities. We can pretend to be free by asserting power over others. Excessive and pretentious claims of power–or knowledge, or even virtue–kill and diminish the human spirit.

The truth of our faith that transcends the facts of our faith teaches us to look for freedom not in the accumulation of power or wealth. We cannot even find it by storing up knowledge or virtue–surely good things. We will never acquire enough to be free. The gospel truth stuns us. To be free means to become a person of truth. The truth is not a statement to affirm. The truth is a person to become. You and I are not free when we believe the right things. Right belief has never set anybody free.

The siren's call to craft a set of right beliefs and hold on to them with all our might is to climb aboard a homemade boat that will be dashed to pieces on the shoals of pain and inexplicable grief. We cannot create vessels of true belief that will free us from dread or disease, from turmoil or trouble.

We play games trying to prove that our "truth vessels," our homemade doctrinal and religious boats, are more seaworthy than others. All our religious creeds and our catacombs of doctrines are rickety vessels that we put together to cross a stretch of life's waters. To be sure, we will always keep making our boats. But they have to be mended again and again because they leak and leave us bailing out water, trying to stay afloat. Our homemade statements of religious truth are frail hand-made crafts for sailing on life's turbulent seas. We keep sailing–scared to death, anything but free. All our theologians are plain people: John Calvin, Paul Tillich, Martin Luther–one of my favorites because he was absolutely nuts–and Karl Barth. Most of them are better shipbuilders than most of us. But they make only human ships. Even with God's help, we can make only human ships.

We are not free because we believe the right things or sail in the right religious boats, whether fundamentalist boats or liberal boats. We become free when we become the right person. Our high calling is to find the truth of our lives. Jesus was not about teaching people to believe the right thing but to see themselves, to see God, and indeed to see one another in a new blazing and transforming light. He brought light by which to see the truth of our being here–the only truth that can set us free.

If we take Jesus seriously, we discover that every person is a gift of God to the world. Your high calling and mine is to find that truth in our lives.

Jesus said, "The truth will make you free." And he also said, "I am the Truth." That means that you and I, too, can become the truth. This truth is not a sermon to believe, not even the Sermon on the Mount. The truth is a person to become.

So, the trustworthiness of truth will never lie in what we say. Words will fail us. We cannot utter words–no matter how golden–that will make us free. Our greatest challenge is not for us to tell the truth. Our higher calling is to become the truth. The truth that sustains and persuades is not the truth we say, but the truth we become.

We cannot build our being together with one another or even with God upon words that are true. Speaking true words is important. Speaking truth words is more important. Truth words are more about relating than speaking. Relationships are far more powerful than words. The gospel is not to tell people that God loves them. That is not a transforming gospel. That is only words. The gospel is actually to love somebody. You can't tell the gospel to somebody you don't care about. The truth is not to tell people that there is hope. The truth is to become somebody's hope.

The truth that makes us free is a radically transforming human experience. The early disciples discovered that following Jesus changed everything. It recast their lives. It changed how they went about fishing in the Sea of Galilee. It changed how they collected taxes. It changed how they met Samaritans. It changed how they understood the temple. It changed how they behaved. It changed their priorities. The truth made brothers out of strangers and the truth made strangers out of family. The truth changed everything.

It takes great courage to step out of the life rafts of easy recitation of religious doctrine or secular certainty in which we comfortably live and step into the raging waters that seem certain to engulf us, of loving and being despised for it, of forgiving and being ridiculed for it. Yes, that is what Jesus invited one of his stakeholders, Peter, to do: "Go ahead, Peter, step out of your boat into the high waves and volatile winds." And wouldn't you know, Peter was just crazy enough to do it? Listen up. When you step out of your boat, it does not mean that you will not sink. But for Peter, sinking was not the last word.

Becoming the truth: it means forgiving and loving and taking care of people who don't appear to amount to a hill of beans. This walking in the truth in the midst of life's most difficult waters does not mean that we will not sink. It means that sinking is not the end of our story. We will fail, but failure is not the end of our story.

Here is the truth, the only truth that will set us free. God is with us when our ships are sailing or when they are broken down in dry dock. That truth can set us free from our panic to make it on our own, on our own knowledge or power, or in our own flimsy boats. We can rest from the absolute panic over whether our life rafts of doctrine and religion will see us safely to the shore. They will not. The hope of life is not that we will somehow believe the right things. We do not. The hope of life is that we will follow the truth–that we will become the truth.

Our calling is akin to that of Peter out in his boat on rough waters. Trust yourself to the Truth. Freedom will not lie in gaining enough knowledge. Freedom lies in the courage to become a person of truth. Jesus said, "I am the Truth." You and I, too, can become the Truth–and becoming the Truth and only becoming the Truth will set us free. Amen.

--R. Kirby Godsey

A GRAVE-DIGGING PREACHER

She prays the Lord's Prayer in French.
She quotes the first eighteen lines of Chaucer's *Canterbury Tales* by heart, in Old English.
She reads the Bible and C.S. Lewis.
She lives on the street.
She digs "The Hill" for scrap metal that she can sell so she will have a little change in her pocket.
She realizes that her addiction causes her to spin out of control sometimes.
She wants to be sober.
She is a mass of contradictions, as we all are.
I have known her for several years.
She is my friend.

Last week, her love died.
Traveler offered her protection from the dangers of the street.
He would often say, "Pray your prayer in French," and was comforted by the words he did not understand.
They were as much a couple as any two people can be.
They sat under the Spring Street bridge and shared these vows:
"Where you go, I will go. Where you lodge, I will lodge."
But Traveler died a couple of weeks ago of a massive brain hemorrhage at the Medical Center in Macon.
There were no other family members other than my very bright and articulate friend who lives on the street.

With conflicted emotions, she offered Traveler's body to others who needed him.
Both kidneys and his liver were used to save others.
The gift gave her a bit of a lift.
But then a great sadness descended. A darkness visible.

On Wednesday I put Traveler's ashes in my car, along with a shovel and a pick.
I picked up my friend, and we made our way to Wilkinson County to bury Traveler's ashes.
When I say bury, I mean bury.
I have never done *everything* that needed to be done at a cemetery.
I did everything on Wednesday.

I have thought about that a lot
And have concluded that I probably need my friend much more than she needs me.
It is her presence (and the presence of some other friends) who save me from being insulated.
Insulation is a dangerous condition for the soul.

So, I took my shovel, pick, Bible, and Book of Worship, and I dug a grave for Traveler.
A grave-digging preacher–that is what I am.
I asked my friend to say the Lord's Prayer in French at the grave, and even to quote Chaucer.
She also recited "The Owl and the Pussycat," one of Traveler's favorites.
I said a few stammering words in the face of death, and I read Psalm 23.
Words of grief, sadness, memory, longing, and hope–"Hope" with a capital "H."

We then drove back to Macon, and I took my friend to detox.
I want her to be well and sober.
She agreed to go to detox.
Actually, it was her idea.

So, pray for my friend.
And pray for me as a grave-digging preacher.
And pray for me as I reflect on covering that grave.
And pray for yourself.

In the midst of the story, I find my heart filled with gratitude.
Can you understand that?
Let those who have eyes, see.
Let those who have ears, hear.

--Tim Bagwell

PROFOUND GRACE – A STAR IN THE EAST

Matthew 17:1-9

A couple of months ago, I found that there is much to be learned in the mountains of Georgia. My husband and I woke up on Sunday, August 19th, showered and dressed for church. We sat down to a breakfast of tomatoes, cucumbers, ham, salami, cheese, bread, cookies, orange-pineapple juice, and Nescafé coffee. This isn't sounding very familiar, is it? We were in Georgia, but we were in a guesthouse owned by the Evangelical Baptist Church of Georgia–Tbilisi, Georgia. We were half a world away from home!

Frank and I had been invited several months earlier to participate in a worship service in the mountains of Georgia, celebrating the Feast of the Transfiguration and the 140th anniversary of Baptist work in that country.

I cannot ever remember focusing my attention on the Transfiguration, though I was aware of the story. Celebrating the Transfiguration–the Feast of Transfiguration–sounded rather liturgical, and a bit foreign to me. I really wasn't sure of what we were getting ourselves into.

We had arrived on Friday night about 10:30 in a new airport. After traveling for twenty hours, we were tired and a little anxious about getting through customs. Fortunately, Frank had been sitting next to a young Georgian woman on our flight from London to Tbilisi. She was a student at Oxford, knew something of our host, and answered many questions about life in her home country.

When we entered the airport, she was ahead of us, and as she finished talking with the customs official, she turned and told us that she had identified us as her friends, hoping to smooth our way. Our luggage was ready for pickup, and we approached another set of doors, hoping that someone familiar would be on the other side.

We were met by our friend Bishop Malkhaz (Yes, a Baptist bishop!), who was wearing a purple robe, sandals, and a cross-shaped pendant. With his long beard, he was the picture of a clergyman, recognizable as such by anyone.

Malkhaz introduced us to his driver, who sped through town on modern roads lined with well-lit advertisements. Without the pictures we would never have understood the signs–the Georgian alphabet is quite unique, round and loopy in character. Once we left the modern roads, though, we were on dirt alleys that led from one residence to another behind stone walls. Following what seemed like a maze of alleys, we finally stopped at a locked door.

Malkhaz knocked, carried on a lively Georgian conversation with two women, obviously about which room we would stay in and what our schedule for the next day would be like. He told us what time we would have breakfast and when we would be picked up, and then we were left behind with the hosts of the guesthouse who spoke no English!

Our room was spacious with two cots for sleeping, an open window for fresh air, and a private bathroom. The shower had no curtain, and the tank of the toilet leaked constantly, but the water was hot and the smiles of our hosts who served us breakfast the next morning were warm. We were surprised when the driver arrived alone to pick us up. He knew no English; we knew no Georgian; and we had to trust that he knew where to take us!

On Saturday morning at his office in the Beteli Center, Malkhaz met us, along with a dozen women from the American Baptist Churches in the United States who were there for the weekend celebration. Though not yet complete, this new facility includes housing for elderly women, space for theological educa-tion, and an iconography center for Christian art.

Baptists in Georgia have embraced the artwork of their cul-ture, and the array of icons being painted at the Center was fasci-nating in style, color, and subject matter. Icons may tell a complex story in a simple narrative scene (the Last Supper or the Trans-figuration), or they may depict individuals of significance–Jesus, Mary, the disciples.

Imagine our surprise in going to the "other" Georgia to find an icon of the Reverend Martin Luther King, who is well respect-ed for his stance on peace and reconciliation, values that Baptists embrace there!

This begs the question–having formerly been a part of the Soviet Union, and now surrounded by Muslim countries, how is it that there are Baptists and other Christians in this country? As we learned, the oldest Orthodox Church building in Georgia was constructed in the fourth century. (Remember that the first Christians to live on our own Georgian soil came in the eighteenth century!)

The country is ninety percent Orthodox with some seeing Orthodoxy as the state religion. A wealthy businessman who does not claim to have a religious faith recently built one very lavish church that we visited.

There are signs of a hyper-conservative bent in church practices developing in the Orthodox Church, and this is in striking contrast to the openness of Georgian Baptists. Baptists have been in the minority for 140 years, yet religious and political leaders alike feel their presence.

Late in the 1980s, Malkhaz was a university professor from Georgia who was in the midst of graduate studies in theology at Oxford in England. When the Soviet Union fell, he was called back home to lead the Baptist denomination in a new and different landscape.

He and local church leaders made a conscious decision to create a Baptist body for the people of Georgia, rather than simply for themselves. They embrace their cultural background, and they seek to model inclusiveness and respect for faiths that are different from theirs. As evidence of this, Bishop Malkhaz invited Orthodox, Muslim, and Baptist individuals to worship, to honor the Baptist presence, and to celebrate the Feast of Transfiguration on the mountain this year—almost unthinkable!

By 9:00 that Sunday morning we were on a bus headed into the mountains, which was particularly fitting since we were celebrating the occurrences on the Mount of Transfiguration. Our bus was part of a caravan of various vehicles, all full of excited men, women, and children.

Once we left the city, efforts to avoid potholes kept us weaving from side to side and bumping up and down. There was a steep drop-off on the right side of the road. When we were on the left, we were passing other vehicles on uphill curves. It was a frightful ride for some of the American guests who had never taken such a trip before, but I was loving it!

After a couple of hours, our bus driver decided that he had

gone far enough. The road was too bad for him to continue, and he pulled off to the side. Fortunately, Georgians are expert users of cell phones and text messaging. A van that had already reached the top of the mountain returned to pick up the first half of our group. Since Frank was a key participant in the service, we were asked to board the van.

Our destination was an impressive monument to Georgia's triumph under the leadership of David the Builder over a large Turkish army in 1121. The surrounding meadows, knee-deep grasses and flowers, were marked by dozens of massive swords pushed into the ground, their hilts looking much like crosses. An amphitheater on the side of the mountain seated those who had come for worship. Stone steps led up to the top of Mount Didgori where our procession would begin. (I now wish that I had counted the steps, but I'm sure I would have been much too out of breath to keep up with the numbers.)

Several willing helpers with suitcases containing gold and white vestments were at the top to dress Malkhaz, Frank, a female minister, and another male minister in what Malkhaz called "full gear." My role was to join others in descending all of those steps I had climbed (using a different set of muscles) and placing bread on the communion table in the amphitheater, while Frank joined in the litany with an interpreter by his side. My understanding of the service was limited to what I could sense without knowing the language.

What did I see? I saw a large amphitheater filled with several hundred people who were there to worship and celebrate together, the inclusion of men, women, and children as worship leaders, the offerings of many shapes and sizes of bread, and the use of a single wine cup for all worshipers who approached the table for Communion. I witnessed the creative works that produced flags for the procession, beautiful vestments for the worship leaders, and liturgical dances by young women dressed in black. There were willing assistants who replenished the bread and wine during Communion with no thought of recognition.

And what did I hear? I heard music and singing, both in worship and following the midday meal, a beautiful language being used to worship our one God, and laughter and friendly words among all the participants.

There was even a wedding, complete with crowns for the

bride and groom. Guests, including me, gave greetings to the crowd. There were people from all across the country and–with us and the American Baptist women–from around the world.

By mid-afternoon we were ready for dinner-on-the-ground (literally), Georgian style! There were breads, cheeses, meats, fish, tomatoes, eggplant, watermelon, wine, and much, much more–all fresh. There was music–strings, accordion, drums, and flute.

So, what was this Feast of the Transfiguration about–and is there something we could learn from these Georgian Baptists on the other side of the globe?

We can turn to accounts of the Transfiguration in scripture. Matthew, Mark, and Luke recorded it, and we heard the account written in Matthew in the worship service today. Recent conversations between Jesus and his disciples focused on the suffering that Jesus would endure and the cost of discipleship. Jesus invited Peter, James, and John to accompany him to a mountaintop to pray.

While there, Jesus' face and clothing took on a dazzling white color, and the disciples found themselves in the company of Moses and Elijah. Peter suggested building tents/shelters/booths for the three holy men.

A voice was heard from a cloud, saying, "This is my beloved Son; listen to him!" Peter, James, and John responded in fear, yet Jesus said, "Rise, and do not be afraid."

If there is anything we can learn about the disciples from a careful reading of the gospels, it is that they were slow–very slow–to understand their leader, his relationship with God, and the Kingdom of Heaven he promised them. You might think that an event like the Transfiguration would make a life-changing impression on them. But let's hold that thought for a moment.

Why Moses and Elijah? They are the best examples of law and prophecy in the Hebrew Scriptures. Their presence affirms the continuity of Jesus' work with previous spokesmen (and women) who represented God to the people.

If we look deeper, we can liken Jesus' mastery of the sea and the feeding of multitudes to stories of Moses' leadership. Jesus' multiplying of loaves, cleansing lepers, and raising the dead conjure memories of Elijah the Prophet. Events in Jesus' life would be interpreted by alluding to events in the history of God's redemption of Israel.

But tents/shelter/booths? Can you imagine the dismay–the sadness–in Jesus' face when his disciples suggested commemorating the event rather than showing more inclination to follow him? Jesus had brought them before God in prayer. He was teaching the hard lesson of obedience to God, and God used this opportunity to clearly affirm his relationship with Jesus.

Surely the disciples felt chastened when Jesus did not respond to the idea of booths. They must have realized that they had not "gotten" the meaning of this holy moment, but determined to do better the next time.

Isn't that what we catch ourselves doing, too? Today we just "don't get it," but tomorrow, yes, tomorrow we will listen more carefully and obey with more conviction.

Thinking back on this day of worship and celebration has taught me more. The service was full of pageantry–Georgian to the core. But it was Baptist pageantry, full of scripture and inclusiveness of all who attended. Everyone was invited to participate–young and old, male and female, well-to-do and not, Christians and Muslims.

There were liturgical dancers with colorful ribbons who told the story of strife between different peoples of the world and the unity they could experience if they follow God's lead and make that effort. Georgia Baptists have become examples for their society of how to help their neighbors in need and to turn the other cheek, and on this day, among those of different faiths, they were able to show their intent.

The service was full of symbolism–Georgian to the core. But it was Baptist symbolism. There was the blessing of an icon of the Transfiguration. Moses, Elijah, Jesus, Peter, James, and John were all included, and all with such expressive eyes–Georgian.

There was the use of a cross, made of nails, reminding all of the suffering of Christ. There were doves that three children held carefully until it was time for them to fly and symbolize the resurrection–God's grace to the world.

There was a message linked to a piece of coal–Georgian to the core. I did not understand its use at the time, so I asked about it later. Bishop Malkhaz raised the coal high for all to see. "This coal lay far below the surface for many, many years before we realized its potential to give energy. Who would have thought that something as small and black as coal could provide warmth for so many people? The energy inside of coal is like the transforming power of Jesus.

"It is like Baptists in Georgia who did not know their potential until later! We need to release this power into the world with respect for those of other faiths and a desire to understand them better. We have come to this mountain to experience God's presence, to acknowledge his ability to work in us, and to join others in prayer and communion.

"Like the disciples, we have failed in understanding God's intentions for our lives; but we are here, back on the mountain to be reminded of the power we hold. Like coal, we need a flame."

In scripture we have a beautiful image of human beings awed by the divine, but encouraged to stand on their feet and not to fear. It is a moment of profound grace. Reminders of what happened at the Transfiguration give new meaning to our lives. Our ambitions may be seen in a new light. A flame may be kindled, and we are renewed. At the time, the disciples did not understand the message at Transfiguration, but they did not stay on the mountain. Duties called, and life moved on.

The Transfiguration affirms the relationship between God and his Chosen Son, but it points us back to our everyday lives, the struggles and the tasks that give our lives meaning, the need to obey God's call. The view at Transfiguration was majestic, but the road calls us back to a life of purpose. The Georgians I met that day could not stay on their mountain either.

I will tell you, the road that calls in Georgia is not an easy one! Georgia is an economically deprived country, and its people suffer. Georgia's standard of living declined significantly when it asserted its freedom from the Soviet Union, and winters have been particularly difficult since Russia cut heating oil/natural gas lines in retribution.

Yet Baptists there are making a difference to the elderly whose monthly pension is only seven dollars; those who are cold in the harsh winters for lack of warm blankets; young ministers, men and women alike, who need training to be effective Eastern European pastors; children who are orphans; and immigrants who are political enemies but who are treated as neighbors–all the while celebrating their culture and the place they hold in representing Christ to the rest of the world.

Our trip back down the mountain was just as bumpy as on

the way up, but I trusted our driver and took a nap. My faith is
in a God who is working among Baptists in Georgia. They have
responded with such grace by going into the mountains to provide
aid to Chechen refugees, people who in centuries past kidnapped
Georgians and sold them into slavery. Moved by their hospitality,
one Muslim imam responded, "When I return home I will do two
things. I will build a new mosque, because ours was destroyed by
the Russians, and I will build a Baptist church, because the Baptists were the only people with us in our time of need."

Orthodox attackers insulted Baptists, burned their Bibles, and
ransacked their churches. Surprisingly, they were brought to trial.
Recognizing that the attackers had no clear understanding of the
Christian faith, Bishop Malkhaz took time at their trial to speak
about the true values of Christianity, the ecumenical movement,
and the importance of religious liberty for everyone.

"What do you wish to happen to these prisoners?" the judge
asked. Malkhaz replied, "I demand that these people be pardoned
and released from the prison. I do not demand anything from them
except the red [communion] wine which we will drink together
when they are set free."

I cannot help but marvel. In a country where Baptists are
a minority and life is hard, it would be easy to fear. It would be
easy to retreat into the church and never come out, to speak among
themselves of God's grace, but never leave the mountain.

Yet, Bishop Malkhaz calls out, "Rise, and be not afraid."
His call reaches further than the boundaries of the Republic of
Georgia. Georgian congregations respond with compassion to
tragedies in other parts of the world (the tsunami, Katrina, terrorist
bombings in Europe, deaths of 9/11 firefighters), holding worship
services to honor those in harm's way and allowing government
leaders to participate and acknowledge suffering that might otherwise be disregarded for political reasons.

"Rise, and be not afraid," Malkhaz speaks to women who are
called to the ministry in a country where such is unheard of. We
worship a God who made himself known through Jesus Christ and
who calls us, male and female, to discipleship.

"Rise, and be not afraid," Malkhaz says as he acknowledges
the Jewish heritage of his Christian faith by displaying a menorah
near the altar of his church.

"Rise, and be not afraid"–I am quite certain that Bishop

Malkhaz has heard this call himself. How else, in the face of violence and prejudice, can he say, "I believe it is a pagan understanding that the activity of the clergyman should be carried on within the walls of a temple only. We as Christian leaders are not attached to the church buildings and walls but rather to the people.

"We should be where the people are suffering. We should be closer to those who are oppressed and humiliated, to those who are determined to fight with nonviolent means against regimes that deprive people of their human dignity."

We in Western civilization do ourselves and others a great disservice in thinking that we alone have the answers to the world's economic, sociological, political, and spiritual dilemmas. We have gone far too long without looking toward the East for revelations of God's profound grace. There is much to be learned in the mountains of Georgia.

--Susan G. Broome

FAILURE

I used to periodically flee from church services, especially from those at Holy Comforter Church in Atlanta. It was there that I landed after a massive ejection from a relationship that, in hindsight, I see, was without fruit, but one in which I had become complacent. I would have been content to stay in it forever–and must therefore be continually grateful to my partner for kicking me out. Hindsight lets me know that it was only meant to be a resting place for me–that to stay and not move on would have been like stepping out of the river that is my life, retreating from its challenges, and therefore from the opportunities presented for me to grow.

I have come to believe that this is the major purpose in all of our lives--simply to grow towards the light, like the avocado plant a friend of mind had that was growing very crookedly because it was stretching itself in the direction of the window. I once suggested she turn it to face away from the window so that it would grow back towards the light, thereby straightening itself up. She replied very, very tenderly: "Oh, no! After all that work?" She did not turn the plant.

My partner had no such tenderness for me. I was contentedly

growing in a steady, easy, not too demanding pattern. Boom! My pot wasn't just turned around–it was thrown out, smashed on the sidewalk, shattered, my roots exposed and thirsty, and no quenching water or nourishing soil seemed to be within my sight, much less my reach.

So I left Columbus, Georgia and headed back to familiar territory–Atlanta. I went to the Episcopal bishop there and asked him to help me find a pot that fit my roots. We talked for a good long time before he directed me to Holy Comforter Church, a little church where the main congregation consisted of mentally challenged people who lived in group homes on SSI or disability checks. I loved that church. The soil was rich and yummy. However, it was a challenging time for me. It was, indeed, like being born again. I am not referring to a momentary euphoria of insight or an ecstatic trip to the front of the church at the altar call. No–this was more like the actual thing: a long, violent, bloody process of being ripped from everything you have ever known and thrust into a new and foreign way of being, involving a lot of wailing and screaming.

That explains the bolting. Sometimes, the presence of God in that place would get to be so overwhelming that, like the psalmist confessing "Whither can I flee from thy spirit?" in Psalm 131, I felt the need to escape from it. For that reason, I experienced a few Eucharistic moments that took place on the church grounds instead of inside the church.

Sometimes one of our troubled congregants would flee first, giving me the excuse to follow as a "caretaker." Once I followed a schizophrenic woman, Mary, who had become upset during the service and had run out shouting something about the Queen of England needing to be told immediately where she, Mary, was. The conversation took place on two levels, like the kind of coded conversation between Jesus and the woman at the well.

"I have living water," Jesus explains.

"But you have no bucket," confronts the woman.

"The Queen is looking for me, but they won't let 'er come!" Mary howled in her cockney accent. She was American born and raised, but I never heard her speak without the cockney.

"And if she would only come?" I ventured.

"Then she would take me to my rightful place," she explained.

"So, this isn't your rightful place?" I queried.

"Oh, no!" she shouted. "Oh no! They brought me here and left me. The Queen, you know–she wouldn't stand for it! She is looking for me, but they don't want 'er to know!"

"I will tell her where you are," I offered.

"She won't 'ear you!" she wailed. "They won't let her 'ear you!"

"They won't recognize me," I leaned in and whispered, a little conspiratorially. "She will hear me, and she will come for you. It will take a while, but she will come. She will do this. (I put my arms around her and rocked her a little.) Then you will know you are home."

Mary made little moaning sounds as we rocked. She graciously clung to my meager consolation as if it were a fragile raft floating tenuously on her great sea of inconsolability.

Another time, when I fled on my own steam, I found myself in the company of another parishioner, a man in his fifties who had followed me out. I don't remember his name, or even the gist of the conversation we were having, probably because of the turmoil in my family relations at the time. What I do remember is the stark statement of truth that poured over me like warm oil.

"I have a sister," he said, "who is very involved in peace and justice work. It is her whole life. Yet, she cannot be in the same room with her family. I have always wondered at that: how can you stand for peace and justice when you hold your own family in such contempt that you cannot even be on speaking terms with them? Where is the peace and reconciliation in that?"

That brings me face to face with my current failure: my present inability to live up to the ideals that my whole life is supposed to be about. I have had the hubris to include myself as one of those people who stand against injustice and for peace. I have struggled and continue to struggle long and hard to reconcile with my family, to learn to forgive on a personal level, which includes learning to forgive and accept myself. And yet, here I am again, face to face with the terrific anger inside myself–staring down the death-grip I have on petty grievances and facing off with my stern unwillingness to forgive and move on.

When I look into the mirror, I see a self-absorbed, control freak of a woman who yells like a nutcase at students who don't even–well, okay, they do–ask for it. They are middle school students, after all. But that's just who they are–and I am supposed to be better than that. And I am not. I am not better than that. This is what I find so very hard to accept.

I feel like I have been such a toady most of my life, the way I have sidled up to God, brownnosing, unctuous with false humility, groveling for an "in" with the Big Guy. I have never even been jealous of everyone being special to God, because somewhere in a shameful corner of my brain and heart, I actually believed I was building up enough brownie points to make me just that little bit "specialer" than anyone else.

The bottom line is that I still just don't get God's Love. I still want God to pick me, just me, love me best. I want to be someone's favorite. Ironically, if I become someone's favorite, it doesn't seem to count–as in, well of course, I'm his favorite; he married me, which just shows how little his opinion counts." It's not enough for me. I want to be the ultimate favorite–God's favorite. Why can't I be?

The better question is why can't I understand love that doesn't play favorites? Why can't I feel that love that doesn't pick me as the favorite? Why is there such a hole in me?

I have heard of the "God-shaped hole" people have and I used to smugly believe that the hole in me had been filled by God a long time ago. But now I am finding out that no relationship is safe, not even my relationship with God. Someone keeps moving my flower pot around and I have to keep relocating the light and reorienting myself to it and growing back towards it and yes–as my tender-hearted gardening friend indicated, it is a lot of work, a lot of work.

I understand that God will never pick me in the way I want Him to–to the exclusion of others. No, I have to pick God–over and over and over again. And it is indeed hard work.

So–is it I or God or just the evil in this world that keeps turning my pot around and around?

I thought I was picking God when I started my new job. I thought I was following the Light. Maybe I was. Maybe God intended for me to crash and burn, to bang up against the hubris that told me I could do anything, with God on my side. That's quite a presumption–the God-on-my-side thing. It has led many a human being straight into Hell.

Maybe I was following my ego, my desire to fix the world,

my desire to be anointed by God to do something big, instead of just listening and making the simple next step I could see on this unclear path. Maybe God really just wants me to fix myself right now, to turn inward instead of spending everything I have to give outside of my own home.

Why isn't there a formula? We walk along a tightrope here balanced between being too outwardly focused in helping our brothers and sisters in need and too inwardly focused, only taking care of our own family and close friends. How does one get the balance right?

I am fifty-eight years old, and I haven't a clue. How could I work this hard and come this far only to discover I haven't a clue? And how do I keep moving forward when I haven't a clue where forward is? Maybe I have lost all sense of direction and am just running and running and running, making concentric circles. If so, my question is whether they are leading me ever closer to the center or taking me farther and farther and farther outward and away?

Again, I haven't a clue. But this I do know: We are meant to continue to stretch our weary selves this way and that, up, down, around, and under, to keep reaching towards the Light of God. We are even graced with a few brief moments of rest here and there, moments when we face it head on, feeling the warmth press against our cheeks, breathing in its health and nourishment, and yes, its bliss. But to stay there is to die. So along comes the mischievous gardener who tends my pot and spins it round again.

And again I know I am alive.

--Mary Palmer Legare

IMAGES OF COURAGE: SERMON NOTES

High Street Unitarian Universalist Church
January 24, 2010

Little did I know during our service in November that honored Universalist Clara Barton, the founder of the American Red Cross (and we had the Red Cross flag draped across our pulpit), that the Red Cross would be playing such a major role in the earthquake catastrophe in Haiti just a few months later.

Little did I know when I sent the title of this sermon, "Images of Courage," to Carole Dixon and Marie Holliday on the 18th of December for our January newsletter that we would be viewing the death and destruction as well as extraordinary acts of courage coming out of Haiti.

Little did I know on the tenth of January, when we talked about Joseph Lister, antiseptic spray, carbolic acid dressings, and the importance of keeping wounds free from infection, that our eyes would be riveted on the makeshift operating rooms in Haiti. And that people would be dying from infection before surgery or after surgery due to infection.

Events like the earthquake in Haiti are profound reminders of how fragile and tenuous all life really is. I have come to believe that every person who wakes each day and lives out his or her life does so with an unspoken but extraordinary courage and resilience. I have come to believe that we cannot survive without courage. Life is filled with too many twists and turns and detours and disappointments. Courage, to me, is our capacity to create meaning and live out our lives in the face of the uncertainties on our journey and the certainty of our death.

For me, the uncertainties on the journey and the certainty of our own finitude create the soil out of which all religion is created. And so for us to ponder and reflect on the subject of human courage is a religious and spiritual act.

I am often drawn to the responsive reading that we used this morning entitled "Impassioned Clay" by Rev. Ralph Helverson. I have read many times the closing sentence of that reading, and it feels appropriate to read it again now as I invite you to think for a while this morning about the subject of *courage*.

Listen now to Rev. Helverson:

We have religion when we have done all that we can, and then in confidence entrust ourselves to the life that is larger than ourselves.

I cannot tell you what, if any, underlying theological groundings may be embedded in that sentence for you; but I can try to tell you what it means to me and how it is connected, for me, to the subject of *courage*. I find myself comforted every time I read those words. I think it is a soft reminder that I am part of a continuum of life–a grand procession of generations. It is a reminder that *in a deeply spiritual sense* I am not alone. *Others have come before me*, have faced challenges and struggles and joys and disappointments, and have, in the course of their life journeys, lived courageously in the face of the unknown, or in face of the known over which one is trying to prevail.

Several weeks ago we shared together the responsive reading by Norman Cousins entitled "The Body is Humankind." Even though the population has increased dramatically since he wrote these words, I find the spirit of his language hopeful: "We are single cells in a body of four billion cells." I draw strength and courage from that kind of image–the picture that all life is connected, each contributing its life force to the common pool of life and energy, that we are all part of a common life.

On the one hand, I am drawn to live as best I know how and moved to being the best that I can be. On the other hand, I am comforted in sensing that when I have done all that I can do, the larger life to which I am connected will continue and that this larger life will be richer for my having lived. It will both be shaped by my shortcomings and failures and absorb them. The larger life will continue as the sum of all the acts of all life before me.

Two weeks ago we installed our new board members and officers for the coming year. The newly installed folks spoke words of promise to the congregation. And the congregation spoke words of commitment back to them. One of the phrases that both sets of promises had in common was this: "We bring our gifts and our flaws and we invite you to accept them both."

As we find ways to live out our lives together here in this religious community, we do and will continue to bring both our gifts and our flaws. The institution has a life larger than our own. We are each vital to its life. It is also large enough and strong enough to be shaped and enriched by absorbing all our gifts and all our flaws. The institution will continue and the world will continue, enriched by our having lived. I believe that our church can be a place that invites us to know, again and again, on many different levels, of the courage that each person has and carries and uses when it is needed.

Courage comes in all sizes and shapes and times and places. Courage is in our ordinary day-to-day living, not just on a battlefield or the site of earthquakes. Learning of the courage of others reminds us of the courage within ourselves.

Several weeks before Christmas, I attended the funeral of

184

two children who died in a house fire here in Macon. One was a twelve-year-old girl. The other was her four-year-old sister. The four-year-old was in my class at Hartley School. The attendance at the funeral was overflowing. I spent the hour outside the church along with many other people. One person with whom I spent the hour was Gloria Jordan. She is the African American paraprofessional in the class of four-year-olds where I read stories and the class the four-year-old who died had attended. It took Gloria Jordan two buses and an hour and a half to get to the funeral from her home.

I learned that forty years ago when Gloria was a young girl, she watched Mercer baseball games from across the street on her aunt's front porch. She had a secret dream of going to college. She will be graduating from Mercer in the spring. I plan to be there to honor her journey, her courage, her accomplishment. She first went back to school as an adult and attended Macon Technical Institute, which later became Central Georgia Technical College. In her article that appears in *Regeneration! A Journal of Creative Writing,* Gloria Jordan confesses her terror during those first few weeks:

> *I felt I was too old, not smart enough, and out of place....*
> *"What kept me going?" you might wonder. A young woman from one of my classes stopped me in the hall one day, commenting, "Ms. Jordan, I love being in class with you. You are smart and funny and make learning fun for me. I try every week to make better grades than you. If you make an A, then I want one, too. I am glad you're here."*

Gloria Jordan, in her essay, testified about the impact of the younger woman's words: *"Utterly amazed that I could so positively impact the lives of others, I fought back the tears."* So, the younger woman in the class blessed the older woman with words of affirmation. And the affirmation called forth a newly discovered sense of confidence. I believe that this kind of encounter, this kind of blessing, can affirm a sense of worth and dignity, and that this strengthened sense of worth and affirmation of dignity can be a profound source of courage just at a time when courage is needed. I believe that the intentionality of the interactions in this church community can also provide blessings and affirmations that are as important and timely and as powerful as the blessing which the young student bestowed upon Gloria Jordan.

Sometimes, courage is called forth from within. Sometimes, it is called forth from the most mysterious and unexpected places, outside of ourselves, beyond our prediction, planning, or sense of possibilities. Ms. Jordan tells us in her article about the awesome experience of being a student at Mercer and being a part of the group of "Regeneration Writers."

> *I have had the chance to research my father, a man I never met, and look into the injustices of his life and the events leading to his death by electrocution in Georgia's prison system. I sat on a panel called "Four Faces from Death Row," representing my father and allowing his story to be heard for the first time.*

Her Mercer experience gave her the courage to find ways to become acquainted and connected to the stories of her biological family, and especially the father she never knew. I hope that all of you who are connected in any way with Mercer will feel a special bond with this extraordinary woman, Gloria Jordan. She says,

> *Attending Mercer has allowed me to be a role model for my children and grandchildren. I will graduate in May 2010 knowing that I am the first in my family not only to graduate from high school, but also to receive a degree from one of the best academic institutions in the world. The habits of inquiry and reflection and the values of integrity, diligence, and community will characterize this grateful and jubilant Mercerian. Glory, Glory Hallelujah! Gloria Jordan is marching on.*

I am indebted to Gloria Jordan for reminding me that courage comes from both external and internal sources. I would like to pause for a moment and invite you to think for a moment about a time when someone spoke with you and shared what you might describe as life-affirming words–your life. And that their words, their blessing, so to speak, restored your sense of confidence, *or gave you a newfound sense of confidence about yourself and the world in which you live.*

I invite you to quietly name and remember the person and their words of blessing and support and care of you. I invite you to be filled with thanksgiving for that special person in your life and what he or she meant to you at a particular moment. Now I would quietly invite you to think about how you might pay that forward. Think about someone in your life right now whom you might find some way to bless, to encourage, to affirm, to support in some words, gestures, or actions today, before the day is finished. The younger student had nice things to say about Gloria Jordan at the very moment when Gloria needed to hear them–and moved her so powerfully that tears came to her eyes. Confidence was created in that moment–in the midst of those tears. You can also choose to be a part of creating confidence that did not exist before by being present, being aware, being compassionate, and being intentional.

Here is a brief scene behind prison bars written by Andrew Legare on Death Row on April 17, 1987. This is part of a poem written for *Regeneration!*:

> *Yesterday I was walking in the prison yard, circling the 100 square feet of brushed and measured concrete enclosed by 12 feet of chain-link fence topped and stranded with barbed and razored wire. The thought about good fences making good neighbors crossed my mind, and I laughed ...*
> *... I looked across the yard to the grass growing so thick and carelessly green outside the fences. I breathed deeply, hoping to partake of the spring freshness and pull it through my veins. A crack in the concrete caught my eye. I looked again at the grass outside the fences, then turned back to look down at one small single-leafed stem rising up from a narrow split in the concrete slab.*
> *My thoughts whirled. My heart jumped. The razor wire glimmered in the sun ... One solitary seed, blown thoughtlessly by the wind or dropped by some passing bird, had fallen helpless into the crack, surrounded by tons of concrete, lacking even the power to crawl free.*
> *Yet, with a uniquely frail tenacity and singularity of purpose–inscrutable, indomitable–it had burst forth, singing its brave face into the blazing sun with a bright green duality of song, proclaiming the pain, the joy, the gift of life. My heart sang out. Even so it sang. Even so sings the human spirit.*

Andrew Legare's poem inspired Yvonne Gabriel, Mercer student and artist from the Netherlands, to paint the picture of the flower breaking through the tough terrain of the concrete–evidence for Andrew and Yvonne of the resilience of life–a fitting visual for a collection of stories entitled *"Regeneration!"*

When I read Andrew Legare's words, I went immediately to my copy of our hymnal and turned to the words of Thomas Wolf, a responsive reading entitled "Some Things Will Never Change" (#555):

> *But under the pavements trembling like a pulse, under the buildings trembling like a cry, under the waste of time, under the hoof of the beast above the broken bones of cities, there will be something growing like a flower, something bursting from the earth again, forever deathless, faithful, coming into life again like April.*

A visceral human response of courage is often called forth at special times of need. And that internally created and called-forth sense of courage can often be strengthened by expressions of care, hope, and affirmations of others.

Some of those special times that come to mind are these:

When a serious medical challenge comes into your life or the life of a family member or friend;

When you are out of work and seeking employment;

When you are beginning a new life after the death of a spouse;

When you move to a new city or town;

When you start a new job;

When you start first grade, high school, or college;

In each of these times, courage is needed.

Courage is needed . . .

to speak your mind on a subject important to you when you know such views are in a minority.

when you are in your first play.

when you sing a solo or you are in the choir.

to serve as president of a congregation.

to claim your sexuality, through words or gesture, if experience tells you it is not safe to do so.

Courage must surely be present when a family experiences the death of a child or young adult and must find ways to rebuild a life beyond such a void.

Courage must surely be present when a family experiences the suicide of a loved one and must find ways to move forward and

188

create a new world.

Courage is needed to . . .

end an unhealthy relationship.

begin a life after being in prison for a long time.

be a parent of a child.

be a teen or a parent of a teen.

be a parent of an adult child who is dysfunctional.

say "I am sorry," and then ask for forgiveness.

to live on the margin, financially.

It takes courage to . . .

be a good parent.

live every day with pain, emotional or physical.

to earn a living and retain your integrity.

live with depression or related challenges.

begin a new relationship.

begin anything new, knowing that it might result in failure and starting over.

end addictive behaviors and begin a life of healthy behaviors that promote wholeness and wellness.

join a Unitarian Universalist church.

These are a few of the images of courage that well up within me as I think about this subject. One thing is sure: we can make a difference for good in the lives of people around us if we will but take the time to be present, to notice, to affirm, to encourage, to bless, to value. Our affirmations make a difference. Our encouragement enlarges the courage of others and adds to their storehouse of strength to face adversity and transcend the abyss of the unknown.

Courage is something we all have, even if we forget.

Courage is something we can help to call forth in another person.

Amen.

--Rhett D. Baird

Hypocritical Resignation

I love your Christ. I do not like your Christians, because they are not like Christ.
--Mahatma Gandhi

All to Jesus I surrender;
Now I feel the sacred flame.
O the joy of full salvation!
Glory, glory, to His Name!

It was the final stanza of the final hymn. Stephen was relieved, as he usually was by this time in the service.

Why does every hymn have seventeen verses? Didn't these hymn writers have enough talent to sum up their thoughts a little more concisely? Even God must get annoyed at some point.

Southern Hills is a throw-back church: large families, traditionally modest attire, and very serious about Jesus. No visitors can possibly feel comfortable, unless they have more than five children and have limited contact with the real world. You can be judged–or feel judged–for any number of reasons. Holding hands with your girlfriend, for instance, is sure to garner some death stares from these faithful servants of Christ. Throw on your favorite pair of jeans and wear them to Sunday service–you might as well be spitting in the face of God. The church has virtually no members from the surrounding community, which is poor and mostly Latino. Southern Hills is made up of white, conservative families, most of whom drive a good thirty minutes to attend Sunday service.

Stephen has many thoughts about the church's lack of involvement in its own community. The motto at Southern Hills is "A Safe Place." The goal of the church seems to be to shut out the outside world and pretend it isn't there.

Are these people blind? Do they not realize their church is in an area boasting the highest crime rate in the city? Wasn't Jesus a friend to prostitutes and tax collectors? Maybe if Southern Hills reached out to the community, the people in the community would stop killing each other.

The people are content with the church being a "safe place"– a haven in the midst of an evil community–and evidently, Stephen thought, God is okay with it too.

Someone announces that it is okay to sit down, and everyone

immediately follows the instruction. Stephen glances over his shoulder as he takes his seat on the front row with the rest of his family. They are the "first family" of Southern Hills church and have sat in that same pew every Sunday for nineteen years. His father is the pastor. The upside of sitting on the front left row is the opportunity to look back and scan the faces of the faithful. The downside is that whenever Stephen is late, which is more often than not, he has to take the walk of shame to the front of the auditorium. Stephen can feel the severe glances, judging him every step of the way. Judgmental stares are not the only consequence for being late–it usually produces an uncomfortable conversation with his father, Pastor Hill.

"Do you not realize," his father begins, "that when you walk into church fifteen minutes late, it doesn't just reflect poorly on you? It reflects poorly on me and your family." Stephen is bigger than his father physically, but he is scared of him all the same. Pastor Hill is like a bulldog. He never gets angry, but he gets very intense, as Stephen explains to his friends.

Plus the possibility of him telling me I'm on my way to hell is always a factor.

Upon meeting Pastor Hill, Stephen's friends unanimously say they are intimidated.

"Do you realize that the Bible says if I can't control my own household, then I am not fit to lead the church? Do you want to be the reason I resign?"

"No, Dad. I don't."

"Do you not want to go to church?"

"No, Dad."

"You do or you don't?"

Hell, no, I don't.

"I do" is what Stephen says out loud.

"Well, that's a relief. But no one would ever know it by your lack of respect, not to mention your countenance when you are at Sunday service. Your mom is embarrassed, because you look like you would rather be anywhere else."

This is true. His mother has asked Stephen a million times, "Why don't you smile when you are at church? Doesn't the fact that Jesus loves you, and you are with your brothers and sisters in Christ, make you happy?"

They're not my brothers and sisters. I can't stand them.

"I don't know, Mom. I don't know why I don't smile all the time."

"Well, it's disrespectful to God, and it's disrespectful to your father."

Stephen often wishes that respect is not just a one-way street. *Why does every rule in the Bible screw me over? Honor thy father and mother. He who keeps the law is a discerning son, but a companion of gluttons disgraces his father. Only fools despise wisdom and discipline. How can I argue with that?*

Stephen snaps out of his daydream state as he realizes that his ass has fallen asleep. He takes a quick glance over his left shoulder as he adjusts himself on the unforgiving, unpadded pew. Five rows back and to the left he spots the Gamal family. Mr. Gamal is wearing his bland navy suit, sporting the required Southern Hills church comb-over. The only demonstration of individuality he affords himself is his novelty necktie.

For some reason, these people deem these ties with depictions of Jesus, the cross, or an angel acceptable. The trend has taken the church by storm. It seems that all the faithful servants at Southern Hills take pride in showing their devotion to Christ with a repugnant, holy depiction hanging around their necks. Stephen hates everything about it.

With her brutal Hillary Clinton haircut and ankle-length floral dress, Mrs. Gamal is beside Mr. Gamal–and then there are the seven clones who are their children.

Freaking hypocrites.

Two weeks earlier, Mr. Gamal sent Stephen an email: "We can't encourage our children to look up to you as a Christian role model as long as you continue to rebel against God with your long hair," was its main point.

Your wife looks like a man-eating lesbian, and you are judging me because my hair hangs over my ears. What world do you live in?

Stephen's father, of course, made him cut his hair. Stephen nearly threw up when Mrs. Gamal came up to him a few days later before the Wednesday night service: "Stephen, your hair looks really nice."

I hate you.

"Thank you" comes out of Stephen's mouth, accompanied by a forced smile.

Mr. Shamon is on the stage giving his best rendition of "If you don't give to the church, then you are probably not a Christian. And if you are not a Christian, you are definitely going to hell."

I've been scared of going to hell since I was four years old—four years old! Can't be healthy for a four-year-old to be having nightmares about hell.

Stephen takes another glance to his left and catches Lindsay Hamilton staring in his direction. She looks away quickly, her face turning red. They have had a crush on each other since they were twelve—something they will never admit. Ever since the "scandal" with Jessica Calaphas, Stephen has made sure any romance in his life happens outside of church. It is just too risky. He and Jessica had been caught holding hands when he was eleven. His father made Stephen apologize to Mr. Calaphas for "defrauding" his daughter and promise that nothing like that would ever happen again. So he and Lindsay have resorted to six years of eye flirting on Sunday mornings, which Stephen thinks is ridiculous for two eighteen-year-olds.

I can't wait to get away from these people.

Mr. Jacobson is doing the announcements. The men will be meeting in building B on Wednesday night, and the women in the main auditorium. The "young men" will be with their fathers, and the "young women" with their mothers.

God forbid they do something specifically for teens. That makes too much sense.

Southern Hills does not have a program for its younger generation. The older generation is absolutely terrified of what their children might do if left to their own devices. The possibilities for debauchery are endless: boys and girls might pair off and "defraud" each other by exchanging phone numbers. The Thompson boy, whose parents allow him to go to public school, might destroy the other teens' innocence by telling worldly stories. Or the young people might get the idea that they can be entertained at church.

God hates for his people to have fun at church.

So Stephen sits with Pastor Hill on Wednesday night, watching a video about the father being the spiritual leader of the household.

Stephen takes another glance over his shoulder, just in time to see the Onkelo family come in late—all twelve of them, with the obvious exception of Mr. Onkelo, who was recently convicted of raping his adopted children. They have five of their own children and adopted five more. Mr. Onkelo just couldn't help himself.

I had dinner at his house. Just when you think you know someone . . .

Mr. Onkelo had not only been a member of the church. He had been a major participant. He ran the sound on Sunday mornings, as well as many other technology-related projects within the church.

Not anymore.

Stephen glances up to the soundboard in the balcony, where two teenage boys sit wearing their headsets. Mr. Onkelo trained them both. Mr. Onkelo is serving twenty-one consecutive life sentences.

I hope everyone in that prison knows exactly what he did. How many conversations did I have with him while he was screwing his own kids? How many times did he sing every verse to "Just As I Am" and then go home and destroy a child's life? More shocking than that, I am not all that surprised. In fact, nothing in this place surprises me.

Stephen is looking at Mr. Gamal and that terrible tie.

By this time, Stephen's father is well into his sermon. Pastor Hill is long-winded. His sermons often surpass an hour and a half. Since most of the church members do not own televisions, no one is missing NFL football.

What time are the Cowboys playing? I hope it's the late game. Dad is on a roll.

A person often gets the feeling that a pastor is preaching directly to him or her–that somehow God has given the preacher a word that is directly intended for that one individual. Stephen doesn't just have a feeling. He knows absolutely, beyond a shadow of a doubt, when his father is speaking directly to him.

"The Lord tells us that we are in the world, but not of this world. Young people, what will you do when you are no longer under the guidance of your parents?"

Maybe I'll give my first, honest "Praise the Lord! Hallelujah!" or maybe even speak in tongues.

"Will you remember God when you are met with the temptations of an evil world? Will you remember the scripture, 'Honor your father and mother,' and that there is no age limit on that commandment?"

Wow. No age limit. Haven't heard that one in a while. He's pulling out the big guns. Please make me feel guilty for being an individual, Dad. Next he'll start talking about how evil rock music is.

When Stephen was fifteen, his father had told him they would have a meeting in the living room at 9 p.m. Stephen spent the rest of the day dreading the meeting, because he knew how it would go. Pastor Hill would "surprise" Stephen by telling him that he had been rebelling against God and his father in some way. It didn't matter what it was. Rock music, secret girlfriend, and disrespecting his mother were the usual suspects. Pastor Hill would then drill Stephen with Bible verses for at least an hour, while Stephen sat silently. Stephen knew it was pointless to voice his own opinion, so he would limit his responses (if a response was required) to two-word answers and head nods.

On this occasion, Stephen showed up first in the living room. He had his basketball with him, a habit he had started long ago specifically for these meetings, so that he would have something to fidget with as Pastor Hill lambasted him for his behavior. Pastor Hill walked into the room with a stack of papers and a CD. It was Stephen's Weezer CD.

And now it begins.

"Is there anything you want to say to me?"

I love that CD.

"No, Sir."

"Do you know what this is?"

Now he's questioning my intelligence.

"Yes, Sir."

"What is it?"

Wow.

"It's Weezer's *Blue* album."

"Where did you get it?"

Stephen just shook his head.

"We will talk about that later. This music is evil. Satan is glad that you listen to this. God hates this music. To show you how evil it is, I printed off the lyrics to several of these songs, and I am going to read them out loud to you."

This should be fun.

Pastor Hill began reading, making sure to give additional

emphasis to certain lyrics that were extra wicked. Pastor Hill droned his way through *The Sweater Song, My Name is Jonas, El Scorcho, Buddy Holly, Tired of Sex, The Good Life,* and, finally, *Why Bother.*

> *I know I should get next to you*
> *You got a look that makes me think you're cool*
> *But it's just sexual attraction*
> *Not something real so I'd rather keep wackin.*

Pastor Hill looked up at his son, whose expression hadn't changed throughout the meeting. His eyes were pointed toward the floor, and he was squeezing the basketball from one hand to the other.

"What do you think about that, Son?"

"I don't know, Dad."

"Son, I have raised you better than this. The fact that you are not repenting right now makes me fearful for your soul. You have to obey my rules in my house. But more importantly, you should be concerned about God's rules. A follower of Christ should not be able to listen to this stuff without being confronted by the Holy Spirit."

The truth was that Stephen had no idea what the lyrics meant. In fact, Stephen had never heard *Why Bother,* because it is not on Weezer's *Blue* album. His parents had been so effective in protecting their children that he had thought "wackin'" must mean punching the wall, or something. At age fifteen, Stephen had never masturbated. He literally had no clue what Pastor Hill, and evidently God, were so upset about.

"At this time, I'm going to ask my second-born son, Stephen, to come up on the stage with me," Stephen hears his father say from the pulpit.

Dear God, why?

"Stephen, as many of you know, has received a scholarship to play basketball. This is his last Sunday with us before moving one thousand miles away for college."

Stephen walks up on stage and stands to the right and a little behind his father. At fifteen, he has surpassed his father in height and is now a good five inches taller.

Dad's going a little bit bald in the back.

"There is no telling what temptations Stephen will meet when he goes to college. It is a public institution. He will hear lies from his professors. Loose women will tempt him. Satan will attack him from every angle. I want to invite the men of the church to come to the front and pray with me for my son. Pray for his innocence to remain intact. Pray that he will not be wooed by this sinful world."

A warning would have been nice, Dad.

Stephen is familiar with this situation. He thinks back to the year before, when he had suffered a severe knee injury. Pastor Hill had called the elders of the church to come to the house and pray for Stephen's healing.

"Is there anything you have done, any sin in your life, for which God might have caused this to happen?" one of the elders had asked.

Are you joking me right now?

"I don't always obey my father immediately. And sometimes I listen to music that I know my dad wouldn't approve of," was the answer Stephen gave. They prayed for healing and repentance for over an hour.

I still had to have surgery and do seven months of rehab. Maybe there had been other sins I should have confessed.

Stephen moves down in front of the stage. The cross that serves as a podium for his father is directly behind him. It is a depiction of Jesus hanging, with the crown of thorns placed on the long hair adorning the savior's head. At least a hundred men came down to the front to lay hands on Stephen. Mr. Gamal stands directly in front. *Please don't touch me,* Stephen thinks, as he makes eye contact and smiles at Mr. Gamal. Anointing oil appears in the hands of one of the elders.

Pastor Hill begins to call out to God.

"Dear God! Please preserve my son's purity. As he goes out from under the protection of his father and his church, cause him to remember who he is. He is my son. He has been promised by me to you. Your commandments have been written on his heart—"

"Hammered" would be a better description.

"—and we know that to whom much is given, much is required. Stephen knows your commandments, and now I am handing him over to you, Lord. Do whatever it takes to keep him within your will. If he strays from your righteous commandments, chastise him, so that he will come back to you."

The entire church is mumbling words of agreement. Stephen wipes away the beads of sweat forming on his forehead. Mr. Gamal's right hand is on top of Stephen's head, jerking it, presumably as the spirit leads him.

I wonder if he's rebuking my hair–maybe telling it not to grow.

The prayer finally ends. Pastor Hill had taken his glasses off. His face is red and perspiring. Stephen is lost in his own thought.

Most of these people believe sports are evil. Most of them believe college is evil. What could they have possibly been praying for that would benefit me? I wonder if God can be embarrassed, because if He can, then His cheeks are a rosy color of red when He sees this church.

Stephen had often thought of the church as unruly children at a grocery store. "Is that your child?" someone would ask his mother. Her face would redden, an expression of momentary regret, and then, "Yes. Yes, that's my child."

And then she would grab her child by the arm, her fingers digging into the meaty part right between the biceps and triceps muscles, and beat the living daylights out of him, right there in the store. At least my mother would—did. Why isn't God beating his children? I will never come back to this place.

Men pat him on the back and shake his hand. Someone begins to sing.

> *All to Jesus, I surrender;*
> *All to Him I freely give;*
> *I will ever love and trust Him,*
> *In His presence daily live.*

Thirty minutes pass, and Stephen is standing in the alley outside the back door of the church. He is thinking of the prayer his father had led.

I hope this is the last time I have to do something like that. God, if you love me, and if you are really there, please don't put me through another one of those–oh shit, the Cowboys game!

Stephen wakes up on Wednesday. He is lying in a bed at the University of Oklahoma trauma unit. The previous Sunday, police had attempted to pull over a truck of local boys in the community of his father's church. They had used the back alley of the church as an escape route and hit Stephen going thirty-five miles per hour, according to the police report. Stephen does not know where he is. Stephen's jaw is wired shut. Stephen cannot not move his legs or feel his fingers. Stephen, in fact, will never walk again.

Stephen's mother is sleeping in the corner of the room. His father walks through the door, followed by the elders of the church, one of whom is carrying the anointing oil. They encircle his bed. They stand silently for a few moments, taking in Stephen's physical condition. Stephen's eyes widen as they follow Mr. Gamal into the room and around his bed. Stephen is straining, not able to move his head or neck, to still see Mr. Gamal as he stops directly to the left of the boy's head.

Mr. Gamal leans directly over him, looking down on Stephen's pathetic figure. Stephen's eyes move down Mr. Gamal's face to his navy suit and the tie which is hanging down, nearly touching Stephen's chest: it is a navy tie. Stephen's eyes fall on the depiction of a man emblazoned on it. He has shoulder-length hair and a shabby beard, and he is carrying a cross. He has one knee on the ground, as if the weight of the cross has made him stumble. He is struggling to stand up. Pious faces, like ghosts, are in the background, sneering at the man as he marches to his death. *What a hideous thing to wear around your neck.*

Mr. Gamal breaks the silence, "If you have any sin in your life that might have caused this terrible incident to occur–" Looking at the wires going in and out of Stephen's jaw, he pauses: "– blink twice."

You have got to be joking me.

Blink. Blink.

--Zach Wells

A FAULKNER DREAM

She awoke in a peaceful disturbance as her mind searched to recapture the vision just now taking leave, just now passing parade-like in regular time while she was thinking, recalling, in slow motion. But she could still see the hulk of a solid, hard man of opaque ebony, old, tired, mean and kind all at once. She could still see him as he walked along a dry and dusty road looking straight ahead, silently, stealthily, moving almost as one would move while standing still on a moving sidewalk–like travelers sometimes do at major airports in important cities. And along both sides of the road in a sepia haze were weary souls of every seriocomic description.

She noticed a man with a sock on one foot and a shoe on the other, wearing a pair of slacks that had once been neatly pleated, pressed, and pinned to hold them onto a thin department store mannequin. Now a rope holds them onto a gaunt addict who had forgotten long ago how to bathe and shave. His filthy, torn, once sunshine-yellow shirt still barely read *Happy Camper.* Other crashing addicts, sniffling and staring, stood around him; none looked at anything but the road and the man walking on the road. Intermingled with the addicts were all manner of the socially unsuccessful–the dropouts whose souls housed twisted scars and open, unhealed wounds.

Children sat eerily, quietly sniffling on the other side of the road; none engaged in the play of childhood save one tiny boy with three green marbles that he lined up and pushed through the loose brown powdery dirt. No child sitting around him had the desire to challenge the ownership of the boy with the marbles; if it had been a chicken biscuit, there would have been a scramble and maybe a bloody nose. Mothers stood by and contemplated how to invite a man with a job and without an addiction into their lives. They weren't talking it over just now as they watched the homeless man pass by. But they were thinking it. They were always thinking it. And they were always thinking it fast, because time refused to slow down, and young girls became new women every day, became new targets and trophies, while *they* became more wrinkled and calloused and their unstraightened teeth became yellow–or became scarce. The window of opportunity closed a little more with each day.

Specimens once human–still human but feeling alien, *still* human but forgetting they were so, *still* human though other humans didn't believe they were so, but believed instead that these on the side of the road had deliberately decided one day to become alien– these continually stared with sunken eyes as empty as those of the steadily forward-moving, bulky hobo; they stared after him with a strange glimmer of hope.

She remained motionless, completely still, afraid that even

a deep breath would make the dream vanish like the scurrying kittens of an alley cat. She was as drawn to the hulking stranger as the forgotten multitudes on the sidelines of the one-lane dirt road. He didn't allow his eyes to meet any other eyes. He just slowly walked, walked, walked on.

Suddenly, but without the jerky suddenness of a magic act, the dusty road was paved and clean, but smaller than before; the ghastly vagrants on the side of the road faded away, and the black man was now the only one in the dream movie. He walked alone for a good while, still at the same meticulous, unchanging pace. Then something began to appear, unfocused and small, growing more and more discernible with every monotonous step.

She waited. Finally, at the end of the road was a broken-down little church, or what used to be a church. The steeple had long ago loosened and broken away in a windstorm; it had fallen and splintered, and the pieces now hid quietly, without power, in the thorny weeds; termites feasted on the splinters in the churchyard and the planks in the floor, which were leaning toward the back side of the little church; the more leaning they did, the more they pushed the cinderblock foundation deeper into the ground, making the entire forgotten structure appear to be looking upward, beseeching the heavens with twin window-eyes on either side of the front door. The road led up to the dilapidated, languid porch and stopped. The man stopped too, once he had climbed the two steps onto the porch.

She held what short breaths she had been allowing, thinking that the creaking porch would fall, would splinter like the steeple in the yard, and would splinter the dream too, before the closing act. But it held, and now her dream was in even more slow motion–like she had pushed the stop-action button on the TV remote. He turned around; she looked at him, but he did not look back. There had been no movie score playing in the background before, but suddenly from somewhere an orchestra crescendo signaled a climax; just before the fade to black, she heard the words, felt the words, saw the words on the slightly leaning nailed-up wooden sign above the door frame, above the troubled, serene hobo's head: *Now there lived in that city a man poor but wise, and he saved the city by his wisdom.*

Then the dream, the vision, the wispy phantom exited as the light of the morning filled her now opened eyes. She didn't know what it meant, but she knew instinctively that she had dreamed no ordinary, every-night dream. The morning light bathed the eloquent, artfully decorated master bedroom with a soft, stationary calm; her heart was quiet but restless. She felt like a child who had always experienced a lovely, gift-filled Christmas, but remained unspoiled and still strained to hear Christmas bells, still listened for them with giddy anticipation.

--Terri DeFoor

Deep Church: The Kingdom of God Breaking into the World

> *Then God said, "Let us make man in our image, in our likeness, and let them rule over the fish of the sea and the birds of the air, over the livestock, over all the earth, and over all the creatures that move along the ground." So God created man in his own image, in the image of God he created him; male and female he created them.*
> Genesis 1:26-27

As a doctoral student in Georgetown University's School of Languages and Linguistics, I was required to take a course in transformational grammar, much of which had grown out of the research of MIT's Noam Chomsky, whose study of the science of language has led him to political action. Indeed, linguistics, I have learned, is a very dangerous field that encompasses the analysis of the theoretical underpinnings of Bible translation and the language strategies used to gain and maintain power—heady stuff for a "little Southern girl," a cradle-roll Baptist who matured on "M Night" and tent revivals in a society segregated in schools and churches, but remarkably more interracially intimate than USA 2016.

That course on transformational grammar posited "deep structures" from which every conceivable sentence can be created by using a set of derivable rules. Having meditated for years on a possible Periodic Chart of the Elements of Meaning, I was immediately taken by Catholic theologian Richard Rohr's description of "Deep Church." Rohr writes, "'Deep Church,' is invariably something shared between a small group of believers, which is probably why he [Jesus] speaks of 'two or three gathered in my name' (Matthew 18:20)." Father Rohr maintains that the "Kingdom of God breaks into this world whenever people act as God would act."

Deep Church has penetrated my very being inside and outside the church–the Kingdom of God breaking irrevocably into my world. Often it has come to me as grace–as something I obviously do not deserve, as in the nurturing kindness of Dorothy, a black woman in my childhood who took in ironing to make a living. Most of the time, my mother required that we add "Aunt" to the first name of older adults–black and white. I don't know why we just called Dorothy and Wilhelmina by their first names but "aunted" Aunt Marthey and Aunt Sarah.

It had not been a good morning for my six-year-old self. When my younger sister Betty had come outside wearing my special store-bought yellow nylon Easter dress with the flocked white flowers, I saw red and hauled off and hit her. Having been born prematurely, Betty enjoyed a specialness that I could never approach. Never addressing the issue of boundaries, my mother picked a switch from the peach tree and began to administer discipline on my bare skinny legs, intensifying her efforts when I stubbornly held back the tears. When she finally laid the switch down, I knew I needed to take a long walk before the wrong words tumbled from my lips once again.

The burning, white Florida sand scorched my bare feet as I moved quickly down the road where I had never before ventured alone. Racing from shade to shade, I saw ahead where another sand road branched off to the right and hoped that there might be more shady spots to bring momentary relief to my blistered feet. Pretty soon I spied a shack at the end of the road and peered into the open door, where a black woman bent over her ironing board with mounds of white shirts all starched and dampened in a basket off to the side. The wood cook stove where she heated her irons stood directly behind her, the smoke wisping from the chimney signaling the existence of a live fire.

As I neared the door, I recognized Dorothy, the woman who helped my mama with the ironing. Forgetting for a moment my burning feet and the now dried blood on my legs, my child-self asked, "Dorothy, is that you?" Dorothy took one look at the skinny tow-headed, blue-eyed, white child and crooned, "Come on in here, Chile. I'se got a sweet tater with yo' name on it."

I couldn't believe my ears. "With my name on it?" I breathed, expecting to see my name spelled out on the sweet potato. Dorothy seated me at the rickety wooden table to the right of her ironing board, pulled a sweet potato from the hot oven, sliced the potato down the bright orange middle, and stuffed a big pat of butter inside. I forgot all about looking for my name. I had never tasted such a delicious sweet potato in my life. Afterwards, Dorothy put down her ironing long enough to tell me about the beautiful oval-framed pictures on her wall. They were all sepia-toned photographs of black people in elegant formal attire, more beautiful than any pictures I had ever seen.

I remember thinking how glad I was that I hadn't happened on Wilhelmina's house. She would have called out, "You been bad again. What you done this time?" Wilhelmina always claimed my mama was mean because she grew the hottest peppers around. Dorothy never mentioned the stripes and blood on my legs. She was careful not to let her eyes look at my legs.

Ever since that day, I have been looking in vain for a sweet potato that is as delicious as the one Dorothy pulled from that oven in the heat of the dog days of summer. I know now that she served me more than a sweet potato. She was the physical presence of God for me. Jesus taught, "In as much as you have done it unto one of the least of these my children, you have done it unto me." I had been to Deep Church. That feeling of unconditional acceptance was never to abandon me.

It was little wonder that years later when Dillard University's Vice President Dr. Elton C. Harrison called me "Chile" in exasperation that the sweet feeling of acceptance swept over me once again. I just happened to be in his office when a student came by to request permission to take the final exams she had missed when her mother had suddenly died. Dr. Harrison berated the student for not having immediately called her professors to make arrangements.

After the young woman left, I sat there abashed, knowing that had it been my mother, I would not have had the clarity of mind to think about a final exam. Characteristically, my mouth opened of its own accord to express those sentiments to the good vice president, who had become a father figure to me after the death of my own father. Earlier he had reminded me that there was a pecking order, intimating that I was not at the top of it. This time he looked at me intensely and almost in a whisper said, "Ms. Eskew, I hope you're around to speak up for me when I need it."

Several years later, the good vice president called me in pain from his hospital bed, where the doctors had not been able to diagnose his problem. At 10:30 in the evening, I found myself seated next to him, asking him to describe his pain for me. I concluded that he was having an attack of appendicitis, a diagnosis confirmed by my doctor when she extracted his appendix with three marks on it for each of the times he had been hospitalized.

I told the Dorothy-story to my students at Mercer. At break time on the last night of class, they asked me to sit down. They pinned a corsage on me and then proceeded to testify about what they had learned in the class. One of the students pulled out two very delicious sweet potato pies and served the entire class. So many of them had come with so many voices in their heads about what they could not do in a writing class–voices that judged them as not "worth a hill of beans" and their English as broken–full of dangling modifiers and fused sentences. I knew they had to confront those voices before they could make the academic progress required of the program. I had gone to class that evening wondering if anything I had worked so hard to communicate had even been heard. I knew that many of the students were not yet where they needed to be. Yet, here they were–reading from the stories they had carefully crafted to honor me. I felt grace wash over me–Deep Church again. The Kingdom of God had broken irrevocably into my world again.

The fervent testimonies of my students took me back in time–all the way to New Orleans. I had helped Veotta Mayo get scholarships to study in France for a year and then a year in Germany. When she had reluctantly returned home, I had helped her get part-time employment at an upscale hotel while she finished her double major in French and German at Xavier University. She had pestered me about coming to her church one Sunday. I told her that I had my own church where I taught a Sunday School class but I would arrange to come to her church for just one Sunday. On the appointed Sunday, I parked my car in Ninth-Ward New Orleans and stepped over needles used for shooting up drugs the night before to get to the door of the storefront church. In the bright sunlight that revealed the ugliness of the scene, I took a deep breath and wondered what I was doing here in a dirty, dangerous drug-infested neighborhood on a Sunday morning. Not allowing myself to hesitate, I turned the doorknob and entered the dimly-lit sanctuary. I finally made out the shape of an empty chair and tried to settle unobtrusively into it, hoping against hope not to disrupt the service already in progress. I realized that I was the only white person in attendance and prayed silently for the time to pass quickly.

A middle-aged woman in her Sunday finery approached the pulpit and in a beautiful, resonant voice announced, "I want to praise God for Dr. Eskew." I felt like crawling under the chair. A second person stood and then a third, all praising God for this white woman at a time when race relations in New Orleans were running low. In a daze of disbelief, I lost track of how many people stood and thanked God for unworthy me.

All my life I had had a fear of testifying in church. When I tried to pray in public, I would hear a voice saying, "Enter into your closet to pray. Do not be like the Pharisee who openly thanks God that he is not like the other people." Without getting my approval, my body rose. I heard my voice start to speak of its own accord. It was asserting that this church had found the secret that was alluding so many on how to keep their children off drugs. It prophesied that they were exercising leadership in effective race relationships at a time when blacks and whites didn't seem to be able to talk honestly to one another. I felt their forgiveness for being part of the race that had enslaved them and continued to devalue them. Now I recognize that what I found there was Deep Church–a community where the Kingdom of God had broken into their lives on a regular basis–and had now broken irrevocably into mine once again.

When I walked into my first class in Mercer's English Language Institute in May 2001, Dayone from South Korea looked up at me and declared, "God sent you to us." I had fully intended to return to New Orleans to teach my classes at Tulane in the fall. Six months later, it would be Dayone who led a delegation of Korean students to my office to talk to me. "Do you know why we like you?" Dayone asked for the group. "Is it because I help you order parts for your car? Is it because I stay late and help you with your homework? Is it because I fix coffee and tea every morning? Is it because I come out at 4 a.m. when you have a problem?" I must have posed a dozen questions, but Dayone shook his head from side to side each time. Finally, he confided, "We like you because you eat Korean food with us."

Now I understand that we had been having communion together. Across generations, cultures, and languages we had experienced Deep Church together. *As often as you eat this bread and drink this cup*–communion, community–*where two or three are gathered together in my name, there am I in their midst.* I thought about Dorothy's sweet potato and the sweet potato pies in that last class. Many of the stories in the Bible center around food. Jesus attended the wedding feast and turned the water into wine. Elijah asked the widow from Zarephath for food, and she used the last of her flour and oil to make a meal for him. Zaccheus invited Jesus to his house for dinner, and Jesus was criticized for eating with a tax collector. The disciples fed five thousand people with a little boy's lunch–all ordinary events that became extraordinary because the Kingdom of God broke through, eradicating the distinction between the sacred and the profane.

Deep Church does not need a sanctuary. It does not need a preacher or even a choir. The Kingdom of God broke through the bars and all the locks the first time I went into a prison in Macon. Coming to Macon from New Orleans signaled a new life for me–no need to let anybody know that I had worked with Sr. Helen Préjean to raise awareness to the injustice of the death penalty. Dot Pinkerton, who founded the Lighthouse Missions, learned from her daughter Lenny that I had written grant proposals and brought in over two million dollars to Louisiana colleges. Dot showed up one afternoon in my office with her sister, and they refused to budge until I promised to write a grant proposal. Once we received $100,000 from the Criminal Justice Coordinating Council, she insisted we revise that proposal and apply for other funds. With my 24/7 schedule in the English Language Institute, I reluctantly agreed, and we added another $100,000 to the ministry coffers. After browbeating me into writing the grants, Dot impertinently announced one day that I shouldn't be writing grants for them when I hadn't ever walked through the doors of a prison.

That's how I found myself handing over my keys before being escorted through six or seven locked doors into the bowels of the prison where a huge roomful of lifers were awaiting the worship service. Anxious, I saw over a hundred lifers, most of whom were murderers–and only two guards on duty. I had been told that a brother and sister would attend to forgive publicly the man who had killed their mother in an East Macon motel over two decades ago. The son, turned policeman, now retired, had held his mother in his arms that night as she breathed her last breath. The daughter who had convinced her mother to work that night so that she could go swimming with her friends had committed suicide from guilt. A second child, a son, had committed suicide a year later. Another daughter had been in a mental health facility for years. The policeman's marriage had broken up, and a third daughter struggled with depression.

Each year the remaining siblings had come together for Christmas, when they would write a letter to the warden of the prison demanding that their mother's murderer not be granted parole. Dot had written a letter to the warden describing the man's repentance and conversion and requesting the man's parole and entry into the Lighthouse Missions program. On the way to pick up his sister, the retired policeman had secretly planned to go into the prison, kill the man who had murdered his mother, and then turn the gun on himself. Upon reading a copy of Dot's letter, he had miraculously begun to think about the changes that Dot had described. If this man had truly become a Christian, then, the retired policeman reasoned, this man was his brother in Christ. After viewing recent pictures of the murderer, he and his sister had supposedly decided together to forgive their mother's murderer.

As I sat there that evening, I began to doubt the sincerity of the retired policeman. A student of World War II and of the language of Adolf Hitler, I knew from research that people say one thing and do another. Telling the big lie is one of the frequently employed strategies of propaganda. I watched intensely as Dot stood and began the service. The new parolee came forward to ask for forgiveness, testifying that he wished he could rewind that night. He claimed he would rather have died than to have killed the woman. An alarm went off in my head when I saw the brother and sister rise and move toward the front. The retired policeman embraced the killer, and his sister embraced the two men. Caught up in the sacredness of that moment, I looked out over the sea of faces and felt the palpable longing of those men to experience such an embrace–a physical sign of forgiveness. Their collective sighs hung in the air. It was a high holy moment–a moment of Deep Church.

In her inimical way, Dot rose and announced that Dr. Eskew would come forward and address the group–the opposite of the anonymity she had promised. Still in a sense of awe and not having prepared anything to say, I stood and made my way to the microphone–with no idea of what would issue forth from my mouth. With the image of the three-way embrace still playing in my head, my mouth opened on its own and out poured the words to a hymn from the *Sacred Harp* tradition that I had sung growing up:

> *I will arise and go to Jesus.*
> *He will embrace me in his arms.*
> *In the arms of my dear Savior,*
> *Oh, there are ten thousand charms.*
> *Oh, there are ten thousand charms.*

As Dot pronounced the benediction, I peered out from half-closed eyes to see a long line of men snaking their way to the front. My eyes followed the line. Shockingly, those men were in line to speak to me. Pressing into my hand notes with their names and contact information, they wanted to know about the ten thousand charms and if I would teach them to write. It had all come full circle. I calculated that in the over 10,000 times I had attended worship services, I had never experienced the forgiveness I witnessed that night. Deep in the bowels of a prison I had once again experienced Deep Church.

My mind shifted to another time when I was learning to write. My oldest sister, Jo, and my second sister, Doris, always held school with the younger siblings when they came home each day. They were frustrated because we had used up all the writing paper, and our mother had threatened us if we took the labels off the canned goods one more time. I could see the light go on in Joan's eye. "We're going outside and write in the sand," she ordered. "If Jesus could write in the sand, so can we," she declared authoritatively, brooking no dissent.

Jo collected sticks for each of us. "Now," she commanded, "copy what I write." In the dirt, she drew a box and wrote in it: "He who is without sin cast the first stone." That lesson has stilled the natural impulse in me to find fault and pass judgment. A veteran fifth-grade teacher, Jo has since held Deep Church in Haiti, Mexico, and many other places around the world. Often Jo's principal assigned the children with the worst test scores to her, knowing that by the end of the year their test scores would outpace those of all the other classes.

Like all the other children in the little Baptist church near the St. John's River, Jo had come under the spell of the pastor, Brother Hubert Taylor. Brother Taylor's Bible stories rivaled Dorothy's sweet potato. From him we learned that we were the children of God–created in the image of God. We believed it.

When I was two years old–the age when I made my first vow to God not to smoke my daddy's cigarette butts any more, not to curse, and not to tell lies, Brother Taylor preached a sermon on grace: *Grace is something we don't earn, but we have to reach out our hands and take it.* He reached into his pocket and brought out a silver dollar. He held that gleaming coin up for everyone to see and promised, *Whoever will come down that aisle and claim this silver dollar can have it.*

I am not sure whether I went down the aisle on my own volition or if my mother gave me a little push. But Brother Taylor did not miss a beat. He reached down, picked me up, gave me the shiny silver dollar, turned to the congregation, and warned them, *Except you become as a little child, you shall not enter the kingdom of heaven.* Brother Taylor practiced Deep Church, and like the spiritual, extended an invitation for all to join him:

> *Get on board, little children!*
> *Get on board, little children!*
> *Get on board, little children!*
> *There's room for many-a-more.*

--Margaret H. Eskew

A VISIT FROM BRITTANY

I walk into my parents' new home. Every brick, nail, and door bought with sorrow–I can smell my mother's scent of flowers and soap drifting throughout the entranceway. The new furniture is placed in a semi-circle around the living room. To my right is the open kitchen–my mother's dream kitchen. I can't help but smile knowing she can find happiness even in the small things. A hall extends off the kitchen, leading to my parents' room and the stairs to my father's personal space. I open the door and go upstairs.

I don't know how I know where to find him. It is just instinct. He doesn't notice me as I walk in. He wouldn't believe it anyway. There he is. The man I love so much. He is tall, and his face wears that familiar mustache and beard. I can feel the way they always tickled my face when he kissed me. He is asleep in his recliner. I stand and watch as his chest slowly rises and falls. I don't want to disturb him, so I just bend down and lightly kiss his forehead.

I turn and walk down the stairs. Once on the ground floor I turn right and make my way to the room at the end of the hall. Mom usually leaves the door open. She knows if I visit that it will likely be at night. I go to the oversized bed where she lies. As I look at her face, she stirs, but doesn't wake up. Maybe she smells my scent–just as hers met me at the entryway. I climb into the bed. The last time I did this, I was a young girl finding comfort in her mother's arms. I embrace her, and as I do, she sighs--it is a sigh of relief and familiarity. Even in her sleep, she hasn't felt this good in years. I lay my hand on her cheek and kiss her on the forehead.

I'm not able to visit my parents as often as they would like, not since that horrible night. I was on my way to visit a friend late at night. All of a sudden a pizza delivery driver came barreling in my direction. He was drunk. I had no time to react; he was driving in my lane, coming directly toward me. Our cars hit head on.

I remember my parents in the hospital–the concern in their eyes. They were crying. The doctor told them there was nothing he could do. I looked at the family I loved very much and surrendered to the light shining in front of me.

--Amanda McCranie

WHAT COLOR IS LOVE?

English teacher Jane Donahue sent me an email from Thailand, requesting that our prayer chaplains at Unity please pray for her and her students: *"I'm speaking to a dead classroom and I don't know what to do to get them excited about learning."* Since I'm married to Jane's only daughter, she likes to keep up with how my education at Mercer is going. One of the core courses in my program is academic writing. I reluctantly signed up for it, even though my son had warned me about taking classes with the professor who was teaching it. The class deals with education as experience and requires that we write about our early experiences. For this class, I had written several stories about working on a farm in North Georgia, where my mother, a single mom, would send me away during the summer months to work. In addition to learning real life skills, I got room and board and earned enough money to buy my school clothes for the next year. I sent Jane one of these stories to help her connect with what I was doing.

Quite unexpectedly, Jane asked if she could share the story with her students. "You're not going to believe this," she reported. "They wanted copies of your story to take home with them to read again." Jane also developed classroom exercises using the vocabulary in the story. When she tested the students, they all got good grades. "Unbelievable," Jane exclaimed. "It's a miracle. I believe God is working through you 2,000 miles away for my class. The students have totally changed and can't wait to answer questions. Please send more stories!"

Within days, I started receiving letters–in English–from the children in Thailand, wanting to know more about Uncle Joe and Aunt Benny, and the boys on the farm. The children related how they had laughed and also how a few things in the story had made them sad. They could not believe that Americans had grown up feeling the same things they had felt.

I called my next story "Toby," which has now been changed to "The Secret." It's a true story about a little black boy who came to live on the farm. Here are some excerpts from "The Secret."

I grabbed the stick and held the barbed wire up while Allen passed through. Then he held it for me while I crawled under. As we walked up the hill toward the house, we could see Uncle Joe with a little black boy. The little boy must have been about eight or nine years old. He had on an old plaid shirt and jeans with the knees worn out. His shoes didn't match–one was brown worn leather and the other looked like an old house shoe. And he didn't have any socks on. Under his arm was what looked like an old stuffed teddy bear. It was dirty, and both eyes were missing. One arm was gone, and someone had stitched it up so the stuffing wouldn't fall out. The little boy held it tight under his arm, and his thumb was stuck in his mouth.

"Boy, get that thumb out of your mouth! I done told you," *Uncle Joe growled. The boy pulled the thumb out of his mouth revealing a missing tooth right in front.*

This story took place in the early 1960s, when there were strict color barriers. I went to an all white school. Whites and blacks were always separated. Whites couldn't befriend blacks without negative consequences. Here's another excerpt from "The Secret."

"Toby, this is your cot. Get in it and stay there till morning," Billy ordered. "If you have to go to the bathroom, you better go now. Uncle Joe don't like us to go downstairs at night."

Little Toby crawled up on the cot next to mine and huddled up in a tight little ball with his knees at his chin and his arms wrapped around his legs. Big alligator tears ran down his cheeks as he clutched that dirty old teddy bear.

I could hear Toby snubbing as I tried to go to sleep. I felt sorry for him not having a family and all. I wondered what it must feel like to lose your mother and to be in a strange place with all white people telling you what to do. I got up, went over to his cot, and sat down beside him.

"C'mon I want to show you something," I said softly. "C'mon. I won't hurt you. It's over here."

Toby reached for my hand as he released his grip on his legs and started to get out of bed. His grip told me that I had his trust.

Strangely, when I reached out and touched Toby's hand, I couldn't tell what color he was. I felt God's love. I felt a relationship like no other relationship I had ever known before. Toby became my brother. In that instant, I realized that what my father and grandfather had taught me was not the truth. Toby and I worked together, played together, and prayed together. We shared our dreams, slept in the same room, and ate at the same table. We became brothers. Whenever you saw me, you saw Toby or vice versa. There were no boundaries between us.

The story describes how some people did not appreciate the situation. The father of two of the boys came and removed his sons from the farm because of Toby. The story reveals the secret of the love between Toby's mother and Uncle Joe when they were younger–a love that could never be realized because of the color of their skin. Uncle Joe had left Iowa because of it.

On my desk at home is a letter from a little girl in Thailand, who asked, "Why does the color of your skin make a difference? Toby could not help that his skin was brown." I have answered many letters from the children in Thailand, but this one is still on my desk.

What do I tell her? Do I tell her that in America we made slaves out of the dark people from Africa and that we treated them like animals? That later we had a war, and thousands upon thousands of young men died over color? Then the government declared them free, but they still weren't? They were "free" but had to remain separate from white people, and the white people had all the control? And that on December 1, 1955, Rosa Parks, a 42-year-old African American woman who worked as a seamstress, boarded a Montgomery City bus to go home from work and, sitting where the black people were supposed to sit, was asked by the bus driver to give up her seat for a white man? That she refused and was arrested? That this started a boycott? That African Americans made up seventy-five percent of the bus riders in the Montgomery area? That the boycott was organized by a Baptist minister, Martin Luther King, Jr., and lasted for 381 days? That when in 1956 the US Supreme Court ruled that the segregation law was unconstitutional, Montgomery's buses were integrated? That this started a Civil Rights Movement that later cost the lives of hundreds, including Dr. Martin Luther King, Jr.?

What do I tell her? What color is hate? Later in the story, Toby asked, *What color is God?* I told him, *I don't know. I used to think God was white like me, but maybe God's brown like you, or maybe God has no color at all–like the wind. You can feel the wind, but you can't see it.*

Dr. King taught us: *Darkness cannot drive out darkness; only light can do that. Hate cannot drive out hate; only love can do that.*

What color is love? Love has no color or boundaries. It is free–like the wind. You can't see the wind, but you can feel it.

--Robert (Bob) Mathis

COLORLESS LOVE

Can you tell me the color of God above?
Do you know what is the color of love?
I know it isn't black or white, or any shade of grey.
What is the color of a sunny summer day?
I'm not sure that there's a color of love at all.
Trying to define it as such is like building up a great big wall.
It keeps people out
That we could be letting in.
It's living in an incomplete world, seeing life through a tinted lens.
So perhaps, it's not that simple to explain–
More akin to the smell of a sudden summer rain.
No priest or poet has any kind of monopoly
On the love that can exist between you and me.
I'm not sure that there's a color of love at all.
Putting love inside a box is going to make this big world small.
It keeps people out
That we could be letting in.
When we love like we're colorblind, everyone can win.
  --William M. (Bo) Walker

This song was inspired by Bob Mathis' essay, "What Color Is Love?"

WHAT SCIENCE CAN TEACH RELIGION

The older I get, the more grateful I become for those unexpected moments of enlightenment that alter my perceptions and broaden my sensitivities. Such moments have the power to move us in new directions, opening doors of insight that, for whatever reasons, had remained closed and hidden from view. My unexpected moments and newly opened doors are no doubt different from your own, but they are surely no more significant or life changing than similar moments in your own experience. I want to share with you three of those important encounters that deepened my understanding of what the world requires of us as educators and gave me a new sense of urgency about my own role as a teacher. First, however, I must tell you something of where I came from and describe for you what was for me, years ago, a way of thinking and believing that, at the time, I simply could not abandon.

I want to confess from the outset that I have a deep appreciation for the positive influence of much, if not most, of my religious upbringing. The exemplary, though not perfect, lives I witnessed every day, year in and year out, in my wise and loving parents made all the difference in how my siblings and I chose to live *our* lives, and we are the beneficiaries of their thoughtful example. I have much, indeed, for which to be grateful. But little, if anything, stays always the same. Times change, and with those changes, unquestioned certainties and traditions often give way to previously unasked questions in search of previously unimaginable answers.

When I was a child in my "growing-up" years at church, I participated faithfully every summer for about a week in what we called our Vacation Bible School (VBS). Included in each morning's opening ceremonies was our "Pledge to the Bible," that went, as I recall, like this:

I pledge allegiance to the Bible, God's holy word.
I will make it a lamp unto my feet and a light unto my path,
And will hide its words in my heart,
That I might not sin against God.

This pledge was followed by the singing of a little chorus, the words of which, as best I remember, were these:

Holy Bible, book divine,
Precious treasure, thou art mine;
Mine to tell me whence I came,
Mine to teach me what I am.

Through the years, accompanying that Bible pledge and that little chorus was an explicit belief in what I learned to refer to later as "biblical literalism," which means, in effect, that whatever is in the Bible is to be believed and accepted as true, without reservation. So I, along with many others, accepted without question that Methuselah really did live for 969 years; that Shadrach, Meshach, and Abednego really did survive the fiery furnace with their hair

unsinged; that a big fish really did swallow Jonah and then vom-
ited him out alive on the third day, with Jonah in a dead run for
Nineveh; and that Jesus really did feed five thousand men, besides
women and children, with five loaves of bread and two fish. I
could go on with an almost endless list of things I thought I really
should believe and never question simply because I found them in
the Bible.

My interest here is not to defend or refute those and similar biblical claims, but to consider briefly the process through
which I began to acknowledge some of the questions that were
forming in my mind about what I had for so long simply taken
for granted as given. It all began, really, when I was a student at
Baylor University and made friends with a fellow student from
the Middle East who turned out to be, of all things, a Muslim. My
friendship with Michael (his adopted American name) was an
eye-opening experience for me, because I soon discovered something I had never encountered before. Michael didn't even have
a Bible, had never read the Bible, and could not, understandably,
share my unquestioned reverence for what I found in the Bible.
In its place, Michael had his Qur'an, and I soon learned that he
was just as convinced about the truth claims of Islam as found in
the Qur'an as I was about the truth claims in my Bible. But did I
have a Qur'an? Had I ever read the Qur'an? Could I have cared
less about the Qur'an? The answer to each of those questions was
"no," and it troubled me that Michael was just as convinced of the
truth of what he believed as I was about what I believed. "Which
of us is right?" I wondered.

I had been brought up to affirm, if not believe, what I was
supposed to affirm and believe, and that did not include reverence
for the Qur'an. I had learned that to acknowledge that I wasn't
really sure about what I claimed to believe and that I didn't really
know much of what I claimed to be *true*–such an acknowledgement was beyond the pale of genuine Christian belief and practice.
Uncertainty, on the one hand, and Christian orthodoxy ("right
belief"), on the other, just did not and could not walk hand in hand.
But the questions kept on coming, and sadly I just kept flounder-
ing, unable to find a firm footing.

Fast-forward twenty years. After four years at Southern
Baptist Theological Seminary in Louisville, Kentucky, and six
years working on a doctorate at Emory University in Atlanta, I

was teaching courses in religion and philosophy at Mercer University's Atlanta campus. A colleague and friend, who taught biology, recommended to me one day a book that he thought my students might find helpful. What I needed, though, at that particular time was not another book to wade through. I had my own books to read and stacks of papers to grade, but I trusted my friend, thanked him for his concern, and began reluctantly to work my way through J. Bronowski's *Science and Human Values*. That encounter with Bronowski was another eye-opening experience, and from time to time, I go back to Bronowski's book and read it again, because in his description of the nature of science and of the human values that flow from and resonate with it, I found and still find clues as to how to respond with integrity to the questions that arise inevitably when a person of any faith acknowledges that there are some things that, contrary to popular hope and belief, we do not and cannot know.

How science works and what it contributes to the world *because of* how it works is the theme of Bronowski's little book. What science has to teach us, he says, is not only, or even primarily, its techniques, but, more importantly, its spirit, the irresistible desire and need to explore, to question what we think we know, in a never-ending search to find out how things really are. Freedom of inquiry, freedom of thought, freedom to speak openly about what we learn from our research, freedom to dissent from established traditions—each of these values demands and honors what Bronowski calls "the habit of truth," which in turn sanctions the critical importance of tolerance for the views of any and of all who live and work affirming the values that are essential to a healthy effort to get at the truth of things.

A third important encounter that helped shape and broaden my understanding of the work of a teacher came much later in my career. It has been only recently, within the past nine or ten years, that I began to take seriously the contributions of the widely known and in some ways beleaguered Oxford scholar, Richard Dawkins. Dawkins' works tend to generate, as perhaps you know, both light and heat, and it is, I'm afraid, too often the heat that gets the attention. But leaving the heat aside for the moment, I would like for you to read a brief passage from his best-selling book *The God Delusion*. The context for this passage is the conviction that scientific "truth" always remains subject to review and revision.

Evidence rules in science, and if the evidence calls into question prior conclusions, so much the worse for those prior conclusions. No self-respecting and responsible scientist would justify holding on to a conclusion that evidence does not support. In this sense, it is safe, I think, to say that it is of the very nature of science to be self-correcting. Now, the quote from Dawkins:

"I have previously told the story of a respected elder statesman of the Zoology Department at Oxford when I was an undergraduate. For years he had passionately believed, and taught, that the Golgi Apparatus (a microscopic feature of the interior of cells) was not real: an artefact [sic.], an illusion. Every Monday afternoon it was the custom for the whole department to listen to a research talk by a visiting lecturer. One Monday, the visitor was an American cell biologist who presented completely convincing evidence that the Golgi Apparatus was real. At the end of the lecture, the old man strode to the front of the hall, shook the American by the hand and said with passion, 'My dear fellow, I wish to thank you. I have been wrong these fifteen years.' *We clapped our hands red.* . . . [My italics.] The memory of the incident I have described still brings a lump to my throat" (*The God Delusion*, pp. 283-84).

The point I want to make here, and the lesson I learned from reading about this encounter, is that it seems not to be in the nature of traditional religion of any persuasion seriously to question its beliefs and practices, to be self-correcting, since whatever challenges orthodoxy is almost by definition not allowed. Seldom, if ever, do we hear from the pulpit anything like an admission that what we have been taught to believe as "true" might well be questionable, or even wrong.

What catches my attention when I consider issues such as these is the understandable but potentially dangerous *certainty* that seems to pervade most, if not all, religious traditions. It was Will Durant, the great American historian and author of the ten-volume *The Story of Civilization*, who pointed out that the natural concomitant of strong faith is intolerance, and that tolerance grows only when faith loses certainty. Certainty, he says, is murderous. Why, if this is true, *is* it true? What is it that drives this compulsion to be right, this drive to protect and defend what we say we believe and which we hope is beyond the reach of doubt?

The only responsible answer I can give to that question

comes, of course, from my own experience, and I cannot, with integrity, speak for you or for anyone else. Let me illustrate in the following way. When I was only eleven or twelve years old, the members of my Sunday School class were challenged by an elderly gentleman in our church to memorize and then repeat for his hearing the entire Sermon on the Mount. I took the challenge seriously and memorized it all. As a reward, he presented me with a small edition of the New Testament, which I still have to this day.

Written on the inside front cover of that little New Testament in the old man's beautiful, flowing script are the words, "God's Simple Plan of Salvation–see page 313." At the top of page 313, he wrote, "You need to be saved," and he circled Romans 3: 23. At the bottom of that page, he wrote, "see p. 430." At the top of p. 430, he wrote "You cannot save yourself," and he circled Titus 3:5-6. At the bottom of that page, he wrote, "see p. 245." At the top of page 245, he wrote, "Only Christ can save you," and he circled Acts 4:12. At the bottom of that page, he wrote, "see p. 152." At the top of page 152, he wrote, "You must repent," and he circled Luke 13:3. At the bottom of that page, he wrote, "see p. 324." At the top of page 324, he wrote, "You must ask Christ to save you," and he circled Romans 10:13. At the bottom of that page, he wrote, "see p. 367." At the top of page 367, he wrote, "Do it now," and he circled II Corinthians 6:2b. At the bottom of that page, he wrote, "see p. 257." At the top of page 257, he wrote, "After you are saved, follow Christ in baptism," and he circled Acts 8: 35-39.

Religion in my church during those growing-up years seemed to be mostly about my eternal salvation, about what might happen to me when I died, and about how to avoid the eternal fires of hell. As a young man, I was scared to death. God, to my young mind and heart, was not really a God of love but a God of punishment, who would, for sure, get you in the end if you didn't get it right here and now. (I understand Martin Luther's early religious experience very well. He and I were much alike in this regard.) So I did my very best to get it right, but it wasn't love that motivated me to get it right. It was fear, and I lived with a crippling fear for years, and that crippling fear birthed my drive for certainty, because I wanted to be sure that I got it right, and my drive for certainty fed my growing intolerance for those who did not believe as I felt obligated to believe for my own eternal safety.

The Sermon on the Mount was not the only biblical passage I committed to memory, and I, along with many of you, can still recite many a favored verse. But as I grew older, I began to understand that there seemed to be a bias in my favorite Bible verses, and I hadn't really spent much time taking seriously the importance of *how I should live in the interim* between the here-and-now and "judgment day." The social consciousness of the Hebrew prophets and of the Sermon on the Mount itself took a back seat to my preoccupation with what I must do to avoid an eternal hell.

NEWS FLASH: "Four young Negro girls were killed Sunday morning, September 15, 1963, by a bomb blast at the 16th Street Baptist Church in Birmingham, Alabama." The culprits were three, perhaps four, white racial separatists, members of the Ku Klux Klan, whose refusal to recognize the basic civil rights of all Americans, regardless of racial heritage, was, and continues to be, shared by literally millions of Anglo-Saxon Christians.

I grew up in a comfortable, though not lavish, neighborhood, and we all looked rather alike with our fair Caucasian skin. Many of us attended church on Sunday mornings and sang together, *Amazing grace, how sweet the sound that saved a wretch like me/I once was lost but now am found, was blind, but now I see.* Most of us, if not all, had no idea about the origin of that hymn. We didn't know–I certainly didn't–that it was written by an English clergyman by the name of John Newton following a shipwreck, that his life had been spared, and that Newton had been involved for years in the African slave trade. Perhaps (but we're not sure) Newton referred to himself as a "wretch" because of his wanton involvement with slavery, though maybe he was just referring to himself as an ordinary sinner along with all the rest of us, and that for some reason God had decided to save his "wretched" soul. I suppose we'll never know for sure. But even after he composed his hymn, Newton, the evidence suggests, continued for several years participating in the sending of slaves to America.

I wish it were true, if it is not, that Newton saw himself as being "saved" from the "wretched" sale and enslavement of Africans for the pitiable sake of the convenience of their white American "masters," who may well have justified their own possession of slaves by one or two of their own favorite verses from the Bible. According to Genesis 9:25-27, for example, the descendants of

221

Canaan, son of Ham and grandson of Noah, were cursed to be slaves to Canaan's brothers from that day forward because Ham had seen the nakedness of Noah, who had become drunk and lay naked in his tent. (Or was it Canaan? There is some question about this.) Christians traditionally have believed that Canaan settled in Africa and that the dark skin of his descendants was somehow associated with the curse. So, weren't all those black people, including those four little girls, cursed by God from the start? What real difference, then, did it make that those innocent lives came to such a savage end at the hands of a small group of angry and bigoted Christians? At any rate, the neighborhood I grew up in was spared the "curse" of those black people, and it didn't really matter, after all, where they happened to live, given that they had already been cursed by God himself.

BREAKING NEWS: "Martin Luther King, Jr. was shot to death this evening, April 4, 1968, in Memphis, Tennessee, where he was attending a gathering in support of striking African American sanitation workers protesting unequal wages and unsafe working conditions." Surely we weren't surprised when we witnessed the deafening silence of many, if not most, of our Christian sisters and brothers, lending tacit approval to the murder of Dr. King.

Through the years it has become clear to me that my own traditional Christian preoccupation with the hereafter blinded me to the serious needs and injustices of our daily life together. When we become convinced that we are the sole proprietors of the truth and that our interpretation of critical biblical texts justifies our denunciation of what we believe to be heretical or socially unacceptable, we run the serious risk of prejudicial thinking that stems from and is nourished by our claims to certainty, reinforcing our own sense of privilege. In our own time, ISIS and Boko Haram and Al-Shabaab illustrate without question the savagery that can come from religious and political arrogance and intolerance. I can't help but think that the name *homo sapiens*–"wise man"–is in serious danger of being justifiably replaced by the name *homo stultus*–"foolish man"–and that the wisdom for which we are named as a species is being sidetracked by religious arrogance, unquestioning certainty, and vicious actions. It is not only non-Christians, of course, as we have seen, who are to blame. American Christians have been persecuting Black African Christians for centuries. When I was growing up, I never witnessed to any significant degree any of these problems, because we had a way of keeping those people "in their place." They were on the other side of town, out of sight and, for the most part, out of mind. My suggestion here is that science might well have something to teach religion. Is that a strange suggestion? Is there something that religious communities can learn from science that might affect our living together in a truly *positive* and less destructive way?

Surely none of us wants to be "wrong," and surely all of us want to believe that we are "right." But how do we determine where we stand regarding rightness and error? Who will demonstrate for us that we may have some rethinking to do, and what will be required for us to acknowledge our complicity in the building of walls between us as we seek to reinforce our own narrow picture of things? In response to whom and to what might we someday "clap *our* hands red" at being shown that maybe we haven't quite yet got it all exactly right? The ability and the courage to look beyond one's own subjective understanding of our world and the recognition that there may well be more to answering our deep and abiding questions than we have envisioned thus far–is that not an approach to the truth of things that science and religion can both affirm with integrity?

Science, at its best, is a way of knowing, a way of learning, a way of getting at the truth, a way that cannot and should not countenance the blind allegiance to what we've always believed just because we've always believed it. Galileo challenged the church's unquestioned understanding of how and why the physical world operates as it does, and papal authority certainly did not embrace him. But why should that have been so difficult for the church to handle? How many Christians do you know who do not believe that the earth revolves around the sun? The technological application of what science can teach us is often, to be sure, questionable and presents us with the need to think seriously about where we are going and what might be the result of our getting there. Hiroshima, Nagasaki, and Auschwitz haunt us still. I am not interested in ignoring the weaknesses and questionable application of scientific discoveries, but I am interested to learn from what science can teach us and in benefitting from its insights.

The most honest response to what we are now learning about this marvelous world is not to ridicule or disparage it, but to be grateful for what we have learned and are learning still because of the commitment of science to discovering the truth about the world we have been given. Science and scientists are at their best when working passionately but humbly before the mystery of all that is. My guess is that we've only just begun to figure it out. I cannot even imagine what future discoveries and research will teach us. To claim to know what we do not know, perhaps *cannot* know, or to refuse to acknowledge what is there for the seeing, only betrays our insularity and our fear of uncertainty. It is not only unwise. It is also self-defeating.

Darwin's critical insight that species develop through the process of natural selection can, and perhaps should, be augmented with the observation that the survival of *our* species is not at the mercy of natural processes alone. Given the madness of today's world, rife with absolutist claims, the human species will very likely survive *only* if it chooses wisely between the options and obstacles that confront it. Our survival is not only about adaptation through natural selection. It is also clearly, without question, about choice. The human race–*homo stultus,* if you prefer–must make up its mind what it will identify as of real, if not ultimate, importance and what it will be willing to do to achieve that end. It's not at all just a matter of chance. We must decide who and what we really want to be and what we are willing to do to make it happen. It is largely, without question, our own responsibility. Furthermore, it will not be wise to pretend that our choices will be of little consequence. They may well turn out to be the most critical of consequences imaginable.

The choices we make in the years ahead will most likely reflect, of course, our conviction that *we* are the righteous ones, and that it is those who disagree with us, who challenge us, that are in the wrong. That much seems clear from a parochial perspective. But we must also realize that those who do not share our history and our traditions most likely believe the same about themselves, so that *we* become the ones in the wrong, and *they* become the righteous. It is not only, or always, about disagreements among the different Christian traditions worldwide. It's everywhere and touches everyone–in the Middle East, in Africa, in Asia, as well as in the Americas–and our religious and cultural conflicts are not likely to go away anytime soon. So, what do we do? Where do we go from here?

I believe firmly that we would benefit greatly from giving

some serious thought to what science has to do with, and might contribute to, responsible human action. But is there any real connection between the two? If there really is a God who acts in human history, why doesn't this God act in some observable way to fix this mess? Is it perhaps, though, only wishful thinking that such a God might choose to intervene and reverse or eliminate the tragic consequences of the many problems to which we human beings have been contributing for millennia? Can we not see, can we not acknowledge, our own contribution to creating a world that we wish, from time to time, we could escape? Could it be, after all, that it's really, in the end, all up to us? Can we truly lay the blame at feet other than our own?

Almost forty years ago now–it was in 1977–a movie came out entitled *Oh, God!* John Denver played Jerry Landers, a young grocery store manager, and George Burns played God. At one point in the movie, Jerry, not quite yet convinced that the character played by Burns really was God, asks how God could stand by and allow such terrible things to happen to so many people throughout the world. If God *can* act as a personal agent, what better reason is there to act than to rid the world of people who commit the kinds of atrocious monstrosities we see all around us? Surely ISIS, Boko Haram, Al-Shabaab–and dare we mention the Ku Klux Klan–deserve their comeuppance. One wonders facetiously if another flood of biblical proportions might be appropriate, so that those of us who are "righteous" might start all over again, vowing to get it right this time.

Why does God allow widespread corruption in high places that favors the powerful few at the callous disregard of those who are weak and helpless? "Why, God, don't you *do* something!" The response is quick and sharp: it isn't God who allows such suffering, such injustice; it's human beings–it is *we*–who, by virtue of our vaunted and cherished freedom to choose, make the decisions that contribute to, and even make possible, so much of what is wrong in the world, allowing it to go unchallenged. "All the choices are yours," God says. So, when we ask why God doesn't do something, we hear in response, "Why don't *you*?" Why don't *we* do something about such conditions? How can we rest content with the *assurance* that it's all about going to heaven when we die, when it's also–perhaps equally so, or perhaps mostly–about trying to do something about the hell we live in here on earth?

It's not a bad thing to admit that I–that *we*–just might be wrong. There was a time when I could not, or would not, make such an admission, but I can't–I won't–go down that road again, and it may well be that the most helpful and honest thing I can ever do is to say, "I really don't know. I have my doubts." I have clearly been wrong about some things. Surely we *all* have at some point. But is it worth killing each other over our disagreements because of our inability–or our refusal–to try our best to work it all through together?

Embedded in the pavement of what is now Broad Street outside Balliol College in Oxford, England, is an iron cross, marking the site of the martyrdom of three prominent Protestant church leaders: Hugh Latimer, Bishop of Worcester; Nicholas Ridley, Archbishop of London; and Thomas Cranmer, Archbishop of Canterbury. In the years 1555-56, these three men were burned at the stake for the "crime" of unorthodox religious beliefs. What was it that Will Durant said about certainty? And the list of such human martyrs goes on almost, it seems, *ad infinitum*. Beware of people who claim to know that they alone are right.

Science does its best work with a *question mark* punctuating its research. Religion, I'm afraid, for all too long, has preferred an *exclamation point*. Is it too much to hope–is it naive to expect that people might respond more positively to an honest and open invitation to dialogue than to a haughty declaration to be passively accepted without question? Dialogue has a way of taking the edge off our certainties, and questions are much less comforting than overly confident affirmations. It is difficult in the extreme, given our fears and confidences and hopes, to acknowledge the real possibility that we could be wrong.

Each of us has a story to tell, and I would be interested in hearing yours, because you just might have something to say that I really need to hear. And if you do, and if you were to say it, I hope I would be wise enough, and grateful enough, to clap *my hands red* at the prospect of being introduced to yet another dimension of what in truth it's really all about.

--Duane Evans Davis

RACE

*There is no such thing as race. None. There is just a human race–
scientifically, anthropologically. Racism is a construct, a social
construct . . . it has a social function, racism.*
--Toni Morrison

*The human race has only one really effective weapon and that is
laughter.*
--Mark Twain

*We may have different religions, different languages, different
colored skin, but we all belong to one human race.*
--Kofi Annan

*For love of domination we must substitute equality; for love of
victory we must substitute justice; for brutality we must substitute
intelligence; for competition we must substitute cooperation. We
must learn to think of the human race as one family.*
--Bertrand Russell

*You must not lose faith in humanity. Humanity is an ocean; if a
few drops of the ocean are dirty, the ocean does not become dirty.*
--Gandhi

*If we are to have peace on earth . . . our loyalties must transcend
our race, our tribe, our class, and our nation; and this means we
must develop a world perspective.*
–Martin Luther King, Jr.

*I wish I could say that racism and prejudice were only distant
memories. We must dissent from the indifference. We must dissent
from the apathy. We must dissent from the fear, the hatred and the
mistrust...We must dissent because America can do better, because
America has no choice but to do better.*
--Thurgood Marshall

*During my lifetime I have dedicated myself to this struggle of the
African people . . . I have cherished the ideal of a democratic and
free society in which all persons live together in harmony and with
equal opportunities. It is an ideal which I hope to live for and to
achieve . . . it is an ideal for which I am prepared to die.*
--Nelson Mandela

"STRANGER IN THE VILLAGE"

James Baldwin's essay, "Stranger in the Village," conjures up a time for me when I was a black girl in a white high school. From all the stories and available pictures adorning the walls, no black girl had ever been captain of the cheerleading squad. I was warned before I auditioned that I was probably just wasting my time because the school was not ready for change. I took this to mean that people of my complexion were rarely seen in a predominantly white school as the head of anything. It had not occurred to me that there could still be people in this day and age who still felt that blacks were beneath them–and that I was just another Negro.

The school had been integrated in the 1960s. Even though blacks could attend, few chose to do so. My grandparents were prominent black leaders in society, so I had to go to Crowns Academy just to live up to whatever status they were trying to achieve. The school was known throughout the state for high academic achievement and student morale. However, my morale plummeted. I dreaded going to school mainly because nobody knew me. I was just a stranger to all the people who looked at me as if wanting to wave their hands, but feeling social pressure not to do so. I was an unfamiliar voice that some were afraid to hear. I was a stranger in a school where education was supposed to be an opportunity for all. I learned that first day that I was a black girl walking down the halls of a white school–a stranger in the village.

The school's only real fame was the cheerleading squad that had come in first place in competitions for over a decade–which explained why they were afraid of me becoming captain and why the other students treated me like I was the chicken pox, with avoidance being the only vaccination. Although my hair was as long as that of the white girls, they still made jokes, claiming that it looked like cotton. I felt like Baldwin did in Switzerland, when he said he "reacted by trying to be pleasant." The only thing I knew to do was to treat the other students with kindness–just as I wanted them to treat me.

I continued to practice for the audition and memorized the routine that the coach had taught us all. I was asked to demonstrate a dance move I had added to the routine and felt that this might be the beginning of a change of heart among my peers. I smiled when the coach praised me for doing a great job, but my peers did not see my sincere smile. They saw only the whiteness of my teeth. However, the stranger in the village was chosen to become the first black captain of the Crowns Academy cheerleading squad.

--KaSann B. Mahogany

STINSONVILLE: SILHOUETTES

When Thomas Wolfe maintained, "You can't go home again," he could have had Stinsonville in mind, especially if he meant that things change from first impressions. On this balmy Sunday afternoon, not quite spring nor summer, the memories hang in the air like thick, bouncy clouds waiting to burst into thunderstorms. The collection of portraits vividly displayed in the gallery of my mind stage their own slideshow in my head.

As far as the eye can see, this "virgin" land sits there like an old maid waiting for her next suitor. The tall grass waving in the wind carries the echoes of children running down Brooklyn Avenue, clutching their pennies as they rush to the A. J. Reid Store for bubble gum, penny candy, or two-for-a-penny cookies. I can hear them now as they come through the "cut" behind Mildred Johnson's house: "Miss Bay! Miss Bay!" they call and cajole long before they reach the store, located behind my mother-in-law's house.

My father-in-law had built this store and named it "Jr. Reid's Place," but it became Miss Bay's store to the children of the neighborhood. Even when she did get a brief chance to sit on her front porch, she could look up those dry streets for two blocks either way and see children coming with drink bottles—long before drinks came in cans. With the urgency of a 911 call, girls in pigtails–half-plaited and half loose–accompanied by cousins, sisters, and brothers, knocked on the door.

"What you want, Sugar?" Miss Bay would call from the kitchen, eyeing the clock as lunchtime neared. She knew Alex, Sr.–or "Hawk" as his friends called him–would be driving up soon in his shiny old DeSoto, looking for his lunch. "I just want some cookies," the little one would say. Before going out the door to the store to sell a nickel's worth of cookies, some bubble gum, and maybe even a drink, Miss Bay would carefully remove slices of fatback or fried pork kidneys from the old, black frying pan. After a morning of cooking, cleaning, and washing, which entailed scrubbing overalls on a rub board, Miss Bay would get ready for work. At about one o'clock she would head for the bus line to get to the College Hill Chi-Chester's Drug Store by two, where she would work at the soda fountain until ten that night. When Hawk couldn't pick her up at the drugstore, she would get the bus back home. By the time Miss Bay climbed into bed, she had easily put in eighteen hours of perpetual motion.

On the weekends the store would really come alive. The jukebox could be heard for a block either way, drawing people from the neighborhood into the yard for dancing, barbeque, fish and sausage sandwiches, hot French fries, and plenty of chit-chat about present and bygone days. For a few hours on Friday and Saturday nights, these hardworking people would throw caution to the wind and become one big happy family, regardless of what their last names were. Even people from Pleasant Hill, Belleview, and other neighborhoods could be seen hanging onto the outer fringes of the group.

And it seemed like "Louse"–Early Sims–always had a game of checkers going in his backyard or on the side of the store. Alex, Jr.–"Tuddy," as most people called him–would be home from college every weekend and would be selling every kind of sandwich his imagination could cook up. The real showstopper, however, was my husband's granddaddy, Arthur Glover. With just enough trips to Miss Sadie's house, he could do any dance from the jitterbug to the twist. He was good as the main attraction until about midnight.

I often find myself reminiscing about how I came to be here. It goes back to being in the right place at the right time–or letting your feet be led by your mind, and your mind by your heart.

Love found me on the campus of Bethune-Cookman College in Daytona Beach, Florida. It was an autumn Saturday morning. I am pretty sure that it was fate that propelled me from my bed and sent me to breakfast that morning. It sure wasn't habit–I always slept late on Saturdays.

While I was waiting in the cafeteria line, one of the fellows from the visiting team of Morris-Brown College walked up to me with the same line that Adam had used on Eve: "Hello there," he said, in a voice as rich as double chocolate. "Don't I know you from somewhere?"

From that moment on, my heart has belonged to one man. For those who don't believe in love at first sight, I can testify that it really does happen. I had only existed until then. After meeting Alex, at last I was really living and aware. It was a born-again experience. Alex Reid, Jr. completely took my heart, my appetite, and my senses–and it all happened so quickly. It really did feel like Cupid actually shot me in the heart. We spent most of that day together, and it seemed like we had many things in common.

After the game that night, we danced and then he walked me to the dorm. The last words he said to me were, "I'll call you on Monday about five o'clock." "Sure," I said to myself. "They (football players) always do." But it was a promise well kept, and he did call–long before five o'clock–and I still thought he was like a sailor in every port. I still didn't think it was more than a weekend fling for some football jock. Little did I know that it was the beginning of a year and a half of long distance courting. We would see each other maybe three or four times a year. We talked on the phone a lot–and, unbelievably, I have a whole collection of letters from him. He wrote me almost every week.

The first time we had a clandestine meeting was at the Arbor Motel in Jacksonville, Florida. It happened on an Easter weekend. I kept looking over my shoulder, hoping not to see anyone I knew. I did. It was Velma Brown, one of my high school classmates, and her parents. I was glad we were at the train depot, because that saved me a lot of explaining and much grief since many students were going on Easter vacation.

The weekend consisted of talking, laughing, take-out dinners, walks, and, of course, unforgettable lovemaking. The thrill of my life is still having him hold my hand while we are walking and kissing me on the back of my neck.

These first years seem almost like yesterday and the day before. They are still touchable in my mind. We were soul mates. He had my heart in his hands and still does. So it was by fate and smooth talking that I ended up in Stinsonville.

On February 8, 1963, my first night in Macon, as we passed by a nice, white two-story house on Brooks Street, my husband informed me that the Mayor of Stinsonville, Mr. Max Brooks, lived there. Mr. Brooks was highly respected by the people of this small community. More than seventeen families lived in his houses, which he clung to like Spanish moss on an oak tree. And the tenants clung to him for the very roof over their heads. The people who lived in his houses usually had large families. At one time, there were over one hundred children from Brooks Street down Brooklyn Avenue.

Max Brooks had recently married Mrs. Annie Brooks and they had a young son, Douglas. Our son, Kevin, was the recipient of many of Doug's hand-me-downs. For a while, Mrs. Brooks befriended me and helped me with my new role as a mother.
--Priscilla Reid

ARTHUR DADDY

If I could admire only one person in this community, it would be Arthur Glover, called "Chief" by his friends and "Art Daddy" by his grandson. He was a master farmer. This would be the time of the year for him to plant peas, collards, okra, corn, and watermelon in a good-sized patch behind Aunt Bea's house. Aunt Bea was his daughter, whom I never saw in his garden. You would have thought that I had enough sense to stay out. In fact, he had warned me that women were NOT ALLOWED in his garden. While we were still living on Brooks Street, I passed by his house on Brooklyn Avenue, spoke to him as he sat on the porch, and proceeded to the garden to get some okra. I looked up, and there he was. It seemed like he had read my mind. Until this day, I don't know how he got there so fast or how he knew where I was going. I learned then that you don't mess with "the Chief." He took no prisoners. My husband tells the story that Chief didn't even keep cows and hogs over a year. A hog over a year old became ham, bacon, and pork chops.

"Granddaddy" lived with a woman named Ms. Doty, who carried laundry baskets on her head much like African women–although he did have a living wife, Virginia–my husband's grandmother, who lived in Jacksonville Beach, Florida. I will always believe that he had a lifelong love affair in his heart with Ms. Doty. The story goes that he was so mean to her that she packed

232

up her things and moved to Jacksonville with the white people she worked for.

Every summer when Grandmama came to Macon to visit her daughters, he would come to Bay's house to talk to her. You could see the love he had for her in his eyes. They would get bright and sad-looking like a hound dog, wishing to recapture the good old days. She talked about him a lot, too. She told me how he would be gone for days at a time on a job and would come back expecting to see a plate of food for every day he was gone–as if to say we did cook for you and expected you back at any time.

His children described how he could communicate so much with just a look. He was the third person I met when I came to Macon, and it seemed like I had known him all of my life. He loved to tease me, but I never knew for sure if he was joking or not. My husband warned never to get on his bad side–he would get you back before he went to sleep. Granddaddy Art would come to our house so many times and knock on the door. When I asked who was there, he always answered, "Nobody." Even after he died, I could still hear him knocking on the door. It had to be him because we lived right across the street from the cemetery where he was buried. I am convinced that he was still playing tricks on me.

After Ms. Doty died, he would get up around five o'clock, eat whatever he had, feed the hogs, and work in his garden until about eight o'clock, when he would come to my house for breakfast. He brought his own eggs and bacon or ham. He liked his eggs sunny-side-up. He would stand right by the stove, giving me instructions on how to cook the eggs, especially when to turn them off.

Different people tried to help me develop my cooking skills. Once, Granddaddy got me to cook an opossum and sweet potatoes. Though it smelled good to me, he never asked me to cook another one. When I became a pretty good cook, I did share many other dishes with him.

Art Daddy and my husband once bought a calf together. At the end of the year when Art Daddy thought the calf was big enough, he decided he wanted to kill the calf the next morning. Even though my husband didn't agree to kill the cow, Art Daddy interjected: "I'll be killing my half of the cow tomorrow." This taught Tuddy not to buy on halves again. There was no argument, however. They killed the cow the next morning. Art Daddy was such a little man to pack such a big punch. His word ruled the house.

Every New Year's morning, Art Daddy would go from house to house and walk from front to back as a means of blessing the house and the family for the New Year. It worked, too–at least for us. We always had food in our freezer and our rent paid. After Art Daddy died, George Taylor tried for a while to carry on the tradition, but the practice faded after a few years.

Art Daddy was a man who was never seen flashing money or begging–he just seemed to float along. I realize no one can live by floating along, but his life was so mapped out that it seemed like he was living on "Easy Street." By the time I came to Stinsonville, Art Daddy was probably the oldest man there, and in this community he was respected and honored by young and old. When our son, Kevin, was born, Art Daddy was so glad to have a great-grandson. He played with him a lot, holding him by his heels or throwing him up in the air and catching him.

One time he put Kevin on Ole Kate, his mule, and the mule took off with Kevin on his back, heading for the woods. Old Kate was not used to anyone riding her. A crowd of people from the store went chasing after them. They caught the mule and managed to get Kevin off unharmed. This was one time his joke backfired on him.

Arthur Glover sure had an impact on my fitting into the community. When others saw how he interacted with me, they began to warm up to me, too. My "in-law" status was done away with quickly, and I just became part of the family. He always introduced me simply as his granddaughter. I took to him like a duck takes to water, with just enough fear of him to know when to stop teasing and an abundance of love for the granddaddy I never had.
--Priscilla Reid

Aunt Bea

Though many voices resound through these streets, one stands out loudly and clearly–the voice of Aunt Bea Tanner. She and her husband lived over the hill and through the woods behind the store. The two sisters, Lucille (Miss Bay) and Beatrice (Bea)

234

spent a lot of time together. Aunt Bea worked mornings and could be heard coming toward home–the long way around–at about twelve-thirty. But many times she didn't actually get home until four o'clock. She was a slow, easy-going person, who stopped along the way and talked casually. I could look up the road toward Max Brooks' house and see her talking to Annie Prince (Mrs. Brooks) or Mrs. Seanett. She would come on down the road, calling out to each person as she passed their house: "Hi, Miss Doty," "Hello, Mildred. How's your mother doing?" She would trudge on down the road past Arthur and Emma Goodwin's house, John and Louise Owens', and Wilma Stephens', never even missing the smallest child. At last she would turn in the drive at my mother-in-law's house. Sometimes we would be sitting on the screened porch, but most of the time she would come out to the store and sit on the old refrigerator that had been turned down there for so long that it was almost rusty. A natural reflex was to brush off a spot and sit down. Whoever was already sitting there always made a space for her.

Even before we had children, Miss Sadie's grandchildren would come up and listen to her talk in her slow, mesmerizing sentences. Sometimes Annie Leola would come as Lillie Mae emptied the dish water out of the back door or fed the chickens. She would always inquire, "How are you doing, Aunt Bea?" Lillie Mae knew not to expect to get away with a one-sentence answer. She had to get settled in for a whole line of "How's Louise? Did you know Miss So-and-So did this, that, and the other thing?" All this time, Lillie Mae would be trying to get back inside.

"Cilla," she would ask me, "Is it about time for the story?" And I would tell her what time it was because by now she had me hooked on "As the World Turns." People would be going back and forth in the store as I tried to keep up with what was going on inside and outside.

Most of the homes in Stinsonville had outhouses; only a few had bathrooms, and Aunt Bea's house was one of those. I would follow her home many a day to get a bath. It's really funny, in a nice way, how I took to the Glovers–my mother-in-law's side of the family. It seems like I was born as one of them.

After a year of living with my in-laws, we moved to Brooks Street, becoming one of Max Brooks' tenants. Aunt Bea then made a detour every day to my house. She was teaching me how to cook. I would take the food out of the freezer and wait for her to come by and get it started. Kevin would be waiting, too. He would hear her talking to Dorothy Williams, who lived two doors down, or Mrs. Nina, who lived next door, and he would start kicking and grinning. She used to call him her "Ivory Soap" baby. He had had a few baths at her house too, and she always kept Ivory soap for him.

Aunt Bea and Uncle Alex didn't have any children, but you would have thought that I was their four-year-old. During the summer of 1963, they took me with them to Jacksonville Beach, Florida. We went to the zoo there and fished at Little Talbot Island. It seemed like they were showing this little kid around as they unselfishly shared their vacation with me. They even left me down there with Grandmama Virginia for a few weeks and came back to get me. Aunt Bea lived for a little more than two years after I came to Macon. The times I shared with her are forever etched in my mind.

It was through Aunt Bea that I became familiar with most of the people of Stinsonville. We would go for long walks in the woods and end up at Miss Jessie Simmons' house on Overlook Avenue. Being with her was like reading a gossip column or a tabloid newspaper: I learned who was kin to whom. This was helpful in knowing when to keep my mouth shut.

Aunt Bea taught me to go to town on the bus to pay bills. She only let me go one place at a time. She would give me directions to the Atlanta Gas Light office where I could pay the bill and catch the Vineville bus back home–I really did want to explore but was afraid of getting lost. The next day she might give me directions to the Georgia Power Office. After a while, I became like a native Maconite, exploring every street and avenue.

The place I loved to go was Dannenberg's Department Store on Third Street, a big, old-fashioned general store. I would go in there whenever I went to town, if only to buy something for my baby: a diaper shirt, a pair of socks, and, of course, orange slices–my favorite candy. I still miss Aunt Bea. I often tell my children what a wonderful person she was. Aunt Bea asked me to name my second child for her if it was a girl. Miss Bay, of course, wanted us to name her Lucille. Stuck in the middle, I made up a middle name to honor both great ladies: Lu'Atrice.
--Priscillla Reid

Neighbors

The people of Stinsonville gave new meaning to the term "nosy neighbors." They constantly and routinely checked on each other without letting on that they were concerned. For instance, my mother-in-law might have been having a cup of coffee in her kitchen while all the while listening to see if Lillie Mae or Louse had come outside. Or she might comment about midmorning: "Did you see Wilma (or Tuddy, as they sometimes called her) leave for work yet? I wonder if she has the day off."

In Stinsonville, it was common to toll the church bell when someone in the neighborhood died. Neighbors would come into the street in various stages of dress to find out for whom the bell tolled. This is how news was passed. As the telephone grew in popularity, this final touch became one of the things that connected us as neighbors and friends.

There were many people of influence in Stinsonville, each with their own expertise. Having served in the armed forces, Mr. Charles Kitchens had seen more of the world than the rest of us. He spent much of his time listening to the fellows in the yard, giving them advice about life. He was considered the neighborhood counselor. I can still hear him saying, "Alex, if I was you, I would–" and his advice was well taken most of the time. The community valued his experiences and opinions.

Charles and his wife, Janie, had two sons, Charles, Jr. and Daniel. To see Mrs. Janie hanging clothes on the line was sheer poetry. It was so natural–like she was waltzing up and down the line with sheets sparkling and billowing out in the morning sun. After Mrs. Janie's two sons left home, she took a liking to my younger son, "Little Alex," and baked cakes especially for him. He remembers fondly that she could make a "mean" cake. It was worthwhile just knowing these people. They were role models long before the term was even coined.

Mr. and Mrs. Kitchens are both gone now. She died first. Mr. Charles spent many days on the front porch conversing with first one person and then another. The last thing we talked about was the birth of my first grandson, Chandler, when Mr. Charles reminded me that he could remember when each of my children had been born. His son, Daniel Kitchens, lived in the home house. The Kitchens brothers own the three houses still standing like an island on that side of Brooklyn Avenue. Typical of close neighbors, many clung together until they were forced apart by reality and the system. After the houses that Mr. Brooks owned were sold and demolished, the independent families lined up systematically and claimed: "Not me. I'll keep my house. I don't need the money that badly." As an outsider, I could only stand there and cheer for each one of them as if they could hold on to the land and the memories forever.

Lizzie Threatt, Bay's cousin, was one of the homeowners adamant in saying that she would definitely hold on to her house. After renting for most of her life, she had only in her golden years acquired her house. Almost daily, she seemed to be negotiating in her mind the plight of the families left behind. Now, the only families remaining in Stinsonville from my arrival in 1963 are Luther Williams and Mose and Emma Jefferson. Lizzie stayed in spite of offers and the temptation to move. Miss Bay (Kid, as Lizzie called her) and Lizzie talked seriously about old times and the current situation. I can hear Lizzie concluding: "Naw, Bay, I'm going to stay right here. It's close to the church and all." No matter what you told Lizzie, her response was always the same: "Naw, Bay. You don't say. Kid, hush." It was like she didn't believe you said it or her eyes saw it.
--Priscilla Reid

A Spot in the Road

Max Brooks lived to be over seventy years old, but I don't think he ever got the message that the people of Stinsonville were working day and night to accomplish the great American dream of home ownership. He could have helped to cement this dream. I feel that he was a bit selfish. I know at least three people, including my father-in-law and my husband, who tried to buy a house or a strip of land from Max. He always refused, maybe not directly, but he would pretend that he was thinking about it for an awful long time and pretty soon the person would forget about it and go on. This is what prompted me to find out how Stinsonville came about. It seemed like there was something magical or mystical that caused one person to want to possess this expanding suburb.

According to the story I was told, Stinsonville was named after Edward Stinson, a freed black man who came to Macon from Virginia, where he was born. His white father had freed him at an early age. Stinson's first stop was Eatonton, Georgia, where he tried to start a school for slave children. Reportedly run out of Eatonton, he arrived here in about 1850, when he bought a large plot of land north of Macon for about five dollars.

Upper-class whites have always surrounded Stinsonville. It was so small that outsiders could easily pass right by it, if they didn't know exactly where to turn. White people sometimes blundered around Stinsonville on Sunday afternoon drives. The most convenient way to enter Stinsonville was from Vineville Avenue to Auburn Avenue onto Brooks Street, which dead-ends at the Methodist Church.

Edward Stinson married and continued to live in the area. Some of his descendants still live in Macon. When I came to Macon, a sixth-generation relative, William Dunn, Sr., lived in the part of town called Pleasant Hill, but he still owned a little more than four acres of land in Stinsonville. At that time, Mr. Dunn's wife supervised the plumbing, construction, care, and repairs for her husband, who was in poor health. Other tenants were Arthur and Emma Goodwin, Roosevelt and Wilma Stevens, and Early and Lillie Mae Sims. Mrs. Dunn also claimed the store since it was their land, even though Hawk had actually built the little building that housed so many memories for not only the Reid family but for others who lived in Stinsonville or frequented it.

Mr. Charles Kitchens owned his home and two rental houses. In addition, there were Tom Johnson's family house, Mrs. Mansena Jackson's house that had earlier been a boarding house, and the houses of Miss Jessie Simmons, John and Carrie Simmons, and John's mother. All the remaining houses on Brooks Street and Brooklyn Avenue, with the exception of Miss Love's house, were owned by Max Brooks. On Grant Street, Mrs. Lockett owned her house, as did Mr. and Mrs. Jimmie Colbert. The Colberts also owned the house directly across the street. Murray Lacey and her family lived in Mr. Colbert's rental house. Mrs. May Lou Tanner died and left her land to her stepson, Alex Tanner. Mrs. Annie Leola Young was also a homeowner in Stinsonville, possessing two houses and a duplex.

Max Brooks inherited most of his land from his father, Professor J. A. Brooks, who founded and taught at the J. S. Brooks School, later becoming Stinsonville Elementary School. The school was then operated as part of the Bibb County School System until it was consolidated with the Pleasant Hill School in the early forties.

Stinsonville was an independent community until 1949. However, it wasn't until the late sixties or early seventies that the citizens were able to enjoy a sewer system and paved streets. About twenty years before the houses were demolished, each was equipped with a bathroom, sticking out like a thumb. It is hard to remember the outside facilities now. It would rain for days, and the next thing you knew someone's truck was stuck in the mud–or the children would get mud splashed on their clothes on the way to or from school. It is good to look back and rewind the film. We cannot be too presumptuous about the future.
--Priscilla Reid

THE STORE

The store asked itself,
As it stood there by the way.
(on the corner)
Not one box upon the shelf,
Not one cookie in the jar,
Not one cold drink in the box,
No more children traveling far,
No more chips going stale,
No one wanting cigarettes,
No one opening up a coke–
I just stand here and ask myself.
"Where's Miss Bay?"
She's not here
To sweep the floor,
To stock the shelves,
To lock my door.
I just stand here by myself.

"Where is all the children's chatter?"
As they hurried to the store,
Huffing, puffing, out of wind,
Wanting candy, chewing gum.
The days are long;
The days are dry,
No more gossip;
No more fun.
Just clouds and angels in the sky,
A lone car passing by.
I just might as well
Shrivel up and die.
Once vibrant,
The store breathed its last sigh–
The bulldozer appeared
And down the store went,
Board by board,
Without a fight–
It wasn't quite right.
The children's last pennies
Have now been spent.
The store is no more–
Not even for rent.
Gone is the icon
Of community caring,
Gone by the wayside
The neighborhood sharing.
Little did we know it at the time
What we had was priceless–
Yes, even sublime.

--Priscilla Reid

TYPEWRITER OR LIGHT BULB?

This story is mostly true. I was an eyewitness to the key
events. I treat it as an act of fiction so that I can take some liber-
ties with it. We all are aware of the great changes that occurred in
our society as a result of desegregation. We take those times very

seriously and often don't talk about them except in hushed and respectful terms. What we often miss, especially those who were not there, is the fact that these were human times with actors who were as human and as flawed as the rest of us. The truth can only emerge when we engage in honest conversation. Telling it like we experienced it–with sensitivity, respect, and honesty intact–can help all of us to come to terms with the great change we were a part of.

I grew up in the racist South. Specifically, I was born in Clarkesville, Tennessee, a town of about 25,000 when I was born in 1946. By the time I started high school, Clarkesville had doubled in size. Like all towns in that area and time, it had two high schools–one white and one black. The assumption was that the capabilities of the two races were different. The entire school board was white. The white community believed that black students could not benefit from the "superior education" offered in the white high school. We had white Clarkesville High School and black Burt High School–on opposite sides of town, as were the white and black communities they served.

The presence of Fort Campbell right outside town was an anomaly. Physically located in Kentucky, it was closer to Clarkesville than to Hopkinsville, the nearest town in Kentucky. Fort Campbell was primarily an Army base. It had elementary and junior high schools, but no high school. When students from the base finished junior high, they came to Clarkesville for high school. The Army had already been integrated, including the base schools. However, when the base students came to town, the white students went to one high school and blacks to another. To my knowledge, no one ever questioned this arrangement.

Times were changing. We all know about Little Rock in 1955 and what came after that. What we don't know about are all the little dramas and comedies that happened in lots of other places. In Clarkesville there was growing pressure to integrate. One leader of that effort was a black doctor who was head of the NAACP, Dr. Russell. A graduate of Meharry Medical School in Nashville, he suffered from the disease that causes black people to lose their pigmentation. Some joked that he was turning white. He bought a house on the white side of town in a lower middle class neighborhood, close to where I lived. There was some grumbling when he moved his family in, but no protests.

242

Dr. Russell continued his efforts to have the schools integrated and in 1963, my senior year, integration was tried. His son Richard was admitted to Clarkesville High. He lived close to the school and he was a good student, so it seemed a safe first step. This was the first time I had ever been in school with a black person. It wasn't even mentioned in the newspaper.

As it turned out, I had chemistry class with Richard. Pleasant and attractive, he wore glasses and was better dressed than most of us. His lab partner was Terry Moore, one of the cheerleaders. A senior, she was a quiet blond. They seemed to get along fine, although there was not much in the way of personal conversation. Richard was personable and outgoing. He had a hard time staying serious and reserved, but we all managed to get along for the first six weeks.

One morning as we were all milling around before the start of class, I saw him approach Terry as she came into the class. He was all smiles and full of energy. I heard him say he wanted to ask her a question. She seemed a bit uncertain, but agreed. He asked: "Would you rather be a typewriter or a light bulb?"

Puzzled, she replied, "I don't know what you mean."

He encouraged her to just answer the question.

"Well, I guess a typewriter," she responded.

Giggling, Richard inquired, "So you'd rather be fingered than screwed?"

Astonished, Terry animatedly stormed out of the room.

The teacher, Mrs. Rice, hadn't heard any of this and started class. A few moments later, Howard, the school bully, came to the classroom door. We later found out that he was a pain killer addict. I had never seen him smile. Howard leaned through the door with the biggest, silliest grin on his face I had ever seen. He searched the classroom until he found Richard. Without saying a word, he simply crooked his finger at Richard and signaled for him to come out into the hall.

End of integration.

Well, that isn't really the truth, but it makes a good story.

The truth was that there were two black students who came to Clarkesville High School that fall. The second one was a young woman who was one of the best students at Burt High. Reserved and serious about her studies, she stayed to herself. I can't imagine how hard it must have been on her, not having any friends and knowing that most people didn't want her there. She graduated the next year with honors.

--Thompson Biggers

MY WHITE KNIGHT

I grew up in the sixties. I lived way out in the country. My mother, brothers, sister, and I lived in a big house that sat back from the road. I was amazed that it never fell off the high rocks that it rested on. Life was very simple and carefree for me. It was a time when I did not understand the way things were.

When we went into town, there were two restrooms. One sign said "White" and the other said "Colored." I asked my mother why, and she would admonish me, "Do not ask questions." At the restaurant, we had to go to the back door to get a sandwich. Of course, I asked why we had to go to the back door and why we could not go inside and sit down like "white people." My mother had this certain look she would give me when she wanted me to be quiet. I got the look and immediately closed my mouth.

I could not even drink from the water fountain in town. When I think about the character Ms. Jane Pittman, I wonder if I should have drunk from the fountain. I laugh to myself. The white people would not have had to say or do anything if this had happened. My mother would have taken care of me.

I still treasure tradition today as I did then. We were having a "big meeting" at our church on the fourth Sunday in October. It was a tradition that everyone would buy new clothing for this great day. People would come from miles around to church on this Sunday. My mother and I planned a trip to Macon to buy new clothing on Saturday. When the Greyhound bus pulled into the bus station in Jeffersonville, Georgia, I was excited at the opportunity to go to the city. At that time, colored people had to ride in the back of the bus. The white people always used over half of the bus space, while the colored people had to stand up when less than half the bus was full.

As I entered the bus, my mother hurried me to the back. As I passed by white people, some of them leaned back as if my color would rub off on them. Their manner forbade me to touch them.

I continued to walk toward the back, while they continued to look at me as if I were a "bug" to be squashed under their feet. The bus began to pull out of the station. Due to the lack of seats in the back, my mother reached up to hold onto the rail.

Out of the corner of my eye, I saw a white man moving toward us. Naturally, one would think that he was going to the rest room located in the back. He stopped right in front of my mother and me and very kindly said, "Madam, you can have my seat."

Mother replied very quickly, "Sir, I thank you, but I can't do that."

He repeated his words very deliberately, "Come, sit down."

As my mother sat down in his seat, she lifted me onto her lap. The kind white man looked at the white passengers and commanded, "Nobody say nothing." He continued to stand over us all the way to Macon. He stood like a knight in armor and with authority. He was in command. When the bus pulled into the station in Macon, he stepped back to let us go ahead of him. He turned and spoke to us after we had exited the bus, "Madam, you and your daughter have a good day."

Mother thanked the nice man and wished him a good day. I trudged along behind my mother, thanking God for my white knight.

--Carrie Mae Mack

THE SMOKING ROOM

Sipping a Diet Coke and reading a newspaper, Keith lounged in the back of the jazz club. It was a hole-in-the-wall joint near downtown Chicago. As the band took a break, a deejay played old school music to the appreciative crowd. Faded pictures of Dizzy Gillespie, Louis Armstrong, and Ella Fitzgerald hung on the stained walls. Keith took a drag off his cigarette as "The Smoking Room" boomed from the giant speakers.

Chaka Khan was belting out the sultry tune and Keith listened to the lyrics with tears in his eyes. Chaka and the band Rufus performed that song with such emotion. Every head in the place was bopping, shoulders swaying, feet tapping. This was the jam:

Here we are alone–in this old smoking
room again. If your highness is your
pleasure, it's alright. 'Cause there's
extra added goodness in my heart for you
tonight, and if there's any such a thing as
God, He must be here tonight. So glad I
got you here to spend some time. Glad I
got you to share my life, baby.

It brought back many memories. Remembering what could
have been was painful. He thought of the times when he had been
in love. Those were the "good ole days." A "brotha" could buy
a pack of Kools for a dollar fifty, a bottle of Mad Dog 2020 for
under three dollars, and a big bag of weed for five.

Keith first saw Elmira as she walked across the campus of
Fort Valley State College the fall of 1974. She was a big-boned
country girl from Guyton, a town near Savannah, and attended
school on a basketball scholarship. Tall and thin with a big booty,
she wore jeans that hung below her waist, hugging every inch.
She wore short halter tops to show off her curvaceous figure. Her
afro-pick with the black power fist was always nearby to keep her
hair neatly in place. She had a walk that made men do a double
take. Her luscious thick lips parted to display a broad, beautiful
smile with a gap between her two front teeth.

Her dialect was Geechee or Gullah creole, a mixture of
Elizabethan English and several different African and West Indies
dialects. Thinking fast and talking faster, Elmira was always one
step ahead of everyone else. Her language was very different.
Sometimes Keith had trouble understanding what she said, yet he
hung on each word.

Elmira explained to Keith that her language was used by
slaves who refused to give up their native tongue when they were
brought over in chains. The slaves could communicate with each
other without Master knowing what they were saying. Families
like Elmira's were brought over on slave ships. When freed, they
chose to stay in that area.

Keith was often amused by the lingo she used. When he left
the window open and the room became cold, Elmira barked, "Put
some draws on that winda."

One night a mouse scurried across the floor as they watched
television in the dimly-lit living room. Elmira looked to Keith and

246

placed her fingers to his lips in order to quiet him. She deftly crept across the floor with the sleekness of a cat, taking long deliberate strides. She grabbed the mouse by the tail, swung it around a few times and flung it against the wall. When the mouse fell lifelessly to the floor, Elmira picked it up, dropped it in the trash, and then sat down as if nothing had happened.

Keith was perplexed when Elmira placed a broomstick by the door each night before going to bed. When she told him that its purpose was to ward off the "hags," he began to wonder what he was getting himself into. Elmira explained that hags were deceased women who roamed around at night looking for souls to enter. Custom dictated that the hag would have to stop and count each straw in the broom. Since there were so many straws, it would be daylight before the hag could finish counting. At first Keith thought Elmira a bit peculiar, but the more he learned about her, the more intrigued he became. Shoot, if a hag entered her house to bother Elmira, he would beat it to death, again.

When she attended the African Methodist Episcopal (AME) Church in her hometown, he gladly went along. When the prayer service began, Keith opened his Bible to John 1:1 as instructed. When the prayer service began, he was pleasantly surprised to learn that he could follow along in his Bible with the reading:

Fo God mek de wol, de Wod been dey. De Wod been dey wid God, an de Wod been God. - De Good Nyews Bout Jedus Christ Wa John Write 1:1. Translation: *In the beginning was the Word, and the Word was with God and the Word was God.*

Keith happily joined in the congregation's performance of the traditional ring dance, pleased to be welcomed into their midst. When Keith asked about her family history, Elmira replied, "my peepl cum frum cross de wata." She brought golden scuppernong and elderberry jelly from home to share. Their meals consisted mostly of red beans and rice. She wove beautiful baskets, an art she had learned from her parents. Elmira was the most interesting person he had ever met.

Keith enjoyed all that she was and looked forward to spending the rest of his life with her. He was not ashamed of being in love and was mocked by the other young men on the campus. They said that Elmira had Keith's "nose wide open," but he didn't care and defiantly joked that he loved her so much he would "drink her dirty bathwater."

They talked about songs that were popular. "What's Going On" and "Mercy, Mercy Me" were hits by Marvin Gaye; Keith loved to debate the true meaning of such profound lyrics. Keith thought Marvin was talking about the Vietnam War and the effects it had on Americans. Elmira just liked the lyrics. She thoroughly enjoyed lying awake at night listening, as he seemed to make love to her through the radio.

Elmira and Keith made love for the first time while they listened to Barry White croon, "Never, never gonna give you up." Keith proclaimed that this would now be "their song" and whenever she heard it on the radio, Elmira got a look of exuberance on her face. The couple hung out with friends at the Shrimp Boat. She loved the fried chicken battered with corn meal mix. They made plans to save the world. Political science was popular; it seemed to be their ticket to the big city of Atlanta. It was a chance to show the world the definition of young, gifted, and black. "Jim Crow" was still alive and well, but they weren't afraid. They were young and didn't have enough sense to be afraid.

While in grammar school, Keith made the trip with his parents to hear Martin Luther King, Jr. speak at the March on Washington in 1963. There was hope for America with Dr. King and President Kennedy working for civil rights. Three months later, President Kennedy was slain. Keith's parents walked around crying for months thereafter. He was young and didn't realize the impact this would have on his life, but he knew it was major. When he learned that Dr. King had been assassinated the next year, he was devastated. Robert Kennedy was murdered two months later. It seemed that the world had ended–at least his world. His parents were painfully quiet. The joy he had always known in his home was gone.

He heard his parents talk about problems they faced in integration of the schools. "Separate but equal" was good enough for the white folks, so that was how many planned for it to continue. In the case of Brown vs. Topeka Board of Education, the Supreme Court ruled that the schools were definitely separate, but inherently not equal in 1954. The Little Rock Nine were the first to integrate schools in Arkansas in 1957. Keith didn't understand why it was so hard to integrate schools in Middle Georgia. One of his friends, Bert, was the first black student admitted to Dudley

Hughes Vocational School in Bibb County in 1963. Bibb County was forced by the Supreme Court to integrate its schools in 1969.

Hanging out in the courtyard on campus, Keith and other students played cards and discussed world events. Many were politically motivated to protest. There was a caravan to the Anti-Vietnam War Rally in Valley Forge in 1970. U.S. troops had withdrawn from Vietnam in 1973. But Keith's older brother, Eric, didn't make it home–at least not alive. His troop had been ambushed in Laos five years earlier. Keith harbored resentment towards the government, not understanding why Eric had to be drafted and fight in an immoral, undeclared war.

Why was it that Eric, and others like him, who weren't treated fairly in the United States, were expected to fight for their country and spill their blood on foreign land? Blacks were drinking from separate water fountains and using bathrooms labeled "Colored," but had to risk their lives for a country that hated them. Keith was bitter about the mistreatment his brother received. He sympathized with Angela Davis, Huey Newton, and the Black Panther Party. Literature about the movement was scattered all over his apartment. He became depressed.

Concentrating in college became so difficult at times that Keith considered dropping out. He was a good student and well liked by his teachers and peers. Elmira was his saving grace. Her faith in him was the motivation to continue his education. She believed in him when no one else did. He was grateful for having such a strong, secure woman at his side.

Keith and Elmira married the month after their college graduation. Elmira received a degree in social services and began teaching school. She coached the girl's high school basketball team. Keith majored in political science and got a job in the police department. They had three children and settled in a modest community.

Listening to a Luther Vandross medley, Keith's eyes glistened. He smiled, tears of joy streaming down his face. The couple had lived a good life. They loved to debate which singer was better, fat Luther or skinny Luther. Both of them were retired from their jobs. The children were "grown and gone" as Keith liked to say. Keith was diagnosed with cirrhosis of the liver and was given three years to live.

Keith put his cigarette out, paid his tab for the sodas he drank, and walked across the street to Grant Park. He was among tens of thousands as he edged his way toward the front. The CNN reporter announced on the teleprompter, "And Virginia goes to Senator Barack Obama." Tears of joy welled in his eyes as he watched the tabulations on the massive screens set up. "CNN predicts that the next president of the United States will be Senator Barack Obama from Illinois."

Keith turned to the stranger standing on his right. They locked eyes, bumped fists and embraced like old friends, both sobbing uncontrollably. Keith's mouth moved in audible prayer: "Thank you, God! Thank you, John, Martin, Bobby, and all who fought and died for this historical moment. God Bless America."
--Elnora S. Fluellen

The Liberation of Education: The Journey of a Southern Black Man

Within a year after my birth, my parents and I moved into a garage apartment, owned by my uncle, one of the few "colored" plumbers in town, and one of only a few black professionals of any kind in the late 1940s and early 1950s. My sister was born there. Sometime after my fifth birthday, we moved to the small town where my parents had grown up and all four of my grandparents lived–my paternal grandparents on a farm outside of town and my maternal grandparents right in town on the major highway through it. We lived with my maternal grandparents in a house that my grandfather had physically built himself. Although they lived right in town, they owned about three acres, from which my grandfather was able to produce some earnings. Even though he, along with my father, worked full-time in the logging industry, they didn't earn very much for such a backbreaking and dangerous job–typical of all black men of that era. Because of his diligence and persistence, my grandfather was able to eke out a nice living. On this small acreage, he grew corn for his hogs and chickens and a variety of vegetables for the family. In the fall he covered sweet potatoes with pine straw and buried them in the ground to preserve them for eating throughout the winter. We also practiced an annual ritual of "hog killing." The women cleaned the chitterlings and prepared some of the meat to be eaten the same day. When we wanted chicken for supper, the women wrung the necks of the chickens and prepared them for the frying pan. We didn't have to guess where our food came from. Sitting at the breakfast table with my maternal grandfather was like a rite of passage for me. Together we would eat a delicious big country breakfast prepared and served by my aunt and grandmother: grits, eggs, some combination of sausage, thick bacon, fried chicken or perhaps even steak, with "red eye" gravy and biscuits–sometimes mixing in hog brains with the eggs. I was learning how to be a man and what a man's responsibilities were.

Even though she had not yet graduated from college, my mother was a teacher in a rural public school. During the winter, she had to make a fire each day in a potbelly stove. Whenever it rained, the car would slip and slide on that old country dirt road leading to the school as the driver tried to keep it from veering into the drainage ditch on either side of the road. One memorable school day, the principal chanced to look up at the sky, and seeing a tornado approaching, he ordered the students to evacuate to their own homes immediately. Within minutes after their hasty exit, a violent tornado leveled the old schoolhouse.

The summer before I started elementary school, my sister, my great-grandmother, and I attended my mother's college graduation ceremony. Although only six at the time, I could sense that this was a special moment for us. I don't know why my father, aunt, or any of my grandparents did not attend the ceremony. I suspect that they might have been somewhat intimidated at going to a college campus.

A full-time farmer, my paternal grandfather owned a lot more land than my maternal grandfather–although not much compared to white farmers in the area. At one point his primary crop was watermelon. Two mules pulled the wagon he used to transport the watermelon to market in town, and I was generously allowed to accompany him. My grandparents lived in an old wooden house with a tin roof, no running water, and no electricity. They had a well out back and a natural spring with clean fresh water not far from the house. The yards of both sets of grandparents were well kept with hedges and flowers neatly arranged. Dogwood, pecan, and fruit trees produced colorful blooms in the spring.

We moved in with my maternal great-grandmother in "the

city" shortly before I started first grade at a segregated Catholic school. My mother continued to teach in that same rural area. Although she was a teacher, she didn't try to teach me how to read or do arithmetic before I started school. I later learned that she didn't believe in pushing children ahead.

Working with my parents and sister to build our own home when I was nine years old increased my confidence in my own abilities. My parents hired a builder, whom we assisted. Most of the work was done during the summer, when my sister, my mother, and I were free to work. My father would work with us until it was time for him to go to the evening shift at his job. My mother managed the project and secured all of the materials. My father mixed mortar and assisted the builder in a variety of capacities. My sister and I carried bricks or other age-appropriate tasks as directed.

Three of my four grandparents died before I turned eleven. After the death of both of her parents, my mother's youngest sister continued to live in their house, providing the opportunity for me to continue spending quality time in the country with her, her husband, and her children, who became like siblings to my sister and me. Occasionally I visited my paternal grandmother, who continued to live on the family-owned farm after my grandfather's death. The outdoor fun with my cousins was balanced with the chores necessary to keep things running smoothly. Working on the farm and developing the skills to perform my assigned tasks contributed immensely to my self-confidence.

Getting to plow with my grandmother's mule helped me mark my advancement toward manhood. I also went out into the fields of white farmers and picked cotton and peaches. It's possible for me to have fond memories of such times since I was only in my early teens and didn't have the task of providing a living for a family as many men had to do. I also never considered doing such work for a lifetime. At that point in our history, most African Americans in the southern portion of the country remained in a position of virtual servitude. Opportunities for advancement in employment or in career opportunities were limited, if they existed at all. Some African Americans owned their own businesses or were professionals, but even among those who might have made the sacrifices necessary to attend college and earn a degree, the prospects of doing very much that was in line with their degree were slim to nothing, except for those who taught, sold insurance, or operated a small business.

Although the conditions of African Americans were deplorable during my childhood, I developed a natural optimism. Perhaps that optimism resulted from gains in the momentum of the civil rights struggle. At last, the black population was beginning to see a glimmer of light that might lead to the end of the tunnel. Despite the hardships she had endured, my mother earned a degree and was actively engaged in a rewarding, though demanding, profession. She always nurtured a positive attitude about the future for blacks in the south. I can never forget the day when my mother drove to the street right in front of Mercer University. Pointing to the administration building, she prophesied: "One day, Charles, you'll be attending that university." I was only eleven or twelve, and the integration of Mercer was still five years away. It was my mother's strong belief in a hopeful future for African Americans that provided the encouragement I needed to apply to Mercer. I thank God that my mother not only saw me attend Mercer and graduate, but that she was there thirty-five years later when I returned to Mercer as a member of its faculty.

I adopted my mother's hopeful anticipation of a more promising future, believing that if I worked hard, I would be able to achieve whatever I set out to achieve. I was convinced that the civil rights movement would culminate in expanded opportunities for African Americans in all walks of life. When I worked in the fields or performed any other type of common labor, I did so with the hope that better days lay ahead for my people. Through the ever present encouragement of my mother, this early hope congealed into a conviction that sustained me and prevented me from falling into despair or engaging in self-destructive behavior as I went about the task of coping with a society that continued to view me and others like me in demeaning ways–and all too often took extreme measures to stifle our efforts to "overcome." Unfortunately, although overt actions to hinder African Americans are not quite as visible as before, institutional racism, ingrained over centuries, continues to hold its grip and retard advancement.

My mother's belief that my sister and I should decide for ourselves about certain matters of importance in our lives gave me the confidence to learn to make good decisions. Church membership was among our freedoms to choose. When I was about twelve years old, my sister and I joined the Catholic Church. I became an altar boy, and during my high school years I participated actively in the Catholic Youth Organization (CYO). This activity provided black teenagers, both Catholic and non-Catholic, with a positive outlet to engage in enriching activities, both on the church grounds and on trips that we planned and executed on a somewhat regular basis. We must have been the only church-based black teenage group to sponsor talent shows and dances at the church open to everyone. Teenagers from across the city often attended.

My father firmly believed that young people need to experiment and discover things for themselves rather than always have adults breathing down their necks, barking out commands and often insisting that things be done only in a certain way or according to a certain procedure. When my mother directed me on how to do a task, my father would frequently admonish her to leave me alone. To my great surprise and pleasure, there were times when she obliged. Sometimes I had the opportunity to explore and learn things for myself in a way that black youth of that era did not always have. My father was an extremely patient man, who never ridiculed us or raised his voice in anger. His demeanor contributed immensely to my disposition as I matured and even influenced the way I currently deal with students. He was truly an educator, even without a degree or an elementary school or high school diploma.

Catholic school provided a sound academic foundation, but it wasn't especially liberating. The black experience in this country did not extend to the curriculum in the classroom. For example, I didn't ever learn anything about slavery through any history book of that period. The playground was the one place where we had a measure of freedom during the school day. Playtime was often unsupervised, effectively encouraging us to learn to develop our own "rules of the game" and police ourselves.

During the summer prior to my entry into high school, my neighbor Leonard and I decided to start our own lawn care business. We combined my family's manual push mower with other tools that belonged to our families and went around the neighborhood, knocking on doors to solicit business. We drummed up enough business to make it worthwhile financially. However, it was difficult to make very much money when we were charging only 35¢ to 50¢ per yard. Initiating a business enterprise for ourselves eventually proved to be invaluable in my case, despite

254

the fact that I did not choose to become a career businessman.

On my first day of high school, students assembled in various classrooms, where the teachers proceeded to ask questions. When the teacher approached me, I immediately stood up, unknowingly soliciting laughter from the other students. I quickly realized that public school students were not accustomed to standing up as a form of respect to teachers. In the Catholic school, we had been taught to stand up anytime an adult walked into the room, no matter who she or he might have been or what his or her status in society happened to be. That was at least one liberating aspect of that school: it instilled in me a strong sense of respect for my elders, regardless of their economic or social status.

Among my first significant acts in high school was enrollment in the band. I took band during my first year of high school. Being able to practice the music during the class left me with time in the evening to pursue other activities, including my lawn service. Band membership entailed a year-round commitment. One band functioned as a marching band in the fall during football season, and a second band presented concerts. Mr. Jordan, our band director, was quite strict, allowing no second chances if students missed practice. It was a great accomplishment for me to move up to the second chair of the trumpet section during the early part of my sophomore year. I learned that hard work and practice pay off.

Mr. Blackshear was perhaps the teacher who made the biggest impact on me during high school. He taught two of my mathematics classes and a physics class. The word was out to avoid Mr. Blackshear. When I was assigned to his second-year algebra class, I immediately observed that some students simply didn't want to work. Mr. Blackshear was big on assigning homework and making sure that we did it. We were required to hand it in to him before school in the morning, and somehow by the time we went to his class that day he had checked it and was prepared to return it to us for feedback. There really was no excuse for anyone not to learn if they simply did the work and put in an honest effort. This was a valuable lesson that prepared me well for college. I must admit that math was always quite easy for me. I actually enjoyed doing it, unlike most students of that era, and apparently most citizens of this country today. During my senior year I took both advanced mathematics and high school physics from Mr. Blackshear. This strong background influenced me to major in mathematics and physics in college.

Ms. Simms was a history teacher, who was a throwback to the time when teachers were quite demanding, but totally devoted to the overall wellbeing of students, both personally and educationally. She was an early proponent of "No Child [or Teenager] Left Behind." Ms. Simms was the only teacher in my experience who included the contributions of African Americans in our history as a discrete part of the curriculum. She selected me to give a speech during our annual Negro [not Black] History Week [not Month] program. She worked with me in the hallway between classes on a daily basis until I knew exactly how to deliver a speech. That experience with Ms. Simms taught me the value of thorough preparation.

My lawn care business had extended into the white community. During the time of the vote in the senate to obtain closure as a way of limiting the debate on the Civil Rights Act of 1964, I was trimming hedges for one of my white customers. The hedges just happened to be right outside the den of the house, where I could easily hear the television as the broadcaster described the events of that deliberation. Joy washed over me as he announced that closure had been reached, meaning that passage of the bill was all but assured.

Another customer, who lived across the street from that house, complained to me that her neighbors were trying to "take" her African American maid from her, claiming, "she belongs to me." This woman seemed to me to be in some kind of time warp in which white members of the community were able to own black members. My aunt, who had worked in the home of a white family and who regaled us with tales of her "boss," shared my sentiments. Social mores are so entrenched that some members of society are not aware of them and the impact they have in the community.

After graduation from high school in 1965, I worked during the summer as a busboy and dishwasher at a downtown segregated, white-only restaurant. Although it had been almost a year since the passage of the Civil Rights Act of 1964, a fellow worker was allegedly fired because he dared to ask if he could bring his girlfriend to the restaurant for dinner.

As I was standing around on campus proudly wearing my freshman beanie during my first week of college, one of the white guys who had served as a host at the restaurant where I had worked was surprised and astonished to see that I was also a Mercer student. After all, what were the odds of a Negro/colored/ black busboy/dishwasher at a local white restaurant of that day showing up at a prestigious university like Mercer, which had just accepted its first two black students two years earlier? He approached me with a degree of enthusiasm and joy that I was a student at Mercer. I had just spent the summer in what was likely the least prestigious job available–even among African-Americans. This was a special moment, highlighting just how far I had come as a member of a society that had a history of putting well-defined limits on people simply due to the color of their skin. That encounter also illustrated that some white citizens were not only tolerating the idea of integration, but were actually embracing it.

During the last quarter of my first year, I took Calculus II from Dr. William Palmer, who had a tremendous influence on me educationally and professionally. My academic advisor, Dr. Palmer probably knew as much about the true essence of education as anyone at the university and beyond. He preferred exploring ideas to presenting facts. His classroom presentations did not resemble the ones fairly standard in colleges and universities. Rather than list a lot of facts and figures on the board and work some examples, Dr. Palmer actually talked with–and not at–us. He tried to help us understand the principles underlying the various topics and concepts. His problem sets, which were carefully designed to facilitate the review and deep contemplation of the course material, were especially helpful to me. Because of them, I learned how to learn more effectively and I performed at a higher level on his exams. In the long run, his methods were far superior to most, if not virtually all, of the others at Mercer. For this reason, I credit much of my liberation process and the great majority of my professional accomplishments to his teaching.

While I was in his math class, Dr. Palmer asked if I would like to work in a new program for mostly African American high school students that was being initiated on Mercer's campus. Little did I know of the scope of the program, the great vision and intense preparation that must have gone into bringing it to campus, and the dynamic impact that it would have on Mercer as an institution, on the faculty and staff who worked in it, the students who participated in it, and society as a whole. That program was the federally funded project, Upward Bound. I was hired to be a tutor-counselor, lived in the dormitory with the students, and worked with Dr. Palmer in the classroom. He was the project's Director of Instruction and one of its mathematics instructors. It was clear that the leadership and hard work of Dean Joe Hendricks was initially responsible for bringing this program to campus, but many others from the campus contributed to its success. It was the most wonderful experience that anyone connected to that project could have had at that point in our nation's history. Working in that classroom under the direction of Dr. Palmer was just as liberating for me as it was for the students, if not more so. He guided them through a set of mathematical discovery activities at a time when this type of activity was just coming into prominence in the profession. Young people of that era were eager and excited to engage in this type of creative endeavor. Other instructors engaged students in creative activities as well, such as the quiz bowl format that was used for a history class. In addition to the subject area courses, all project participants were assigned an afternoon activity, such as drama, art, or chorus. Then, at least once per week, students were taken on local field trips, and perhaps twice during the summer experience they were taken on a major trip out of town, including excursions to Washington, DC and Florida.

The initial Upward Bound class was about eighty percent black and twenty percent white with a mainly white staff. This was at a time when blacks and whites continued to struggle with the notion of associating on a personal basis. Wherever we went, people noticed the makeup of the group. There were no significant race-related incidents until we stopped at a drive-in restaurant in South Georgia to get something to eat. There happened to be a group of young white males hanging around who didn't take too kindly to the idea that a group like ours would have the audacity to stop in their town and eat at one of their restaurants. Fortunately, staff members intervened, preventing any physical conflict.

Among the major occurrences on and around campus was the incident at Tattnall Square Church. The church building actually sat on a corner of the main campus, although it had no formal connection to the University. I wasn't aware of what was in the making, but one of the white tutor-counselors had arranged for two Upward Bound students to accompany him to church one Sunday. This event caused a major upheaval in the church, with most of

258

the congregation in one corner and the minister of music and the pastor in the other. The pastor received notoriety from the presentation of his views about the controversy in a little book entitled *Ashes for Breakfast*. By this time, Sam Oni, who had come to Mercer from Africa as its first black student, had graduated. He returned to campus from California to join in the protests. Oni had come all the way from Africa to help integrate Mercer. Here we were, at least four years after the passage of the Civil Rights Bill of 1964, and so little had been accomplished through all the struggles of the millions of Americans, including the deaths of several, who had fought so hard for social justice in this country.

One of my regrets during my years at Mercer was not getting to see or hear Alex Haley when he came to campus. At the time, he had gained notoriety for his collaboration in the writing of *The Autobiography of Malcolm X.* I did go to see Dick Gregory when he came to campus. He was not very far removed from having transitioned from an overweight comedian to a highly respected activist, humanitarian, workout/training specialist, and nutritionist. I don't know of anyone whom I've heard speak who has made the kind of impact on me that he did during his presentation. He spoke to a packed audience in Willingham Chapel, then Mercer University's largest auditorium facility. He didn't mince words simply because the audience was mostly white. He didn't hold back at all in criticizing our government and various institutions in this country due to their racist policies and actions.

The statement that had the most impact on me was what he said about his reaction to the strike by teachers in Kentucky. He maintained that teachers and preachers should be among the best paid professionals in this country, but that they don't deserve a dime more unless they go out and fight for the students instead of themselves. I was involved in education through the Upward Bound project and about to embark unawares on a lifelong career in education. Gregory's statement profoundly influenced my entire perspective on teaching from that day to this, and he helped me understand that teaching is not about teachers themselves but about the lives of the students with whom they gladly work.

--Charles Roberts

CANNON RIDGE STORIES: BURNIN' DAYLIGHT

My eyes opened to a dark room. It was early. I could hear the large iron skillet clank onto the stove as Mother began preparing breakfast. Yesterday had been the last day of school. I was hoping Mom would let me sleep a little later today. It was not long before I got my answer. "Bobby, get up and eat your breakfast before we have to leave for work. I have a list of things for you to do," Mother yelled from the hallway.

"Ah, shoot! Why do I have to get up?" I mumbled to myself. I moved in slow motion to the side of the bed, my body half on and half off the bed, and dozed for a couple of seconds. Another clank of the iron skillet rudely interrupted my half slumber. I grudgingly pulled my pants on. With no shirt, socks, or shoes, I crept to the breakfast table–only to be sent back immediately to my room to make myself half decent. Pausing for a half second to admire the model car I had worked on the night before, I heard Mother's ultimatum: "Don't make me come back in there!" With only a few seconds to live, I threw on my shirt and socks and scurried to the table.

"I don't see why I have to get up. There's no school today. Where is Ronnie? Why ain't he up?" I whined.

"You are not supposed to say 'ain't'! Your brother has a part-time job this summer. I can't go to work and just leave you here in bed. Here's a list of things that have to be done today without fail. Uncle Joe will pick you up in the morning at 5:00 to take you up to the farm to work this summer."

We always called him Uncle Joe, but he wasn't related to me in any way. He had been my scoutmaster. Now that I was ten years old, I had dropped out. Mother couldn't afford to keep buying the uniforms. She complained that I was growing like a weed. Mom and Dad both worked, leaving no one to keep an eye on me during the summer. It was decreed that I go to North Georgia to work on Uncle Joe's farm. I went in May and would not return until school started in September. I was the youngest in the family. My oldest brother, Walter, and my sister, Susie, were married. The brother next to me in age was Ronnie, and now he was old enough to go to work. That would leave me home alone all day. My mother allowed as to how an idle mind is the devil's workshop. She and Dad wanted to make sure I didn't have any free time to get into trouble.

At 5 a.m., still in the best part of my sleep, the sound of Mama's wake-up call rudely interrupted my dreams. "Heck, it's still dark!" I complained inaudibly to myself. Back talk would land me in serious trouble for sure. I sat outside on top of my little suitcase, waiting for Uncle Joe's big ol' red truck. I had to wait outside because Uncle Joe did not like to get out of his truck and come to the door. He was always in a hurry.

It was deathly quiet. Not even the birds were up. It was like I was the only one in the world. Suddenly, Uncle Joe's big truck split the silence. I could hear it coming afar off, getting closer by the minute, louder and louder, until the headlights pierced the darkness. I told my ol' dog Sandy good-bye as the truck ground to a stop in front of the house. I glanced back toward the house to see if anyone was around–nothing but a few lights was on.

"We're burnin' daylight, Boy!" Uncle Joe yelled. I hurriedly picked up my suitcase and darted toward the truck. I could barely reach the door handle. The door was so heavy that it took both hands to pull it open. I threw my suitcase up into the truck and slammed the door shut. I was still hoping somebody would come out to tell me bye. I guess they were all too busy getting ready for work. What if a wild animal had come and eaten me up? They wouldn't find out until September. I would just be a greasy spot in the driveway.

Uncle Joe was a man of few words, but when he did talk, everybody listened. Sometimes I was a bit afraid of him–mostly when he got mad. He taught me how to do almost everything. He was more like a father to me than my own dad was. Dad worked hard as a truck driver and didn't feel like having kids around when he came home. Us kids just stayed out of sight in our rooms and did our homework and stuff.

Uncle Joe was good at everything. He would take time to teach the boys who worked on his farm. Every summer there would be five or six boys from age ten to fourteen working on the farm. At first, I hated it. We worked long hours, the work was hard, and the weather hot. It made a man out of me. I learned enough to take care of myself and eventually of a family.

"We've got to pick up Tony and Allen in Austell and then we

can head home," Uncle Joe explained.

"How many guys will we have this year?" I asked.

"Only six this year. Tommy, Billy, and David will already be there when we get to the farm."

It was just a few minutes before Tony and Allen climbed into the truck. I always felt sorry for them. Their house was small and looked like it was about to fall in. Their dad came and went. They never knew when he might be home. He would stay gone for weeks, sometimes even months at a time. And when he was home, he was real mean to them and their mother. Tony told me that his mother had to go to the hospital one time when his dad hit her. Sometimes the children had to sleep outside and didn't get anything to eat until they got to school. Once they got a whipping because the school came out to collect the money for their lunches. After that, the school never came out again. I wondered if they just quit eating or whether they got free lunch. I didn't ask any questions. On the farm, they would eat well and be safe until September. I felt sad because Tony and Allen both became my good friends, almost like brothers. All three of us fell asleep, leaning on each other.

I woke up a few miles from the farm. I could tell we were in Cannon Ridge when I smelled the air. The short-needled pines made it smell like Christmas. As we came closer, there were no more houses or stores or anything–just trees and more trees until the road changed to dirt. As we turned onto the road to the farm, we could see the large sign over the road that read "God's Heaven." The sun was already up in the sky. Tony and Allen woke up. Allen began to cough as the dust blew into the cab of the truck.

"Looks like we ain't had no rain, Uncle Joe," I commented.

"We sure ain't. I want all of you boys to work on the yard up close to the house. Billy can drive the tractor. We've got to cut all the high grass. I hate snakes. I got to see 'em so I can kill 'em. Leave your things in the truck. You can get 'em later. Y'all get out the truck. We're burnin' daylight!"

"Hey, Billy, Tommy, and David!" I yelled. We all had our small reunion and immediately got to work. The grass was high in the yard all the way up to the house. It was an old two-story frame farmhouse, painted white except for the shutters, which were a powder blue–Aunt Benny's favorite color. It had a long porch on the front with two bench swings on each end, where we spent our

Sunday evenings.

All the guys slept on the top floor. Uncle Joe, Aunt Benny, and their daughter Alice slept downstairs. Uncle Joe did not like for the boys to go around Alice. He didn't even want us to talk to her. She always worked in the house and helped with the cooking. All of us dreamed that someday we would marry her and inherit the farm.

Out in the yard Billy fired up the old Ford tractor, black smoke belching from the exhaust. Billy yelled, "Yeeeeee-Haw! We're back!" Billy loved that old tractor and kept it running like a top. Sometimes I'd ride with him and watch him drive. I couldn't wait to be old enough to drive it. We had to put the big bush hog on the tractor to knock down the grass. It was like a big lawn mower, except a tractor had to pull it. After the grass was cut with the bush hog, we used two lawn mowers to cut the grass closer to the ground. Uncle Joe wanted to be able to spot a snake a mile away. In a couple of hours, the grass was cut and we began to pick up the limbs that had fallen. There was a large fire pit in the back where we could pile up all the dead limbs to burn.

When Uncle Joe rang the bell, we dropped what we were doing to go eat lunch. Outside the house was a large sink for us to wash up. It was a strict rule to clean up before we ate. Aunt Benny always reminded us, "You all might not be the best lookin' boys, but you can be clean." The kitchen was right off the porch. Inside was a large table at least fourteen feet long with benches on both sides where the boys sat with Uncle Joe and Aunt Benny on each end. Alice had to serve and was not allowed to eat until the boys had left the house. We could always feel Uncle Joe watching us to see if we were looking at Alice. I kept my eyes straight ahead unless someone asked me something. That kept me out of trouble with Uncle Joe.

"Well, Tony, by the looks of your face, I guess your daddy's home," Aunt Benny surmised. "Hope your mother looks better than you."

"No, Ma'am," Tony confessed. "She's been in the bed for two weeks. He hit 'er in the back. He said he weren't gonna spend good money on doctors. I worry about my mama when we're all the way up here."

"Don't worry. He won't kill her. He wouldn't have nothin' to beat on," Aunt Benny consoled him.

"Alright! That's enough ratchet jawin'. Git to eatin'. We're burnin' daylight," Uncle Joe grumbled. "The train of failure usually runs on the track of laziness!"

I think Uncle Joe had a big heart and didn't like listening to those stories. He really did care about all the boys who helped out on the farm. One day when Uncle Joe was sitting around on the porch with us, Allen started telling a story about his daddy coming in drunk and hitting him across the face with a lamp. I glanced up to see Uncle Joe's response. He claimed he had gotten something in his eye and had to go in the house to wash it out. I knew he was starting to cry but didn't want us to see his tears. He was a hard man with a big heart. We always felt safe with him.

After lunch, we spent the rest of the day working in the fields. It was spring and the new corn was only about three or four feet tall. Soon it would be well over my head. We were pulling the weeds from in between the corn stalks. Since the weeds had gotten a head start, I knew that we wouldn't finish until dark. It was just spring and already felt like a hundred degrees with no breeze or anything to cool us down. The hottest place in the world has got to be a cornfield in the summer. It feels like you can't breathe, and when the stalks get taller, it's easy to get lost—almost like in a maze.

Last summer, Tony had lost his knife and went back to find it the next day. After an hour or so, we could hear him yelling. Uncle Joe called out, "Tony, stay where you are. We'll come to you. Jus' keep on yellin'!" In a few minutes they both came walking out of the field. Tony was soaked to the bone in sweat. I learned to break some of the stalks so I could find my way out.

David whimpered, "We'll be lucky if we get to go to bed tonight. I see where the deer are stompin' down the corn over there. Uncle Joe will make us stay up all night watchin' for 'em."

"Let 'em have the dumb ol' corn!" Tommy suggested. "I feel like somethin' the cat dragged in. I'm gonna split the sheets tonight."

As the sun began to go down, we were relieved to hear the clang, clang, clang of the bell, announcing that it was time to wash up for supper. After supper, Uncle Joe told us to go on to bed—that we looked like ninety miles of bad road. I *felt* like ninety miles of bad road. I could barely drag myself up the steps. Upstairs was a large room with ten army cots spaced evenly apart. I would always get the one closest to the window box. I loved to look outside at night when there was a full moon. Sometimes I would catch sight of a deer walking around in the yard.

One year, when I had been at the farm for the Christmas holidays, I looked out of the window at the new moon shining on the fresh snow. I spied a deer that stood very still, almost as if he knew I was watching. The colors all around were dark and light shades of blues. It looked like a Christmas card with "Peace on Earth" written at the top. I sat there in the window box for hours as tears ran down my face, wishing I were home with Mama. I prayed that someday I would be old enough to stay home with my family.

"Alright! Git your butts up! We're burnin' daylight!" Uncle Joe boomed.

Had my head even hit the pillow? What daylight? It's totally dark outside. I knew Uncle Joe would not come back a second time. I had better get up and wash and get to the table as fast as I could. If we were late for breakfast, we got to work on an empty stomach. That was no picnic. It was a long time to lunch. Once when Allen had not buttoned his shirt all the way up, he was asked to leave the table and was not able to eat until lunch. That never happened again.

"The horses got out last night from the lower pasture," Uncle Joe reported. "All you boys will help me round up the horses and fix the fence. Bobby, you take care of the cows. Aunt Benny and Alice will go to town for more supplies. Hurry up with your food. Let's go! We're burnin' daylight!"

What's the big deal with all this daylight burning? Why do I have to stay here and work the cows all by myself? I never get to do the fun stuff. I'll be glad when I'm big enough to go with the rest of the guys. I angrily kicked a rock across the yard. I dared not say anything to Uncle Joe. The boys threw a few tools on the truck and they were gone. Aunt Benny and Alice left right behind them.

The silence descended. The sun was just beginning to separate the light from the darkness. The dew was on the grass, meaning I had to be extra careful going through the electric fence. I had touched it once before, and it had knocked me down to the ground. I looked around for a stick or something to push up on the barbed wire to make a place large enough for my body to slide through. I could walk all the way down to the gate, but that would be sissy. All the boys would sure have fun with that if they found out.

As I got closer to the barn, I could hear a low moan or groan. Was that one of the cows? I hoped that a stupid old possum hadn't got into the barn last night and hurt one of the cows. I carefully pulled the big door open. Squeeeak. The door hinge needed some oil. A person could never sneak up on someone with this door. All was quiet again. I didn't hear a sound as I moved slowly into the barn. Then I heard it again–that low moan. I looked high and low, hoping there would be no possum. I hated those things. The moan seemed to be coming from Essie, the big brown cow. She looked fine, just bigger than I had remembered. Then she made another low, low moan. I couldn't see anything wrong with her except that she sure needed milking. I gave her some water and went around to the other side to get the bucket for the milk. That's when I saw it! I thought I saw it. Oh, my God! Essie had a leg sticking out of her backside! All I could do was stand there and stare at it–for what seemed like a long time.

My mind was spinning. Do cows eat other cows–or was she growing a new leg? Freak! I didn't know what to do! There was blood everywhere. My mind went from spinning to slow motion. Maybe Essie's having a baby? At ten years old, I didn't know much about these things. All I knew was I had to get some kind of help–and quick! Everybody was gone and I was the only one here. Oh, Lord! What do I do? Essie just kept on moaning. I knew she was in pain, and I had to get help.

I ran out of the barn and looked in the yard. I knew the lower pasture where everyone was working was too far to walk. I saw the big ol' Ford tractor sitting in the yard next to the well house. There was a first time for everything. I had always wanted a rea-son for driving that ol' tractor. I knew I was too small to reach the pedals. Somehow I had to figure that out. I would worry about that when I got to it.

This time I was not so careful going through the electric barbed wire fence. Blam! I hit the ground as 110 volts left my body. Shake it off! Shake it off! I was limp in the wet, dewy grass trying to get my head together. I had to get help for Essie. I slowly stood up, my back wet from the dew, still shaking from the shock. Walking slowly, then a little faster and faster, I went into a full run until I reached the tractor. I felt smaller than ever as I stood looking up at the large tractor.

Climbing up into the seat, I discovered that the key was not there. It was on the nail in the house. I climbed back down and ran as fast as I could to the house. I grabbed the key and away I ran, hearing the screen door slam behind me. Reaching the tractor, I positioned myself strategically. Standing and leaning back against the bottom of the seat were the only way I could reach the pedals. I stuck in the key and turned it clockwise. The tractor jumped three times, grinding the side of the big wheels up against the well house.

Oh, yeah. I remembered I had to press in the clutch. Holding the steering wheel with a tight grip, I used my left foot. I barely weighed enough to press the clutch in. I turned the key, and the motor started. Black smoke belched out of the exhaust pipe as I eased off the clutch. The tractor jumped three more times and choked to a stop. I had forgotten the gas. I tried again. When the motor cranked, I gave it a little gas with my right foot while easing off on the clutch. Miraculously, the tractor began to move. My problem now was trying to steer the enormous machine. With the clutch now all the way out, I increased the gas and rode off at a pretty good clip.

Bouncing through the field of corn, I was making a path. Uncle Joe was going to kill me, but all I could think of was getting some help for Essie. I slowly turned the tractor toward the lower pasture. Looking behind me, I could see the path through the corn all the way back up to the house. It was not a straight path. I had snaked around all over the place. What a mess I had made. My life wasn't worth anything. Uncle Joe would kill me dead for sure. Finally, I could see the big red truck and the horses and then, over to the left of the truck, Uncle Joe and the boys came into view. They were all frozen in shock, trying to figure out what in the world I was doing. I let off the gas, and the tractor choked to a stop, nearly knocking me off.

"We got to help Essie. She's having a baby," I shouted as loud as I could.

Uncle Joe didn't say a word. He just jumped in the truck with Tommy, David, and Allen following quickly behind him.

Billy yelled, "I'm proud of you, Boy! I'll drive. Come on, Tony! Jump on. Let's get to the barn! We've got a baby calf a comin'. Yeeeeeee-haw!"

We slowly made our way back up to the house. Aunt Benny and Alice were at the house when we got there.

"Aunt Benny, Essie's having a calf!" Billy yelled. "Uncle Joe has gone to get the vet."

"Alice, you unload the car and start lunch. I'll be down at the barn," Aunt Benny commanded.

At the barn, Essie was still making those low moaning sounds. It sounded like she was dying.

"That's alright, Girl. We're gonna take care of ya," Aunt Benny cooed with love. "You Boys, go up to the well and haul me some buckets of water down here. We've got to get her cleaned up. The ol' girl's got a lot of pride. And watch out for that electric fence!"

Don't worry, I thought. *That fence is only going to get me once.*

By the time we had carried the water down to the barn, and Aunt Benny had started cleaning Essie up, Doc Mason arrived. He reached into his case and brought out this big needle, filled it with medicine, and stuck Essie in the neck. Essie was already in so much pain that she didn't feel a thing. Seeing the huge needle, we all backed up a little bit. Doc Mason put on some rubber gloves that went all the way up to his armpits.

"Joe, get me some rope," Doc Mason ordered.

I could not figure out what he was going to do with the rope. He took the rope in his right hand and stuck it in Essie's rear end. Then he took his left hand and stuck it in until he was up to his elbows in Essie. Somehow he tied that rope around the calf and then pulled his arms out.

"Okay, Joe, grab the rope, and when I tell you, pull."

Uncle Joe and Doc grabbed the rope.

"Alright, on three: one, two, threeeeeee," Doc yelled.

Out popped a bloody, ugly, messy calf. It flopped to the ground. Aunt Benny grabbed it and started cleaning it up.

Essie turned and gave a look, as if to say, "Glad that's over." She stopped that chilling, low moan that I will never forget.

"You boys stop staring and clean this barn from top to bottom. We have a new resident," Aunt Benny commanded.

"Come on, Doc. I'll buy you a cup o' coffee!"

"I'm gonna stay here and help the boys," Uncle Joe said.

"Glad that didn't take long. I got here just in time," Doc

Mason offered. "That little feller will be up walking around soon."

After a couple of hours, the barn was looking pretty darn good, and the smell was gone. Uncle Joe told us to sit down and rest for a while. Tony, Allen, Tommy, Billy, David, and I sat in a circle on the ground recapping what had taken place.

"I always wanted a path through that old corn field, but I kind of hoped it would be straight," Uncle Joe joked. We all started laughing.

"I couldn't watch where I was goin' for trying to make sure I was pressin' the right pedals," I explained.

"I think he did one heck of a job," Billy bragged.

"Is that how a woman has a baby?" Allen asked.

"I'm sure not going to be a doctor when I grow up," David declared.

"If I was a doctor, I'd wear one o' them deep-sea divin' suits," Tony chuckled.

--Robert (Bob) Mathis

The Secret

I grabbed the stick and held the barbed wire up while Allen passed through. Then Allen held it for me while I crawled under. As we trudged up the hill toward the house, we could see Uncle Joe with a little black boy who appeared to be about eight or nine years old. The boy had on an old, faded, red plaid shirt and jeans with the knees worn out. His shoes didn't match–one was scuffed-up brown leather, and the other looked like an old house shoe. He didn't have any socks on. He had something under his arm, but I couldn't make out what it was. It looked like an old, stuffed teddy bear. As we came closer, I saw that it was filthy, and both of its eyes and one of its arms were missing. It was obvious that some-one had stitched the bear up to keep the stuffing from falling out. The little boy held the teddy tight under his arm, and his thumb was anchored just as tightly in his mouth.

"Boy, get that thumb out of your mouth–I done told you!" boomed Uncle Joe.

The boy reluctantly pulled the thumb out of his mouth,

revealing a missing tooth right in front. We heard the tractor with all the other boys on it stop not far from the house. They jumped off and came running, forming a circle around Uncle Joe. Tommy, Billy, David, Tony, Allen, and I all stared at Uncle Joe like he was some freak in a circus sideshow. Aunt Benny and Alice came out of the house as wide-eyed as we were.

"Good God! What in the world do we have here?" Aunt Benny exclaimed.

"This is Toby," Uncle Joe explained. "His mother was a good friend of my family back in Iowa. She was a good Christian woman. We used to play together when we were kids. Seems that she up and died a couple of weeks ago and didn't have any family left. Nobody knows where the boy's daddy is. They found a piece of notepaper where she had written my name, so somebody sent him to me."

"I know I'm not the smartest man in the world, but, ah—he ain't got nobody. Not nobody! So here's what's gonna' happen. Everybody, listen up! I'm only gonna say this once. Toby's my problem, and we always work out problems around here. We will work this one out, too. Benny, you gonna have to git this boy some clothes and some shoes. Feed 'im first. He's gonna work here jus' like everybody else. You boys, you teach 'im. You teach 'im everything I've taught you. And I better not git any lip from y'all. Jesus said, 'to the least of these.' Right now, he looks pretty 'least' to me."

"Where you want 'im to sleep?" Billy asked.

"He'll bunk with y'all. That's jus' what I'm talking about. Git it through your heads–he's here to stay. He's got nowhere else to go! He's one of us now!" Uncle Joe insisted.

Aunt Benny saved the day.

"Well, come on, Little Toby. Let's go find you something to eat. That must have been some kind of bus ride."

Aunt Benny's voice faded away as she and Toby went into the house with Alice trailing behind.

"If you boys can't find something to do on this big ol' farm, I guess I'll find you something," Uncle Joe threatened.

"Oh, yeah, we got plenty to do. We're gone!" I quickly responded.

All of us boys scrambled and headed for the tractor, not saying a word. We didn't want Uncle Joe to find us work. We knew he'd have us cut a cord of wood before dark. We quickly scampered off for the lower pasture, where the fence always needed work. The rest of the day we pulled barbed wire tight and nailed it to the fence posts. Not one of us uttered a word about Toby. It was nearly sundown before the bell rang out, announcing that it was time to wash up for supper.

As we entered the kitchen, Toby was already sitting on the bench at the supper table. He had on new jeans and shirt and even new boots. He still had that old teddy bear stuck up under his arm. It was so dirty that I was surprised Aunt Benny let him bring it to the table. There was very little conversation at the table that night. Everybody felt uncomfortable around a stranger. After supper, all the boys headed upstairs to go to bed. Toby trailed behind us.

"Toby, this is your cot. Git in it and stay in it till morning," Billy ordered. "If you have to go to the bathroom, you better go now, 'cause Uncle Joe don't allow us to go downstairs at night."

Little Toby crawled up on the cot and huddled there with his knees at his chin and his arms wrapped around his legs in a tight little ball. Big alligator tears ran down his cheeks as he clutched that dirty teddy bear.

Tommy walked over to Toby's cot and menacingly commanded, "Gimme that ol' teddy bear. It stinks! I'm goin' to throw it out de winder."

"No! It's mine! No! Mama made me dat bear!" Toby shrieked.

"STOP! You want to git Uncle Joe up here. Tommy, git back to your cot and leave Toby alone. Uncle Joe will bust your butt. Now, GO!" Billy ordered.

Toby huddled up in his ball with the tears gaining momentum as they flowed down his cheeks. Tommy slowly made his way back to his cot, and all the boys began to settle down. Silence finally came and then sleep. Toby lay sobbing in the cot next to mine. I genuinely felt sorry for him, not having a family and all. I wondered what it must feel like to lose his mother forever and to be in a strange place with all white people telling him what to do. I got up, went over to his cot, and sat down beside him.

"C'mon, Toby. I want to show you something," I coaxed. "C'mon. I won't hurt you. It's over here."

Toby released his grip on his legs and started to get out of bed. I reached for his hand, and his grip told me that I had won his trust. We went over to the window where I had spent many a night crying and wishing I was at home and wondering what my family might be doing. So many nights I had sat in the window, hoping to see a deer or another wild animal playing in the yard.

We both crawled up into the window box. Soon Toby's tears ceased. We just sat there, not saying a word. Soon a buck crossed the yard and paused as if to say, "I'm here for ya." I looked over at Toby's sad little face and saw the excitement in his eyes as it began to move across his whole face. A big wide smile appeared.

"See, I told ya!" I said.

A few minutes passed, and the deer ran back into the woods. Toby soon fell asleep there in the window box. I carefully covered him up and left him there for the night. It made me feel good to be able to help him a little. I knew that nothing I could do could take away the pain he must be feeling. Sleep finally came.

"Alright, get your butts up! We're burnin' daylight," Uncle Joe bellowed.

At the breakfast table, Uncle Joe started lining up the day for everybody. "Billy, you and Tommy take the tractor down to the lower pasture and try to finish up that fence. Bring the horses up here to the cow pasture for grazing. David, you, Tony, and Allen git the ladders and git some o' them green apples off the trees before they split. You can feed the apples to the horses and pigs. Bobby, you and Toby–"

"I know," I interrupted, "take care of the cows and clean the barn."

"Yeah, and you take your time and teach Toby where every-thing is. Alright, let's go now. No playin' around. We're burnin' daylight!"

"Toby, will you trust me to clean up that ol' one-armed teddy bear?" Aunt Benny gently prodded. "I'll take extry care with it. I might even have some old buttons 'round here to give him some eyes. I think your mother would be proud to see him all cleaned up."

Toby reluctantly gave her the bear, trusting her with all that he had left from his mother.

As we grew closer to one another, Toby would often tell me stories of how his mother had sung old hymns to him and fried him apple pies. At times she would pick him up and dance around the house with him. Those were happy times for him. Sometimes

272

his mother would take Toby with her when she cleaned people's houses. He would look at all the fine things they had and wonder what people had to do to be so blessed–why some people had everything and others had nothing, and why God had made people different colors. Only life and time would begin to answer his questions.

"Whatever you do, don't touch that fence!" I warned.

"Why?" Toby queried.

"It's electric. It'll knock the livin' daylights outta you!" I cautioned.

We had a special stick with a fork at the top, perfect for holding the fence up so we could scramble under. We always kept the stick right next to the post so that the next person could use it. Toby seemed to be afraid of that old barn. The closer we got to it, the wider his eyes got.

"C'mon," I cajoled. "It's just a dumb ol' barn with a bunch of dumb ol' cows. You'll git used to it. Help me git this door open."

The door squeaked ominously as it began to budge.

"It's haunted—ah ain't goin' in dere!" Toby shrieked.

"Oh, come on. You cain't stay out here all day. That big ol' chicken hawk gonna come down and pick at your head," I warned. "You got to quit bein' so spooky."

"You got me skeered," Toby whined.

"There ain't no way I'm a goin' back and tell Uncle Joe that we're too skeered to go in that barn. I think I see that chicken hawk right now!"

Toby didn't lose any time scooting into the barn. I took extra time to show him where the tools and the feed were kept. The time flew by. Before long we were all in our cots again ready for sleep–everybody except Toby. He was back in the window box. Everybody was too tired to make conversation.

Without warning, the door suddenly blasted open, and the overhead light pierced the darkness. Tony and Allen's father was standing in the middle of the room.

"Tony! Allen! Git up! I'm a bringin' you home. My boys ain't sleepin' with no niggers!"

"You'd better watch your mouth in my house!" Uncle Joe warned. "They're your boys, and you can do what you want, but they're better off here."

"You know I can come right back here with the sheriff. Then

the whole town will find out what's going on here!" he threatened. "Allen! Tony! I'm not tellin' you again. Git your butts in the truck!"

With those parting words, the three of them left. Uncle Joe looked up at Toby in the window box, cut the light off, and shut the door. The silence was so thick we could have sliced it with a knife. I crawled up into the window box with Toby. We watched as Tony and Allen got into the truck. Their dad and Uncle Joe were still arguing out in the yard. In a few minutes, their dad got in the truck and screeched his tires as he raced off. Still stunned by the events of the last few minutes, we watched as the taillights faded into the distance.

"Dey ain't nuttin' but trouble ever where I goes," Toby complained dejectedly.

"It ain't always gonna' be that way," I consoled him. "Now be quiet. That ol' buck won't come back while we're makin' noise."

With Tony and Allen gone, our workload got even harder and the days hotter as time marched on through the summer. One day as Toby and I were cleaning out the barn, we got so hot we had to take time out to sit down and cool off.

"Ahs got a secret," Toby confided.

"Yeah? What kinda secret?" I inquired.

"'Bout Uncle Joe and my mama," he whispered conspiratorially. "One night Mama she drink too much apple cider–I tink it be apple cider. She tell me how her and Uncle Joe play together when dey be kids. Uncle Joe be de husban' and she be de wife. Mama make mud pies, and Uncle Joe et some o' one."

"That's funny, but it ain't no big deal," I countered.

"Dat ain't it," Toby persisted. "Well–ah–dey growed up a little. When dey bes teenagers, dey bes out behind de ol' wood shed–and dey kisses!"

"No way!" I whooped.

"Mama tell me dey kisses," Toby affirmed. "And guess what? Uncle Joe's daddy see 'em. He beat de fire outta Uncle Joe with a bullwhip across his back. Ah jes' bets he still got de scars to dis day. Dey lock my mama up in de tool shed fer tree days without no food or water. Dey warn 'em dat whites and blacks not spose ta be together."

"No way–no how," I agree.

"Guess what? Dat don' stop 'em. Uncle Joe sneak out late at night and tap on Mama's winder so dey kin be together. Mama tell me dat she kin never love a nudder man. Dat why ah ain't got no daddy. Mama say, she rape and dat how ahs gits here. Ah don' know what 'rape' mean. Ah gonna 'members it, till ah finds out. Mama says ahs a wonderful blessin' from somethin' bad, and if anythin' ever happen to her fer me to find Uncle Joe–dat he bes a good man and he do right by me.

"Mama start sneakin' out de house at night and goin' down to de juke joint. She tink ah was sleepin', but ah kin hear de doh' shut. One night dey foun' her dead out back behin' dat ol' joint. She never come back home. Ahs wait fer her tree days and nights. Den de tird day de preacher come and tell me what done happen. He say dat she don' look like herself no mo'. He say ahs cain' see her no mo'. He tell me Mama confess to him 'bout Uncle Joe. He foun' Uncle Joe in Cannon Ridge, Georgia, where de south make dem cannon fo' de Silver War. De church collec' some money and gimme a bus ticket to here. Dat's my big secret–and you cain' tell nobody."

"Don't worry! I ain't a tellin'," I solemnly promised.

--Robert (Bob) Mathis

RAIN

The clank of the big iron skillet hit the stovetop as Mother began breakfast. The kitchen was right next to my room. I could hear everything. I soon smelled the wonderful aromas coming from the kitchen as the bacon hit the skillet. I knew in a short time I would have to drag myself out of my warm, cozy bed. The breakfast would be well worth it. It would be so nice if Ronnie, my older brother, would just sleep a little later so I could have Mama all to myself.

Some mornings I got up at the first clang of the skillet just to be alone with Mother. She worked away from home all day, came home, and immediately started dinner. After she cleaned the kitchen and ran a load of clothes, it was time for bed. If I got up early enough, she would tell me wonderful stories about her childhood. At ten years old, I had a hard time imagining her as a little girl with issues of growing up like I had. Mother was always so serious around the house–I often wondered if she could be as silly as me.

"Good morning, Mama."

"Hey, Baby!"

"Mama, I'm ten years old. Why do you still call me your baby? It's embarrassing."

"You'll always be my baby."

"Even when I'm a grown man?"

"It don't matter how old you git. You'll always be my baby. Now eat your breakfast. Your eggs are gittin' cold. When I was a little girl, my mother would send me and two of your uncles up to a neighbor's house. Mama would tell us to sit on the back porch and maybe—just maybe they would have some table scraps left over. After we sat there forever, I would hear the lady say, 'Those Mote kids are out back again–like old dogs.' Then she would come out and give us an old sack full of greasy table scraps—even food they had partially eaten. I didn't care–I was hungry. Mother would take the sack, warm the food, and put it on a plate for us to eat. Sometimes, there were very few scraps to divide with eight kids. Most of the time I went to school hungry. Everybody would turn around and look at me when my stomach growled.

"Eat your breakfast, Baby. I'll tell you what we're gonna do. I'm gonna take the day off work, and we're goin' to Atlanta to the picture show. Then we'll buy you some new clothes–and maybe I'll have enough money to get you a toy!"

"Just me and you, Mama?"

"Just me and my baby!"

"Alright, get your butts up. We're burnin' daylight!" Uncle Joe yelled.

"Uncle Joe, what's he doin' here?" I thought. "Where's Mama? I'm not at home. I'm on the farm! I was just dreamin'."

I had to sit on my cot for a few minutes to focus. I missed Mama so much and wished we could spend some alone time together. I looked up at the window box, and there was Toby beginning to stir. Across from me was Allen and beside me was Tony, all slowly coming to life. Every morning Tony would stand up, slide on his pants, bend over close to the wall to pick up his socks, and raise up fast, bumping his head on the roof rafters. It felt good having Tony and Allen back on the farm. One day a policeman

276

had driven them to the farm. He told Uncle Joe that their daddy had killed their mama and was going to be in jail a long time.

"Oh, shoot!" Tony cried. "That roof gets lower ever' day."

"You're right on schedule," I laughed. "Maybe you're jus' growin' up and gittin' taller."

"Toby, you been sleepin' in that darn winder box long enough!" Billy declared. "Tonight you need to sleep in your cot. You been wearin' the same clothes for three days now. It's past time for you to take a bath and put some clean clothes on. Give the rest of us a break. Jeez!"

"Okay, ahs–but ahs jus' gots dese here broke in," Toby stuttered. "Ahs likes to sleep in dat winder box–it make me feel safe. Ahs likes ta be high up over ever'tang."

"It's time you growed up and sleep like the big boys," I added. "That winder box is my special place. I jus' let you have it for a little while cause I felt sorry for you. You been here long enough now to sleep in your own cot. You'll git used to it. I promise. Ain't nuttin' gonna happen to ya. You can hang on to your ol' teddy bear."

"Well, ah–okay," Toby agreed hesitantly.

"Why don't you jus' sleep with Bobby? You two so close and ever'tang," David jeered.

"Ah, shut up, David," I yelled. "You always pickin' on us. Jus' leave us alone. I hope Uncle Joe works the fire out of you today. Maybe the rest of us wouldn't be so tired at night if you'd pull your weight aroun' here."

"I'll show you who's pullin' their weight."

"Knock it off," Billy interjected. "Let's jus' go eat. David, you stop pickin' on 'em!"

At breakfast, there was always plenty of everything: scrambled cheese eggs, bacon, ham slices, grits, and homemade biscuits with gravy, with honey, jellies, and real butter made by Alice. Farm life can be hard, but we always ate well. When Aunt Benny and Alice weren't cooking, they were canning food for the winter months. The farm ran like a well-oiled machine. We all had our jobs and we did them without question. If somebody got sick, we picked up the slack.

"It's startin' ta rain," Toby announced.

"Yeah, ain't it great," Uncle Joe exulted. "That's music to a farmer's ears. I love to see a good rain after the crops are in their beds. You ain't worried about a little water, are ya? It might help you ease into that bath tonight."

Toby looked shocked, but kept on eating. "Uncle Joe, you hears evertang," Toby said with his mouth full.

"Toby, you gots ta swallow before you talk. That sure looks ugly," Aunt Benny scolded.

"Y'all finish up, and let's get ta work," Uncle Joe ordered. "We're burnin' daylight. There's rain gear on the back porch. Don't forget your hats. You sure gonna need 'em today."

The rain started gentle as a mother's kiss. We watched as the dry and dusty road turned from red to muddy brown. The air smelled fresh and new. The water started collecting on the roof of the farmhouse and then slowly began to run down in streams. All the low places in the yard began to fill with water as the rain changed from light to steady. The corn in the fields was glistening, and the leaves reflected light and dark as the wind blew through them–like a perfectly choreographed dance. We stood on the porch and watched as the rain began to come down even harder. The day got darker instead of lighter.

"Uncle Joe," I yelled. "We're down to jus' a couple bales of hay and we're 'bout out of feed."

"You and Toby jump in the truck," Uncle Joe responded. "We'll jus' run down to the shed and load up while I still have the trailer hooked up to the truck."

We jumped off the porch and ran toward the old red truck. Toby had to jump into every puddle along the way, testing out his rubber boots. I could hear Aunt Benny laughing from the porch. The rain seemed to bring out the kid in all of us. I jumped up and grabbed the door handle with both hands and rode the door as it swung open, dangling from the handle, my feet not touching the ground.

"Oh, ahs gots to do dat!" Toby screamed.

"Jus' one time," I cautioned. "Uncle Joe will be here in a minute."

When I slammed the door, Toby jumped up, grabbed the handle with both hands, and rode the door as it swung open. He dangled for a moment and then fell down into a big puddle.

"Now you got to work all day with wet underwear on. Get up! You're soaked to the bone, and we ain't even started the day."

"Now ahs don' have to take no bath, and my clothes be

washed," Toby declared.

"Nope, don't count. You still gotta have a bath and clean clothes."

We sat on the passenger side close together. I liked to sit by the window so I could see out. Toby sat in the middle with his short legs, giving Uncle Joe room to change gears. It didn't matter to Toby. If there was something he wanted to see, he'd just push right over me.

"Hold on. Here we go," Uncle Joe warned.

Uncle Joe turned the key, and the truck shook as its massive motor cranked. We both felt the rush of excitement as Uncle Joe shifted into first gear, and the truck began to move. We both felt important because Uncle Joe had picked us to help with the hay and feed. Normally, he took the bigger boys. The windshield wipers mesmerized us as we watched them move from side to side pushing the water off the windshield. Too little–we couldn't see over the dashboard what was coming down the road, although we could see through the side window that the trees were blowing in the wind and the rain was getting harder. Uncle Joe pulled the truck up close to the front of the shed.

"You boys go inside, climb the ladder to the hay bales on the second level, and jus' push 'em out that big door. I'll stack 'em on the trailer."

It took both of us to take down a bale, slide it to the door, and push it off. We'd watch as it fell down to the trailer where Uncle Joe would grab it and stack it. Soon we had about twenty bales on the trailer.

"Okay, Guys, that's enough. Let's get the feed," yelled Uncle Joe.

Uncle Joe had to carry the fifty-pound bags of feed. There was nothing much for me and Toby to do, but watch. After Uncle Joe threw about five bags on the trailer, we covered the load with the tarp and tied it down, ready to head back to the barn. The rain was coming down in buckets. The day got even darker as we headed back up the muddy road.

"This is the hardest rain I've seen in a long time," Uncle Joe declared. "I can barely see through the windshield. The wipers can't keep up. I'm going to have to stay in the ruts so we won't 'fishtail' with the load on the trailer. The wet bales make it even heavier."

"Look out," I screamed. "Deer!"

The deer was galloping at a steady clip, jumping out of the woods right in front of the truck. Uncle Joe swerved to miss him, but the deer clipped the right front headlight on the truck. The tires could get no traction, and the truck slid sideways into the ditch. The county had just cleaned out the ditches, so they were plenty deep. The truck and trailer were stuck sideways in the ditch.

"You boys jump out on your side," Uncle Joe ordered. "I can't get my door open on this side. Let's see what the damage is."

I could see the deer on the bank. "Don't look like he's movin'."

The truck was covered in mud, and the wheels were buried about halfway up. Toby and I ran to help the deer. As we got closer, the deer jumped up and ran back into the woods.

"Guess he's okay," Uncle Joe grunted. "Looks like we lost a headlight. You boys stay here while I walk up to the house and get Billy and the tractor. We'll try to pull it out."

The rain was so loud hitting the truck and leaves on the trees that we had to yell at the top of our lungs just to hear one another. Toby walked over between the rear of the truck and the trailer to try to get a shovel out of the truck bed. Then he jumped back and ran toward me.

"Sump'ns ovuh dere!" he yelled.

I walked over toward the trailer hitch and looked at the side of the trailer up against the bank. When the mud began to move, I jumped back. Then I eased back up for another look.

"Ah tink it be a big ol' snake!" Toby screeched.

I just nodded my head and carefully positioned myself to get a better look. I could see the mud move again and heard a weak yelp.

"It's a dog!" I shouted.

"A dog?" Toby repeated.

I pulled back some of the mud and could see the face of a black and white dog. I carefully cleaned the mud from his eyes and mouth. The water in the ditch was rising and the dog's head was almost under water.

"Toby, git me dat shovel. Dis dog's gonna drown if we don't pull him out. He musta been chasin' dat deer and jumped between

280

the trailer and de truck. He's stuck under de wheel of de trailer and his head's goin' under if we don't git him out."

My head went under water as I tried to feel under the tire. I could tell his leg was under the wheel. Coming up for air, I saw blood on my hand. I filled my lungs with air and went back down, trying to free his leg from the wheel. It just would not come loose. "Gimme that shovel!" I said to Toby. "You git down there and pull on that dog. I'll pry with the shovel and maybe the trailer will move jus' a little. Pull hard at the count o' three. Okay–one, two, threeeeeeeee!" I put all my weight on the shovel. Unbelievably, the whole trailer moved a little—just enough that Toby was able to pull the dog out.

"He be out," Toby yelled.

We got the dog out of the ditch and up on the shoulder of the road. He was covered in blood, the rain making him look worse than he really was.

"Let's pick 'im up and carry 'im home," I yelled. "You git his backend. Be careful of his leg–I think it's broken."

Toby and I started up the old muddy road with the injured dog. Soon we could see Uncle Joe and Billy coming with the tractor. Uncle Joe jumped off the tractor and came up to us.

"The dog musta been chasing that old deer and jumped between the truck and the trailer and got stuck under the wheel," I explained over the loud rain.

"Let me get 'im."

Uncle Joe reached for the dog and ran all the way back up to the house. Uncle Joe put the dog in Aunt Benny's car and raced off to Doc Mason's for help. Billy, Tommy, David, Allen, and Tony went back to the truck to pull it out of the ditch. Toby and I went down to the barn to start our chores.

It was getting late, and the livestock needed food. The rain never let up. Water was standing in the pastures, and the ground was saturated and muddy. It felt good to be in the barn and out of the rain. The rain beat down on the tin roof, making it impossible to hear each other talk. Knowing what to do, we went right to work without saying a word. I know Toby was thinking the same thing as me–hoping and praying that the dog would make it.

"Hey, I think the rain's beginnin' to let up," I said with relief. "Now maybe we can hear ourselves think. Let's take a break and sit down and talk a minute. Toby, we got to pray for that dog."

"What do God look like?" Toby asked.

"I don't know exactly," I answered. "I always thought he was like an old wise man with white hair and a long beard–like we see in those pictures. You know–those pictures they have in church and in Bibles and thangs."

"What color be God?"

"I don't know. I always thought he was white like me–maybe that's just 'cause I'm white. Who knows? Maybe he's your color–kinda brown. Who really knows if he is a 'he'? I heard this preacher man say one time that God is spirit and ain't no man or woman."

"Spirit? Like a ghos'?"

"No–like the wind. You can't see the wind, but you can feel it blow on you. Sometimes, the wind blows real hard–like God is mad or somethin'. But God is in the air–ever'where, even in this ol' barn with the cows and the chickens. God's all around us, Toby–all the time."

"You means, God knows when ahs ain't take no bath?"

"Yeah. God knows ever'thang!"

"Ah hopes God take good care of my mama!"

"I don't always like ta pray, but we gotta pray for that dog."

"I don't know hows ta pray."

"Guess, I'll have to show ya. Close your eyes and bow your head and think real hard about what I say. Don't let your mind wander. Dear God, I don't really know what I'm doin', but–uh–can you look after that ol' dog and make 'im better? See, we–uh–kinda need that ol' dog here on the farm ta help us with these dumb ol' cows. They're always wandering off, and we have to go after 'em. It surely would be good if we had that ol' dog to help us. Me and Toby will be real good and take our baths like we s'pose to. Amen."

"Why you has ta go and stick in dat bath stuff! Let's do dat prayer over."

"No! Too late. You gotta take a bath, Toby."

"Well, if dat dog live, I gonna name him 'Rain.'"

That night at the supper table the phone rang, breaking the silence. We all listened as Uncle Joe picked up the old black phone:

"Hello. A broke leg? Cuts and bruises? You think he'll be fine. When can I pick 'im up? Okay. See ya tomorrow. Thank you, Doc Mason. Bye."

"Ol' Rain can sleep in my cot, and ah jes' goes back to my winder box," Toby offered happily. "Dat God do some purty good tangs. But ah guess ahs still gots to take dat bath."
--Robert (Bob) Mathis

THE STORY BOX AND THE LITTLE GOLD LOCKET

"I don't know where you little fellers put all that food," Aunt Benny exclaimed in amazement. "Toby, you and Bobby are always the last ones to leave the table. Guess I'd better pull out the sewing machine. You're both goin' ta have a growing spurt the way you're puttin' the food away. I think I'll make you each a pair of shorts to wear around the house. You'll still need your jeans for workin' in the barn."

"Here, Toby. Eat the last of these beans so I don't hafta throw 'em out," Alice requested, as she cleaned up the kitchen.

"Yeah. Ahs gonna grow ta be dis tall!" Toby boasted as he jumped up on the table.

"Lord, Chile! Git yourself down from that table before you break your neck!" Aunt Benny yelled.

"It's not far 'nough up ta break anytang," Toby argued.

"It's just a plain fact. You don't stand on tables," I countered.

I watched Aunt Benny take out an old pie plate and load it with our leftovers as she emptied all the big pots for Alice to wash. Then she placed another plate on top of the first plate, so the flies wouldn't get into the food.

"When you two git finished eatin', I want you to take this food up to Old Widow Johnson's house," Aunt Benny requested. "Toby, she don't know you, so you be real nice and polite. Be sure to say, 'Yes, Ma'am' and 'No, Ma'am.' Mind your manners! And don't you two git off the road goin' up there. Go straight up there and back. Do you understand me?"

"Yes, Ma'am," I promised.

"How about you, Toby? Do you understand?" Aunt Benny glared.

"Oh–ah–yes, Ma'am," Toby answered with a mouth full of food.

"What'd I tell you about talkin' with your mouth full!" Aunt

Benny reprimanded Toby.

"Well, maybe don' ax me nuttin' while ahs eats," Toby suggested softly.

"I can't git mad at you. You're so darn cute," Aunt Benny cooed with love. "Sometimes I wish you boys would never grow up–just like a couple of cupcakes, one vanilla and one chocolate. Oh, well, better pull out the sewin' machine and git started on some bigger pants for the both of you. You're both growin' like those weeds around that okra out there. I've gotta git ta that as soon as I can. Lord, where does the time go?"

"Take this sack of stuff when you go," Alice said.

"Alright," I agreed.

"Come on, Toby, you're gonna love Ol' Widder Johnson."

We both left the house full of energy and full of food. I had the plate of food, and Toby had the sack of stuff. We walked down the driveway under the sign that said "God's Heaven" and out to the dusty dirt road. Old Widow Johnson lived about a mile and a half up the road. Toby found a stick and made it his walking stick. I knew sooner or later that he would get bored with it. Then he'd make it into a gun, begin hitting rocks with it, or maybe make it into a bat or something. One thing for sure I could bet the farm on–he would end up hitting me with it.

"Looks, Bobby! Ahs gonna hit a home run."

"Just be careful you don't hit me!"

Smack! Toby missed the rock and hit me right across the forehead. I nearly dropped the plate of food. I went straight down in the middle of the road. I saw stars.

"Oh, Bobby, don't die! Ahs so sorry. Please, God, don' let Bobby dies. Ahs sorry. You my bestes' buddy. Wake up, Bobby!"

I opened one eye and said, "I'm gonna kill you!"

With that, Toby took off running up that old dirt road as fast as he could. I've seen a lot of things run in my life, but I don't believe I've ever seen anything or anybody that could outrun Toby. He became a little black speck. I got to my feet, reached up, and felt my forehead. I had a huge "goose egg." Toby was now completely out of sight. I began staggering up the road with the pain shooting through my head. A little further up the road, I could hear Toby sobbing behind a tree.

"Come on out here. I know you're back there!"

"No, youse gonna kill me. Ahs don' means to. Ahs sorry!"

284

"I'm not gonna kill you. Now come on out here. I was just mad. Toby, I've never seen anybody with so much energy. You're always into somethin' and gittin' inta trouble. You have to behave when we get to Ol' Widder Johnson's house. Oh, yeah–don't call her 'Ol' Widder Johnson.' We jus' call her that behind her back. You call her 'Mrs. Johnson.'"

"Why?"

"I dunno know. Aunt Benny tol' me to call her 'Mrs. Johnson' when we are in her presence."

"Youse don' say nuttin' 'bout 'presents.' Is wes gonna git presents?"

"No, Toby. That jus' means when we are with her to call her 'Mrs. Johnson.'"

"Why we gots so many rules?"

"I dunno know. Please jus' do what I tell you. I'll figure out some answers later. How's my head look?"

"You looks like somebody hits you wid a stick."

"We're almost there. Please, behave."

A little further up and just beyond the woods, we could see the grassy yard. Soon the house came into view, an old two-story white house with black shutters and huge columns all across the front. The largest house in Cannon Ridge, it had been a working plantation with over two hundred slaves before the Civil War. Mr. Johnson had owned the cannon manufacturing company in town that was destroyed during the war. Out front near the walkway to the front porch was a statue of a black jockey holding a lantern.

"Why does dey wants a boy dat looks like me a holdin' a light?"

"I knew you was gonna ask me that. We don't have time to talk about it now. Just please behave when Mrs. Johnson comes to the door."

"No times fer dis and no times fer dat. Ahs ain' nevah gonna know da answers."

"Please, Toby. Just be quiet! Mrs. Johnson, we brought you some supper," I yelled.

In a few minutes, a figure appeared in the doorway. Mrs. Johnson was truly the last of the "Southern Belles." She was wearing a long dress that dusted the floor. Its long sleeves had lace at the wrist where she tucked her hanky. The front buttoned up to her neck, and the sleeves were puffed at the shoulders. Her face was worn and wrinkled by the years. Her grey hair was pulled back into a bun. She was very much a lady with her Southern charm and style.

"Oh, mercy me!" said Mrs. Johnson, in a thick Southern drawl. "What do we have here? Bobby, did you bring me some supper? This little feller must be Toby. I've heard a lot about you. If you ain't the cutest thing I've ever seen, there ain't no cows in Texas. Let me git a good look at you. And you got a front tooth missing. Ha!"

"Nice to meets ya, Mrs. Johnson."

"Oh, goodness! We've got a perfect gentleman," Mrs. Johnson beamed.

"Sees, Bobby. Ahs don' call her 'Ol' Widder Johnson' like you says," Toby pronounced proudly.

Blood rushed to my face, and not a word could escape my mouth.

"Bobby, what in the world happened to your head?" Mrs. Johnson inquired.

"Well, ah–me and Toby was playin' on our way up here, and I got hit with a stick."

"Ah hits him, Mrs. Johnson, but ahs don' means to," Toby confessed.

"Let me git you a cold washrag to put on your head," Mrs. Johnson gestured kindly. "Just put the supper over there on the table. Come into the kitchen with me so I can tend to that head."

As I followed her into the kitchen, I realized that Toby was not behind me. I turned around to see Toby making his way toward the living room.

"Toby, don't be messin' with nothing," I scolded.

"Why do everthang has sheets over it?" Toby probed.

"I don't have a lot of visitors. So I don't have to keep dusting everything, I put drapes over the furniture. It's what we used to call in olden times 'closing the house,'" Mrs. Johnson explained. "It's just me here, and the only rooms I use are the kitchen and master bedroom."

"Bobby, sit down here and put this cold washrag on your head. Maybe that goose egg will go down a little. Do we have time for me to get out my story box?"

"We have ta be home before dark," I cautioned.

"I ain't walkin' down no roads aftuh dark," Toby chimed in.

Mrs. Johnson left the room and returned in a moment with an old wooden box. The wood was worn and scratched. It looked like many people had handled it. It had a little hasp on the front with two tiny hinges to secure the lid. Mrs. Johnson sat down at the table between Toby and me. Holding the rag on my head, I sat there watching Toby stare at the box. I knew he couldn't wait to see what might be inside.

"Toby, when I open the box, I want you pick out something," Mrs. Johnson instructed.

Toby's eyes were filled with excitement as he gazed into the box. There were all kinds of odds and ends: pieces of jewelry, pictures, and even some old nuts and bolts. Toby's hand crept in and drew out a gold locket in the shape of a heart. We looked up at Mrs. Johnson. Tears filled her eyes as she took the gold locket from Toby's little hand.

"Don' cry, Mrs. Johnson," Toby pleaded. "Ahs picks sometin' else!"

"No, we have to follow the rule. I am required to tell you boys a story about the little gold locket," Mrs. Johnson explained.

"My father built this house himself in 1847. It is well over a hundred years old–you'll have to pull a bent nail out of the box for me to tell you that story. I was born in this house on April 9th in 1865, the very day Lee surrendered and the Civil War ended. A terrible thing happened when I was about nine. The year was 1874 or 1875. I had a little friend who lived up the road, almost where God's Heaven is now.

"Betty Sue and I were about the same age as you two. We were like sisters. We did everything together. We even walked to school together and back home. She would spend the night here, but I was never allowed to go to her house. Betty Sue's house was torn down about fifty years ago. It was on this side of the road, opposite from the farm. Nobody ever wanted to live in it after the terrible thing that happened.

"One morning on my way to school, I was waiting in the road for Betty Sue to come out of her house. Mr. Thomas, her father, came out the front door going to work. Betty Sue was right behind him. She said, 'Here's your lunch, Daddy.' That's when he hauled off and slapped her across the face. He hit her so hard it knocked her front tooth out, and she fell to the ground. Toby, she looked like you with that front tooth missing.

"Bobby, I was just shocked. I couldn't make up my mind to run or just stand there. I hid behind a huge tree beside the road. I saw Mr. Thomas stand over her and scold her: 'I'll just bet the next time you'll give me my lunch before I get out of the house.' Then he turned away, got on his horse, and rode off.

"Betty Sue slowly got up and went back in the house for a few minutes. I was so filled with emotions. I don't know if I was angry or afraid. My father had never hit me. I had never seen a grown man hit a frail little girl. In a little while, Betty Sue came out ready for school. Her face was bright red, and there was a little blood in the corner of her mouth.

"'Betty Sue, are you alright?' I asked.

"'Yeah, I'm okay,' she lied.

"'Why did he hit you like that?'

"'Cause I forgot to give him his lunch. Look at this.'

Betty Sue pulled up her shirt. Her back was black and blue. It was the worst thing I had ever seen.

"'What happened?' I pried.

"'Every night when he comes home, he makes me go to my room and take off all my clothes except my underwear. He has a rope tied on each of the four posts of my bed. He makes me lay face down and ties my hands and legs to the bed, and leaves me there. I pray that he won't come back. Sometimes, about the time I fall off to sleep, he comes crashing back in to beat me. He says that kids are like horses: you have to break their spirits. I'll be glad when I lose my spirit.'"

"I didn't understand. Father never tried to break my spirit.

"Betty Sue confided in me, 'I really like school because I can eat and play with other kids. On the weekends my daddy ties me to the bed and won't let me eat. Mother has to sneak food into my room when he leaves. I'm afraid that he's going to kill me someday. He hates me. Here, I want you to have this. You're my best friend and the only one I can tell things to.'

"'It's your little gold locket!' I exclaimed.

"'It would make me happy if you would keep it for me. I never had a chain for it. If he finds it, he will take it away from me. My mother gave it to me.'

"About three weeks later, I was standing out at the road one morning waiting on Betty Sue to walk to school with me. Mr. Thomas came out to the road and said: 'Betty Sue won't be goin'' to school today. She's sick.' I didn't say anything. I started up the road toward the schoolhouse. When I got far enough out where he couldn't see me, I doubled back and walked behind Betty Sue's house and hid behind the well. I was planning to tap on her window to make sure she was okay. I heard a noise, crouched down, and hid behind the shed just beyond the well.

"I spied Mr. Thomas coming out of the house with a big bundle wrapped in an old bedspread up on his shoulder. I was shocked to see him drop the whole bundle into the well. I could hear it splash into the water when it hit the bottom. Before he went back inside, Mr. Thomas looked around like he was checking to see whether anyone had witnessed what he had just done.

"I hightailed it back to the road and ran all the way to the schoolhouse. I was breathing hard and shaking inside. All I could think about all day long was Betty Sue. She didn't come to school the rest of the week. I knew something was bad wrong. On Saturday, when my father came home for lunch, I heard him tell my mother: 'That little Thomas girl fell in the well and drowned.'

"I ran into the kitchen and blurted out: 'Mr. Thomas done killed her. She showed me where he beat her and told me how he tied her to the bed and would not give her any food. One morning I saw him hit her in the face and knock out her tooth. Please believe me!' They wouldn't take my word.

"Mr. Thomas was a deacon in the church. My parents claimed that he would never do anything like that. Betty Sue's mama had also said that Betty Sue had slipped playing on the side of the well and had fallen in. She confided that they had admonished Betty Sue many times not to play on the well.

"I know what I know. I know Mr. Thomas killed Betty Sue and threw her body in the well. But nobody would believe a little nine-year-old girl. All I have to remember her by is this little locket. Later, the Thomases moved to Athens, Georgia, and we never heard from them again."

I looked over at Toby, and his eyes were as big as saucers.

He jumped up and shrieked: "Ahs ain' hearin' no mo!"

He scrambled out of the kitchen through the living room to the porch and down the sidewalk. All the eye could see was dust spiraling down the road.

"I gotta catch him, Mrs. Johnson. I hope you like your supper."

I couldn't catch up to Toby. When I got back to the farm, Uncle Joe and Aunt Benny were sitting in the kitchen with that deer-in-the-headlights look.

Aunt Benny shook her head and exclaimed, "Toby claims he ain't going back to Ol' Widder Johnson's house. He's up in his winder box again."

--Robert (Bob) Mathis

GOING HOME

I've been lying here wide-awake for hours. Shining through Toby's window box, the full moon illuminates the whole room. I look over at the cot next to me where Toby is all sprawled out, hugging his teddy bear. I pick up his sheet from the floor and cover him up. Just a few months ago we saw him for the first time. He was standing in the driveway with Uncle Joe. A little eight-year-old black boy from Iowa, Toby had on shoes that didn't match–one was brown worn leather and the other was an old house shoe, and he didn't have on any socks. Under his arm was an old dirty teddy bear that his mother had made him.

After Toby got to know me, he shared a shocking secret about the love between our Uncle Joe and his mother–a love that had forced Uncle Joe to leave his home in Iowa, a love that could never be realized because of the color of their skin. After the murder of Toby's mother, he didn't have any family left. Finding a piece of paper with Uncle Joe's name and address on it on the mother's body, the preacher sent Toby to Georgia to live with Uncle Joe.

In the short space of a summer, Toby had become like a brother to me. None of us on the farm could even imagine what we had done around there without our Toby.

I look at every boy in the room and realize that they are family to me. We had formed strong bonds as we worked hard to get our tasks on the farm done. The farm was economic survival for our families. Billy is the oldest of all the boys and kind of like a foreman or second in command around here. We all look to Billy for advice or instructions. He's from a little town in South Georgia called Plains with a population of about 425 people.

Billy likes to talk about this peanut farmer named Jimmy

Carter. He said the Carters were the only people offering any kind of work in the area. His mother continued to live there after his daddy went North to look for work and never came back. Billy always sends his mother money–almost everything he makes. Billy's a kind spirit who never gets angry with us. One time when I was sick, he did all my work for me and never told Uncle Joe. He likes to pick Toby and me up by the backs of our shirts and brag, "This is how I work my arms out." It works, too. His arms are as big as my waist.

Tony and Allen are always ready to lend a helping hand. They are brothers from Austell, Georgia, a little town northwest of Atlanta. Their daddy is very mean and likes to beat on them and their mother. I don't understand why. They are good boys. They worry a lot about their mother. Uncle Joe and Aunt Benny like to give them extra attention. They buy their school clothes, because they know that the boys won't get any clothes if they don't. I found out that Uncle Joe went to their school and paid for their lunches for a whole year. I heard him say to Aunt Benny, "At least they will get one meal a day."

David and Tommy are always telling us jokes and making us laugh, when they're not playing tricks on Toby and me. They are from somewhere in Alabama. Their families are very poor. What little money they make here on the farm will be used to feed the family. Uncle Joe always makes sure to ship food to them first, before it's all sold at the farmers' market. Uncle Joe also divides the pork and deer meat with their family.

David said that he can see outside through the cracks in the wall. He uses old newspapers to fill the cracks in the wintertime, which doesn't help much because he still freezes and has to sleep in all his clothes, even his boots. With all their hardships, they are still the jokers in the bunch and always seem happy. Maybe they are just happy to be on the farm with us–people who love them and care for them. It's going to be hard to say good-bye at the end of summer.

The house is quiet and all are asleep as I make my way downstairs and through the kitchen, then out to the back porch. Here comes ol' Rain to welcome me to the backyard. Nothing moves in this yard without Rain knowing about it. He jumps up and licks my face as if to say, "Boy, I'm going to miss you." Rain thinks he owns the farm, although he is the newcomer. Nothing gets past him. We all feel a little safer with him on guard.

I sit down in the yard swing and look at all the wonders around me: the empty corn stalks as far as you can see, the old barn down in the south pasture where Toby and I share our secrets, the chicken coop, and the pig pen–all are quiet and peaceful. Everything's asleep except Rain and me. The huge trucks are all loaded with the best and sweetest corn in the South, ready for the farmers' market. The corn for feed is loaded in the silo, and pigs will be heading for the slaughterhouse. There's still a lot of work to keep a farm running, even in the winter. I wonder what it's like to be here all winter.

Uncle Joe told me that they get a fair amount of snow, being at the foot of the mountain. It hardly ever snows where I live. We always pray for a snow day so we can get a day off from school. I'll bet if I lived here, Uncle Joe would get us to school even if he had to take us on the tractor. I can't believe I'm thinking this, but I'm going to miss this place–Toby, most of all. I wonder what school will be like for Toby. I just hope he behaves and everybody accepts him like we did. It's going to be hard for Toby. If anybody can do it, he can.

"Rain, I just heard the rooster crow. Let's go and get the boys up. We're burnin' daylight!"

When we get upstairs, Rain jumps up on Toby's cot and starts waking him up by licking his face. Toby starts to giggle and then breaks into full laughter as Rain continues to lick.

"Oh, boy!" Toby says quietly. "Ahs gonna gits ta say it! Alright, gits yo' butts up. We's burnin' daylight," Toby yelled at the top of his lungs. Toby laughed harder and harder as everybody threw pillows at him.

I feel sorry for anybody who even tries to break Toby's spirit. Toby has made the farm a better place to live and work. All the guys will be sorry to leave this year. Billy will be up for the draft and most likely will go to Viet Nam. I worry about his safety. There is no way the farm will be the same without him. He always helps us little guys. He taught me a lot. But things have to change. People grow older. Uncle Joe always told us, "Challenges can be stepping stones or stumbling blocks. It's just a matter of how you view them."

At the breakfast table, Uncle Joe asks, "Well, Toby, you think you can take my place around here?"

"Uncle Joe, you hears evertang," Toby says.

"The people in the next county heard you," Uncle Joe says.

"I'm not one for speeches. Billy, you've been workin' on this farm for ten years now. I can't believe that little eight-year-old boy has grown into a strong man that will be servin' our country. You make us proud, boy! You helped make God's Heaven what it is today. I've got a little present here for you."

Aunt Benny starts to cry and leaves the table. Toby's eyes are as big as saucers–again. I don't think he understands that everybody will be leaving today. Uncle Joe reaches down and brings up one of his old guns.

"We want you to have ol' Betsy. You've always loved this gun, and this is the gun I taught you to shoot with. This was my daddy's gun, and now Benny and I would like you to have it. Kind of somethin' to remember us by. Ol' Betsy will always protect you wherever you go."

"Uncle Joe, I can't take ol' Betsy," Billy declares.

"Oh, yes, you will, and I'm not gonna hear another word about it. This is normally the time that I give out the daily chores.

"Billy, Tommy, and David, I have your bus tickets home.

"Bobby, Allen, and Tony, y'all ride with me in the red truck. I'll drop you boys off on my way into Atlanta.

"All of you did a great job for God's Heaven this year, and y'all know that we are just a phone call away. I don't care what kind of trouble you get into, just call me–I'll come a runnin'," Uncle Joe promises in his determined way.

With that, Toby jumps up and runs out of the house with Rain right behind. I start to get up and chase after him.

"No–give him some time to think," Uncle Joe advises. "He's got to learn to make it around here all by himself. The little feller has a rough road ahead of him.

"You boys, get your things together and get your bus tickets. Benny will take you into Ellijay to the bus station. Don't forget that next summer, before you can start work, I have to see that report card. You must have A's, B's, or C's to work here. Just do the very best you can, and I'm sure it'll be enough. Remember, 'success' only comes before 'work' in the dictionary.

"Bobby, you'd better go find that boy and bring him back."

I go outside to see an empty yard. It is still early, and the sun is just beginning to light the other side of the mountain. I know if

I can find Rain, I'll find Toby. My first guess is the barn. I lift the barbed wire to ease my body through. I don't want to get a shock on my last day. I can see Essie down in the pasture with her calf "Cupcake." When I pull the old barn door open, I can hear Rain inside. He is running around looking up at the loft.

"It's hard to hide from anybody with ol' Rain around," Toby pouts.

"Come on down here so I can talk ta you. I'm not climbing all the way up in the loft to get ya," I warn. "Don't take all day about it."

"Youse dumb ol' dog! Youse tell ever'body where ahs bes!" Toby growls.

Toby slowly climbs down from the loft and sits down leaning on the barn wall where we always have our little talks. His face is soaked with tears.

"Toby, we talked about how I would have to go back to school someday. I know you just put it out of your mind like you do all the bad things that happen. I wish I could take you home with me, but I can't. We have got to face facts. Today is the day I have to leave and go back home."

"Everybody has a home ta goes to 'cep' me. Why my mama hasta die?"

"I wish I knew all the answers to all your questions. Boy, you sure do have a lot of questions. Things have to change: seasons, people, even animals and plants. Just like ol' Rain–he's not going to be with us forever. We just have ta enjoy him while we've got him."

"When I was 'bout six or seven, Mama had a friend who used to keep my older brother and me during the summer before I started comin' up here. She was an older woman named Rose. She was the grandmother I never had. Both my real grandmothers died when I was a baby. Most days I'd be down on the floor playing with my toys, and she would come in the living room, sit down in the big platform rocker, and say, 'Now why in da world would you wants to stay down on dat floor, when ahs got dis big ol' lap to sit on? C'mon, Chile, git in my lap and let me rock you.' Then I'd crawl up in her lap, and she'd put her arms around me and sing me to sleep. She sang those old church hymns. I loved to hear her sing, especially 'Amazin' Grace' and "Softly and Tenderly.' When she cooked, she would make me two small baby biscuits.

"My older brother, Ronnie, was always real mean to me and would take my stuff away from me. He wouldn't do it when Rose was there. She'd get him good.

"One day I got mad at Rose cause she wouldn't rock me or sing to me. She complained, 'Ahs jus gots too much to do with dis ironin' and stuff.' When it got time for her to leave, I could hear her callin' me, but I just hid in my room and acted like I didn't hear her. Finally, she just told Mama, 'Ahs jus spen' some extry time with him tomorrow.'

"I felt like I had Rose right where I wanted her. I knew she wouldn't let another day go by without rockin' me. But there wasn't another day. The next morning Mama woke me up and told me that she would be staying home from work and that she'd have to find someone else to keep us. Then Mama started crying. Rose had died in her sleep and wouldn't ever be comin' back. I feel bad to this day for not hugging Rose's neck and telling her bye. Now I can't make it up to her. I loved her so much. Nothing was the same after she died. My brother didn't even care that she had died. Now, I got to live with that and I can't change what I did.

"Toby, we never know when the end is near. I learned this lesson early in my life. Now I try to live like there might not be a tomorrow. You have to go up there and hug Billy's neck and tell him how much you care, cause you don't know if he's comin' back from Viet Nam. I know things are rough on you, but Billy's gonna have it a lot rougher. We gotta be big boys and say our good-byes."

"Youse cries when Rose dies?"

"Boy, did I ever. I feel like crying right now. Guess we'll have a lot of Roses in our lives. Uncle Joe told me that sometimes we are so busy adding up our troubles that we forget to count our blessings. You're really lucky, Toby, that Uncle Joe and Aunt Benny have given you a home. If you were still in Iowa, who would be taking care of you?"

"Yeah, guess youse right 'bout dat!"

"Come on, Ol' Buddy! Let's go tell 'em bye."

We come out of the barn and see Billy, Tommy, and David standing next to Aunt Benny's car, waiting to get in.

"Youse can't leave. Youse gotta tell me bye!" Toby yells at the top of his lungs.

Toby runs up the hill and jumps up into Billy's arms. Billy

swings Toby around and around beside the car.

"Thought you didn't love me anymore," Billy teases, holding Toby in his big arms. "You're my little man. Wish I had time to take you huntin' this winter. We'd kill us a deer!"

"Youse cain' hurts no deer!" Toby yells.

"Well, Little Feller, there's lots for you to learn about around here," Billy says. "One thang Uncle Joe will have to teach you is that if we don't kill off the deer in the winter, they will eat the crops next spring. And if they eat the crops, you don't eat–and I know how much you like to eat."

"I'll bet you'll be as big as we are next summer," David declares.

"I'm gonna have some brand new ghost stories, when I come back next year," Tommy jokes.

"Ifn it bes de same ta youse, leave dem ghost stories in Alabama," Toby requests.

"Bobby, Ol' Buddy, you be sure and make good grades this year," Billy says as he picked me up. "Maybe you'll get better with that tractor. Keep it runnin' just like I showed you. Uncle Joe, I can't believe you're going to break up our little 'salt and pepper' set. Looks like just pepper will be runnin' around God's Heaven from now on. I love you boys, and when I come back from Viet Nam, I'm gonna teach you both how to shoot a gun–just like Uncle Joe taught me."

The guys get into Aunt Benny's car and take off. Uncle Joe gets something in his eye again and goes into the house to wash it out. We load our suitcases on the back of the truck and wait for Uncle Joe to return. Toby seems to be doing better. I notice that Toby will not look me in the eye–most likely for the same reason that I can't look him in the eye.

"Get your butts in the truck," Uncle Joe orders. "We're burnin' daylight!"

Tony and Allen climb in the middle this time, and I get the window, or what we used to call "shot gun." When Uncle Joe starts the thundering engine, I can feel my heart pounding as I look at Toby's sad little eyes. Standing there in the driveway with the sun at his back, Toby looks so little–all alone, except for Rain. I watch from the back window as we drive down the driveway. Toby just stands there with tears running down his face. He gets smaller and smaller as the dust from the road blurs him from my vision. It is just as well. I don't want him to see me cry. I turn around in my seat, and my heart is aching for those good ol' summer days on the farm. Barely out of sight, and I'm wanting to go back where life is real, and we laugh and cry together as a family.

--Robert (Bob) Mathis

EXCERPT FROM FOUNDERS' DAY

February 5, 2014: Fiftieth Anniversary of the Desegregation of Mercer University

I have spent most of my years, since graduation from Mercer, in Washington, D.C., a city best known today for its manifest dysfunction, gridlock, and partisan hot air. So last year when President Underwood told me on the eve of the shutdown of the federal government that the Student Government Association had invited me–a Washington lobbyist–to come down from the nation's capital to share my Washington wisdom, I thought, "Wow! The Student Government Association has a really good sense of humor."

That assurance gave me the courage to accept this gracious invitation. I turned it into an opportunity for me to take a journey, back in time and back to the main campus that I had not visited in many years. I spent time in the Tarver Library. I reached out to a number of my classmates of 50 years ago, some of whom were also Mercer Cluster colleagues: Sam Oni, Don Baxter, Larry Maioriello, Colin Harris, Larry Couey, Kathy Holmes, Edward Simmons, and Ben and Ellen Jordan. Some of them are here today, along with my daughter Louisa, and my wonderful wife Virginia. President Underwood, if my wife or daughter asks to see all of my transcripts and grades, please tell her those are restricted by the Federal Privacy Act of 1974!

The most fun for me on my campus visits was the opportunity to talk with a great many current Mercer students. Those included the impressive young men and women who are the elected officers of your Student Government Association, along with the current editor of the *Cluster*, Emily Farlow, and her staff editors, and with some of your excellent Minority Mentors. Thanks to all for their patience and time.

Much of what I rediscovered about the past and learned about the present surprised me. Some of it shocked me. Some things about my time at Mercer in the 1960s made me proud. Some things made me ashamed of myself and others.

But first, let me put things in the context of life on this campus fifty years ago.

In 1962, the United States and the old Soviet Union came to the brink of nuclear war during the Cuban missile crisis. The military draft was in effect, and Mercer ROTC students graduated in uniform and were sworn in as Army officers as part of the ceremony.

Most of the time when a student was in this beautiful auditorium, it was because he or she had to be. Chapel attendance was mandatory, three days per week. Staff from the registrar's office stood in the balcony, taking roll to see that your assigned seat was occupied—either by you or someone else.

In 1963, one of the big headlines in the *Cluster* announced that Mercer was raising tuition by $25 per quarter. That brought the total fees for room, board, and tuition to a whopping $1,380 for the full academic year.

Freshmen, in retrospect, should have gotten a discount because they were supposed to wear a goofy orange and black beanie hat for the first couple of weeks of the school year.

Dorms were not air-conditioned, but that wasn't a big deal because most folks had no air-conditioning at home. Parking was not a problem because most students did not have a car. There was no I-75, but there were passenger trains.

Fifty years ago the *Cluster* ran a story about long lunch lines in the Connell center. Some things never change. There was also an article about whether the Administration Building was haunted. That's silly—of course, it's haunted. Like today, we had a great basketball team. But we had a small library, no swimming pool, and a campus quad that could not hold an aesthetic candle to that of today.

But while talking about 1963, here's the hardest job: trying to explain to a Mercer student today the bizarre terrain of race relations in the South and the nation fifty years ago.

My daughters, ages seventeen and twenty, have listened politely to my stories of white-only schools, white-only drinking fountains and rest rooms, and white-only restaurants and hotels. But when I have tried to explain how a system of such stark racial discrimination was somehow an accepted norm by most white people, I get the universal teenager put-down: a big eye-roll to heaven and the comment, "Really?"

I believe my kids think that we all must have been crazy. And maybe an insanity plea would be the best line of defense. Early evidence of that would be the incident in 1954, featured in Dr. Andrew Silver's documentary play, "Combustible/Burn," about the early civil rights movement in Macon and at Mercer. That's the story of Richard Scott, an African American graduate of Talladega College in Alabama, and Clifford York, a white Mercer ministerial student. They were arrested on charges of "suspicion of a misdemeanor." Basically, when the neighbors saw a young black man having dinner at a white person's home in Macon, they called the cops.

Upon their release, an NAACP spokesman explained, "The deputies honestly thought the two young men were breaking a law by dining together." Sherriff Wood said his deputies made the arrest out of fear of violence that might occur in the neighborhood if the biracial dining experience had become widely known. And I suppose they would have been right about one thing–trouble was brewing. By the time I came to Mercer in 1961, the South was catching fire from the searing injustice of racial prejudice.

Let's recall the times.

In 1961, a mob of about 100 students threw rocks, bottles, and fireworks outside the dorm of black student Charlayne Hunter, when she and Hamilton Holmes desegregated the University of Georgia.

In 1962, James Meredith could have been killed for his efforts to desegregate the University of Mississippi. A mob of a thousand gathered there and attacked a hastily assembled band of 300 federal marshals with rocks, bottles, and rifle and shotgun fire. Two people were killed, and of the 300 marshals, 160 were injured–twenty-eight by gunfire. The next day, 23,000 soldiers were stationed around Oxford.

The ultimate horror came a year later, on the morning of Sunday, September 15, 1963, the same month that Sam Oni, Bennie Stephens and Cecil Dewberry became my classmates at Mercer. Four members of the Ku Klux Klan planted a box of dynamite under the steps of the 16th Street Baptist Church in Birmingham. The explosion came as twenty-six children were walking into a Sunday School class. Four little girls—three were fourteen years old and one was eleven–were killed and twenty-two others injured.

Many blamed Alabama Governor George Wallace for the killings by inflaming the racial prejudice that spawned such violence in his state. A week before the bombing, he famously told The New York Times that to stop integration, Alabama needed "a few first-class funerals and political funerals."

The use of such language was calculated–Wallace had been defeated for governor in 1958 by a racist candidate who was endorsed by the Ku Klux Klan, and who attributed his victory to Wallace being soft on integration. Indeed, Wallace had been endorsed by the NAACP. In winning the governor's office in 1962, Wallace had said, and I quote directly, "no other son-of-a-bitch will ever out-nigger me again."

I repeat those despicable words just as he spoke them to try to give you a sense of the world of social, moral, and political turmoil that was smoldering just outside the boundaries of the Mercer campus.

For me, as a reporter and editor with the *Cluster*, and especially as an intern and later regular reporter with *The Atlanta Constitution*, now *The Atlanta Journal-Constitution*, civil rights stories were big news.

But it would be wrong to think that this was a subject that dominated the attention of the all-white Mercer student body. We lived in the comfortable bubble of the university's world-within-a-world. In the minds of most 18- to 21-year-olds on campus, desegregation was not at the top of the priority list. I feel confident that if we had taken a campus vote in support of Sam Oni's admission to Mercer, it would have passed. But few of us had any peer relationship with blacks, so this was just not a front-and-center issue in the minds of the majority.

I contrast that with the African American students at historically black colleges in Georgia and across the South. They were both the foot soldiers and the strategists for the demonstrations that ultimately broke the back of segregation. Education meant power and progress for African Americans, then as now. That's why fifty years ago, so-called separate-but-equal education had been kept as separate and unequal as possible.

And so it was a little more than fifty years ago that Mercer stood at an important crossroads on what to do with respect to one of the great issues of the twentieth century. The easiest course would have been to do nothing.

It was not foreordained that Sam Jerry Oni, a student from Ghana, would be admitted to Mercer. It was public universities, not private colleges and universities, which were the subject of landmark desegregation litigation and court orders. Mercer in 1963 was bound by charter, money, and tradition to the Georgia Baptist Convention, which itself was on record in opposing integration–albeit in the gauzy, polite language of the day.

The Convention reviewed part of Mercer's budget, and every year voted to set its own important financial contribution to the university–a dollar number that was always a headline in the *Cluster*. Powerful alumni bitterly opposed desegregation and made it clear that their financial support would dry up if the school embraced integration.

The easy choice would have been to go slow, which was the mantra of the day in the South. But there was something special in Mercer's character, then and now, that made a difference.

At the same time the Bibb County deputies were locking up Richard Scott and Clifford York for dining together in 1954, Mercer Professor of Religion Mac Bryan was among those challenging Mercer students to learn the art of critical thinking and Christian conscience on race and religion.

Dr. Bryan would school a generation of Baptist ministers, many of whom would go on to lead Georgia churches and play a key role in supporting Mercer integration. Harris Mobley, the Mercer-trained Baptist missionary who would recruit Sam to come to Mercer, famously said, "Dr. Bryan invented me."

Also in the 1950s, Joe Hendricks had arrived at Mercer as a student and returned to campus in 1959 as dean of men after studying theology. Joe would become one of the seminal figures in Mercer history, and certainly in the history of racial justice.

So it was well before 1963 that the strategy was formed. Desegregation at Mercer would happen in the context of faith and shared human dignity. It was not just that Mercer would desegregate, but how Mercer would do it that became important.

The key actors by the time I was at Mercer were Joe and Jean Hendricks, Ray Brewster, Willis Glover, Tom Trimble, Bob Otto, Harold McManus, Bobby and Mary Wilder, and many others. They were the campus radicals who would seek to save Mercer's soul, and they were the administration and faculty of Mercer.

They were quite the band of brothers and sisters–great scholars, but also fun to be with in a classroom. I remember Dr. Glover, the history professor, teasing Dr. Otto, who taught logic. He said, "Bob, history teaches us that logic is not important. Students don't need to learn logic. They need to learn to use fallacies effectively."

At the top of this faculty food chain was a man who does not always get his full due–Mercer President, Dr. Rufus C. Harris. He was a Mercer graduate, former dean of the Mercer and Tulane University law schools, and president of Tulane University for more than twenty years. Most people thought that he came to Mercer in 1960 as a pleasant way to transition into retirement. He fooled us all, serving as president until 1980. With his patrician bearing and quick mind, he set the course that navigated Mercer desegregation with, through, and around trustees, Baptists, alumni, and the media.

And the media very much included the Mercer *Cluster*. In hindsight, whenever I interviewed Dr. Harris, I was like a simple-minded border guard in a *Star Wars* movie talking to Obi-Wan Kenobi. I was no match for the Jedi master of interviews, and of course he was too smart to let me figure that out in real time. Basically, whatever Dr. Harris wanted me to write is what I ended up writing.

President Underwood, having seen you in action, I now know that you also are a Jedi master, so I presume that is a skill passed on in secret with each presidential transition. May the force be with you!

In the pre-*Twitter* world, the *Cluster* was the major conduit of information about all things Mercer. The earliest article on desegregation I have seen was February 2, 1950, when a student, Jim Young, wrote an almost full-page column with a strategy to phase in desegregation. He said, "the chief obstacle is not the sentiment of the college student bodies, nor that of the faculties or even that of the administrations. The chief obstacle is the sentiment of the financial masters of the administrations–the trustees and the general public."

There was a companion article on the same page by another student, Ms. Laurice Walker, and together these two pieces were a stunningly direct exposition on how to counter racism, and all founded on the teaching of Jesus. Ms. Walker said of desegregation that it would cause conflict, but that "New social conditions are born like people–there's some misery attendant upon the birth," and she added that we should be mindful that Jesus said in Matthew, "I come to bring not peace, but a sword." Wow. Props to Laurice–strong words for any era, much less 1950.

I look back with mixed emotions on my own work on desegregation as editor. We covered the run-up to the desegregation decision aggressively, ran editorials and columns in support, and left no doubt where we stood. My predecessor as editor, Larry Maioriello, took a good bit of heat from his law school classmates for his early stand in support of desegregation. Some called the *Cluster* staff "Maioriello's Menagerie." Larry was and still is a tough guy, and he just ignored it.

In hindsight, I give myself a decent grade for the journalism of the initial coverage of this issue on my watch, but I get a C-minus for weak follow-up. I was shocked to learn in later years about the visit of the Tattnall Square church pastor to Sam's dorm room immediately after he arrived, delivering the message that he would not be welcome in the congregation.

I talked to Sam about that recently, and basically apologized for being a pretty sorry reporter for not having known or written about that incident. He said that at the time, he and his white roommate, Don Baxter, were so shocked that they said little about it. But a good reporter would have been in touch with Sam and following his life on campus. I think after Sam, Benny, and Cecil were on campus, we treated it as a story that was finished, which it was not.

For my own part, editorials in support of desegregation were in my comfort zone because I had grown up in a family where it was made clear early and often that racial bias was a sin. My father, John Hurt, was the editor of the state Baptist newspaper in Georgia, *The Christian Index*. The *Index* was one of the largest circulation weekly publications in the state, sent to more than 100,000 subscribers. Dad had a strong editorial voice, and he used it decisively in support of the Mercer desegregation.

He had pushback from some of his readers and some denominational leaders. I never thought much about the courage it took for him to do that, as he was an employee of the Georgia Baptist Convention. It was only later that I learned from my older brother, also a Mercer graduate, that our mother was very concerned that

Dad would lose his job over his editorials. I was probably focused on the fact that he had better sources than I did. He broke the story of the application of Sam to Mercer that sparked the follow-up stories around the country and in *The New York Times*. The media was just one part of the strategy that the faculty and Dr. Harris crafted to break the Mercer color barrier. Not by accident, the heart of the strategy was to leverage the powerful Southern Baptist tradition of sending missionaries overseas, and using that tradition to teach a lesson. When Georgia Baptists, or any good soul, looked into the mirror handed to them by the Mercer-trained missionary Harris Mobley, they would see the dazzling smile of Sam Jerry Oni. As Harris would say later with delight, "Our preaching caught up with us."

But journalists or university presidents were not the ground soldiers in this fight. The ground soldiers in the fight were Sam and his white roommate, Don Baxter, along with day students Benny Stephens and Cecil Dewberry. They were the Seal Team Six for a hostage rescue of this university, and they did not escape without injury. Sam's faith was shaken by the hypocrisy of churches that would not accept blacks. Also disgusted by religious hypocrisy, Don abandoned his plans to be a minister.

Desegregation was to be a shock wave in congregations all over the South. At Mercer, the Rev. Tom Holmes, teacher and administrator, staked his professional career in 1965 on his ability to bring Tattnall Square Baptist Church through the tumult by accepting that all were welcome in God's house. For preaching truth, he was called "lower down than a dog" and fired. His wonderful book, *Ashes for Breakfast*, tells the story.

He was not alone. Many preachers all over the South lost their pulpits in the same way. They became pastoral refugees. My first pastor in Washington, D.C., Bob Troutman at Riverside Baptist, had been run out of his church in Memphis.

But the die was cast in Macon. Mercer would not only desegregate, it would establish an on-campus tutoring program for black students who wanted to attend, but who had been denied the same standard of a high school education as their white classmates. Today, Mercer's minority enrollment of more than twenty percent is by far higher than virtually all of its peer institutions in the South.

We speak today of Dr. Harris and the faculty of that time as the seminal figures in desegregation here, and they were. But fundamentally they were teachers. Race relations were just one of the lessons in the syllabus, and their lives and lessons transformed a generation.

Ellen Jordan, my classmate in 1963, sent me an email when she learned about the topic of my remarks today. She wrote, and I quote, "Here's a snapshot from the perspective of a naïve little Baptist girl who had no independent thought until I got to the Mercer quad ... Happy with the status quo, an over-achiever, high school nerd, product of segregated neighborhoods and schools, afraid to leave the box, feeling always that religion would carry me along, I came to Mercer with no expectations. Just another comfort zone.

"And then I went to Ray Brewster's class. He turned the world upside down in the most quiet and shocking way. Sitting on the edge of the desk, feet propped on a trashcan, tattered book in his hand, he gave me 'a whole new life.' To this day."

Ellen closed by saying that Ray, his colleagues, and Dr. Harris "symbolize the Mercer experience," and that "they chose the right side of history at that moment in time. I am touched that nearly a half century later, here we stand ... Mercerians–from different backgrounds somewhat, with similar experiences mostly–and the circle is unbroken. Maybe Mercer is still doing that today."

Ellen, I think, knows that she can rest easy. Mercer is continuing that tradition.

I know that students, faculty, and President Underwood have made it clear that the observance of the fiftieth anniversary is not a time for self-celebration and resting on laurels. And, indeed, no white man or woman today should expect a pat on the back for helping end a practice of discrimination that defies modern understanding.

But the simple truth is that the campus radicals of my era– mainly the faculty and administration with the support of students– plowed up the weeds of systemic discrimination at this university and did so in a way that new things could grow from that work.

It is a very good thing that most students in 2014 find the racial terrain of fifty years ago to be ancient history. It is a good thing that the name of Governor George Wallace draws blank stares from most teenagers today. But it also should be good for them to know that George Wallace, late in life, became a born-again Christian, renounced racism, ran for governor yet again, was endorsed by the NAACP, and won the majority of the black votes in Alabama on his way to victory.

Don Baxter, who had turned away from the ministry to medicine, said in this room that his experience at Mercer with Sam changed his life forever–and for the good. Sam said in this room that he found renewal in his faith and in this university when he returned years later to see the changes that had taken place.

Charles Richardson, an African American who is editor of the editorial page of *The Telegraph*, told me that Mercer today is a life force in Macon, radiating a vibrant and progressive power in this city and state. This community depends on Mercer for progress.

My classmate Colin Harris, who retired recently from the Mercer faculty, reminded me that on Founders' Day we should be mindful that "founding" is a process more than an event. Founders are present in the life of a community in every generation.

To students today, of all races and national origins, you have the opportunity to know each other as friends and partners in life in a way that just was not possible in my time. Right now, at Mercer, you have the opportunity to live, study, and socialize together in what for many of you is probably the most unselfconsciously integrated environment you have ever encountered. It is an opportunity for you to develop the friendships of a lifetime.

The end of the story of the fiftieth anniversary is not really an ending–it's a beginning. You attend a much better, much stronger, more compassionate and impactful school than the one I attended. You have access to programs that reach around the world. You have a student body strengthened by diversity to deal with a world of diversity, and you have a faculty of great accomplishment.

Now it's your turn to write the storyline of a Founders' Day that will unfold some years from now. I do not know what the social, economic, cultural, or public policy challenges will be that you choose to take on. But I am confident that in your task, you will be able to draw on the strength to do so from a university that was changed for the good by the campus radicals who saved Mercer's soul.

--Robert H. Hurt

RHYTHM, RHYME, & DRAMA

The drama is complete poetry. The ode and the epic contain it only in germ; it contains both of them in a state of high development, and epitomizes both.
--Victor Hugo

If ... it makes my whole body so cold no fire can ever warm me, I know that it is poetry.
--Emily Dickinson

Poetry is boned with ideas, nerved and blooded with emotions, all held together by the delicate, tough skin of words.
--Paul Engle

The poet is a liar who always speaks the truth.
--Jean Cocteau

Poetry is the art of uniting pleasure with truth.
--Samuel Johnson

Poetry involves the mysteries of the irrational perceived through rational words.
--Vladimir Nabokov

All poetry is putting the infinite within the finite.
--Robert Browning

A film that is a true work of art transcends theatre and heartwarmingly changes lives.
--A. D. Posey

Out of the quarrel with others we make rhetoric; out of the quarrel with ourselves we make poetry.
--W. B. Yeats

If you spend a hundred bucks, or more, to go to the theatre, something should happen to you. Maybe somebody should be asking you some questions about your values, or about the way you think about things. Maybe you should come out of the theatre, something having happened to you. ... But if you just go there, and the only thing you worry about is where you left the damn car, then you wasted a hundred bucks.
--Edward Albee

DELLA'S PRAYER

Lord,
When my sons are all grown and have families of their own,
Help me be accepting of their spouses and respectful of their
houses
To be loving, kind and caring and not overbearing
To let them live their lives without adding any strife.
Most importantly, and the least of all,
Don't let me be like my mother-in-law!
--Diane Lang

NO ONE WANTS TO PASS ON THIS PAIN

I feel alone, as though no one understands.
Sanity is close yet alludes no command.
Alone and confused in my thoughts,
I need help before I am lost.

No one wants to pass on this pain.

From the inside I don't understand
How to stop these intense commands.
Why am I crying? Why am I sad?
Mommy and Daddy think I am bad.
No one understands the pain I'm in.

No one understands my pain.

I do, Baby! I understand,
Mommy still struggles with these intense commands.
First I'm happy–then I'm depressed,
It feels as though I'm lost in distress.

I'm sorry you feel this pain.
When you find yourself hanging in the dark,
Let me ease your heart.

I never meant to pass on my pain.
--Amanda McCranie

Songs for the Living: He's Been Gone Two Weeks

Sometimes I think I'll go insane
With your ceaseless, childish chatter
Prodding at my benumbed mind all day,
It's "*Mommie, this*" and "*Mommie, that*"
And the steady, absorbed dwelling
In your childhood worlds and fancies
And food and fights with friends and
Pleas to spend the night
Or go skating or over to Mary's,
Or else the latest movie plot
And what the other kids are wearing.

From far away I hear my voice–Is that my voice?
"*Not just now, Love,*" "*We'll talk about it later*"–
Mechanical and in the distance, heavy
With the sudden shock of hurt.
Children, don't you know that Daddy's gone
And never will return?

Of course, you know.
But childhood brings its own relief
During the daylight hours.
Only at night you let that knowledge come
And muffled in your beds,
You cry.

When did it end? I don't remember.

Just sometime. After days and nights
Breath came to me once more
And life began again. That was
His answer. Only the ache
Remained.

Interim

You were my Rhinestone Cowboy,
All glitter and swagger,

Speaking a language of love
And fluent, easy caring.
That I believed. I didn't see
That your façade was just that:
Façade–
Charade–
The empty kiss, the empty words,
The empty touch and empty sharing.

You were not real–not even to yourself.
Too late I see the rhinestones,
Cowboy.

QUESTIONING

Could I have walked this path before?
The hurt is so familiar. If so,
Why did I not recall its lesson
Before it was too late?
"Don't give your heart to anyone or anything
For it will hurt you
Later."

No. That was not the lesson.
It must have been: "Don't cling."
Let the old past go. The hurt
Is part of life–like joy.

So here I go, each life and always
Offering my heart. Maybe someday I'll learn
To feel the joy, to know,
But never again
To cling.

THE DAYS

I think
Sometimes it's like a nightmare,
Totally unreal and out of joint
From which I never waken.
I walk with fright these days,
Pushing it daily back and back
Out of my mind

To the far reach of consciousness
But it's never really gone.
What was it like, I wonder?
Those days of little cares
Like "What's for dinner?" And
"Are my shirts all pressed?" And "Honey,
I can't find my socks."

Don't tell me things go on
Just echoing, unreal
And very like a nightmare.
I don't think that I could bear it
Right now.

The Court

We sat before the Judge
In that hushed and echoing room
They call the Court.
And in his robe, the Judge looked back
At us
In silent sympathy, yet stern and quite
Impersonal.
Oh, your face, my love–you looked so grim.
Was it all so bad? Those days,
That life we shared
Dissolving now around us?
Now gone
In cold, judicial words, the final gavel rap,
Finality.
Goodbye.

Inside your mind
I wonder if you heard the sound I heard
Inside my mind, across the years,
From far away, a silver sound–
A happy family
Playing?

Packing the Moving Boxes

Somewhere–Isaiah, I think–it says
"Remember not the former things."

Well, God, help me not to remember
These touching tributes of love
Fashioned by their little hands
During their toddler years
And brought to me in trust.

I hold each one a while before it goes
Into the trash. It has to go.
But, oh, my God, let me not remember
Those other years when I was happy
But much too busy with life
To know it.

DEPARTURE

The moving van pulls out.
Goodbye to all we knew–
The house, the trees, old friends
Beside the sounding Bay.
And Christmases and dinner parties
And camping on the beach.
Oh, well.
I guess it didn't matter
To you.

I turn the car lights on
And hush the kids, the dog,
Two cars–
New life, here we come. I'm scared.
"Lead, Kindly Light"–we're following,
I hope.

REALIZATION

It seems over all these years
I've been unfair to you.
Seeing more in you than you were,
Building up an image of you
That wasn't you at all–
Only me.
I looked at you expectantly
Thinking I really knew you

And didn't really see you.
Or when I did, withdrawing
From your reality and substituting mine.

Oh, unfair! The burden was too great–
The denial far too sharp.
Across the years and wonderings
I see it now, and say to you,
I'm sorry.

VISITATION

Whenever you come to see the children,
It's almost more than I can bear.
I watch the small one try to woo you
With childish treasures of great importance
To her
That she tries to share
With you,
Dark eyes anxious and hopeful,
To your every mood alert
And of feigned interest
Aware.
And when you go, she smiles distantly–
Distantly to match your
Distance.

I don't know which is the worse to watch–
The young one or the older one.
One tries so hard to please;
The other doesn't care,
She says.
Hah.

AUTUMN WIND

Listen, they are singing–
Standing on the hilltop, small arms flung wide,
Sharing the wind, the smell, the fell
Of autumn.
And round their shoulders
The golden leaves fall down,

Down, down, into golden heaps
That rustle in the wind–
Too sweet an invitation
For childish heart to spurn.
They roll and shriek and scuffle
Among the leaves. We sit and laugh
All crowned with leaves and out of breath
And watch, while down below
The valley darkens, and the lights
Come on.

Where are you, love? I miss you so.
Too bad you couldn't stay with us
And join in with our song.

OUR DAUGHTER'S FOURTEENTH

Happy Birthday, Love! Today you are fourteen.
And I recall across the years
Your tiny, newborn self
And the promises we made you,
Your father and I,
Supreme in pride and confidence
Of life together,
And you never would know anything
But security and love.
Well, sorry about that, child.
It didn't work that way. Who knows
What happened? Or why
You became a statistic? We all
Became statistics.

But anyhow, Happy Birthday.
I want you to know I'm proud
Of you, for through it all
You stayed
A source of caring and never lost
Your love and sense
Of you.

CHRISTMAS

Christmas was so strange this year
And peace so far away. You called
And voiced your loneliness,
While tears so close to words
Welled in your voice, speaking
Of Christmas past–not long ago–
Another place, another time–two people
Now different people, hurting, yet
Unable to be one.
I told you then I loved you. The door
Has never closed. My hand
Extends to yours. Your voice stiffened
And silence was your answer,
Then tumbling words of rage. I fled.
"Peace on Earth, and mercy mild,
God and sinner reconciled."
God and sinner–not man and she
Who once was wife.

In silence, then, upon that hill
That overlooks the city's lights,
I knelt and prayed for peace
For two who couldn't reach it–
Not alone.
God, are You still there
For all of us who hurt
And hurting, hurt each other?
The night wind whispered, "Yes."

Silent Night, Holy Night. Amen.

CONTINUING EDUCATION

I'm learning more these days
Than I ever wanted to know
Of changing tires and car repair
And life insurance and
How to build a fire in the fireplace
And taxes and all the things

315

You coped with, and I took for granted.
Lord, how education
Hurts! Was I so blind to all you did?
Maybe so. But never blind
To all you meant to me. I thought
I really tried to share
The ups and downs of marriage
With you and let you know
I cared. I guess I failed.
And so, I'm learning more these days
Of lots of things, but most of all,
Appreciation.

I wonder if you're learning
To do the laundry.

BLOCK PRINT SESSION

Well, I wish you could see them—
Crouching over newspapers on the floor,
Whooping with delight at each new print,
Standing on one foot to press their blocks
Onto clean white paper,
Onto smudged grey paper,
Onto shopping bags,
Construction paper—
Rags—
Printing joyously onto surfaces
Never meant for ink—exploring
Color, lines, textures,
Or else carving their designs,
With faces all screwed up
In concentration,
Muttering to each other
In intense conjecture
Over how it will print out—
Neighbor children coming in to watch,
Then joining in the action,
Dark heads, fair heads, eyes alight—
And neat rows of prints
Drying in the sun.

At times like this, I miss you,
As you are missing
Them.

The Nights

There was a time–it seemed forever–
I thought I could not breathe
Against the searing pain,
And breath was shallow. There was
No sleep, and night streamed out
With the mindless ticking of the clocks
And the circling, weary
Why?
No answer. God, are You there?
Is anyone there? No.
Only silence, and in their rooms beyond,
The children lay asleep.

Transactional Analysis

God, you make me mad!
Can't you see I'm trying?
What more do you want
Of me? Well, what?
Just tell me that. It's so mixed up.
It really isn't fair, you know,
And it makes me so damned mad.
But then, of course, You know,
God.
Through gritted teeth I tell you
Thanks. It's hard to say
And harder still to feel.
But hang in there with me, Baby.
I'm trying.
Don't leave me now,
God.

Cougar's Ninth Birthday

Your birthing day dawned bleak, and no one
Thought

The two of us would make it.
Unknown to you, to me, our world
Already was unraveling, though to you,
It must have seemed so new, so bright and harsh
After the womb's dark warmth
And comforting, steady heartbeat.

Well, the heart's still here
And steady still in love
For you are learning now a grief
That many children
Are finding,
And from which I cannot shield you.

Oh, little one, was ever child
More filled with love to give
Than you?

So Happy Birthday, sweet–I cannot give you
The only gift you want: a father's loving presence,
Looking on with pride
At the year you have accomplished.
But I can give you still
What nourished you before:
A heart, steadily beating
Love
And warmth
And care.

Hush, Hush

Hush, hush, my little one. Your blessings are few.
Daddy never considered what would happen to you.
Too old for the daycare,
Too young on your own,
Just what do you do until Mommie gets home?

You wander the neighborhood to find someone to play,
In fair weather or bad, 'cause you're locked out all day.
If school gets out early
Or Mommie is late,
You've lost the last house key, so outside you wait.
Hush, hush, my little one. Your blessings are few.

Daddy never considered what would happen to you.
Too old for the daycare,
Too young for the key,
What will happen to you if something happens to me?

No one to come home to
And no one to share,
You're the throw-away child.
And it just isn't fair
For all the throw-away children.

Situation–Outreach

For Jane

Listen, kid, if I can make it,
Then so can you. It hurts.
You dared to love–to take the chance,
And loving brought you pain.
Okay, I know. I've walked that way–
Like you, rebelled and wept a while,
And rose to love again.
To you, these words seem stupid now,
While you struggle to go on–
Presumptuous words, and shallow, trite,
Of comfort bare, and that's all right.
I only know I've faced the night
And out of night
Comes dawn–I think.

--Barbara Anne Winkler

Looking Back and Moving Forward

*I write these lines hoping that my family will one day realize
who I really am and how my heart feels. Perhaps a day will
come when my children understand the why of their father.
These words, some written while a student at Mercer University,
reflect who I am and reveal the positive and negative waves I
have created. I offer special thanks to my brothers–I miss you
guys.*

Fatinah: Flash Memory of a Kind Face in Iraq

Your dark hair plays inconspicuously with the wind, free and careless. Your sun-doused forehead is fair and entices me to look at you. Yet I know I must not stare. Eyes brown and deep with a glaze of honey distract me from my course–beautiful eyes, filled with hurt. I can see how the pain of warfare has hardened you. As I approach, there are only about five feet between you and me, but I can sense your gaze is kilometers away.

The status of your town makes my heart ache. I'm distraught. As I continue to patrol, I cannot cease the thought of wanting to speak to you–this my mission does not require, and your culture forbids. I turn and examine my sector and with arduous scrutiny inspect my men. My squad's formation looks good–combat ready.

The sudden sound of a dull and muffled pop catches my attention. We quickly react, hearts flutter from the adrenaline rushes, eyes widen. Before we react, I notice a punctured, slow-leaking futbol, kicked by the street children to relieve the tension of a chaotic war-torn day, bounces once and rolls near your small, sandaled feet. Your face is unchanged; reality does not dissipate your defiant stare.

Despair and pain surround you. Emotionless, you kick the ball, removing it from your sight.

Iraqi winds full of dust and sand fill the air. A sudden gust of wind forces that pesky hijab to flaunt your face. I'm astonished, for it reveals a small, pointed nose, majestic olive-tan skin, and full, well-defined lips that make your semblance my most coveted delight. I force a smile and know that you can see the pain in me. "Our mutual ground," I say to myself. Then I think, "No! How dare I compare my flicker of grief to your lasting anguish."

I turn to take one last glance at you since soon you will no longer be in sight. Then you amaze me with a genuine smile that brightens my day. Your mouth flattens. Your smile is so wide that it seems to reach from one ear to the other, forcing your amber eyes to close a little and to form lines at the edge of your thin, sculpted brows.

You are no longer in sight, but my spirit lifts as I have reached Nirvana. You've become my Lotus, my Sphinx. Your memorable face is forever sketched in my mind's eye. You have become my solace in my pilgrimage through life, the one person I owe so much. I know that I will never find you to thank you for giving me hope amidst bedlam.

REFLECTION

My mind feels empty; I search for a thought, an idea, some glimpse of light that might guide my train out of the darkness and into the creative print. My fingers forge with a pen. What am I to do if even frustration does not materialize creation?

It has been tough for me these last couple of weeks, especially since mental pain and the sadness of my soul bear heavy on my heart. Last Christmas was spent away from my children, yet in the chaotic presence of my father's love. He is such a hard man— short, stubborn, and broad. The thought makes me smile.

Although my father admits to feeling love, he has never been able to transmit it in a public manner. I know this might seem strange. It is not love that is hard for him to transmit or demonstrate. It is the act of loving that he has a problem showing.

I know this is still confusing, even to me as I try to explain it. My dad shares his love—just not what I expect of love. In hard times, he will share an anecdote. In sad times, he will share an anecdote. My father does not share any anecdotes of a happy time. It is as if showing gratitude for the happy will only bring pain and sorrow.

I understand, now that I am grown. I clearly see how the happy moments of life in life can devastate the proud condition of being man.

Man provides. *Man* is master of his fate. *Man* works hard and never complains. *Man* this, that, and the other—the list goes on and on. What a man is, what he does, and how he does it seem to be genetically imprinted. This code serves as measuring stick and provides a list of qualities from which to judge and to be judged. He is too much like this, too little like that—too manly, not manly enough, a substandard man, and that one over there is possibly gay.

Man is a delicate condition. It teeter-totters on finite balance and once the balance beam leans to one side or the other, falling from man is imminent and permanent. There is no greater threat to man and to the status of man than remembering happy moments. Nostalgia, Great Evictor, you have single-mindedly tossed man into despair and then taken with you his title. Nostalgia, Great Machine of Warmth and Comfort, you have taken away my father and replaced him with cold-man. Cold-man does not feel nostalgia and is quick to *regain balance* at the *onset* of such feelings.

Woe, how I long for happiness and resist nostalgia.

What will become of my son and daughter if they, as my father and I have modeled, are reflections of their father?

UNDER

My watch is constantly stopping,
Yet I cannot catch up with the time.
And time wears on me,
Constantly wearing me down.
And gravity feels stiff–
The gravity of its shackles is prison-corrupter of hearts
That allows me to feel failure, as if I have not done my part.
Torn into pieces,
I am falling apart–
No longer social,
Cold is my heart.
Yet pain I do feel.
It seems to be
My soul's only meal.
How am I?
You know me–
I'm always doing good.

He was such a good man.

ONE DROP: AN INVISIBLE HEREDITY

Contrast in its essence–in its core
One drop can break a rock's steel ore.
It can stain and relegate,
Or it can help bloom and germinate.
The disparity between white and black
Is one drop of color or one drop of bleach.
One drop makes the variation in speech.
Perspectives change–some have and some lack.
Inclusion, exclusion, exclusive admission

Advance a melting-pot fission.
Oceans gather into a whole;
Humanity separates–breaks the mold.

What drops are part of me–
Have made me who I am?
Am I merely a drop in the vast sea of man?
Does the constant beat of a drop break the stone,
Or is it the fate of one person alone?
Are not all drops equal parts of a fraction–
Or are they individuals straining toward action?

Por Amor He de Querer

Tonto ha de nacer
Aquel quien en busca de amor
Ha de vivir con dolor
La pena de la vida.
Esa gran profunda herida
Que nunca ha de mermar
Y solo engrandece como el Mar
Con sus ríos en desemboco.
El llorar queda poco
A una vida sin armonía.
El alma en agonía
Por aquella que,
He de querer.
--Maximo G. Wharton

A HEALTHY LESSON

This play for children was written by Albany State University's Acting II professor and coordinator of Speech and Theater Division, Dr. Florence Lyons, and her students in the Acting II class, who also made up the cast: Hillary Scales, Bruce Edwards, Caroline Grant, Beauvyon Swain, Nicolle Burke, Theodore Holmes, and Christopher Atkins. The play premiered on December 8, 2010 for three- and four-year-olds at the Early Learning Center in Albany. Dr. Lyons served as a consultant in several Mercer writing classes.

Cast (*in order of appearance*):
MRS. SUNFLOWER
BASHA
PRINCESS
PRINCE
GERM MONSTER 1
GERM MONSTER 2
MR. CLEAN

Setting: Kingdom of Kindness and Good Manners

(Mrs. Sunflower appears downstage right. She is wearing a flowered print dress and has a sunflower in her hair. After yawning and stretching, Mrs. Sunflower sighs. She seems surprised to discover the audience.)

MRS. SUNFLOWER: Oh, good morning, Children! You are all so colorful today. You look like a beautiful garden of tulips, daisies, and roses. I'm Mrs. Sunflower. How are you on this fine morning? You all look so happy and healthy. I, too, feel happy and healthy. Do you know how to stay happy and healthy all day long? You should wash your hands before you eat, after you eat, and after you play. You should also cover your mouth when you sneeze and cough. If you don't, you could spread germs. Germs make you sick. Raise your hands if you have ever had a cold. Germs cause colds, and we're going to call them–Germ Monsters. Oh, (*MRS. SUNFLOWER looks at her watch.*) it's almost time for my daily watering.

BASHA: (*yelling from offstage*) Mrs. Sunflower! Mrs. Sunflower!

MRS. SUNFLOWER: Do you hear that, Children? It's Basha, coming to water me!

(*Basha enters, wearing a turban, shirt, bow tie, and khaki pants. He speaks with an Indian accent.*)

BASHA: (*Basha looks at the audience.*) Hi! (*Basha begins watering Mrs. Sunflower near her feet with an empty watering can. As he waters her, he shakes his head left to right and looks worried.*)

MRS. SUNFLOWER: What's wrong Basha? (*Basha stops watering.*)

BASHA: Trouble in the castle!

MRS. SUNFLOWER: What? Oh, no! (*Mrs. Sunflower crosses downstage left to a large pail, and Basha follows.*) Let me look into my magic pail. (*Mrs. Sunflower looks in the pail and gasps.*) Those Germ Monsters are at it again! (*Mrs. Sunflower addresses the audience.*) Would you like to see what I see? Cover your eyes. After we count to five, you will be able to see what's going on in the castle. (*She counts slowly.*) One. Two. Don't peek! Three. Four. Five.

(*While Mrs. Sunflower counts, the Prince and Princess skip in and sit at a table with toy blocks. Once Mrs. Sunflower and the audience finish counting, Mrs. Sunflower and Basha cross downstage right to watch the actions of the Prince and Princess who are seated center stage. The Prince wears a crown, a shirt with a bow tie, and pants. The Princess wears a tiara and a royal blue dress with a rhinestone belt. They both play with the blocks on the table.*)

PRINCESS: I like playing with blocks. Ahh-Chew! (*Once the Princess sneezes, Germ Monster #1 appears. The Prince and Princess don't notice Germ Monster # 1.*)

PRINCE: Me, too!

(*Germ Monster # 1 walks menacingly toward the Prince and Princess and sprinkles confetti above their heads. The Prince and Princess are seemingly unaware of the Germ Monster.*)

MRS. SUNFLOWER: Look, Basha! There's a Germ Monster! He came because the Princess didn't cover her mouth when she sneezed.

BASHA: Yes!

(*The Prince and Princess continue playing for a while.*)

PRINCESS: I'm hungry. Let's go eat! (*She stands.*)

PRINCE: Okay. (*He stands.*)

PRINCESS: Wait! Shouldn't we wash our hands?
PRINCE: No, it's okay.
(*Germ Monster #2 appears and sprinkles confetti on the Prince and Princess.*)
MRS. SUNFLOWER: Look, Boys and Girls, there's another Germ Monster! See what happens when you don't wash your hands before you eat?
(*The Prince and Princess exit stage right.*)
BASHA: Bad germs. Bad!
GERM MONSTERS #1 AND #2:
We spread our germs on other people!
We spread our germs on other people!
(*The Germ Monsters give each other a high five.*)
GERM MONSTERS #1 AND #2:
Cough, cough, sneeze, sneeze. Put your germs on everything!
Cough, cough, sneeze, sneeze. Put your germs on everything!
(*The Germ Monsters walk slowly toward the audience. Mrs. Sunflower and Basha block the germs from getting to the audience. While the germs are trying to get to the audience, the Prince and Princess enter. Once the Prince and Princess are seated, Basha and Mrs. Sunflower move to the side of the stage and observe the Prince and Princess.*)
PRINCESS: Uh-oh. I don't feel so good.
PRINCE: Me neither.
GERM MONSTER # 2: Now we can make the whole Kingdom of Kindness and Good Manners sick!
Monsters:
Cough, cough, sneeze, sneeze. Put your germs on everything!
Cough, cough, sneeze, sneeze. Put your germs on everything!
BASHA: What can we do?
MRS. SUNFLOWER: This looks like a job for Mr. Clean. Come on, Children, call him with me: Mr. Clean! Mr. Clean! Mr. Clean!
(*After the audience calls for Mr. Clean, he appears.*)
GERM MONSTER #1: Something smells–clean!
GERM MONSTERS #1 AND #2: (*in unison*) Oh, no! Not Mr. Clean!
(*Mr. Clean appears. He is dressed in white hospital scrubs, a yellow cape, and yellow dishwashing gloves.*)
MR. CLEAN: Did somebody call Mr. Clean?
MRS. SUNFLOWER: Yes! The Prince and Princess did not

wash their hands before eating, and the Princess sneezed and didn't cover her nose and mouth. Now the Germ Monsters have made them sick!

MR. CLEAN: This looks like a job for–Mr. Clean!

(*Mr. Clean wrestles the Germ Monsters for a while and he wins.*)

MRS. SUNFLOWER: Yay! Mr. Clean has defeated the Germ Monsters! So what did you learn today? *(Mrs. Sunflower goes to the audience and lets them answer.)* Children, sing with us!

(The entire cast assembles in a line, as if for a curtain call. They encourage the audience to sing with them.)

CAST and AUDIENCE:

Wash, wash!

Clean, clean!

Wash off all the bad things!

Wash, wash!

Clean, clean!

Wash off all the bad things!

Wash, wash!

Clean, clean!

Wash off all the bad things!

(The cast hold hands and bows.)

CURTAIN

--Florence Lyons

JOINING THE ACADEMIC CONVERSATION

Thought is more than a right–it is the very breath of man. Whoever fetters thought attacks man himself. To speak, to write, to publish, are things, so far as the right is concerned, absolutely identical. They are the ever-enlarging circles of intelligence in action; they are the sonorous waves of thought.
--Victor Hugo

Rarely do we find men who willingly engage in hard, solid thinking. There is an almost universal quest for easy answers and half-baked solutions. Nothing pains some people more than having to think.
--Martin Luther King, Jr.

If we encounter a man of rare intellect, we should ask him what books he reads.
--Ralph Waldo Emerson

The man who does not read has no advantage over the man who cannot read.
--Mark Twain

The book you don't read won't help.
--Jim Rohn

In a good book the best is between the lines.
--Swedish Proverb

Books serve to show a man that those original thoughts of his aren't very new after all.
--Abraham Lincoln

There are worse crimes than burning books. One of them is not reading them.
--Joseph Brodsky

Once you learn to read, you will be forever free.
--Frederick Douglas

Books are like mirrors: if a fool looks in, you cannot expect a genius to look out.
--J.K. Rowling

CIVILITY: WHAT I LEARNED FROM COHORT 40

January 23, 2010

The following reflections on civility are rooted in my conviction that I learn much from being with students. I am grateful to them for giving me that opportunity. A colleague suggested that my reflections reminded him of Oscar Hammerstein's lyrics in *The King and I*:

> *It's a very ancient saying, but a true and honest thought,*
> *That if you become a teacher, by your pupils you'll be taught.*

Some eight years ago, I made a presentation to a class on the topic of civility. Over the years, I thought many times about that presentation and the discussion that it generated. When I returned to the classroom full-time in the fall of 2009, I consulted my notes from eight years earlier and wrote a reflective piece concerning what I had learned from my earlier experience with students. It was entitled "On Learning to Be Together: Some Observations on Civility and the Formation of Communities of Learners." I shared my written reflections with the new group of students I would be teaching and mentoring for the next sixteen months. Like the earlier group to whom I gave my original presentation on civility, these students were mid-career adults who were studying leadership. As a class assignment I asked them to develop a civility covenant that would define and guide their relationships as a community of learners at Mercer University. I wanted them to incorporate their own ideas, lessons, reflections, and experiences into the covenant. I was moved by the seriousness with which they undertook this assignment. The outcome of their discussions in the fall of 2009 is a document that they created and signed entitled "Civility Covenant."

I asked adult student learners to think specifically about creating a covenant rather than a creed. I thought that it was important that the words they wrote "become flesh," that is, the values and ideals expressed in their covenant would guide their conduct as members of a community of learners. A creed is a set of beliefs; a covenant defines an intimate relationship. Because they were members of a lock-step cohort in a degree-completion program, they would be together for an extended period of time.

The discussions this new group of students had concerning the meaning of "civility" and how it can be lived was an intense one. The students acknowledged that civility had diminished during their lifetimes and that for the most part public life in the United States had become uncivil. Consequently, they thought the assignment was relevant and important, and they embraced it in important ways.

What did I learn from them?

First of all, they made "respect" the cornerstone of their definition of civility, not manners or politeness. They embraced a concept of "respect" that went beyond the idea of someone having to "earn respect" in order to "get respect." A phrase in the their covenant speaks about "unconditional respect." Second, they viewed "conviction" and "responsibility" as two sides of the same coin. The students concluded that the values and ideals used to judge and evaluate them as members of a community of learners should be those identified in their covenant: unconditional respect, hospitality, humility, tolerance, empathy, and care. They were careful to distinguish "tolerance" from "indifference" toward others. Third, they applied what they had learned in class to the ideals expressed in their covenant. To many of the students, the first line of the last paragraph was the most important sentence in the covenant: *"We promise to care for each other and for ourselves–listening, offering suggestions, celebrating successes and 'encouraging the hearts' of others."* The students' reading of James M. Kouzes and Barry Z. Posner's *The Leadership Challenge* (2007) influenced the sentiments they articulated in that sentence.

The fourth lesson I learned came when I met with the students again two months later in a research course that I was teaching. I asked them whether the "civility covenant" really influenced how they behaved toward each other since they had completed writing the document. I had made a bet with myself that they had forgotten all about the covenant–not because they weren't good and decent people, but because the spirit of the times with its market orientation and egocentric and narcissistic spirit undermines civility in insidious and debilitating ways. My assumption proved wrong. I worried that I had hurt their feelings by not thinking more positively about their commitment to the ideals and values in their covenant.

I was surprised that the students had found the assignment

personally important and that it had made them conscious of their behavior not only as members of a community of learners, but also as leaders and followers in the organizations where they were employed. I am convinced that their experiences in writing a covenant will have a long-lasting impact on their personal and professional conduct. I believe that significant learning took place.

I shared my reflections with colleagues, friends, and other students and was surprised by the responses (and nonresponses from valued colleagues). The most gratifying comments came from students in other classes when I asked them to read and reflect on the "Civility Covenant" that fellow students had composed.

This leads to the one big lesson I learned. As a university, we have a responsibility to teach civility. A good starting point for us as teachers, administrators, and staff members is to commit ourselves to civil conduct. Perhaps as a community dedicated to teaching and learning, we also need to develop our own inclusive civility covenant. The ideal and practice of collegiality among faculty lead us in that direction, but training, leadership, and an organizational culture and structure that reward individualistic and self-centered values often undermine it. Consequently, collegiality does not seem to lead to civility. A student reminded me of Gandhi's mantra: "We must be the change we seek."

As a human being, a teacher, and, for more than thirty years, an administrator, my engagement in this project on civility has helped me understand the deep, personal consequences incivility wreaks on the lives of others. We are a violent society. *Incivility, I have learned, is a form of nonphysical violence.* For important and understandable reasons, our attention in our communities is on reducing physical rather than nonphysical violence. Both are injurious to body and spirit. Both attack the identity and integrity of other human beings. As a professional, I also came to understand, as a result of the dialogue I had with students, that organizations, communities, and leaders themselves allow, encourage, and perpetuate incivility. That is true within the walls of the academy as well as outside, which makes our efforts to teach civility problematic.

Incivility is hurtful conduct deeply rooted in the fabric of our lives. It is important for us to understand that judgments concerning whether an act or situation is uncivil rest not with the perpetrator but with the victim or victims. Sadly, when we–as perpetrators of incivility–believe that we are the sole judge, we are able to justify without compunction conduct that is often deliberately cruel, hurtful, and unacceptable.

--T. E. Kail

EDUCATION: OPPRESSION OR LIBERATION?

Author and educator Paulo Freire offers a scathing analysis of the traditional education system in his essay, "The 'Banking' Concept of Education" (1970). Freire asserts that educators often treat pupils like depositories: students "receive, memorize, and repeat." The oppressive nature of the banking concept dehumanizes students and can prevent them from engaging their minds beyond regurgitating information deposited. Freire offers an alternative method that truly liberates students. Called the "problem-posing" concept of education, it allows students to think beyond themselves, engage the world, and reflect on their positions in that world. Educators should ask themselves whether their teaching styles oppress or liberate.

Picture any typical classroom. Students sit uncomfortably in desks and stare up at teachers who tower over them and indoctrinate them with information that the educators choose or interpret based upon nothing more than a state mandate. Blandly, as teachers offer their assessments of texts, students take notes and memorize these interpretations in order to pass arbitrary exams and to move on to subsequent levels, and to the new teachers who will do the same thing next year–and the next year.

On the surface, this doesn't seem like a really bad thing. It is good for students to memorize information in order to succeed on exams. Is this not the way it has always been done? However, Freire saw beyond the seemingly innocent nature of this style of education and offered his analysis, calling it the banking concept of education.

Freire describes the banking concept of education as "narrative," identifying its major characteristic as the pleasant sounds of spoken words, not its power to transform learners. In learning math concepts, for example, students record, memorize, and repeat the math facts without understanding the principles. In geography, they memorize lists of the countries and their capitals without having any understanding of what it means to be a capital. Rather than using this information to build the students' cognition of the world, the teacher simply treats these topics as data. No longer is the student a living, breathing, active being; the student is, instead, stagnant, dormant, and intellectually deteriorating due to the oppressive nature of the process.

Oppressive? That would seem a little harsh. Why would Freire use the term *oppressive* to describe the banking concept of education? He maintains that memorization and regurgitation inflict physical changes in the brain. Thoughts run along pathways of nerves located in the brain. As students use memorization and regurgitation, the critical thinking pathways become more difficult for thoughts to travel whereas the nerves used for memorization are etched deeper and deeper, almost like an old bumpy, uneven brick road versus a new, well-maintained asphalt road. The oppression is such that students do not even realize that they have been rendered incapable of complex thought; the driver drives along the brick road, ruining the car with contentment because it's the only road that the driver has ever used. Ignorant educators using the banking concept see themselves as liberators of the mind. There is a liberating aspect to education, but it is not found in the banking concept.

Freire, instead, offers a different method of education that does truly liberate the student: dialogue centered around the solution to problems in the lives of students. He calls this method "problem-posing." It regards students as "conscious beings." Imagine a classroom in which a young student is asked to think critically and respond to the idea and logistics of collecting apples for harvest, rather than simply counting them. Freire warns that teachers must "abandon" the educational practice of "deposit-making" and opt instead for articulating the problems of human beings "in their relations with the world." Problem-posing education encourages students to engage actively in uncovering their own realities in the world.

Unfortunately, either consciously or subconsciously, many teachers refuse to empower their students by employing the problem-posing concept of education. They instead rely on the banking concept. The banking concept of education leaves educators in complete control of the learning process. Educators who utilize the problem-posing concept of education show their students how to take the knowledge from the classroom and apply it to every part of their lives. To oppress or to liberate—that is the choice for the educator.

--David D. Toliver

RAYMOND HAMRICK: MIDDLE GEORGIA SACRED HARP COMPOSER

Even after his death at ninety-nine on November 24, 2014, Middle Georgia music treasure and Macon native Raymond Cooper Hamrick continues to make waves all around the world—sound waves, that is. As time ticked toward his centennial birthday, downtown Macon watchmaker Raymond Hamrick continued to compose music in the Sacred Harp tradition and repair watches for Andersen's Jewelers, the store where he began work in 1935 and that he purchased in 1963.

The use of notes in the shape of triangles, ovals, squares, and diamonds perched on the traditional five lines and spaces of the music staff characterizes the Sacred Harp musical tradition. Over his lifetime, Hamrick composed more than two hundred "fasola" tunes, six of which appeared in the 1991 revision of the 1844 *Sacred Harp*, used in singings throughout the world. Georgia Sacred Harp singers John Plunkett and John Hollingsworth convinced Hamrick to allow the publication of his tunes in a volume they entitled *The Georgian Harmony*, which now comprises two editions. In the index to the second edition of *Georgian Harmony*, 178 tunes are attributed to Hamrick. A major contributor to the 1991 *Sacred Harp*, Hamrick composed several of the tunes currently sung most frequently at Sacred Harp singings.

One of the most prolific composers in the Georgia Sacred Harp musical tradition, Hamrick embraced the tradition only after returning to Macon following a four-year stint in the Air Force. The legendary friendliness of the singers, their extraordinary culinary skills exhibited in the generous food offerings at the traditional "dinner on the grounds" that punctuates morning and afternoon singing sessions, and the dedication of the singers to the music initially influenced Hamrick to join in a singing in 1946, the year he attended his first singing school in south Bibb County, a school taught by Primitive Baptist elder Monroe Denton. Hamrick learned that no harp is involved in the Sacred Harp tradition–the human voice is considered the "sacred" harp. Singers gather in a square formation according to voice parts (treble, alto, tenor, and bass) and are led by a singer who stands in the "hollow" square formed by the arrangement of the singers. Facing the tenors, the leader in the hollow square or another delegated singer gives the pitch for the song. Without any accompaniment, the assembled group sings through the notes the first time using their names: fa (triangle), sol (oval), la (square), and mi (diamond). The leader uses up-and-down hand motions to maintain the rhythm, turning to signal the entrance of the various parts. Singers indicate upon registration their willingness to stand in the hallowed hollow square to lead a song. Men, women, and children lead. No song is repeated. The secretary of the singing maintains a record of each leader and song and forwards the record and the minutes of the singing for publication in the *Minutes of Sacred Harp Singings* for that year.

Hamrick worked for the *Macon News* and later as an assistant to the manager of the Macon Auditorium after graduation from Lanier High School for Boys in 1933. In 1935 he began what was to become his life's work as a watchmaker at Andersen's Jewelers on Second Street in downtown Macon. Shortly after the Japanese attack on Pearl Harbor on December 7, 1941, and the nation's subsequent the entry into World War II, Hamrick joined the Army Air Corps, serving from 1942 to 1946. His technical skills as a watchmaker qualified him to attend the top secret Norden Bombsight School in Denver that developed the bombsight used in the Hiroshima bombing. Upon graduation, Hamrick was assigned to a B-24 heavy bomber outfit stationed at various stateside bases and eventually at the B-29 base of the Twentieth Air Force in Guam.

Hamrick returned in 1946 to Andersen's Jewelers. That same year after attending his first singing school, he became active in the South Georgia Sacred Harp Singing Convention, serving at various times as vice president and president. In 1952, he met and formed a close friendship with Hugh McGraw of Bremen, Georgia, the widely acknowledged national leader of the Sacred Harp singing tradition. He and McGraw became active in composing music for Sacred Harp singings, sharing their songs with each other for feedback. Marcus Cagle (1884-1968), one of the foremost composers of Sacred Harp music, also influenced Hamrick. In the early 1950s Hamrick began corresponding with the leading scholar of the Sacred Harp tradition, George Pullen Jackson of Vanderbilt University. He and Jackson first met when Jackson was guest speaker at West Georgia College's commencement in 1952. Hamrick began to collect books, articles, and letters pertinent to the history of early American music. His collection included a number of early shape-note tune books, which he donated to the Pitts Theology Library of Emory University, where it is available for research projects. Hamrick served as a consultant to authors of books and dissertations related to the Sacred Harp tradition and wrote articles describing its performance. In addition to Sacred Harp music, Hamrick was active in barbershop singings for twenty-nine years with concerts throughout the southeast.

According to Jesse P. Karlsberg, who completed a dissertation at Emory University on the Shape Note tradition, Raymond Hamrick

> *influenced the 1960 edition to the Sacred Harp by suggesting a song from the Southern Harmony for inclusion and composing a song, MILLARD, dedicated to Millard Hancock, which appeared credited to Joyce Harrison as "Mrs. Raymond Hamrick." The song was removed in 1966. Raymond contributed A PARTING PRAYER and PENITENCE to the 1966 revision of the Sacred Harp. A PARTING PRAYER was replaced by EMMAUS in 1991; a version of it appears as a PRAYER FOR PARTING in the Georgian Harmony. His alto part to STAFFORD appeared in 1971.* (Email from Jesse P. Karlsberg, August 6, 2015)

Hamrick served on the Board of Directors of the Sacred Harp Publishing Company and as the company president. His work on the Music Revision Committee resulted in the widely used 1991 edition of the *Sacred Harp*, which includes six of his compositions: CHRISTIAN'S FAREWELL (347), INVOCATION (492), LLOYD (503), NIDRAH (540), EMMAUS (569), and PENITENCE (571). His most popular piece, LOYD, had its origins in a dream, which Hamrick described as follows:

> *While sleeping one night, I dreamed of a great throng of singers, their faces hidden by cowls, singing a melody that I*

recalled on waking. I jotted down the tune, and later harmo-nized it and named it LOYD after my friend and fellow singer Loyd Redding.

In 2010, a collection of ninety of Hamrick's compositions was published in an attractive hardcover edition as *The Georgian Harmony: A Collection of Hymns and Fuging Tunes in the Shape-Note Tradition.* This book was typeset and edited by John Plunkett and John Hollingsworth. The second edition of *The Georgian Harmony* was published in 2012. In the preface to *The Georgian Harmony, Sacred Harp* leaders John Plunkett and the Hollings-worth family provide an apt description of Raymond Cooper Hamrick's contributions to *Sacred Harp* singing and a testimony to his personal character:

> *For decades his contributions to the South Georgia singings were enormous. He gave the appropriate pitch for each song, he taught singing schools, and at singings (when requested) he helped singers of all parts learn how a new song should sound. His singing skills (honed in a large barbershop singing group in Macon) were legendary. Those fortunate enough to sit by him at a singing realized that his singing was a live demonstration of how a song was supposed to be sung. Once . . . a long-time Sacred Harp singer, a very good bass singer in his own right, commented that "Raymond Hamrick is the best bass singer I ever sat by." Indeed!*

> *Raymond Hamrick began writing music in the 1960s and continues to the present. We love his music, and it is a great joy and honor to work to bring this music to the singing com-munity. Our love for the person is even greater. Raymond's talent and intellect are combined with modesty, kindness, and generosity. He is a scholar and a gentleman, and it is always a great pleasure to visit him. In abundance, he has earned our appreciation, affection, and admiration.*

> *Sacred Harp singers from Georgia to California and Maine to Florida sing Raymond Hamrick's tunes. His tunes are lifted in Poland and in England, in Canada and in Ireland, among others. This unofficial Georgian goodwill ambassa-dor gave the world timeless harmonies that build friendships and create community wherever they are sung.*

Sacred Harp singings promote community among the singers around the world. Singers travel together to singings and sing and eat together. A number of singers considered Raymond Hamrick "family." In addition to this wide extended singing family, Raymond Hamrick's family includes two daughters and sons-in-law: Mrs. Susan (Terry) Hatfield of Port Lavaca, Texas, and Mrs. Patricia (Charles) Dancy of Jackson, Georgia; a granddaughter: Mrs. Melissa (Torrey) Thorsell of Bedford, Texas, and two grandsons: Justin Byrd and Joshua David Byrd, both of Macon, Georgia.

--Harry Eskew

REGENERATION WRITERS EDITING TEAM

KARL S. ADAMS

A native of Macon, Georgia, Karl Adams has spent over two decades working in multiple factories in Bibb County. Perhaps due in part to a hearing impediment since birth, Karl has developed strong analytical skills along with a rich vocabulary, a ready wit, and the ability to express himself in a way that often catches listeners off guard. His writing creates a strong empathic bond with readers, seldom leaving them unchanged by the experience. Able to write in multiple genres, Karl relates easily to both children and adults. Karl hopes to one day see his work displayed in bookstores across the country and in digital format for e-book readers. He has often been described as having the demeanor of a small town preacher. A seeker of truth, Karl is a dedicated family man who draws his inspiration to write from his relationships with his wife, Kim, and their two children, Katherine and Kole.

MARGARET H. ESKEW

The recipient of Mercer University's 2016 Joe and Jean Hendricks Award for Excellence in Teaching, given in recognition of "challenging and inspiring teaching in and out of the classroom, active engagement of students in the process of learning, discovery, and leadership; caring mentoring to motivate students to achieve their highest aspirations;

and supporting junior faculty in becoming exemplary teachers," veteran teacher Margaret Eskew is a linguist, writer, speaker, and publisher. Fluent in German, she analyzed the language of Adolf Hitler, determining the language strategies he used to gain and maintain power in depression-era Germany. Part of her research is documented in *The Syntactic Preferences of Adolf Hitler*, published by Peter Lang. Her research centers on the intersection of education and totalitarian language and is rooted in the study of history, race, and economics in World War II Germany.

ROBERT (BOB) MATHIS

An artist who creates beauty out of wood, turns dilapidated historical buildings into magnificent edifices, and piddles with painting, sculpture, and carving, Robert N. Mathis, Sr. is a natural storyteller. A native of Mableton, Georgia, Bob spent many summers of his childhood at "God's Heaven," a farm in Cannon Ridge near Ellijay in North Georgia, where he was intimately involved in the beginnings of integration in the South. There he also developed building, woodworking, and management skills, a love for people and animals, and a consciousness of the need to take care of the earth. A tireless volunteer in the community, Bob has served on several university-wide committees at Mercer and has presented two research projects at the Mercer University Research Conference in Atlanta. Bob's stories, whether in narrative, poetic, or essay form reflect the joys and struggles of his youth and of a region coming to terms with the economic and freedom issues that define it. Bob discovered that his skills in constructing houses could be transferred to writing. Bob is married to Dr. Mary W. Mathis, a leader in public health in Macon and a member of the Mercer faculty. They have two children: Robby and Amanda.

Sharon McElhaney

Retired from the United States
Postal Service, Sharon McElhaney
brings to the journal tremendous
skills in organization and task com-
pletion. In her first year at Mercer
University, her research project
involving the collection and analysis of local stories of homelessness
was accepted for presentation at
the Mercer Research Conference in
Atlanta in April 2015. She organized the collection and editing

of the writings in this journal. Sharon has a passion for those on
the fringe of American society. After researching the services of
Hull House in Chicago, she developed a vision to open a similar
facility for the marginalized in Middle Georgia. She ministers to
young people in need of direction, providing them the assistance
they need to succeed. Engaged in the study of religion and writing,
Sharon is preparing to enter law school upon graduation.

Anna M. McEwen

The second daughter in a blended family of ten children, Anna
McEwen developed early in her life high-level skills in listening
to others and intuiting their feelings. Her compelling honesty
invites confidence and catalyzes meaningful conversation. In the
dark hours of her young life, she turns to poetry to probe her hopes
and fears and find her pathway. Even when she was a third-grader,
her teachers and peers recognized her gifts in writing, inducting
her into Young Authors for her winning entry, "Walking, Talking
Crayon." Anna's contributions to editing *Regeneration II* are
seamlessly woven into the volume. Although her plans for the
future are still emerging, she is certain that they will include her
inclination for creative writing.

Ray Sapp

Ray Sapp is living proof of the transformative power of faith and the resilience of the human spirit. On his own since the age of thirteen, Ray's strong work ethic and native ability insured his continuous employment. Watching others with fewer skills and less mental acuity receive promotions over him, Ray made the choice to gain a formal education. He obtained a GED and then enrolled in Penfield College at Mercer. Determined that his rough start in life would not dictate how far he could advance, Ray finds tremendous support from his wife, Marylin, and in his church. Ray has found his voice in writing. His stories capture the intense emotion of traumatic events and elicit thoughtful introspection. Through writing, Ray has come to terms with the forces that initially shaped him and is taking the power from them to forge a bright future for himself and his family. Ray gives physical manifestation to the power of regeneration.

David D. Toliver

Accomplished in audiovisual production and in radio, David Toliver brings a wealth of experience to the editing and publishing process. A native of St. Mary's, Georgia, David has traveled around the world to work in many events, such as the Super Bowl game in Phoenix, which he covered for the St. Mary's local radio station, The Lighthouse, where he provides an early morning weekday sports commentary. His audiovisual expertise has taken him to Ireland, Canada, Zimbabwe, states on both coasts, and everything inbetween with GNTV Media Ministry in Macon, Georgia. David's strong analytical skills and his tactful honesty have added immeasurably to the value of the journal.

WILLIAM M. (BO) WALKER

Bo's engaging smile belies the weight of his experience and his deep probing for meaning and pattern. The fun boils up in his writing, sometimes frothing the deeply serious nature of his underlying questions. A Renaissance man, Bo delights in composing music, singing and playing, and writing poems, essays, and short stories. He fashions elaborate costumes for Star Wars characters. Reality proves stranger than fantasy as Bo recounts the stories of his mattress deliveries in Middle Georgia. Bo's wife, Caitlyn, and their two sons put the sparkle in his eyes and the urgency in his educational endeavors, beginning with a Bachelor of Liberal Studies with concentrations in writing and literature.

MAXIMO G. WHARTON

Maximo Wharton spent most of his childhood traveling back and forth from his native Puerto Rico to the United States. The cultural disconnect between home and school activated his penchant for expressing those conflicts in writing, particularly in poetry. At the age of eighteen, Maximo graduated from Marine boot camp and served in the Marines for almost a decade before joining the National Guard for an additional eight years of national service, followed by six years of work in the prison system. It was not until he came to Mercer University in 2014 that Maximo began writing short stories and remembered how much he enjoyed writing. A veteran of two wars, a father of two, a writer, and a perceptive and diligent student, Maximo is pursuing a degree in criminal justice.